Battlefield Russia

Book Five of the Red Storm Series

By

James Rosone & Miranda Watson

Copyright Information

Disclaimer

This is a fictional story. All characters in this book are imagined, and any opinions that they express are simply that, fictional thoughts of literary characters. Although policies mentioned in the book may be similar to reality, they are by no means a factual representation of the news. Please enjoy this work as it is, a story to escape the part of life that can sometimes weigh us down in mundaneness or busyness.

Table of Contents

Chapter 1
State of Shock

Washington, D.C.

White House

Vice President Walter "Wally" Foss was finishing up his daily five-mile run on the treadmill at his residence at the Naval Observatory when a member of his Secret Service detail walked up to him and signaled somewhat frantically that he needed to speak with him. Wally hit the stop button on the treadmill and pressed the pause button on his smartphone, stopping the playback of an audiobook about Teddy Roosevelt.

Taking his earbuds out, he asked, "What's going on, Jim?"

Just then, three other agents walked into the room, spreading out to sweep the room for any potential threats. This unsettled Foss a bit—he had never seen a Secret Service agent anything other than calm, and one of them was visibly sweaty as he searched the room.

The first Secret Service agent explained, "Mr. Vice President, we need to move you to the White House Situation Room. The vehicles should be pulling up in a few minutes." The agent handed him a towel to wipe the sweat from his face.

Foss sighed as he stepped off the treadmill. "That's fine. Just give me a couple of minutes to get a quick shower and put some more appropriate clothes on."

Mike Morrel, the head of his Secret Service detail, shook his head. "Sir, there isn't time," he asserted. "We have to get you to the White House immediately. We were just informed a couple of minutes ago that there was an attempt on the President's life at the rally in Michigan. We don't know if the President was hit, but we do know the Secretary of State was shot, and it has been reported that he was killed." Agent Morrel guided the VP out of the fitness room and toward the stairs that would lead them to the main entrance of the building.

Within minutes, the procession of agents in black suits, black sunglasses, and clear earbuds had the VP out of the building and into the waiting motorcade. While the sirens wailed, VP Foss's mind raced. *"What the hell is going on? Did I really just hear what I think I did?"* he thought in shock.

They raced down the road at top speed. The Vice President started thinking more about how many traffic laws they were violating than anything else. In what seemed like the blink of an eye, the sea of Secret Service agents was ushering him out of the vehicle and borderline shoving him down the hall. Before Foss knew it, he was down in the White House bunker.

"So, now what happens?" he asked.

Agent Morrel replied, "I just received word that the President was indeed hit, although we don't know his status yet. The Chief Justice is traveling here now. Until we know more, the Twenty-Fifth Amendment is going to be invoked."

The weight of what had just been said sat on the Vice President's chest like an elephant. He had always known he was a heartbeat away from the presidency, but truthfully, he'd never wanted to ascend to that office in such a dramatic way. *"Please let this be temporary..."*

A few minutes went by with no new information. Foss started checking every possible source, turning the various televisions in the room to different news channels, hoping to find out something new.

His phone rang, startling him. He looked down and saw that the caller ID said Tom McMillan.

"How bad is the President, Tom?" Foss said, not waiting for the usual conversational cues.

"I don't know yet," said the National Security Advisor. "All I know is he was covered in blood and one of the doctors said they couldn't feel a pulse, and then the elevator doors closed. I honestly don't know, but I'm going to stay here until I do," he replied.

The Vice President took a deep breath. "OK, keep me informed," he said, trying to sound more positive about the situation than he felt. "The Secret Service has just taken me down to the bunker. The Chief Justice is also on his way. They are going to invoke the Twenty-Fifth Amendment for the time being until we know what the President's status is." Despite his best efforts, he recognized that his voice sounded a bit shaken as he spoke.

"You'll do fine, Sir," Tom McMillan said reassuringly. "We have a good team in place, and we'll get through this. I'll call you as soon as I know more."

The phone clicked, and the call ended.

Almost twenty minutes went by. The Chief Justice still hadn't arrived. Foss was getting really antsy. He started pacing the room.

Finally, he couldn't take the anticipation any longer, and he got the attention of Agent Morrel. "Do we know how the President is doing yet?"

Lifting his cufflink to his mouth, Agent Morrel stated, "Hoosier wants a status update on POTUS."

What seemed to Foss like an hour, but was really more like five seconds, dragged by. Suddenly, the Vice President noticed that the facial expressions and demeanor of Agent Morrel changed. He looked at the other agents— their faces were ashen. Morrel lowered his hand and then looked up at the VP with a look of sorrow in his eyes.

"We just got confirmation, Sir," he finally said. "POTUS is dead. You are now the President." He paused for a second, then added, "I've been instructed that we are to take you directly to the Oval Office. The Chief Justice just arrived at the White House to swear you in. The Secretary of Defense is also on his way here."

The Vice President sat down in a chair for a moment, absorbing the information. He wasn't sure what to say, or what to think for that matter. Forty minutes ago, he had been on his last leg of his five-mile run, just like any other day. The President was supposed to give a campaign endorsement in support of the GOP challenger in Michigan as they looked to flip that Senate seat. *"How could he have been assassinated?"* he wondered. It had been 55 years since a US president had been assassinated. It didn't seem like this was really possible.

Given the situation, the agents did give him a moment. Then Agent Morrel put his hand on his shoulder. "Sir, we need to move," he said gently.

Foss nodded and stood up. Soon, they rode the elevator out of the bunker, and he was quickly led down a series of hallways until they entered the Oval Office. The moment he walked in the door, everyone stood out of respect. A few people were wiping away tears; others were obviously still in a state of shock themselves. Before he could say anything, his wife walked in with another agent and his two children.

She gave him a quick hug and whispered, "I'm so sorry, Wally. Hang in there. You can do this, and we're here to help you. We have your back." His two children wrapped their arms around the two of them and they shared a family hug.

Just then, the Chief Justice of the Supreme Court finally arrived. He gave a moment for the family reunion, then he walked over with his hand extended. "You have my deepest sympathies, Mr. Vice President," he said. "I still can't believe that someone would assassinate our President like this, but please, we have to get you sworn in. Do you have a Bible you want to use? If not, I brought my own."

Wally's wife, Dana, produced the Foss family Bible. In minutes, Vice President Walter Foss was sworn in as the 46th President of the United States of America. A handful of pictures were taken of the event, and someone from the White House communications department video-recorded the swearing in. Soon these images would be posted to the official government websites and social media accounts. It was imperative that people know the government was still functioning despite this horrific event.

Once the ceremony was complete, the Director of the CIA and the Secretary of Defense urged him to join them and the rest of the national security staff in the briefing room. They had urgent matters to discuss and they needed his authorization. President Foss said a quick goodbye to his wife and two children and quickly followed the men to the Situation Room.

Upon entering the briefing room, the new President took his seat at the head of the table and motioned for everyone else to take their seats. Not looking at any one particular person, he immediately asked, "Could someone please give us an update on what happened in Michigan? Do we know who is responsible? Is the Eastern Alliance involved?"

Maria Nelson, the Director of the FBI, spoke up first. "Mr. President, the information we have presently is incomplete. We are still in the early stages of identifying who the shooter was, and if he was aligned with any of the Eastern Alliance powers or other political groups," she replied.

Maria had just taken over as the new Director of the FBI three weeks ago. She was the first woman to hold the position at the agency. She had previously served as the head of the Science & Technology Directorate at the Department of Homeland Security before President Gates had appointed her to replace FBI Director Flagman, who opted to resign when it had become known that he was the subject of a Department of Justice investigation. When it had become public knowledge that he had tried to cover up the number of foreign agents that had been working within the government, the only way to recover was to step down. Besides, he had failed to investigate the plethora of elected officials who had obviously leaked sensitive and classified information to the press and to American adversaries. Flagman had become persona non grata in the public sphere.

When Gates had nominated someone new to head up the FBI, he had wanted someone who could bring a heavy technology background and fresh perspective. His goal had been to bring someone in who could bring the FBI's way of solving crimes into the 21st century and restore public and political trust back to the agency. Not even a month on the job, and Director Nelson would now have to handle the death of a President and the continued threat of foreign intelligence and Special Forces actively carrying out attacks within the country.

While Foss felt for the situation that the new director found herself in, he wasn't going to give her a lot of extra room. "I need more than that, Maria," he told her bluntly. "What do you guys have so far?"

Director Nelson squirmed in her chair for a second. She looked around to the others in the room before she returned her gaze back to the President. "What we know right now is that the shooter fired multiple shots at President Gates. The first shot hit the President in his bulletproof vest, knocking him to the ground. The second shot hit the Secretary of State when the President's security detailed jumped on top Gates to protect him. As the agents moved to secure the President in the Beast, the shooter fired a third shot. This one struck Gates's bodyguard, went through the agent and hit the President, ultimately killing him."

She sighed, realizing she would have to reveal her hand. "We believe we know who the shooter is, but we are waiting on a few more pieces of information to come in before we make it official. Preliminary reports indicate the shooter is named George Philips, an American citizen. So that means we are not dealing with a foreign national. Mr. Philips is currently in his final year as a PhD student at Brown University, where he was also the university president of the local antifascist or Antifa group. We have agents raiding his apartment in Providence, Rhode Island, right now."

Several of the people near the President grumbled some obscenities. She overheard someone mutter somethings about Antifa having gone too far this time in their political disagreements with the government. President Foss silenced the comments with an icy stare.

"Do we have the shooter in custody yet?" asked Foss.

She shook her head. "No, Mr. President. Not yet. We set up a large cordon around the shooting, but we are not optimistic about capturing him inside of it. There was just too much chaos happening around the area when the shooting started. People started scattering and running every which way, making it incredibly hard to seal everyone inside our search perimeter. I am, however, confident that once we determine he is in fact the shooter, we will apprehend him within the next couple of days. Mr. Philips is not trained in how to evade capture, and he's about to become the most wanted man in America," she added.

Sitting back in his chair for a minute, Foss needed a few seconds to absorb the information. "*What am I supposed to do next?*" he thought.

"OK, here is what I want to happen," the President said. "I want every trail, link, and associate of this Mr. Philips tracked down. We need to find out if he is a lone wolf assassin or if he had help."

Foss then turned to his generals, adding, "I want everything that was going on with the war prior to this shooting to continue. We are not going to alter our plans unless something on the ground changes. In the meantime, I need some time to be brought up to speed on the status of the war, where we stand, and what our next steps are. I want to know everything the President had previously agreed to, what he had turned down, and any additional options that were to be brought up to him prior to the assassination. Let's reconvene the war council in two days, once I've had some time to get caught up. Director Nelson, I want hourly updates from your office and Homeland on this manhunt."

With his first orders as President issued, Foss got up and left the Situation Room to return to the Oval Office and try to figure out exactly what he was supposed to do next.

****

Staten Island, New York
Arthur Kill Inlet, Kinder Morgan Terminal

Mikhail Fedorov ducked his head slightly and moved into the small cabin of the speedboat he and his colleagues would be using for this operation. It was still relatively dark, and the others wouldn't arrive for at least another twenty minutes, but he wanted to make sure everything was ready. He reached down and grabbed several fishing poles and brought them out to the main deck. Once there, he assembled the poles before placing them in the six trolling pole holders, three on each side of the open-air cabin.

Running his hand across the side of the cabin wall, Mikhail had to admit, he really loved this boat. He had purchased the 42-foot Boston Whaler fishing boat two years ago and had really taken to the sport. He'd go out several times a week with friends he'd made through work and genuinely enjoyed his time out on the water. In many cases, he'd head down the Arthur Kill Inlet, which was part of the waterway that surrounded Statin Island and was fed by the Hackensack, Passaic, and Rahway Rivers from New Jersey. It was more of an industrial channel than a commercial or recreational one, but he made sure to use it often, so his boat became a normal sight there.

Hearing some voices coming closer to him, Mikhail looked up. He smiled as he saw that his three compatriots had found the marina.

"Mikhail, you're a lucky man to live here. This place is beautiful," Artem Petrikov said. He tossed his duffel back to Mikhail, who caught it with both hands, grunting as the weight of the bag hit him. The other two Spetsnaz men near Artem climbed aboard the boat, handling their four-foot black hockey bags a lot more gingerly than Artem had.

Shaking his head, Mikhail asked, "What the heck is in here?"

Patting Mikhail on the shoulder, the ringleader Artem coyly answered, "The tools needed to complete this next mission." Then his facial expressions became more serious. "Is Daria ready to meet us?" he asked. "It's important that she be ready to pick everyone up and know how to get us to the safe house once this show starts."

"Daria is ready. The van is fueled, and we've checked everything: headlights, taillights, and blinkers. There should be nothing that draws attention to the vehicle by law enforcement. She'll get you to the safe house,"

Mikhail replied, annoyed at being questioned for probably the fifth or sixth time in the last two days.

Artem nodded. "Mikhail, I only ask about these details because these are the issues that often lead to people being stopped. This is perhaps the most dangerous mission my team has embarked upon. We need to do our best to make sure we survive so we can carry out future attacks as directed. There are not many direct-action units left in America, so the ones that are still alive and operating need to make sure we do what we can to keep carrying out missions for the Motherland."

Mikhail nodded, then changed the subject by pulling up the news report. The assassination of President Gates was all anyone had been talking about the past couple of days. Apparently, the shooter was still at large, despite the authorities having released his picture and name the same day the President had been shot. There was a massive manhunt underway across the country.

"How long do you think it will take them to find the President's shooter?" inquired Mikhail.

Thinking about that for a second, Artem replied, "A couple more days, tops. I'm not aware of the shooter being a part of any of our teams, and I don't believe Moscow would have sanctioned an action like that. From what the media is saying, the shooter appears to be a leader with the American antifascist group." Chuckling for a second, he added, "I find it funny that he was ultimately killed by a PhD student, an academic." He shook his head in disbelief.

Mikhail untied the last line that had been keeping the boat tied to the slip before turning on the engine. With a half dozen fishing poles hanging off the side of the cabin, the twin 300-horsepower engines purred softly as the boat cut gently through the water, leading them to the Hudson River, toward the Arthur Kill Inlet and their primary target.

An hour went by as the four of them drove the boat down the Hudson until they came to the inlet. The sun was fully up at that point, and it had turned into a beautiful morning, with the sun glistening off the skyscrapers of Manhattan to their left and the Statue of Liberty and Ellis Island to their right. When they turned to head closer to their target, two of the Spetsnaz soldiers went below to the galley and began to get their weapon of choice for this operation ready.

"We are almost to the target now, if you want to see it," Mikhail said to the two men who were getting the Kornet-EM missile ready. One of the soldiers brought the tripod launcher up to the front of the boat to set it up, while the other brought the tube with the missile. The two Spetsnaz soldiers got the antitank missile system configured deftly, like practiced professionals. Unlike the Sagger missile systems of old, the Kornets were true fire-and-forget missiles. The specific version they would be using for this attack was the EM Thermobaric, which packed a 10-kilogram high-explosive warhead, perfect for what they wanted to blow up.

As they got the missile set up on the bow of the ship, the soldiers looked at the Kinder Morgan Terminal and smiled as they saw the 37 fuel tanks, which housed roughly 2,900,000 barrels of gasoline.

Letting out a soft whistle, Artem turned to Mikhail. "I fully understand why you said this target had to be destroyed with a Kornet-EM," he said. "If we tried to use an RPG, we'd all be killed when that place goes up." He obviously had a new appreciation for the work the GRU agent had done ahead of time.

Mikhail smiled, happy to have his efforts recognized. "I'm going to get us roughly 8,000 meters from the terminal," he explained. "Once the missile hits, I'm going to floor it down the inlet to try and get as much distance between us and the terminal as possible. Even still, I can't say with certainty that we won't be consumed in the blast if that entire place goes up at once. If that tanker farm is full, then it can hold nearly three million barrels of petrol. I can't even imagine how big of a bang that place will set off."

He brought the boat speed down to just a couple miles per hour, enough to steer and hold it in position. One of the Russian soldiers turned the missile seeker on and identified its target. "I sure hope you calculated this out, Mikhail," Artem said nervously. "If not, we're going to die in a fiery blast." With that, he nodded toward the soldier who was going to fire the missile.

Pop. Whoosh!

The Kornet-EM ignited and shot off the bow of the boat, headed right for one of the fuel tanks. As soon as the missile had cleared the boat, Mikhail gunned the engine, racing down the rest of the inlet, doing his best to place as much distance between them and the fuel farm as humanly possible. The 1,400-horsepower engine roared as the boat picked up speed. Mikhail snuck a peek over his shoulder and spotted the missile completing the last leg of its journey as it slammed into one of the fuel tanks, causing a small explosion. The initial blast suddenly ballooned as the petrol caught fire, causing the entire tank to explode. Seconds later, more tanks blew up, adding their own mayhem to the growing conflagration, until the entire terminal detonated in one gigantic cauldron of fire that rapidly expanded beyond the terminal, engulfing a second oil wholesaler terminal across the inlet. That terminal, which housed an additional twenty fuel tanks, also exploded, adding to the growing firestorm. Fires began spreading across fuel pipelines to the other tank terminals nearby.

While Mikhail was doing his best to race down the inlet and maintain control of the speedboat, he felt the concussion of the blast. The heatwave rippled across his body and the boat, and he almost lost control when a large wave nearly pushed them into the bank of the inlet. Turning to look back one last time, he saw the fireball had grown enormous as it reached for the heavens.

"*I knew those terminals were all connected,*" he thought smugly, satisfied with his work. After years of covert effort, now all that was left to do was escape.

"We did it, Mikhail," said Artem with glee. "How long until we reach the marina?"

"A few more minutes," Mikhail responded. "Daria is waiting for us with a vehicle once we get there. She'll drive us to the next drop vehicle at a park maybe three miles away. From there, we'll largely stay on country roads as we drive to the cabin we'll be using as a safe house."

Nodding in approval, Artem just smiled. Mikhail knew exactly what he was thinking. They had just destroyed a major part of the Northeast's fuel supply and storage terminals. This would surely hurt the Americans.

****

Washington, D.C.
White House, Oval Office

The weather was dreary. As President Foss stared out through the bulletproof windows of the Oval Office, rain suddenly started pouring down. In the distance, he could still see people gathered outside the perimeter fence, holding vigil for the deceased President Gates. The formal funeral had taken place earlier that day, with the President's body having been brought from the capital building to lie in repose at Arlington Cemetery, where the other bodies of assassinated presidents had been laid to rest.

Knock, knock.

The sudden noise pierced his inner thoughts, pulling him back to reality. Turning, he saw his personal assistant standing in the doorway. "The Director of the FBI, Homeland and the National Security Advisor are ready. Shall I send them in?" the aide asked.

Nodding, Foss signaled with his hand for them to be brought in. He then took his seat behind the desk as the three individuals walked into the room and stood before him. Looking up, he simply asked, "Is he in custody?"

Smiling, Maria Nelson replied, "Yes. We just caught him thirty minutes ago. We're about to break the news to the media."

Foss let out a deep breath, obviously relieved. "What more do we know about him?" he asked.

"We've looked into all of the people he's been in contact with and his past activities. We know from the initial interviews we've conducted of his associates, fellow classmates, and professors that he believed President Gates was a fascist that needed to be stopped, and he felt compelled to act out of fear that his younger brother, who had been drafted into the Marines, would die in Asia if the President was not stopped."

"Do we know if he had any foreign support or help? You had told me that he was an Antifa leader at his university."

"He had led and organized a series of protests and work stoppages at a number of defense manufacturers in his local area. In doing so, he routinely met with the Northeast director of the organization and the international leader, a man by the name of Peter Talley who's based out of London. As we dug further into Mr. Talley's background and coordinated our findings with MI5 and MI6, we discovered that Mr. Talley had also been on their radar for several years. Apparently, they believe he may in fact be a man by the name of Vasily Smirnov, a major in the Russian GRU."

Tilting his head slightly to the right, the President asked, "Are you saying the GRU is organizing or controlling the Antifa organization?"

Tom McMillan, the National Security Advisor, replied, "Not exactly. We don't believe Antifa is an overtly Russian-backed or Russian-sponsored organization. However, they are being heavily financed and influenced by the GRU. The Russians' goal is presumably to leverage any domestic groups, both liberal and conservative, that are against the war in order to disrupt or negatively influence the war effort."

Clearing her throat, DHS Director Molly Emerson added, "The problem we have with Antifa is we now have credible evidence that their international director, a man who has traveled and met extensively with other Antifa leaders in the US, is a Russian spy. He personally knew and worked with George Philips. Mr. Philips was also receiving a monthly stipend of $5,000 a month from the international Antifa organization as a university leader. When we inquired further into the organization's finances, we discovered that there are only three other Antifa leaders in the US receiving a stipend from the international organization. All the other leaders are doing this pro bono, volunteering their time and skills."

Director Emerson continued, "In March of 2018, Mr. Philips purchased the rifle he used to kill the President. The rifle and the optical system he used, combined with the four months of shooting lessons he received, cost roughly $9,000. Several weeks prior to his purchasing the rifle, Mr. Talley, aka Major Smirnov, had wire-transferred that exact amount to Mr. Philips. Right now, we are working under the assumption that Major Smirnov knew Mr. Philips was susceptible to recruitment as an assassin and provided the material support needed to make that a reality. It is my assessment, and my department's assessment, that the GRU ordered the assassination of President Gates and used Mr. Philips to achieve that goal."

An awkward pause sat in the room. *The Russians ordered the assassination of our president, during a time of war?*" thought Foss incredulously. He couldn't wrap his head around that reality.

After a moment, Foss turned to Maria Nelson. "Is this the FBI's assessment as well? Do you guys have an alternate theory, or is this where the evidence is leading you too?"

Maria took a deep breath in and slowly let it out before responding, "I'm not yet 100% ready to make that same leap. The information we have is pointing in that direction, but we need to interrogate Mr. Philips first. I want more evidence before we firmly come to that conclusion."

President Foss frowned a bit. He appreciated Director Nelson's thoroughness, but it wasn't the answer he wanted to hear.

"Mr. President," interjected McMillan, "I concur with the FBI that they need to identify more definitive links between the GRU and the assassination of the President. However, the intelligence community and Homeland Security are not responsible for building an evidence-based case for a criminal conviction in this situation. We need to look at the circumstantial evidence that is not always sufficient in a court of law. Right now, we have corroborating information from MI6 and MI5 that Mr. Talley is a suspected Russian spy. We know Mr. Talley is the international organizer, financier and lobbying point of contact for Antifa. We also know he met and worked with Mr. Philips for more than a year. The intelligence suggests that Mr. Talley had at least provided material support to the man who assassinated the President. We don't know if he directed the assassination, but at this point it doesn't matter. He provided the assassin with the financial and material means to do it, which makes him just as culpable in our eyes. With your permission, I would like to move that we place Mr. Talley on our Top Most Wanted list, both domestically and internationally. We need to take him into custody and question him further."

Maria's countenance had changed during McMillian's speech, as if she were visibly changing her opinion. "Mr. President, I agree with the NSA on this one. We need to apprehend Mr. Talley at once," she urged.

"OK, let's pick Mr. Talley up," the President agreed. "Where is he currently?"

"Philadelphia," answered Molly. "We're tracking down the exact location, but we'll have it shortly. We know he flew into Newark three days prior to the assassination. He spoke at Antifa rallies at Columbia University and the City College of New York. The day before the assassination, he led a protest march at Global Container Terminals in Jersey City. Their goal for the day was to shut down the port's activity by chaining themselves to the terminal gates and creating human barricades across the streets leading to the container terminal. They essentially stopped the port operations until the police could break them up," Molly said.

"What is that port terminal doing to support the war?" inquired the President.

"This terminal, along with many others on the East Coast, is responsible for loading the dozens upon dozens of transports moving munitions and other war stocks to Europe," explained Molly. "What's suspect about these types of protests is they always seem to happen when a Global Defense Force convoy arrives from Europe. If they were just targeting this one particular port, we could move the operation to another one. The problem is these protests hit every port on the East and West Coast that's being used to support the war efforts in Europe and Asia."

President Foss rubbed his chin. He had only been doing this job for eight days, and it still felt like he was drinking from a firehose. He'd heard a bit about protests from the nightly news, but his attention had been focused on other situations until now. He leaned forward. "Are other antiwar groups participating in these types of work stoppages? How much of an impact are these activities having on the war?"

Molly and Maria both turned to Tom, gesturing for him to take that question. "Antifa is the main culprit, but there is a large conservative group that also joins in from time to time, called Southerners Against the War. They largely carry out these types of work stoppages at the Southern ports. As to what kind of effect are they having on the war…a lot. Let me put it this way, Mr. President. A tank round is produced in a factory in Pennsylvania on Tuesday. On Thursday, the round arrives in port and is loaded onto a ship that same day. Saturday, that ship leaves in a convoy, and it arrives in Antwerp seven days later. Five days after that, the round is loaded into an M1 Abrams battle tank, and two days later it's fired at a Russian tank. The time from when the round is produced to when it's fired by one of our tanks is roughly seventeen days. If we flew that round on a cargo plane, then the time from factory to firing would be reduced to seven days." He sighed. "We are so low on munitions in Europe that these work stoppages truly have the potential to be the deciding factor in whether our front-line forces have enough ammunition or whether they're forced to retreat or surrender because they ran out of bullets or tank rounds."

The President sat back in his chair digesting what Tom had just said. "*Gates really shielded me from a lot,*" he realized. He wondered how his friend had managed to stay so calm under all this pressure, and how he had managed to hide the dire circumstances of the war.

Looking at Tom and then Molly, the President's eyes narrowed. "This has to stop. We can't allow these organizations to pose this significant of a risk to our winning this war. I have no problem with people exercising their First Amendment rights, but not at the expense of putting our soldiers' lives at risk. Director Emerson, if you can find a legal link between these organizations' activity and the Russian GRU, then I want these groups disbanded and labeled as GRU-sponsored groups. If people participate in these types of activities—stopping the day-to-day operations of a factory, port, or any other function that would result in the delay of war stocks arriving at the front lines—then I want those people charged with providing material support to the enemy during a time of war. Is that understood?" he asked.

The three of them nodded.

Shaking his head for a second, President Foss waved his left hand slightly. "I'm sorry that I got us distracted down that rabbit hole," he said. "Where is Mr. Talley at this point?"

Molly took her cue. "The day of the assassination, Mr. Talley traveled to Chicago. He gave a speech at the

University of Chicago the day after and then participated in a work stoppage rally at Boeing's downtown office, which happens to be where their design team is for the various suite of military drones we are currently using. As of right this moment, he is scheduled to give a speech at the University of Pennsylvania tomorrow morning and then catch a flight back to London tomorrow night."

"Apprehend him tomorrow before he gives his speech," the President ordered. "Try to do it quietly if you can, maybe do a raid on wherever he's sleeping."

The group talked for a few minutes more before the directors of Homeland Security and the FBI left, leaving just the President and his National Security Advisor. Looking at Tom, the President commented, "What you told me about the supply problem is really disconcerting." He paused, then blurted out, "Why is the problem so bad? Why are we not able to keep our army properly supplied?"

Tom briefly turned away from the President as he grabbed one of the nearby chairs and pulled it up to the President's desk and sat down. "I'm sorry, Sir—my back is killing me," Tom said as he got comfortable in the chair. "The issue with supply chain is our capacity to meet the demand. We've drafted millions of young men and women into the military. The ammunition needed to properly train this new army of millions of people is incredible. We are actually consuming nearly as much ammunition in training as we are in combat operations in Europe and Asia. The other problem is that we have active battle campaigns underway in the Russian Far East involving more than 200,000 soldiers, an active campaign in the Philippines involving more than 180,000 soldiers, and two campaigns in Europe involving 360,000 soldiers. Our forces are spread too thin, and we aren't able to concentrate on any particular theater because we're being hit on so many different fronts."

"What did Gates want to do about this problem prior to being killed?" asked Foss, running his fingers through his hair.

"He wanted to slow the war down," McMillan answered. "He'd ordered General Cotton to place everything on hold in Europe and stay on defense. Gates prioritized the invasion of Taiwan over everything else. His thinking was that once Taiwan was back in our hands, we could shift our focus back to Europe while we continued to grind the Chinese economy down through cyberattacks and precision airstrikes."

Foss leaned in. "Why prioritize Taiwan over Europe?"

"It comes down to weather, Mr. President," explained Tom. "From November to March is considered typhoon season in Taiwan. If we don't land our forces and establish a beachhead before the prolonged severe weather sets in, then we risk starting a major invasion and possibly having a typhoon interrupt our ability to support the ground force. If we wait to invade until the spring, then we just give the Chinese another eight months to entrench themselves, and they'll be that much harder to remove."

The President grunted.

McMillan continued, "As it stands, combat operations are starting to peter out in the Russian Far East as winter creeps ever closer. We have to remember that most of that is Siberia—incredibly poor infrastructure and horribly cold temperatures. With the defeat of the Indian Army a month ago, the priority threat to our forces there is now going to be the freezing temperatures. As operations there come to a close until spring, we can shift more of our resources to Taiwan and Europe."

"How soon until we're ready to invade Taiwan?" asked the President. After the assassination of Gates and the horrific attacks on Statin Island and Jersey City, the country was reeling. Foss wanted to be seen as decisive in the face of all this chaos. The country needed a win.

"We had planned on launching the invasion on October 1st, Sir," said McMillan. "In light of everything that has been happening here, we can probably move the invasion up by fifteen days, but I wouldn't try it any sooner. We should also speak with the Chairman of the Joint Chiefs and get his opinion to make sure the military is ready."

The President crossed his arms. "Set up a meeting for tomorrow with the war council, then," he ordered, "but call the chairman today and let him know that I want to launch the invasion of Taiwan at the soonest possible date."

Foss stood, indicating the conversation was over.

"Yes, Sir, Mr. President," Tom answered, and they walked out together, ready to get to work.

Chapter 2
Battle of Taiwan

Luzon, Philippines
Clarke International Airport

Loading another thirty-round magazine and placing it in one of his front ammo pouches, Staff Sergeant Conrad Price smelled the pungent scent of jet fuel intermixed with the humidity and smell of death that still permeated the air around this hard-fought military base. Sprawled out in the recently repaired cargo hangar were the men of Bravo Company, 2nd Battalion, 75th Ranger Regiment, the US Army's premier shock troops. The Rangers had just finished their preflight briefing and were now doing their final equipment checks before they would load up into the C-17 Globemasters that would ferry them to their drop zone.

Price looked down at his right hand, his trigger hand, and saw a slight tremor. He quickly flexed his fingers and went back to loading another magazine before anyone noticed. His nerves were starting to get the best of him as his mind wandered back to one of their earlier combat jumps. No matter how hard he tried to push the image out of his mind, he kept seeing his best friend, Joe Perez, lying in his arms, bleeding out from multiple bullet holes. Joe had saved him that day, and he'd paid the ultimate price for his country and his fellow Rangers. The look of fear on his friend's face as his eyes had pleaded with Price for help would often cause him to break down emotionally when he was alone. He couldn't afford for those emotions to surface now, not before a mission.

That was eleven months ago, but it still felt like yesterday. *"How many friends have I lost in this war? Too freaking many!"* he thought.

Sergeant Price angrily rammed another 5.56mm round into his last magazine. He desperately fought to turn those emotions of sorrow, pain and loss into a burning rage toward the enemy that had taken so much from him. That smoldering anger had kept him alive up to this point. He'd even been awarded the Silver Star for savagely charging and taking out an enemy machine-gun position in Siberia three months earlier. In his private moments, he'd secretly wished he'd been killed so that the pain would end, but since that hadn't happened, he'd brutally killed the occupants of the fortified position with his trench knife when his rifle jammed.

With his magazines loaded, Price reached over and grabbed six fragmentation grenades and fastened them to his chest rig, making sure he'd wrapped the pins with at least one strip of tape. He firmly believed in the power of Murphy's Law, and he wasn't about to be that soldier whose pin got caught on something and the grenade went off.

Now that his personal kit was ready, he made sure his rucksack was packed with three changes of socks packed in Ziploc bags, a thousand rounds of ammo, two bricks of C4, four MREs, and the rest of the stuff needed to survive for several days, in case they were unable to get a quick resupply. Fastening his last piece of equipment to his ruck, he hoped the troops hitting the beaches would be able to relieve them according to the plan. Snorting to himself, he remembered something his dad used to tell him: "Everyone has a plan until they get punched in the face, son." It seemed like an apt comment at that point.

Seeing that his own equipment was ready, Price walked over to check on the eight other guys in his squad. They had nervous looks on their faces like him, but also that sense of duty and purpose as well. Like him, they had all volunteered to serve in the Rangers, to be the tip of the proverbial spear and carry out the high-risk missions. Of course, the extra $750 a month in special pay was an added bonus.

"How's my face paint look, Staff Sergeant?" asked Specialist Michael Cochran as he finished rubbing some OD Green paint on an exposed part of his neck, lowering the small mirror he was using.

"I think if you stand still, you could pass as a tree," Price replied, drawing a few laughs from the others and cutting the tension in the room.

One of the other privates chimed in, "Tell us this isn't a suicide mission the brass is sending us on, Staff Sergeant."

Specialist Alistair Waters, the squad comedian, interjected, "Since when is doing a night jump onto an occupied enemy air base a suicide mission? It would only be a suicide mission if we did it during the day—at night, it's a walk in the park." He got a few more chuckles from the Rangers around them.

A few minutes later, they heard the roaring sound of a C-17 pulling up near the hangar they were huddled in. After just a couple more moments, a total of four of the aircraft had positioned themselves near the hangars, their rear cargo ramps dropping down so the Rangers could load on in. Two platoons were slated to pile into each plane, giving them some extra space so they would have room to set up their parachute rigs once they got closer to the drop zone. They were going to be in the air for close to seven hours, too long to stay strapped to their rigging.

Prior to the soldiers moving to board the C-17s, several fuel trucks drove out to the planes and topped off their tanks for the flight. They'd be making one midair refueling before they reached their final destination.

They were all abuzz with adrenaline. The 2nd Battalion, 75th Rangers had been given the inglorious task of capturing the Taiwanese Air Force base just north of the city of Taitung, on the southeast side of the island. The battalion would land on and around the air base and secure the area for follow-on forces. While that was taking place, two Australian infantry battalions would land near Taitung and move in to secure it. Following their attack, the US Army's 63rd Infantry Division would land and assist in securing the southern half of the island. Once the Rangers had secured the air base, a brigade from the 82nd Airborne would start to arrive and bring with them a series of light armored vehicles and artillery support.

"Everyone up! It's time to load up," yelled their platoon leader.

The Rangers dutifully carried their gear and parachute rigs with them to the transports. They'd assemble their parachute rigs once they got closer to the drop zone;

until then, they'd contemplate the inevitable jump and what awaited them once they landed.

****

120 Miles off the East Coast of Taiwan

Aboard the USS *Gerald Ford*, Captain Patricia Fleece poured herself another cup of coffee from the hot pot in the combat information center or CIC. She was still grateful that the last massive battle she had participated in had turned into a victory, even if it hadn't been as decisive as it could have been. If things had gone even slightly differently, she wouldn't be standing there drinking a mug of java. She constantly remembered how lucky she was to be alive and still have command of a ship.

On the big board, she could see the destroyers and cruisers were in the process of firing their Tomahawk cruise missiles at the various land targets on the island. Above them, the Commander Air Group, or CAG, was in the process of launching the carrier's airwing of F-35s to go in first and take out the known enemy air-defense sites. This would be quickly followed by a squadron of F/A-18s that will be conducting Wild Weasel missiles, trying to get an enemy radar to lock on them so they could fire a HAARM missile, specially designed to follow the enemy's targeting radar to its source and destroy it. As they destroyed more and more of the Chinese's targeting radars, their air-defense systems would crumble until they no longer posed a threat. Then, the real bombing attacks would commence.

"How much longer until the ground invasion starts?" Captain Fleece asked Admiral Cord, who was nibbling on a small sandwich the galley had brought up for the crew.

"A couple of hours," she replied. "You see that track of aircraft that just entered our bubble in the south?" she asked, pointing to a new cluster of aircraft that were slowly making their way toward them.

"Yeah, I see it," Fleece responded.

"That's the lead airborne element of the Rangers," Cord explained. "They're going to try and seize that PLA Air Force base down in Taitung City, where those Tomahawks are about to hit. If the rest of the fleet times everything right, the first wave of Australians should be hitting the beaches near there about the same time the paratroopers hit the airport. To the north, the Marines will land near Luodong." She spoke as if instructing a class of naval officers at Annapolis—except this was a real invasion, not some tabletop exercise. While the invasion of Luzon was the largest naval invasion since World War II, the invasion of Taiwan was significantly larger.

Admiral Cord took the last bite of her sandwich, then asserted, "I'm going to order the strike group to start moving in closer to the shore. I want our ships closer to the landing force. Do you have any objections?"

"No, I think it's a good idea to move in closer to land in case some of our fighters sustain combat damage and need to make an emergency landing," Captain Fleece replied. "I wasn't too keen on being this far out from where our fighters were striking either—it limits the payload they can carry."

"Things are about to get real crazy for the next couple of days," said Cord, smoothing back a hair that had fallen out of her bun. "I need you to stay on top of your people. If you see someone getting too tired, swap them out for a fresh body. We're going to have tens of thousands of soldiers and Marines landing in what will likely be a very contested landing."

Fleece nodded. "We're ready, Admiral. You can count on the *Ford*."

****

The water was relatively calm as the Marines of Echo Company, 2nd Battalion, 6th Marines loaded up into the amphibious assault vehicles or AAVs that would ferry them to the beach. Due to the heavy presence of enemy air-defense systems, it had been determined by the brass that the Marines would only conduct a seaborne assault, so they wouldn't risk losing dozens of troop transport helicopters. This, of course, meant the AAVs would have to make several trips to the ships to get everyone ashore, but it was a small price to pay until they were able to neutralize the enemy air-defense systems.

Checking his own equipment one more time, Captain Tim Long ducked his head slightly as he climbed aboard the vehicle that would ferry him to the shore. This would be his second seaborne invasion of the war, and the third time he was part of the first wave of an invasion. He wasn't sure if he should feel honored, nervous, or worried that his luck might run out this time.

"Third time's a charm, or something like that," he finally determined.

Five minutes after sealing the hatch to the vehicle, they rumbled toward the back ramp until they reached the inevitable edge and drove right off. The AAV briefly dipped under the water before popping to the surface like a buoy. The driver effortlessly turned the vehicle toward the shore and gave it some juice. In short order, their vehicle fell into formation with the other AAVs that made up the first three waves of the assault. Following those initial waves were the larger LCACs, hovercrafts that would bring their tanks and other armored vehicles ashore.

While their vehicle slowly made its way to the beach, one of the privates asked, "Do you think the Chinese will be waiting for us at the shore?"

Captain Long turned to look at the private and saw that everyone else in the vehicle was now looking at him, waiting to hear what he would say.

"Probably," he answered matter-of-factly. "This is my third invasion. Each time, the PLA was waiting for us. I would suspect they'll be waiting for us here as well. However, we've trained for this. We all survived the Philippine campaign, and we'll survive this campaign as well. Remember your training, and do your best to look out for each other. Work as a team, and we'll come through this." As he spoke, he did his best to convey strength and optimism to them.

The vehicle sloshed around a bit in the waves as they got closer to the shore, and the motion pushed their vehicle forward. One of the Marines got sick and puked in a barf bag that the vehicle commander had handed him when they'd boarded. Apparently, the crew was tired of cleaning puke out from seasick Marines, not to mention having to drive around all day in a vehicle with vomit swishing around on the floor.

"We're approaching the beach!" yelled the gunner from his perched position.

"*Strange. I'm not hearing any explosions or machine-gun fire,*" Long thought.

"Hang on, we've reached the beach," the vehicle commander told Captain Long. "We're going to drive up a bit and get you guys closer to the actual city before we turn around and go back for the next load."

Seconds later, their AAV hit the soft sand and increased speed up the beach. Even as they moved up past the shoreline onto rockier areas, there still had been no reported contact with the enemy. It was quiet—no heavy machine guns, no artillery, rockets, or mortars. It was eerily silent. The hairs on the back of Captain Long's neck stood straight up. Something about this situation just seemed wrong.

A few minutes into their drive, the vehicle commander halted the track and dropped the rear hatch. In seconds, everyone was out. They found themselves at the edge of a row of condos and other buildings that faced the ocean. There were no civilians or enemy soldiers there to greet them, not even a stray dog.

"Everyone, fan out and start clearing these houses," Captain Long ordered. "We need to get the beachhead secured!"

Long turned to find his radioman. "Tell the other platoons to begin searching the nearby houses and make sure they are cleared. Also, send a SITREP back to the *Wasp* and let them know we're on the beach and securing it. Tell them we haven't encountered any enemy resistance as of yet."

Captain Long searched the nearby faces until he located his sniper team lead. "Staff Sergeant Jenkins!" he shouted, waving his hand.

The staff sergeant heard his name and ran quickly to Long. "Sir?" he asked.

"Get your snipers deployed on the roofs of these buildings and start scanning those hills and ridges. I find it hard to believe the PLA would willingly give up the beach without a fight. I think we just walked into a trap," Long explained.

"We're on it, Sir!" shouted Jenkins as he motioned for his sniper teams to get moving.

Ten minutes went by with Captain Long's company clearing one building after another along the coastal city before they made their way inland. During that time, the second wave of Marines had landed, bringing the other two battalions of their regiment forward. The LCACs were going to wait to bring their armor ashore after the third wave landed, but with the first two waves not encountering any type of resistance, they opted to move in and get the tanks and LAVs ashore before their luck turned.

Captain Long led his Marines further inland until they came to Qinqyun Road, the main road that separated the oceanfront part of the city from the more inland part that ran all the way up to the mountains. It also divided the east coast of the island from the west coast and the city of New Taipei. Looking up at the rising mountain scape they were walking toward, Captain Long thought he saw a glint of something. Several areas of the mountain had thick, black, oily smoke rising to the sky—a cruise missile or airstrike must have found something of value to hit.

Boom, boom, boom. Thump, thump, thump…

Suddenly, the world around Captain Long's company exploded. Artillery and mortar rounds landed all over the part of the city his men had just walked into. Chunks of buildings, parts of parked cars, and clumps of dirt and concrete were thrown around in all directions like flying pieces of shrapnel, adding further chaos to the carnage that was being unleashed upon the Marines.

"Take cover!" Long shouted. His men were already seeking shelter against the sides of the buildings that hadn't been pulverized during the initial barrage.

Captain Long turned back and scanned the ridgeline for the source of the barrage. Then, further up the mountainside, he saw the cause of their peril—cleverly hidden bunkers firing down on to them.

Screams for corpsmen pierced the air as the wounded called out for help. Looking back to the beach, Captain Long saw dozens upon dozens of explosions rocking the beach where his Marines had just been ten minutes earlier. Several of the LCACs that had zoomed in to land their armored vehicles had been hit on their way off the beach and now lay in the shallow waters as burning wrecks.

Some of the tanks that had made it ashore trained their main guns on the bunkers that were firing on the beach, sending well-aimed shots right back at the enemy. Several of the bunkers—the ones with artillery guns hidden in them— were starting to be blown up by the Marine tanks.

Knowing his Marines couldn't stay where they were, Captain Long yelled, "Everyone, move forward!" They needed to get closer in to the hills and the mountains if they were to escape the deadly artillery fire that was still raining down on them.

Steadily, Captain Long's Marines made their way through the now torn and destroyed seaside city to the rolling hills at the base of the mountain range that separated the island. When they reached the edge of the city, they were met by yet another nasty surprise. One of the fireteams ran to the base of the first hill, only to be ripped apart by machine-gun fire. The weapon of death that shredded them to pieces was one of the Chinese Hua Qing miniguns, which launched 7.62×54mm rounds from its multiple barrels so quickly that the soldiers were decimated before they even knew what had happened. This fearsome weapon then turned toward the rest of his company of Marines, and they immediately dove for cover in the mounting rubble of the city.

Captain Long grabbed his radio receiver and contacted his heavy weapons platoon. "Lieutenant Lightman, get your mortars set up and start pounding those bunkers up here!" he shouted.

Raising his own rifle to his shoulder, Long took aim at the machine-gun bunker with the Hua Qing minigun in it and fired several rounds at the location where he thought the gunner must have been. For a few seconds, the gun stopped firing, and Captain Long thought he might have been successful in his efforts. Then the shooting picked back up again.

"*Crap!*" thought Long.

Green tracer rounds zipped over his head and stitched up the buildings and anything else his men were using for cover. Aiming for the same spot he had just sent a few rounds into, Captain Long squeezed off another four or five rounds. The gun went silent again. This time, one of his Marines fired off an AT-4 rocket, which hit just below the gun slit, throwing a lot of shrapnel and fire into the bunker.

Just as another fireteam charged forward, two more hidden machine-gun bunkers opened fire, killing two of the Marines outright and wounding the others. Several of his Marines ran out there to help drag the wounded to cover, only to be cut down by the PLA soldiers, who were now going to use those wounded Marines as bait to kill more of his men. Before Captain Long could say anything, a handful of mortar rounds hit the area around the bunker.

A moment later, Long's radio crackled. "Pit Bull Six, this is Dog Catcher Six. How copy?" He recognized the voice on the other end as Colonel Tilman, his regiment commander.

Slouching down behind the half-destroyed wall of the building he had taken cover in, Captain Long hit the talk button on his radio. "This is Pit Bull Six. Send," he responded.

"Is the path to the base of the mountain clear?" asked Tilman.

"Negative, Dog Catcher. We've encountered several lines of well-camouflaged machine-gun bunkers protecting the base of the mountain. Some of the bunkers are equipped with miniguns, which are tearing us up. I've got dozens of wounded up here," he replied.

Long heard a sigh on the other end. He knew that Tilman would not be happy. The guys on the beach were probably getting pounded. He'd probably hoped that if they could push through to the base of the mountain, they might be able to get some reprieve from the enemy artillery fire.

"Copy that, Pit Bull," Tilman said after a slight pause. "We have fast movers inbound from the fleet. Their call sign is Angel Eight. Use them to clear out those bunkers in front of your position and advance to the base of the mountain. We need to clear a path off this godforsaken beach. How copy?" Colonel Tilman shouted to be heard over the explosions in the background.

"That's a good copy, Dog Catcher," replied Long. "I'll contact you once we're past this line of machine-gun bunkers."

He put down his receiver and turned to his radio operator, who had a separate UHF radio that was designated for air support. Sadly, the ground forces operated on one set of radio frequencies and radio system, while the Air Force and naval aircraft operated on a different system entirely, which required the ground forces to have either two radios or a forward air controller who could speak directly to the fighters overhead. The battalion and regiment had a FAC, but not the individual companies.

Once his radioman had set the right frequency in place, he handed the handset to Captain Long, who proceeded to make contact with the F/A-18s that had just been assigned to him.

"Angel Eight, this is Pit Bull Six. We have troops in contact," he began. "Requesting danger close mission at grid TA 5764 4765, enemy machine-gun bunker. How copy?"

There was a short silence. "Pit Bull Six, that's a good copy," the pilot responded. "How many targets do you have for us?"

"Angel Eight, I estimate at least five enemy bunkers to our immediate front," explained Long. "However, I have eyes on at least twelve bunkers nestled into the mountains that are hitting the beach with artillery fire. What type of ordnance do you have?"

After another brief pause, the pilot's radio had caught up. "We have a mix of 500-pound and 2,000-pound JDAMs. We'll drop the 500-pounders near your position and save the big boys for the mountain bunkers. Send us the coordinates for the other bunkers, and we'll hit them on our next pass across the island." The pilot's voice sounded so nonchalant from the safety of his high-altitude perch.

Five more minutes went by as they fed the planes somewhere above them the coordinates to seventeen separate targets. Then, one by one, the bunkers were hit. Many of them were completely blown apart. Within seconds of the bombs landing, more than half of the artillery fire that was devastating the beachhead ceased. The machine-gun bunkers directly in front of his company front had also been destroyed. By this time, another company of Marines had pushed through the enemy artillery fire to reach their position. With the bunkers destroyed, or at least temporarily taken offline, the Marines charged forward, quickly overrunning the enemy positions as they pushed their way to the base of the mountain.

The fight to liberate Taiwan was on, and it was going to be another bloody campaign before it was over.

****

East Coast of Taiwan

High above the coastal city of Toucheng, there was an old Buddhist temple that sat just off the Fudekeng Industrial Road, halfway up the mountain that divided the Island of Formosa. It was at this little piece of paradise that Brigadier General Lee Jinping and Major General Xian Loa were observing the American fleet advancing toward them.

"It won't be long until they begin to land their Marines," General Xian thought in anticipation as he looked at the ships approaching the coast.

"When do you want our anti-ship missile batteries to start attacking the American warships?" inquired General Lee.

Xian lowered his binoculars and examined General Lee's face. He seemed eager to put his fortifications to the test. "Soon," General Xian responded. "Right now, the Americans have no idea what we have waiting for them. We want to let them deploy their ships, offload their ground force and then hammer their ships. What I want our forces to do right now is to be patient. We must wait for the Americans to land a substantial ground force. Then, when they are lulled into thinking we have abandoned the coasts to them, we unleash everything we have. We will sink their ships off the coast and pummel their ground forces. By the end of today, the Americans will accept that they can't recapture Formosa from us, and they will withdraw."

Xian, who had been given command of the 41st and 42nd Armies by General Yang, was thoroughly confident in Lee's work and in his men. They had laid an elaborate trap for the Americans, and now they just had to stay patient and let it play out.

For the next hour, jets roared overhead. He listened to a myriad of precision-guided munitions and cruise missiles hit targets near the coast, along with a few positions further up on the mountain fortress. Most of the targets that had been hit were actually elaborate decoys. The Chinese knew the Americans would be hunting for targets, so they gave them a plethora of marks to hit. It was part of their strategy to deceive the Americans and to camouflage their true intentions. For now, the Americans would be led to believe they were crippling the island's air defenses and destroying key bunkers and strongholds. When they were satisfied, they would send in their ground force, and then the real fight would begin.

****

10 Miles from Taitung

"My butt is killing me, and this rigging is tearing into my back and shoulders," reflected Staff Sergeant Conrad Price. He tried unsuccessfully to shift positions for what must have been the hundredth time since they boarded the flying deathtrap of a C-17 nearly seven hours ago.

"We're five minutes out! Everyone, stand up for equipment check!" shouted the jump master, who was standing near the exit of the plane.

"Finally!" Sergeant Price thought, barely keeping himself from exclaiming aloud.

Standing up, Price checked the man in front of him to make sure his equipment was properly set up and ready. He could feel the guy behind him doing the same to his gear and then felt the familiar pat on his shoulders letting him know he was good to go. With these formalities taken care of, the jump master yelled out a string of additional commands as they prepared to jump.

Catching a glance out the window, Price could see the sun was starting to break through the evening sky. Soft yellow, red, and blue hues were ever so slowly trying to push the blackness of the night away, bringing with it a new day. However, this would be a day filled with sheer terror, excitement, and uncertainty.

A couple of minutes went by, and then the lights inside the cabin turned from a light blue to red. Seconds later, the two side doors they'd be jumping out of were opened. The chilly, humid air buffeted their faces as it quickly circulated throughout the cargo hold of the plane.

To Sergeant Price, the aircraft looked like it was still too low for them to jump. The water whipping past them looked practically close enough for them to land on.

"Man, these pilots aren't messing around," he realized.

Without warning, the aircraft's engines decreased power and the plane shifted sharply upward in altitude, forcing the paratroopers to grab for anything they could to keep themselves from falling over onto each other.

"A little warning would have been nice," Price grumbled to himself.

Seconds later, the plane leveled out and the jump light turned from red to green. The jump master started screaming, "Everyone, get off the aircraft as fast as possible!"

Not knowing if the plane was about to be blown up, the Rangers practically shoved each other out the jump door to try and get on the ground.

Following the lead of the soldiers in front of him, Sergeant Price quickly made his way out the door to the wild blue yonder below. Less than a second after exiting the plane, his chute opened, jerking him hard and preventing him from becoming a six-foot lawn dart. Looking around, Price saw strings of green tracer fire reaching out for the planes that were now flying across the runway of the airfield, dropping Rangers as fast as humanly possible.

With the sun not fully up just yet, they could easily spot the illumination flares going off several thousand meters above the air base, which further illuminated the paratroopers who were dangling from their parachutes and the planes delivering them. The AC-130 Spector gunship loitered above and behind them, then suddenly opened fire on the enemy antiaircraft guns that had shown themselves, silencing several of them before they could down any of the American aircraft.

Craning his neck to his left, Sergeant Price saw what appeared to be three ZU-23 antiaircraft guns that the gunship had not silenced yet. A dizzying rate of fire crisscrossed the sky above the runway. One string of rounds tore into one of the C-17s, causing it to explode before its human cargo had a chance to jump.

"*Holy crap. That was two platoons' worth of Rangers*," Price thought in horror.

Seconds later, the AC-130 gunship obliterated the gun positions, but the damage had already been done.

A minute later, Price found himself quickly approaching the ground and positioned himself to tuck and roll just as he had done in dozens of practice jumps. Before he knew it, he was on the ground, and his body had instinctively done what it had been trained to do.

Once on the ground, he quickly brought his weapon to bear. He'd spotted a machine-gun position that a handful of PLA soldiers were running to, and he wanted to take them out before they could start mowing down his fellow Rangers. Just as Sergeant Price was about to fire, a hail of bullets rained down from the sky and the running figures evaporated, cut to pieces by a five-barrel 25mm Equalizer cannon, which spat out thousands of rounds a minute. With the immediate threats neutralized, Price went to work on getting his pack strapped to his back and rounding up his squad.

Glancing back up toward the sky, Price saw the horizon continue to fill up with parachutes as the rest of the battalion arrived. He also spotted two smoke trails streaking up nearby and watched as missiles headed straight for the gunship that had been providing them with direct fire support. The AC-130 turned hard to one side as it spat out flares at a high rate of speed as it quickly changing altitude and revved its engines. Then, one missile successfully impacted against the plane, and one of the engines exploded and caught fire. The second missile was diverted by one of the flares and detonated harmlessly away from its intended target. However, the gunship was now trailing smoke with an engine out as it lumbered out of view. Price wasn't sure what happened to it, but he knew he needed to get his squad moving to their next objective. He could contemplate what had happened to the Spector gunship later.

Seeing the other members of his squad unstrapping their parachutes and grabbing their packs and weapons, Price shouted, "On me!"

He swiftly led them toward the opposite side of the base. Their objective now was to clear the munition bunkers and then press on to secure the western edge of the base perimeter before expanding out further up the ridgeline that overlooked the base.

As they approached the road that led to the munition farm, his squad nearly ran straight into an enemy machine-gun position, which appeared to have been hastily manned, since the Chinese soldiers there were still feeding a belt of ammo into the gun.

At once, Price brought his rifle to his shoulder and fired at them. He was quickly joined by the members of his squad, killing the four enemy soldiers before they were able to react to their presence. With the enemy gun position taken out, they pressed on, now joined by at least two other squads of soldiers.

They continued unhindered until they reached the building that led to the entrance of a massive bunker complex. The relative silence was broken by a fuselage of enemy machine-gun fire.

Zip, zip, zang. BOOM.

Bullets and grenade explosions struck everywhere as the two sides fought it out in relatively close quarters.

"Frag out!" yelled Price. He threw one of his grenades at a cluster of enemy soldiers that had just arrived from deeper in the bunker complex.

BOOM.

"On me!" he shouted. He raised his rifle to his shoulder and fired a string of shots into the gun slit on the bunker, then charged.

Bang, bang, bang!

The sounds of his rifle echoed off the surrounding cement walls of the bunker system. Price slammed his body against the cement wall just to the left of the gun slit, then reached down and grabbed another grenade from his vest.

"Frag out!" he shouted as he tossed the second grenade inside the bunker. He had held the grenade for a couple of seconds before he threw it in, trying to cook down the timer. This would give the soldiers inside very little time to react to it.

BOOM!

Dust, air, and flame rapidly blew out the gun slit. Then a few cries of pain and agony groaned out, indicating the fragmentation grenade had found its mark. Price dropped his now-empty magazine, placing it in his drop bag, and pulled another out of the front pouch of his vest. Once he loaded the fresh thirty-round magazine, he slapped the bolt shut, loading the next round. Then he flicked the selector switch from semiauto to full-auto. Sergeant Price placed the barrel of his M4A1 into the gun slit and proceeded to empty his thirty-round magazine into the compartment. Pulling back against the wall, he dropped the empty magazine and slammed a fresh one in place.

"Damn good assault, Sergeant Price," he heard from behind him. He glanced back to see Lieutenant Rafael

Martinez, his platoon leader. More men were stacking up against the bunker wall his fireteam had formed up on.

Price nodded in acknowledgment, then turned to his squad, signaling with his hands that they were going to breach the bunker. Once they had finished stacking against the wall next to the bunker entrance, one of his soldiers pulled the door open slightly, throwing a grenade in and slamming the door shut. A second later, the grenade went off, and the private opened the door again, allowing the team to rush in and begin clearing the first room.

That first area of the bunker complex turned out to be the gun room, so they scarfed up some additional weapons before moving to the next entrance. Before they moved down the hallway and deeper into the complex, they threw a hand grenade down the hall and waited for the explosion. They rushed through the entrance, weapons at the ready, and found the next room. The other members of their platoon weren't far behind Sergeant Price's team. Together they would clear the complex much more quickly. Ten minutes went by. Aside from two enemy soldiers who had surrendered, they didn't meet any further resistance.

Walking out of the fortified positions, the men of Second Platoon moved to the edges of the bunkers and climbed up the grass-covered sides to gain a better view of what lay around them. As he looked back toward the runway, Price could see the burning wreck of at least one C-17. Further out, he spotted a gravy train of aircraft lining up for their approach.

"These guys must be bringing in our light armored vehicles and other heavy equipment," Price reasoned.

Parachutes were still descending over the runway with each pass of one of the cargo planes. Swarms of soldiers on the ground were busy unwrapping a pair of JLTV vehicles, which looked to be equipped with M2 .50-caliber heavy machine guns.

"OK, enough lollygagging," Lieutenant Martinez announced. "We need to push the perimeter out. You guys see that string of roads and cutbacks leading up that ridge? We need to secure it. Battalion wants us to set up a position on top of the crest before nightfall, so we need to hoof it if we're going to make it up there by then." Martinez gestured toward an incredibly tall and intimidating ridgeline, part of the Dulan Forest. Various parts of the ridge provided exceptional overwatch of the air base, which would be very helpful since it was unknown if the area was still occupied by enemy forces lying in ambush, or if it was truly empty.

The soldiers grumbled a bit but eventually threw their packs on after the short break and fanned out as they made their way into the tree line that led to the outer perimeter road. As the platoon made their way up the forested ridgeline, they heard an increase in gunfire maybe a couple of kilometers to their right. Clearly, one of the other platoons was in the thick of it. More gunfire was still sounding off in the distance to their left, where the main city was located. That beach was being hit by an Australian infantry unit, so it wasn't Price's concern, so long as the Aussies did their job and secured the city. The airborne had the air base and the Dulan Forest to secure. It was rough terrain and would be a challenge, but it was a challenge the sky soldiers thrived on.

******

Nanfangao Lookout

The last two weeks had been filled with terror and anxiety. The Americans had been dropping bombs all over the place, hitting God only knew what. From time to time, a bomb or missile would land near the bunker complex Sergeant Lei Wei had been calling home for the past two months. It especially irritated him when he was trying to write a letter home to his family. His unit would be ordered to man their weapons and be ready to repel a possible enemy invasion. Each time their officers told them this might be it, the time when the Americans would finally land their vaunted Marines on the beach to steal the rightful territory of Formosa from China's bosom.

Lei felt proud of himself, and he knew his parents and elders back in the village were extremely proud of him as well. After his herculean efforts and bravery during the invasion of Formosa, he had been awarded the Order of Heroic Exemplar by the lone political officer who had survived that day of days. Once Formosa had been captured, Lei had been specially flown to Beijing, along with nearly fifty other soldiers who were being awarded the medal. They were presented their award by President Xi himself at a formal ceremony. For his part, Lei's exploits that day were widely publicized in his home village and region as an example of what a young man, a lowly farmer, could achieve and do for his country. The Communist Party had promoted Lei from a militia member to the rank of sergeant in the 40th Motorized Infantry Brigade, which was traditionally stationed in the province he was from.

That particular brigade happened to be a jungle warfare brigade, and they had been placed in charge of a large swath of the eastern shore of Formosa. They would be the frontline force against a naval invasion. Lei felt immensely proud at being promoted into this unit, though he was not exactly thrilled with the tough odds they would be facing against any Allied force that sought to liberate Formosa.

For nearly eight months, everyone had thought the Americans would leave Formosa alone and focus their efforts elsewhere. Then rumors had spread about a massive military defeat in northern China that had cost the lives of over a hundred thousand soldiers. The more recent gossip was that the PLA forces were being defeated in the Philippines. Sergeant Lei recognized that if the Americans had recaptured the Philippines, then it was likely just a matter of time before they tried to steal Formosa.

One of the privates broke Lei out of his reflections. "Sergeant Lei," he said, "do you think the Americans are going to invade soon?"

A few of the other soldiers perked up as they heard the question, waiting to hear what their sergeant would say. Putting his pen down, Lei looked up and saw the scared expression on the young man's face. Lei replied, "The Americans will come. I don't know if it will be today, tomorrow, or next month…" Just then, a series of explosions blasted in a not-too-distant area. He continued, "…but rest assured, the Americans will come, and when they do, we will throw them back into the sea from which they came."

The soldiers in the sleeping quarters of their bunker complex nodded in agreement. Before the men could ask any more questions or ponder what he had said further, the general quarters alarm sounded, alerting them that they were to man their battle stations. Getting up from his cot, Lei cinched his boots back on, then pulled on his body armor and reached for his QBZ-95 rifle. The men quickly filed out of the sleeping quarters section of the complex and made their way to the gun positions their squad had been assigned to.

Walking through the maze of tunnels in the complex, Lei could hear and feel the bombs hitting the earthen fortifications above them and around the nearby area.

"This is a much heavier bombardment than anything we've seen up to this point. I wonder if this really is it," he thought.

His squad of soldiers moved through the tunnel, past other groups of soldiers running to and from various other sections of the underground maze.

Bang! Boom!

A series of large explosions rocked the mountain their fortification had been carved into, knocking most of the men in his squad to the ground. Bits of the ceiling crumbled down, letting in some small segments of dirt. Looking ahead of them, they could see a rush of smoke billow into the tunnel from one of the gun bunker positions, which was right next to the section his squad had been assigned to defend. Several soldiers stumbled out of the bunker room. Some of them held their heads, one braced his arm, and another limped out on an injured leg. Many of the soldiers in his squad rushed toward their comrades see what had happened and to help them.

Sergeant Lei spotted one of the other sergeants he had taken a liking to and ran up to him. "What happened, Yin?" Lei asked.

His friend looked dazed at first, unsure who had asked him the question. Then he slowly recognized his friend and fellow sergeant. "I think it was an American bomb or missile. They didn't hit us directly, but the explosion was close. Oh God, I still have wounded soldiers in there. We need to get them help," he replied, suddenly remembering the rest of the reality around him.

Before Lei could send his own men in to help, a group of medical soldiers ran past them into the bunker room, and their captain walked up to them both. "Sergeant Lei, get your men into your bunker room and prepare to repel the Americans," he ordered. "We'll handle Sergeant Yin's men." The captain had a concerned look on his face that betrayed his true feelings. He looked scared, like the rest of them.

"Yes, Sir!" shouted Lei, who then barked orders to his squad to man their positions.

Racing into their own bunker room, he saw the three soldiers he'd left on duty, looking out the gun slits with pairs of binoculars. When the rest of the squad ran in, they turned and excitedly explained what they were seeing, pointing at dozens upon dozens of enemy warships that had not been there even a few hours ago.

Grabbing one of the binoculars, Lei saw what looked like mini-aircraft carriers, with too many small craft to count circling around them in a holding pattern. Then he spotted several destroyers and cruisers, which were using their five-inch guns to fire directly on their positions. Hearing the roar of a jet engine, Lei looked up and saw an American war plane swoop in and release a pair of objects from under its wings. The payload struck the fortified positions near the Suao Lighthouse on the opposite side of the naval base and harbor. That had been one of their key strongpoints to keep the Americans from being able to capture and use the former Republic of China naval base, piers, and docking cranes.

Lei could smell the air, charged with burnt dirt, metal, cordite, and sulfur, wafting in through the gun slits. The atmosphere around them was already filled with the odor of battle and high explosives, a smell that would only grow thicker throughout the day. His nose also detected the putrid smell of burnt flesh, feces, and urine from those who had been killed and had lost the will to hold their bowels during their demise. Snapping out of the apocalyptic scene unfolding before them, Lei knew he had to get his men ready to defend their position.

"We need to get the guns ready at once!" he shouted. "Assistant gunners, make sure you have the extra barrels ready to swap out when the time comes. Also, make sure you have enough water nearby to help keep the barrels cool. They are going to heat up quickly, and we need to make sure we don't melt them. Where's my ammo runners?"

"Here, sergeant!" the trio shouted as they ran up to him and stood at attention, waiting for his next set of orders.

"Get the ammo cart and grab four more boxes of ammo for the Hua Qing. I want two extra boxes next to each of the guns! Understood?"

"Yes, Sir," they replied and ran out to grab the extra ammo.

Taking a moment to survey his position, Lei felt confident about their chances. His bunker room was six meters wide and ten meters in length, with ten meters of rock between them and the next bunker room. To their front, the gun slits looked like sideways Vs, opening the aperture of the gun slit further away from the opening; this provided the gunners with as much protection as possible from the outside and gave them exceptional fields of fire and the ability to raise or lower the angle of their fire, depending on where the enemy was.

It also had a wall that divided the room in half, to help ensure that a single rocket, missile, or cannon round wouldn't kill everyone in the bunker with one lucky hit. Inside the bunker, they had two of the coveted Hua Qing miniguns. The guns were electrically run six-barrel killing machines. Sergeant Lei had been told that they were a knockoff version of a similar gun system the Americans used. Because of the incredible rate of fire, each of these weapons had a five-hundred-pound wooden crate/ammo box sitting next to it, which were self-designed by the PLA soldiers who would be manning and using them in the bunker complexes.

Each of these boxes of ammo had fifty 100-round belts attached to them, giving the gunner 5,000 rounds before they needed to swap out ammo boxes. Outside of the bunker complex, this little idea of stringing that many belts of ammo together would never work, but for their purposes, it was brilliant. The commander of their bunker complex had considered the idea important enough to share with the rest of the island defenses, which definitely said something.

They also had two W-85 heavy machine guns, which fired 12.7×108mm rounds, similar to the American M2 .50-caliber machine gun. Between these four killing machines, Sergeant Lei was confident his twelve-man squad would be able to prevent the Americans from successfully landing at the portion of the coast they were designated to protect. He just hoped the other areas would be equally protected.

Lei's biggest concern, since they hadn't practiced for it in any of their training drills due to the cost of ammunition, was making sure they would be able get rid of the sheer volume of spent shell casings these four machine guns were going to create. The bunker had two slits in the floor next to the outer wall, which had been cut in the rock on each side of the bunker for this purpose. The goal of these fixed positions was to be able to fight in them for a long time. Knowing that, the engineers designed a way to get rid of the brass casings as quickly as possible, so they wouldn't clutter the floor up and make it nearly impossible to walk. Each of the guns had a trash can next to them and a flat metal shovel. One of the ammo carriers would also man the shovel and trash can. When the cans got full or there was a lull in the shooting, they would lug the trash can to the slit in the wall and dump the spent casings down it. The casings would then land outside the bunker and gather below to be picked up at a later date, assuming, of course, that they successfully repelled the Americans.

One of the soldiers backed away from the wall and put his binoculars down. He looked nervously at Lei. "This looks like it's it," he said, "the big invasion you and the captain talked about. That looks like a lot of enemy soldiers." He motioned to the small landing craft still circling around their mother ships. "Do you think we can stop all of them?" he asked.

Sergeant Lei walked up to the young private and put his hand on the man's shoulder. "We'll stop them," he said, trying to display as much confidence as humanly possible. "You need to stay focused on doing your part. Don't worry about what the others are saying or doing, just concentrate on your piece of the puzzle, and we'll get through this. Besides, you're the lucky soldier that gets to use the minigun." His mouth curled up in a sarcastic half smile.

Unlike a lot of the PLA sergeants, Lei felt he could accomplish more with honey than vinegar. Maybe it was his small country villager attitude, but he seldom yelled at his soldiers unless they needed it. His squad, and a lot of the other members of his company, had taken an immediate liking to him. Not only was he a hero and good luck charm, but he was also a nice guy to be around.

"They're heading to the shore now!" shouted one of the soldiers excitedly as they watched the smaller amphibious assault vehicles and troop landing ships begin to head toward the shore. Several of the destroyers fired smoke rounds into the village and port area just in front of the shoreline in an attempt to obscure their view of the landing.

"*That smoke may hinder the bunkers near the coast, but it won't affect us,*" Lei thought as a devilish smile spread across his face.

As the landing force got closer to the shoreline, a pair of fighters flew in low and fast, releasing a series of long, tumbling bombs. They hit right on top of where Lei knew a line of bunkers and trenches had been built. The bombs exploded in thunderous flames that grew in intensity and stretched across the entire trench line. Horrible walls of fire intensified as the firestorm consumed everything in its path.

"Dear God, is that what napalm looks like?" Sergeant Lei wondered. His palms were suddenly very sweaty. The Americans had begun using that horrible weapon early on in the war, especially as the fighting had intensified in the Pacific.

Ten minutes went by, and then the first American landing crafts hit the shoreline, disgorging their human cargo. Lei watched in amazement at how many American Marines charged up the shoreline and how quickly they did so.

"Should we open fire, Sergeant?" asked one of the corporals who manned one of the machine guns. So far, none of the other bunker rooms had started shooting yet, so as not to give away their positions.

Lei shook his head. "Not yet. Our orders are to wait until the third wave of Americans lands. Then we are to unleash death and destruction on them."

The corporal nodded, though he clearly wanted to start shooting at the American invaders. It felt like forever elapsed as they watched the first wave of Americans rush forward to be met by what remained of their initial defensive line; it was fascinating and terrifying at the same time. Watching those American Marines scream and charge their positions in such a ferocious and fearless way sent shivers down Lei's back.

"*These men fight more viciously than the Taiwanese did, and they are more skilled,*" Lei realized nervously. He started to wonder if it would really be possible to make it out of the bunker complex alive.

The second wave of Marines landed and joined the fray. To Lei and his comrades' horror, they watched as the Marines quickly overpowered and overwhelmed the first defensive line with speed and ease. Lei really earnestly began to question if they could hold this position, or if he was already surrounded by his tomb. This bunker complex they were in was manned by only 230 soldiers, and they only had five-gun bunkers. Once they were taken out or overrun, that was it for their part in the war.

Twenty minutes after that second group landed, the third wave of landing craft arrived. This wave brought with it multiple hovercraft or LCACs, which proceeded to offload dozens of eight-wheeled light armored vehicles and main battle tanks. Just as Lei was about to order his bunker to start shooting, he saw dozens of helicopters approaching the shoreline.

"Machine gunners, focus your fire on those helicopters!" he yelled. "When they come in to drop off more Marines, light 'em up!"

One of the minigunners angled his weapon toward one of the Osprey tiltwing helicopters and let loose a string of bullets that looked more like a laser beam reaching out for the helicopter than it did machine-gun fire. In seconds, the Osprey was sliced through by hundreds of rounds, tearing it apart. The chopper blew up in spectacular fashion over the beach, crashing down onto the Marines below.

The corporal turned to fire on the next helicopter, although at this point, the cluster of helicopters took evasive maneuvers as they broke off their assault. However, Sergeant Lei's bunker was not the only one to fire at the Ospreys—a total of three were downed before they managed to head back to the sea from which they had come. The soldiers manning the machine guns then switched to shooting at the swarm of American Marines who were moving inland.

Suddenly, the field phone attached to the wall rang. Lei grabbed the receiver, straining to hear who was on the other end and what they wanted. As he focused all of his attention, he could barely make out the voice of his captain. "I need to speak with you immediately," Lei heard.

Shaking his head in confusion, Sergeant Lei responded, "I'll be there shortly."

He tapped on the shoulder of one of the other sergeants. "You're in charge until I return," he said.

The other sergeant just nodded and went back to making sure the four machine-gun positions continued to rain death and destruction down on the Marines who were now moving their way up the incline toward their position.

When Lei had traveled halfway down the hallway to where their captain was, the bunker complex shook violently, throwing Sergeant Lei to the ground. Parts of the roof above him gave way, dropping down chunks of rocks and dirt. Looking behind him, Lei saw a ton of smoke and debris coming from his bunker room. A single soldier emerged, stumbling out of the room before collapsing.

Lei quickly ran to his soldier and asked, "What happened?!"

"I don't know what hit us," the young private said, still in a state of shock. "One minute we were killing those Marines, the next moment the entire room was hit with something that blew apart the roof and walls. Had I not been on my way to get more ammunition, I'd be dead."

As Lei got up, he tried to look into the bunker room and saw that most of it had collapsed. There was no fire, like he'd have expected to see from an explosion, just a lot of debris. Whatever had hit them had also caused a lot of damage to the rock, which Sergeant Lei hadn't thought was possible without a missile or a bomb. In that one moment, all but one of his soldiers were gone forever.

****

Commander Mark Gray of the DDG-1001 *Michael Monsoor* was on his third cup of coffee, and it was only 0900 hours. When his ship had approached to the Taiwanese coastline, he'd insisted on being present either on the bridge or in the CIC. His ship was screening for the larger troop ships and would be employing its railguns for the first time as they identified targets of opportunity. As the invasion fleet approached the shoreline and moved into position, the coast stayed silent for several hours. No missiles or projectiles were fired at them, and it appeared as if the enemy had simply walked away from the beach in favor of a protracted inland fight.

The invasion appeared to be progressing smoothly, or at least predictably, according to the intelligence and operation planners. As the captain of the second *Zumwalt*-class destroyer in the Navy, now that the PLA Navy had been summarily destroyed in the Battle of Luzon, his task was to support the Marines' ground invasion of Taiwan. While they had fired off some of their Tomahawk cruise missiles prior to the landings, their primary job now was to try and test their railgun against those hardened targets the ground forces were having a harder time destroying.

With that goal in mind, the camera monitoring of the landings by the CIC members was critical. As they found hardened points, the ground forces would call them, asking for a fire mission. Once the target had been identified, the *Monsoor* would fire one of its railguns and take it out.

As Commander Gray watched a couple dozen Ospreys and other helicopters head toward the beach, he suddenly witnessed the violent destruction of two of them. His stomach sank as the fireballs descended down to the earth below, right on top of some of the Marines. Gray scanned the horizon. His eyes were suddenly drawn to a suspicious area on the side of the rock.

One of the other battle managers in the CIC must have spotted the same thing seconds before him. "Zoom in on that position!" he shouted, directing everyone's attention to the spot. In seconds, they all saw where the enemy fire was coming from. Carved into the side of a steep ridgeline was a heavily camouflaged bunker. Looking more closely, they saw what appeared to be several bunker positions.

"Weapons! Take that position out now!" yelled Commander Gray.

The first railgun fired, slamming its projectile into the first bunker, silencing it quickly. The second gun quickly followed, hitting the next bunker and successfully ending its reign of terror. Unfortunately, another Osprey was torn apart by what appeared to be a minigun firing from the third position before the first gun could spool up again fast enough to take it out. Seconds after the Osprey lit up like a Christmas tree, that bunker was also obliterated by the railgun.

"Make sure to put a few extra rounds into the bunker system," ordered one of the battle managers.

Commander Gray then walked toward one of the petty officers, who was manning a monitor. "Begin scanning the entire ridgeline for any possible signs of gun bunkers," he ordered. "If you think there might be one, we're going to light it up with a railgun."

"*Worst-case scenario, we might blow up a few extra rocks and trees,*" Gray thought. In any case, if they eliminated other bunkers, they would definitely be saving lives.

The rest of the day was spent with the crew feverishly looking for enemy strongpoints and hammering them with their railguns. Their ability to provide direct kinetic support to the Marines as they moved inland was proving to be invaluable as they ran into one enemy strongpoint after another.

Chapter 3

Armored Fist

Kiev, Ukraine

Clty Clinical Hospital #12

Lieutenant General Mikhail Chayko was smoking his ninth cigarette of the day as he looked over the battle plans one final time. In six more hours, he and the other men of the 1st Guard's Tank Army would launch the largest military offensive since World War II.

The sudden change of government in Britain prior to the summer had thrown the Allies into disarray. The British PM had ordered the withdrawal of British forces from the continent, including the North Sea, which had forced the remaining NATO Allies to put their large summer offensive on hold. This pause in combat operations in Ukraine, Belarus and the Baltic States had given Chayko the time he needed to get more forces moved into Ukraine for his own grand offensive.

Brigadier General Mikulin, the 4th Guard's tank division commander, walked up to join Chayko in looking at the map before him. "Are you confident the northern line around St. Petersburg is going to hold when we launch this attack tomorrow?" Mikulin inquired. He wasn't sure if he liked the idea of trusting such an important sector to a largely untested Indian army, especially in light of how poorly they'd fought in the Russian Far East.

"If our offensive stalls or doesn't achieve our goal, then yes, I'm very concerned about our northern flank," Chayko answered. "However, if we're able to drive deep into Poland and the Czech Republic, then we'll be able to relieve that pressure on our northern flank." Chayko paused for a second, running his fingers through his thinning hair. "This entire offensive is a gamble, Mikulin. If we can achieve our objectives, then we'll give the politicians a stronger hand to work with at the negotiation table, but we need to conclude this conflict before the end of the year."

Mikulin rubbed the stubble growing in on his chin. "I'm concerned that it won't matter how much land we grab or hold—the President won't accept or pursue peace. We've already met our military objectives for this war eight months ago. We should already have our forces resting back home, dealing with the domestic problems. Instead, we're still fighting on, with no clear objective. Mikhail, you have to make them see reason before we all end up dead."

Chayko was a bit taken aback by Mikulin's sudden reluctance—he was his best field commander, and he needed him focused on defeating the Americans, not worrying about politics back home. "I understand your concern," Chayko finally said, being careful to speak very tactfully. "I have a call in an hour with General Egorkin. I was going to bring these points up to him as well. You need to stay focused on achieving the military aims of this offensive, and I'll work the political aims. To that end, is your division ready to execute the plan?"

"Yes. My division is ready to hit the Americans," answered Mikulin, speaking with a tone of regret. "Per your instructions, I've kept the Zhukov drones hidden. They'll be providing overwatch for my armored formations. My main concern is the Allies' Air Force. If we are not able to keep the enemy fighters off our backs, they're going to tear my formations apart."

Chayko nodded. "I've been told that with the added help from the Indian Air Force, that problem should be taken care of, or at least mitigated. They've provided several squadrons' worth of surface-to-air missile systems to move with our forces and two hundred additional fighter aircraft. Their Jaguar aircraft are exceptional ground-attack planes. Say what you want about the French and British—they make fine warplanes. And in this battle, we'll have them on our side."

The two of them talked on for a short while before General Mikulin left to return to his command. The start of Operation Armored Fist was about to begin.

****

Ternopil, Ukraine

Childers spotted Lieutenant Colonel Tim Schoolman finishing up his first cup of coffee for the day. He had a very puzzled look on his face.

"Penny for your thoughts, Sir?" asked Childers.

Schoolman looked up at his Sergeant Major. "Intelligence says the Russians are going to start a new offensive sometime today. It just doesn't make sense, though. They've achieved all their military objectives in Ukraine. They know we don't have the force to push them back to Russia yet, but if they attack us now, they will squander the only forces they have holding us at bay."

"You're assuming their offensive won't be successful," said Childers, crossing his arms. "What if they're able to push us completely out of Ukraine or cut deep into Poland? I imagine that would have a profound impact on our ability to push them out of Ukraine."

"I don't think they have the steam to launch a sustained offensive—"

Schoolman's reply was interrupted by the shriek of incoming rockets. The early-warning system sounded, halting any further conversation.

Boom, boom, boom!

Thunderous explosions rocked the front lines a couple of kilometers to the front of their positions. As the explosions grew in intensity, the artillery barrage walked closer to their current location, forcing everyone to seek shelter in their foxholes.

While the artillery was keeping people's heads down, the aerial dance of death between Allied and enemy aircraft began overhead as the Russian and Indian Air Forces battled to clear the skies for their ground-attack planes to rush in and begin to clobber the Allied positions.

****

Mons, Belgium
Global Defense Force Headquarters

General Cotton rubbed his temples, trying to ward away the migraine that was beginning to take hold. He realized that he had been clenching his jaw and attempted to relax his face. The sense of calm confidence he'd felt just a day earlier was now replaced by a feeling of surprise, dread, and uncertainty. The Alliance had finally gotten over the shocking assassination of President Gates when the Russians, who up to that point had appeared like they were merely going to try and hold on to their previous gains in Ukraine, had opted to go on the offensive and try to grab more land. Rather than spreading their forces out to hit the Allied lines across multiple sections, they had balled their armored forces up into a giant wrecking ball and summarily punched a hole in their lines.

In twenty-four hours, the Russians had broken through the Allied positions at Ternopil, bypassing the provisional Ukrainian capital city of Lviv. Now they were pushing their way into Poland. The French 3rd Armored Division had been caught off guard but had managed to stop the Russians at the critical road junction in Radymno, Poland, before they could advance any further. What troubled General Cotton most about this offensive was not knowing which direction the Russian Army was going to drive toward. Until he knew whether the Russians were moving their troops toward Kraków or Warsaw, he didn't have a clear choice on where he should order the German armored divisions he had been holding in reserve.

Turning to look at his operations chief, Cotton asked, "What is the status of our air forces? Are we able to send any additional fighters to help blunt the Russian offensive?"

A French colonel pulled up a screen on his computer, showing a real-time readout of the aircraft currently in the air, and the ones being sortied over the next several hours. Looking over the air packages, he quickly saw that a squadron of French Mirage 2000s and a squadron of Italian Eurofighters that had been slated for ground support missions were twenty minutes from taking up station over the battlespace.

"Sir, we have two squadrons that should be in position within twenty minutes," answered the colonel. "Do you want me to have them vectored to a specific sector?"

"Two squadrons? Surely that can't be all we have in the air right now," General Cotton thought in disgust.

"Yes. Have them support the French 3rd Armored Division at once," he answered. "Send an order that they are to provide whatever support the division commander tasks them with. Also, we need to get more squadrons in the air *now*. What additional aircraft do we have that can be scrambled?" General Cotton spoke with a sense of urgency that he hoped the others in the command center were picking up on. He needed these guys to realize how much danger the

Allied positions were in. If they couldn't contain the Russian offensive, it would unravel their entire line.

The French colonel scanned the electronic roster. "With your permission, two squadrons of American A-10s are returning from a ground support mission, Sir," explained the colonel. "They were supposed to have several hours of downtime, but we can order them to return to the battlespace immediately if you'd like. Also, there's a Dutch squadron of F-16s that can be reconfigured for ground attack as well. They're currently slated to replace a squadron of German Eurofighters that are performing an air supremacy role. Would you like me to have the orders sent retasking all three squadrons, General?" he asked.

A smile spread across Cotton's face. "You said two squadrons of Warthogs?" he verified.

The colonel nodded. A grin appeared on his face as well.

"Yes, Colonel. Send the orders to the squadrons and get it done," ordered Cotton. "Tell them they are to report to the French sector and provide them with as much ground support as possible. Also, send a message to the 23rd Fighter Group that until they are told otherwise, their A-10s are assigned to the French 3rd Armored Division. We have to stop that Russian offensive before they gain too much ground."

Feeling more confident about the air mission, he looked over at his logistics team, which was being run by a US Army colonel. Colonel Cobb had proven to be a logistical wizard since being assigned there, and he was a National Guardsman to boot. In the private sector, he'd worked as the Northeast logistics chief for UPS, so he was certainly no stranger to the world of logistics.

General Cotton walked over and got Cobb's attention. "Colonel Cobb, how are we doing on ammunition for the French and German divisions at the front right now?" he inquired.

Colonel Troy Cobb was a short, portly man. Had he not been in his last year before retirement from the New York National Guard, he probably would've been kicked out for his weight. As it was, his guard unit was letting him finish out his last year so that he could qualify for his retirement. He was happy to be a part of this mission and smiled as Cotton approached him.

"Ah, General. I'm glad you asked about that. Both divisions are good on ammunition right now, but I'm having a devil of a time getting a service contract approved through the Pentagon. Normally, I wouldn't even be dealing with something like this, but a colleague of mine at UPS reached out to me and asked if I could possibly intervene for them since I work on your staff."

General Cotton held up a hand up to stop Colonel Cobb. "Whoa, I'm not sure I can directly get involved in something like that. I know you work for UPS and all, but we can't use our positions to get preferred treatment or contracts like that. You know how it works—it has to go through the proper channels at DoD."

"I understand, General, but I'm not sure you realize how dire our ammunition situation is. We're burning through munitions nearly as fast as they're being produced. Right now, the Pentagon is shipping the vast majority of our ammo through the Global Defense Force convoys. When a convoy arrives, we find ourselves flush with munitions, so that's not the issue. The problem is the time to transport it. Right now, it's taking close to three weeks from the time a unit of ammunition is produced to the time that it's shipped and transported across the ocean to us. That's also assuming none of the freighters moving our munitions aren't sunk or heavily damaged on their way across the Atlantic. We need this contract approved if we're going to keep ourselves supplied," Cobb explained.

"OK, what's the hold-up, then?" Cotton inquired, arms crossed.

"UPS has a contract to transport munitions to Europe and Asia, only they need an amendment to the contract, and the Pentagon isn't wanting to give it to them. The contract says they can't provide delivery of munitions to any location that's within 300 kilometers of the current front lines. While that sounds fine, we need that ammunition to be delivered a lot closer." He pulled out a map that had a number of yellow stars written on it denoting supply depots.

"As you can see, that demarcation places all of Poland, Romania, Denmark and the Nordic states completely out of bounds."

General Cotton nodded. He suddenly understood exactly how vital this was.

Colonel Cobb pressed forward. "If you can get the Pentagon to approve the amendment, Sir, then UPS is willing to have their pilots fly in as close as 50 kilometers from the front to deliver much-needed munitions."

Cotton took a deep breath. "All right, you sold me," he relented. "Get me the numbers of the people I need to talk to and I'll make the calls later today. In the meantime, I need you to work your magic and make sure we don't run out of food, fuel and munitions. Got it?"

Cobb nodded and set to work.

Chapter 4

Russian Underground

Pushkino, Russia

The cool October air blew in through the window in the kitchen. It was a welcomed sign after an unusually long and hot summer. Looking at the morning paper, Alexei Kasyanov could not fully determine if the news reports were truly accurate about the most recent Russian offensive, or if this was just more spin by a government that was slowly crumbling from within.

Finally, he decided, *"The Petrov regime is in its death throes. It just doesn't know it yet."*

Putting the newspaper aside, Alexei poured himself another cup of tea, adding just one sugar cube. He then pulled out his notebook and began to read over his notes from his recent meeting with a Russian FSB major. Alexei had spent the better part of two months trying to arrange a meeting where he and the major could speak and not worry about being detected, which was hard to do in Moscow these days. While it was incredibly risky meeting someone from within the FSB, Alexei had felt it was time to start making new friends in high places that would be pivotal to him removing Petrov from office, preferably without bloodshed.

His CIA and German BND minders had obviously cautioned him against meeting with anyone from the FSB, lest they betray him to the authorities. To his credit, Alexei had managed to convince the men in charge of the Moscow garrison, two Russian colonels and a major general, that when the time came, they should side with him. Of course, he had promised them high positions of authority in the new government once the coup had been completed.

Unfortunately, the information the FSB man had provided the night before was most troubling. It required an emergency meeting with his American and German handlers. A soft rap on the door frame let Alexei know his first handler had arrived. Seeing the familiar face, he waved his friend in. Alexei wouldn't say that he and Mitch Lowe had become friends, but dodging death squads and spies across Moscow and the surrounding area had a way of strengthening the bond between people, much like what soldiers experienced in combat. The two of them had developed a deep and smooth-working relationship. Mitch was his contact with the outside world, and the intelligence shared with each other was bringing the removal of Petrov closer with each day.

Smiling as he walked in, Mitch helped himself to a cup of tea from the kettle on the stove and then took a seat opposite Alexei. "You said you had something important to talk about?" he inquired.

"Remember that FSB major I told you I was going to meet with last night?" asked Alexei.

"Yeah, I remember him," Mitch answered. His face suddenly looked concerned. "The Germans were providing security for your meeting," he stated. "Did everything go according to plan?"

Waving his hand as if warding off Mitch's concern, Alexei replied, "No, there was no problem. The Germans are exceptional security guards. I know you don't fully trust them, but they are very competent. Anyway, at the meeting, the FSB agent told me he had critical information about the British prime minister, but he would only share it if he could be guaranteed certain things."

Mitch leaned forward. His interest had obviously been piqued. "What does he want? And what does he have to offer?" he asked.

Alexei smiled. "A secret recording between the British PM and the head of the FSB in Britain," he responded.

A short pause ensued as Mitch tried to wrap his head around what Alexei had just told him. "Interesting," he finally replied. "You know that would have to be vetted to make sure it was true. What does the recording supposedly say, and what does he want in exchange for it?" he pressed.

"He wants $5 million USD and asylum in America," Alexei answered. He was nervous to state these terms. In all reality, he wasn't sure if this was sincere or just a ruse by the FSB to draw him out, and maybe expose those who were helping him stay on the lam.

Mitch let out a soft whistle as he leaned back in his chair. He stared at Alexei for a few minutes, assessing him. "Alexei, what does your gut say about this guy? Is he legit? Do you believe him?" he asked.

Now it was Alexei who sat back in his chair. He looked at his teacup and reached down to take a sip, more to stall his response than anything else. He played through every moment of the previous night's conversation and analyzed every facial tell he had observed. "I think the major was scared," Alexei finally answered. "I believe he's looking for a way out but doesn't have a clue about how he can get out without getting killed or giving away his intentions."

Mitch nodded. "Fair enough. I need to hear the recording before I can possibly agree to his terms, though. I need to at least know he's not BS-ing us. Is it possible for us to hear the recording?" he asked.

Alexei dug around in the pocket of his trousers for a second before he produced a micro SD card. "The major said he put a sixty-second segment of the recording on this. He told me the rest of the forty-five-minute discussion will be made available once we agree to smuggle him out of Russia and he has his five million dollars." He pushed the SD card toward Mitch.

Mitch examined the card closely. Alexei knew he was probably wondering if it was even safe to place the card in one of his devices. He eventually pulled out a small pocket audio recorder, which was probably deemed to be of low enough value, and then he opened a small dust cover on the side of the device. Once the card was in, Mitch turned the recorder on and hit the playback button.

It was the first time Alexei was hearing the recording, too. He had been too afraid to risk one of his own electronic devices. Sure enough, the voice on the recording did sound like Prime Minister Chattem. The other voice was unknown. As they continued to listen, Mitch's eyes grew wide as saucers. The questions that were being asked and the agreements that Chattem had made put him in a very untenable position.

"If this ever came to light, it would topple Chattem's position as prime minister," thought Alexei.

Once they had turned the recorder off, Mitch looked at Alexei with a fire in his eyes. "Tell your FSB major that I need to run this by my headquarters, but he should plan on packing a bag and being ready to move when I say."

"So, you think this is real?" Alexei asked.

"I think it needs to be further analyzed before that assessment can be completely made. I don't have the equipment or personnel to do that here. I'll get this electronically sent to Langley, and I'm sure we'll know something shortly," Mitch replied.

With that, their meeting ended. Mitch left to head to his own safe house and get the content of this SD card encrypted and sent back to the States for analysis.

Twenty-four hours after sending the file back to Langley, Mitch received a short message: "We will pay the five million for the rest of the recording, and we will work to smuggle the Russian agent out of the country."

Based on the quick turnaround of the intelligence analysis and decisions that required a certain level in the chain of command, Mitch understood that not only was this deal a go, but they wanted it done as quickly as possible.

Chapter 5
British Awakening

Washington D.C.

White House, Oval Office

Prince Andrew felt the Gulfstream G650 lurch forward as it came to a halt inside a large hangar on Andrews Air Force Base. When the engines turned off, the flight crew opened the door, allowing the prince and the other British passengers to exit in relative secrecy. Once all ten passengers had exited the aircraft, they were guided to a helicopter nearby.

"She'll take you the rest of the way to the White House," said one of the men as he ushered them forward.

Prince Andrew scanned the scene, then nudged his brother. "Philip, check out the level of security. Not only do we have our own small contingent of bodyguards, but check out all of those dozens upon dozens of soldiers wearing full body armor who are guarding the facility. They are armed to the teeth."

Prince Philip nodded but didn't say anything. Prince Andrew figured his brother must not want to draw attention.

A moment later, they stepped onto the large Sikorsky VH-3D Sea King helicopter that was waiting for them. Prince Andrew and his brother exchanged glances of approval. This helicopter was plush and comfortable. As soon as everyone was aboard, the pilots spun up the engine.

"You hear that?" asked Prince Philip.

"What do you mean?" asked Prince Andrew.

"Exactly my point," Philip explained. "You can barely tell the engine is running with all the soundproofing in here."

Prince Andrew smiled. Both he and his brother were helicopter pilots themselves, so they knew a thing or two about flying.

Prince Philip turned to one of the American Secret Service agents. "Is this the same helicopter the President flies on?" he asked out of curiosity.

The agent turned to look at them and nodded. "The President sent his personal helicopter to come get you. Sorry for having you land at Andrews instead of Reagan International, but this airport is more secure and private."

Prince Andrew suddenly realized that this meeting must be an even bigger deal than he'd originally thought if the President had sent his own helicopter. Besides, they were also accompanied by the former director of MI5 and a Tory MP.

"*If Chattem found out about this meeting, he'd be piping mad,*" Andrew thought. A smirk spread across his face.

When the helicopter flew over the White House, Andrew caught a glimpse of the outside. While a lot of tourists were snapping pictures of the iconic building, his eyes were immediately drawn to the one-meter-tall sandbag wall that had been built around the perimeter of the building. He also spotted several menacing-looking armored personnel carriers as well.

As Marine One circled the building and came in for a landing on the South Lawn, a sudden gust of wind hit them, bringing with it a torrent of rain. Once they had settled on the ground, Andrew noticed that the rotor blades wound down much faster than on a normal civilian model.

A couple of guards came walking over to the helicopters with umbrellas, ready to shepherd them to the portico and side entrance to the White House.

Once the British party made it into the building, they were led to a meeting room near the President's office.

One of the staffers at the White House brought them a tray filled with tea and light finger foods. "All right, gentlemen, wait here for a moment and we will let the President know that you have arrived."

****

As the President waited for his British guests, he observed the shower pounding on the windows outside the Oval Office. A dark set of storm clouds had moved into the Washington area, providing some much-needed rain. The sudden tempest seemed a bit too symbolic of his mood at the moment.

"How do I tell these gentlemen that their PM cut a deal with the Russians?" he wondered. It still seemed almost bizarre to him that Chattem had made an agreement to withdraw armed forces from the war in exchange for his position of power.

Knock, knock.

The President looked up and saw the National Security Advisor, Tom McMillan, stick his head into the room. "Sir, our guests have arrived. Do you want me to bring them in?" he asked.

President Foss nodded, not saying a word. He was still trying to figure out what to say. Then he suddenly remembered that JP, his CIA Director, would also be there. JP had been so quiet as he'd sat on the couch, drinking his second cup of coffee and reading over documents to prepare, that Foss had actually forgotten he was in the room.

When the British contingent walked in, the usual greetings were exchanged. After all hands had been shaken, the President signaled that they should all take a seat. A few additional chairs were brought in to make sure there was enough room, but then the four British bodyguards found their way to the door to wait outside the room with the Secret Service agents. They had enough sense to know this needed to be a private meeting, even without being told.

George Younger, the former head of MI5, opened the discussion. He turned to his former counterpart, JP, and asked, "So, what is so hush-hush that you had the lot of us secretly whisked away from London to meet you here in Washington under such cloak-and-dagger means?"

The two young princes placed their cups of tea gently on the table in front of them and then leaned forward, obviously eager to hear the response.

JP opened his folder and produced some documents he'd planned to give as handouts. As he began to pass them out, he explained, "We brought you here under these circumstances because what we are about to brief you on is incredibly sensitive in nature, and frankly, we're not sure how to proceed. We are seeking your guidance."

The Brits looked at each other with perplexed expressions.

JP continued. "We have a deep cover agent in Russia who acquired some rather interesting information about the Prime Minister." He held up a hand to stop any questions. "The document you now have in front of you is a dossier on Max Weldon, a Managing Director for the Rothschild Group. If you will continue to peruse the information, you'll find that he is also known as Maksim Sokolov and belongs to the Russian Federal Security Service. Take a few moments to briefly scan the pages before you—I'm sure you will all come to the same conclusion that we have, that this Max fellow is a grave threat."

Pages rustled as everyone rifled through the dossiers.

After a moment, Younger looked up. "Prior to being forced out of MI5, I knew of this character. We'd known about him for some time. Our continued hope was that he would lead us to some big fish, and we could find someone to turn and then get them to start feeding him false information. Why are you Yanks so interested in him now?" he asked.

JP then pulled up some images on his Microsoft Surface Pro, turning the tablet around so everyone could see the series of images that showed Chattem moving across

London, wearing a variety of different disguises and ultimately ending his escapade at the Oxford Cambridge Club. He then played a video that showed the two men arriving at the same hotel room.

"They arrived separately, of course," conceded JP, "but they were clearly meeting to discuss something."

"Do you have audio of the meeting?" inquired MP Rosie Hoyle, the opposition leader in the House of Commons.

"We do, but not from the video. The FSB would have detected such a device if we'd used one that could record and store both audio and video. The recording we have was taken by Maksim Sokolov himself, probably to use as blackmail at a later date and time. Between the video and the audio recording, you can piece together what is happening pretty well. Our analysts have run their voices through our recognition software, and we came back with 100% matches."

JP then proceeded to pull a small digital recorder from the breast pocket of his jacket. As he placed the device on the center table between them, he hit the play button.

The group sat there listening intently to the two of them talk. At first, it seemed to proceed innocently enough as Max asked Chattem what his position on the war would have the cruise missile attack, and him agreeing to the separate peace deal, and subsequent withdrawal from the war. It's cut and dried that he is guilty of high crimes."

She pulled a stray hair away from her face. "The challenge I see is how will the public might react to this. People were already angry about the losses we had sustained in the war, and then they became angry when we pulled out from it. Once they learn of this recording, they will go absolutely barmy," Hoyle asserted.

George Younger interjected, "We need to get this recording verified and then distributed to MI5 and MI6. We have to arrest Max Weldon before he knows we are on to him. He's probably a veritable wealth of information that we desperately need to mine. I can guarantee, there are going to be a lot of other people involved in this soft coup that the Russians have essentially been able to pull off."

Younger then turned to face the two royals. "Sirs, Ms. Hoyle is right. When this news breaks, it's going to devastate the country. We're going to need help from both of you in calming the people and helping to unify the country behind a new government. It may be difficult to explain why Britain will most likely return to the Alliance and become involved in the war again."

The princes nodded.

be if he became the PM. However, when the conversation turned to what would need to happen in order for him to obtain the position of prime minister and Chattem specifically mentioned the assassination of several Tory MPs and a cruise missile attack against their country, their jaws hit the floor.

When the recording was done, the President looked at his guests, who were obviously in a state of shock. "Now that we have acquired this information and shared it with you, what are we supposed to do with it?" he asked.

"That traitorous bastard," Prince Philip said under his breath.

"We have to remove him," Prince Andrew replied.

Tom McMillan leaned in. "That's why we brought the four of you here. This is a British problem, one we can't solve. We want to know what we can do to help you."

MP Rosie Hoyle cleared her throat. "First, I would probably move to have the PM brought up on charges of treason. We'll obviously need a copy of this recording, so we can verify it. Once that has been done, the Ministry of Justice will want to hear it and then determine if they want to prosecute. I am confident they will. It's clear that Chatte suggested several MPs be assassinated, and that happened, so there's a clear link to the events that transpired. Then

"We'll do our best to manage the mood of the people," Prince Andrew stated.

The Brits and Americans continued to talk for a few more hours before the meeting ended. Once the British delegation left the Oval Office, Tom turned to the President. "That went about as well as I thought it would," he said.

President Foss snorted. "We blindsided them. They have to act, especially now that they know we know what transpired. The bigger question is, how will the average person respond to the knowledge that their prime minister colluded with the Russians to become PM and withdraw the UK from the war?"

Before the two men could talk further, the President's Chief of Staff, Josh Morgan, stepped into the room. "The delegation just left for Andrews," he confirmed, "and the generals are also down in the war room and are ready for you."

When Vice President Foss had been sworn in as the new President following the assassination of Gates, he'd brought his own chief of staff with him and replaced Gates's man. It wasn't that he hadn't liked Gates's Chief of Staff; he'd just wanted his own guy in the position. Josh Morgan was someone he'd worked with for many years, and he felt comfortable with him.

"I guess that's our cue," the President said. He, Tom, and JP got up and followed Morgan to the Presidential Emergency Operations Center, or PEOC. It had been unofficially dubbed "the war room" for a few months now, since nearly all the meetings in there revolved around the world war.

Walking to the elevator that would lead them to the subterranean room, Foss couldn't help but marvel at how the engineers had had to build the new addition to the White House. With so many changes in technology, from fiber optics to wireless technologies, the Situation Room and the presidential bunker had gone through some major overhauls.

Walking into the PEOC, the President saw that his military leaders and advisors were standing next to their chairs, waiting for him to arrive. As Foss took his seat at the head of the table, everyone sat down. Then he motioned for Admiral Peter Meyers, the Chairman of the Joint Chiefs, to proceed.

The admiral stood and cleared his throat. "Mr. President, this is your evening brief of the war and where the situation currently stands. There are several key decisions that require your approval. I'll go over those decision points as we reach them," he said. Then he went through a quick outline for the briefing before beginning his presentation in detail, which was something President Foss had insisted upon. He was not a fan of the more freewheeling discussions that President Gates had been known for, and he preferred everything to be much more formal and organized.

Eventually, Admiral Meyers brought up some images of Europe on the screens. One map showed the latest Russian offensive, and where their army was driving toward. "The Russians launched their Armored Fist Campaign seven days ago. As you can see, the offensive was able to punch a hole in our lines at these three points," explained Meyers, using a laser pointer to bring attention to the problem areas. "Presently, the Russians' offensive has stalled in front of Rzeszow, Poland, roughly 160 kilometers from Kraków. In the north, the Russians broke through the French positions near Lublin. They're falling back to a new defensive position roughly 60 kilometers from Warsaw. We've moved a joint Dutch-German brigade to reinforce the line there. We should be able to contain them roughly one hundred kilometers southeast of Warsaw while the French division regroups.

"In the north of Poland and Lithuania, we managed to stop the Russian offensive before it was able to really get going. Once we caught wind of their plans, we specifically went after the enemy's fuel dumps. Without diesel and gasoline, their offensive ground to a halt before it really got going."

The President interjected, "If you guys were able to knock out their fuel dumps in the north and this prevented their offensive from progressing there, then why were you not able to do the same thing in the south, where their larger army group is located?"

Admiral Meyers tipped his head to the side. "Mr. President, the army group in the south had significantly higher concentrations of surface-to-air missile systems and other air-defense assets," he explained. "With the introduction of the Indian Army to the war, we're facing a lot stiffer air defense. The Russians also concentrated a lot of the Indian armor units with their main offensive in the south, which greatly bolstered their offensive capability. We've moved the Ninth Army Group to stop the Russians in the south. With the bulk of V Corps comprising armor and mechanized infantry, they should have the armored force to handle the Russian and Indian armor units."

The President grunted and then nodded.

Admiral Meyers paused a second. "Sir, with your permission, I'd like to move forward with inserting a Special Forces unit near the Caspian Sea to go after the Russian oil and natural gas pipelines," he asserted. "We'd like to go after their ability to move the product to their factories. This will further grind their economy to a halt and reduce the likelihood they can sustain their offensive."

President Foss looked at Meyers for a second, turning to gauge the mood of the other generals before replying. "I'm concerned that if we do this, the Russians will retaliate by hitting our pipelines in Alaska or the Midwest," he began. "It's bad enough that they blew up the petroleum facility in New York—that attack killed over 800 civilians. Besides, how would we even get our Special Forces or Navy SEALs to the Caspian Sea?"

"We would send a Romanian SOF unit in to make the attack. It would be them and the Georgians," Meyers explained.

Tom jumped into the conversation. "And exactly how are you going to get the Azeris to allow a Georgian unit to operate off their coasts? Don't they hate each other?"

"I believe you are mixing the Georgians up with the Armenians," the President's Chief of Staff asserted. "The Armenians and the Azeris are the ones that hate each other. The Georgians and the Azeris get along just fine."

"Ok. Let them be the ones to carry out the attack," said the President hesitantly. Then he unfolded his arms before changing the topic. "I want to move to Taiwan," he said. "How are the landings progressing?"

The staffers changed the maps to show Taiwan. The scene looked like a hot mess with a swarm of red and blue icons all over the place and arrows to match.

Clearing his throat before proceeding, Admiral Meyers began, "Forty-eight hours ago, we began the liberation of Taiwan. The force we landed in Taitung City on the southeast side of the island has secured our first beachhead. The Australian Army captured the city while our paratroopers secured the enemy air base and the city airport. The paratroopers are now moving to secure the mountains that overlooked the valley and city below. Once this area is captured, it's going to create a safe corridor for us to position ground-attack aircraft and helicopters. It'll also provide us with a buffer zone to start landing more heavy armor units. As we get more troops ashore, they'll move up Highway 9 and the coastal highways to link up with our northern force."

Meyers hit a button to zoom into a different area of the map. "Moving to the landings further north—we hit Yulan County with multiple landing points, so our forces wouldn't be bunched up." He paused for a moment, taking a deep breath. "Our forces are taking a beating there right now, Sir. We're two days into the landings, and the Marines have only captured roughly a kilometer inland in some areas, and as far as six kilometers in others. We're in the process of moving more naval and air assets to support the ground attack now—"

The President interrupted, "—What's the holdup? Why are our forces still stuck on the shoreline?"

"The city of Yulan sits in kind of a low-lying basin if you will. On nearly all sides, it's surrounded by large ridgelines and mountains. The PLA has built a series of bunker complexes throughout this area, and they're able to rain down a lot of death and destruction on our forces. Our Marines have to fight their way to the ridgelines and mountains, and then fight their way into these bunker and tunnel complexes to clear them out. It's going to take us a little while to root them out and secure the area. Depending on how many soldiers the PLA wants to commit to this battle, it could take us several weeks or even a month," he replied.

The President squirmed in his seat uncomfortably, then seemed to be lost in thought for a moment.

After an awkward pause, the President had a look as though a lightbulb had just gone off in his head. "Admiral, when my father was in World War II, he said they had some guys in their unit that used to use flamethrowers against these bunker complexes," he explained. "I don't mean to micromanage, but are we using some of these older weapons that worked well during the past wars to help solve this problem?" Foss clearly wanted to look for a way to contribute to the effort rather than just giving permission for the generals to do something.

General Kyle Stirewalt, the Chief of Staff of the Army, jumped in to answer this question before anyone else could. "We are using some of the older weapons of the past, Mr. President. However, we also have some newer stuff we are using as well. I will admit, at first, we didn't realize how difficult of a problem these bunker complexes would be. We'd been hitting them with bunker-busting bombs, but some of these complexes are dug so deeply into the mountains that they aren't easily destroyed. While we may demolish an entrance or outer bunker, we haven't been effectively striking deep inside them. Short of using a nuclear-tipped weapon, it's hard to reach that far down. So, yes, Sir, we have started to reissue flamethrowers again—albeit, much safer and better versions of those weapons, but yes, we are reissuing them. Another new weapon we're also looking at using is gas."

The President stiffened when Stirewalt mentioned the word *gas*, but he didn't stop the general from speaking, and neither did anyone else.

"We're going to try an experiment down in the south to see how it will work," the general explained. "The type of gas we're going to test is called SP-5. When a person breathes it in, it immediately renders them unconscious for several hours. It won't kill them, but it will put them to sleep for a while. Our intention is not to slaughter everyone inside the bunker if we can avoid it, but rather to render them incapacitated until our troops can get inside and take them prisoner."

Foss let out a short breath and smiled once he learned the general wasn't proposing they use some sort of WMD. He would've shut that down in a New York minute if that had been Stirewalt's intention. But a gas that would render a person incapacitated until they could be taken prisoner, that was something he could live with, especially if it saved American lives.

"OK, General, you have my permission to move forward with that option," Foss responded. "However, I want to know immediately how effective it is, understood? If it does work, let's see if we can look to incorporate it in some other manner that might allow us to incapacitate the enemy elsewhere. Perhaps we can find a way to end this war soon without it getting any further out of control."

Foss turned to eye Admiral Meyers. "What are we going to do about India? They've sided with the Eastern Alliance, and that's a problem for us. With India and China inexplicably working together now, nearly half of the world's population is now at war with the West. Our troops are already fighting each other in the Russian Far East and now in Europe. What are our options?"

Katelyn Mackie, the President's Chief Cyberwarfare Advisor, responded, "We're working on that right now, Mr. President. Our hackers are going after their logistical network and doing what they can to infiltrate their network-connected technologies to shut down various segments of their economy. We're pinpointing our efforts to disrupt the production of war materials that are dependent on one or more components—for example, a special computer component used in a surface-to-air-missile that's also used in a tank, or an aircraft. If we're lucky, we can cause a shortage of the part, or hamper the production of the part entirely. We're also looking for ways to insert malware code or kill codes into the software or hardware of the components of these types of systems. It's a very technical process, but it will have an effect on their ability to produce their war materials and to sustain the war long-term."

Admiral Meyers added, "While the introduction of Indian troops in Russia has complicated things, I'd like to note that we handed them a crushing defeat in Siberia over the summer. I won't dismiss their impact in Europe, but it's been a year since former president Gates reinstituted the draft. It had been slow at first, getting troops trained and to the front lines. However, they're now starting to show up in much larger numbers. In Siberia, our forces have hunkered down for the winter. We're still sending replacements for the losses they took, but they're nearly back to one hundred percent strength. In Korea and northern China, we've also suspended our offensive operations for the time being. We're consolidating our gains and continuing to hit them with precision-guided strikes with our B-2s and B-1s.

"Our focus now is on supporting the liberation of Taiwan, and Russia," Meyers continued. "The US Ninth Army in Europe has now surpassed 280,000 soldiers. The Fifth Army, which is still marshaling in France, has now reached 195,000 soldiers. This latest attack by the Russians and Indians is a last gasp, a desperate gamble on their parts to put us on defense. We may lose ground, but it'll be recaptured in the coming months. The Russians know that, and the Indians know that," he concluded.

Josh Morgan's left eyebrow rose conspicuously. "If they know that, then why are they launching this offensive?" he retorted. "Why wouldn't they try and hold those forces back to defend their border and make our counterattack more costly?"

"The same thing was asked during the Battle of the Bulge during World War II," Meyers responded. "In reality, the Nazis would have been better served by using those forces to defend the Rhine. They could have prevented the Allies from crossing the river for many more months. Instead, they chose to launch this last major offensive in hopes of cutting our forces off in the Low Countries, to grab the supplies at Antwerp, and to throw the Allied army into disarray. They truly believed that offensive would have altered the course of the war, or at least put them in a better position to negotiate a peace deal. I believe the Russians and Indians are of the same mindset with this current offensive. If they can divide our forces and thrust deep into Europe, they believe they'll be able to fracture the Alliance further and give them a better position at the negotiation table."

"The only way we're ending this war is when Petrov surrenders," Foss reiterated. "I agree with President Gates—

the Petrov regime needs to be removed and a new government installed, one that is willing to be a part of the global community and not a belligerent bully."

He paused for a moment, looking at the tired and worn out faces of his military advisors. He knew they were doing their best with what they'd been given. The fact that they'd somehow held the military together after all it had been through was a testament to their skill and ingenuity. As he stood, he added, "You all have done an amazing job executing the war. Please pass along my thanks to the others, and let's end this war…Tomorrow is election day, a day that may force us to make some changes in how we prosecute the war. One year from now starts the next presidential election cycle. I know it's a tall order, but I'd like us to work toward concluding this war by this time next year. The last thing our nation and the world needs is a sustained global war during a US presidential election." With that, President Foss stood and left the room to attend to other matters of state.

Chapter 6

From Georgia, With Love

Makhachkala, Republic of Dagestan

Russian Federation

The weather had recently turned cold and miserable in the relatively sleepy seaside town of Makhachkala. Major Gogaza pulled another cigarette out from his pack, stopping briefly while he cupped his hands against the wind to light it. He took a long pull to make sure the tobacco stayed lit. Gogaza let the smoke fill his lungs and reveled in the feeling as his body absorbed the nicotine. Then he continued his leisurely walk near the trainyard. Looking past the fence, he saw the petrol tanks and the network of pipes that connected them to the offshore oil rigs in the Caspian Sea.

Major Gogaza made a mental note of the security around the facility, noting the pair of soldiers casually walking a German shepherd along the perimeter. The fence itself was nothing too remarkable—a single-layer fence roughly six feet in height with three strings of barbed wire in a forked pattern on the top. It was designed to look tough, but it wouldn't keep an intruder out. Returning his gaze to the sidewalk and street he was meandering down, Gogaza spotted a small coffee shop and decided this would be a good place to stop and observe the guard schedule for a while.

Seeing an empty seat next to the front window, he slipped into the café and placed his windbreaker on the chair, along with a copy of the local paper. He then placed an order for a macchiato and a local baked delicacy and settled into his seat to read the daily paper. Gogaza spent a total of 72 minutes there. To be safe, he ordered a refill on the macchiato and downed a second pastry. While he was there, he noted that a pair of guards walked past the perimeter with a dog roughly twenty minutes apart. He stayed long enough to see four pairs of guards and dogs walk past the fence at nearly the exact same interval, with almost no variation.

Major Gogaza smiled to himself. *"These guys are either bored or sloppy,"* he thought.

After leaving the café, Gogaza took a very meandering route back to the house that had been rented for his team to use for this operation. The structure was dilapidated, but it would serve its purpose of not attracting attention to the ten Georgian Special Operations soldiers who were staying in it.

****

Three days went by as Major Gogaza's team surveilled the target of their operation. They developed a series of plans and discussed everything that could go wrong with each scenario. Then they constructed and ran through the alternative plans. It became clear that the best way for them to gain entry into the facility and accomplish their mission in the stated timeframe was for them to cut a hole in the fence near a section of shrubs on the northern side of the facility, then move quickly to place their explosives at the base of the storage tanks. A separate two-man team would infiltrate at a different point and look to blow up the pumping station to the pipeline.

Gogaza pointed to three of his team members. "You three will need to stay behind to provide sniper overwatch on this small crest," he ordered, pointing to a map. "It has a perfect vantage point to observe the fence we will be breaching."

"Yes, Sir," they responded.

"That gives us two snipers and one spotter," Major Gogaza continued. "If all goes according to plan, we will destroy the pumping facility, three million barrels of oil, and a critical junction in the pipeline. That will put a serious dent in the Russian petroleum business."

They all smiled, excited to be a part of degrading the Russian capability to support this horrible war.

****

The night air was cool. Cloud cover obscured the moon, which, for Major Gogaza's team, couldn't have turned out any better. They had driven to a small dirt road that was less than a few hundred meters from the perimeter fence they had chosen to infiltrate. All of them did a mic check to make sure that their throat radios were operational; they could clearly hear each other whispering as if they were talking right next to each other in a normal tone of voice. Then his men adjusted their night vision goggles before they exited the two vans. The special operators quietly snuck out of the vehicles and moved quickly and stealthily through the small trees and underbrush until they reached the fence.

The two-man team that was going to gain entry further down the perimeter drove their vehicle down the road another two kilometers until they reached their own infiltration point. Once there, they would wait for their overwatch team to let them know it was safe to cut the fence and move to place their explosives near the pumping terminal.

While Major Gogaza desperately wanted to penetrate the facility with his men, he knew he could serve them better by staying with the sniper team and managing the small surveillance drone they had brought with them. When the rest of the team got close to the fence line, he and the sniper team split off from the rest of the group.

Once they reached the hill, the snipers immediately unslung their packs and went to work setting up their rifles and other equipment. They removed the thermal-resistant blankets they would cover themselves with to prevent their body heat from showing up on any infrared or thermal security cameras. Before Gogaza crawled under one of the large blankets with his sniper team, he pulled the small surveillance drone out of the backpack, quickly unfolding it and turning the power on. Once the system check was complete and the drone was paired with the controller, he turned the little engine on, pulled his arm back and threw it for all his worth into the air.

The drone took off and established a circular holding pattern until Major Gogaza took direct control of it. With their eye in the sky in place, he crawled under the safety of the blanket. Flicking the night vision camera on, Gogaza quickly found the roving guard patrols. From what he could see, there were four roving patrols that moved around the perimeter of the fence.

Once the first patrol passed, he contacted his operators. "Cut the fence and begin to infiltrate the storage tank facility," he ordered.

They needed twenty to thirty minutes to place enough charges inside the tank farm to make sure the entire facility went up. If all went according to plan, his team would also place multiple charges at a lot of the oil pipeline terminal sections, which would tear apart the actual pipeline shutoff junctions. That would in turn cause petrol to continue to flow past the destroyed sections of the pipe, into the raging inferno they were about to create. With any luck, this fire would rage for days if not weeks, depriving the Russians of a critical fuel source.

Five minutes into the operation, they spotted their first sign of trouble. One of his team leaders contacted Gogaza. "OP1, Alpha Two has eyes on two tangos with a dog moving toward my position. I'm going to be spotted. Please advise if you're able to neutralize the dog. I'll take out the tangos."

Major Gogaza cursed under his breath. "That's a good copy. OP1 will neutralize the dog. Stand by," he replied. He gently nudged the sniper to his left, who had already zeroed in on Alpha Two's position and found the tangos and the dog.

Despite using a silenced rifle, the sniper's shot was still audible when he fired. Because of the range needed for this situation, he could not use subsonic rounds, which meant the silencer could only partially muffle the sound.

Major Gogaza suddenly felt nervous and exposed. *"At least the infiltration team on the ground is in a range to use their subsonic rounds,"* he thought.

The sniper's round successfully struck the German shepherd center mass, killing it instantly. Before either guard could react to what had happened, the operators of Alpha team appeared from behind one of the fuel tanks and fired short bursts from their silenced rifles, hitting both guards in the chest and killing them before they could fire a shot or alert their comrades to the attack that was underway.

Knowing their cover was blown, Major Gogaza called an audible and changed the attack plans. "Alpha, move immediately to place your charges on the pipe control junction *now*! Bravo, find one more fuel tank to place your explosives on and head back to the rally point. Charley, get your charges placed on the pumping station ASAP and then meet back at the rally point. How copy?"

One by one, the three teams reported in and raced to get their explosives rigged. Then, to Gogaza's dismay, the drone detected several additional guards exiting a small building, heading toward his Alpha team's location, probably to investigate the single gunshot they'd heard.

"Alpha, you have six tangos heading toward you. Set your charges and get the hell out of there!" he said urgently.

He watched nervously as the guards fanned out and moved toward the pipe control junction.

Gogaza keyed his mic. "OP1, OP2, you guys are going to have to cover them on the way out." The two snipers used their foot to tap, letting him know they understood and were standing by.

It was killing Gogaza to watch everything take place over a drone feed and not be on the ground with his men. He'd been in Special Forces his entire military career, and he lived for missions like this. Sadly, rank and command meant he was spending more time doing activities like this than actually being the shooter directly on the ground.

His radio crackled ever so slightly. "This is Charley. Explosives have been set. Exfilling now. Will meet at rally point."

"Thank God, at least the pump station is rigged to blow," thought Gogaza. Now they just had to get their other two teams out.

To his surprise, the guards that were headed toward Alpha were either walking slowly or just completely missed them as they made their mad dash to the fence line. In either case, both Alpha and Bravo teams made it out of the facility before the second perimeter guard patrol got near them. Then, as he and the rest of the teams packed up their gear and headed to the van, they all heard the facility alarm go off.

Gogaza sighed. *"They must have found the bodies,"* he realized.

"Blow the charges now, and let's go," he ordered as they all piled into the van. It was time to go meet Charley at the rally point and then head to their exfil point and hope their ride out of Dagestan was still possible.

As the alarms of the facility vibrated in the air, the darkness of night was broken by a brilliant flash and a thunderous boom. The first petrol storage tank had exploded. This initial blast was quickly followed by several more glorious explosions. Within minutes, close to a dozen more tanks had blown up. The night sky turned to day as the roaring flames now reached thirty or forty meters high into the sky.

Major Gogaza's team sped along the side road even faster. The perimeter of the flames would only increase, and they had to pick up Charley Team before they too were engulfed.

A mischievous smile spread across Gogaza's face. If the guards had survived the immediate attack and managed not to be thrown to their deaths by the shockwaves, they would surely be much more interested in trying to live or finding a way to stop the flames than in catching him.

A few seconds later, Gogaza's van twisted to a stop, kicking up dirt. Charley Team jumped in and they closed the door. They would all be drinking that night.

****

Volgograd, Russia
Lukoil Oil Depot

Warrant Officer Third Class Tiberius Petre held the 120mm mortar round over the top of the mortar tube, waiting for the order to release. Within seconds of indicating he was ready, his commander, Major Constantine Prezan, gave the order to him and the two other mortar teams. Tiberius dutifully dropped the mortar round and bent down to grab the next one.

Thump, thump, thump.

The mortars shot out of their tubes and headed toward one of the largest oil depots in Russia. Seconds after the first mortar fired, Tiberius dropped the second round in and repeated the process as quickly as he could until all his rounds were spent. In the span of three minutes, the three mortar teams had managed to fire off 36 mortars into the tank farms, causing many of them to explode. Soon, the fires and explosions were ripping across the nearby facilities. Within twenty minutes, the entire area was torn asunder as millions of barrels of petrol and the refineries nearby were reduced to a burning inferno.

Tiberius swelled with pride. With his mission complete, it was now time for them to work their way back to their safe houses and see what other mischief headquarters had in store for them.

Chatper 7
The Big Switch

Moscow, Russia
National Control Defense Center

A technician finished changing one of the halogen lightbulbs in President Petrov's office, under the close supervision of two FSB agents and a set of personal bodyguards. Once the agents had made sure there were no listening devices somehow being inserted into the light fixture, they let the poor man leave so he could go about the rest of his duties in the underground bunker, ensuring all the lighting and HEPA filters were functioning properly.

Since the assassination of the American president two months ago, Petrov had become paranoid that the Americans would try the same thing against him. The Yankees had managed to effectively piece together the assassin's history and find the link between the Russian GRU and the antifascist organization that had been running roughshod on the American and European college campuses. Once Foss had been able to see the full scope of the work stoppages, antiwar protests and general civil disruption that Antifa was having on the American and European war efforts, the new administration immediately moved to crack down on the organization. There had been so much anger and outright hostility toward Antifa after Gates had been assassinated that what had been a horribly dysfunctional American Congress had somehow managed to unite around banning Antifa as a violent Russian-sponsored organization.

However, what really had Petrov on edge was the fact that the Americans and the British had uncovered the FSB plot to remove the former Tory government in favor of one that would end the United Kingdom's involvement in the war. To that end, he had called an urgent meeting.

"These answers had better be good," he thought as he stared at some fish in his aquarium, fighting over a piece of food. He couldn't help but think how the world situation was not unlike the struggle he observed before him.

"Everyone is ready in the briefing room," one of Petrov's bodyguards told him, breaking his temporary trance. He stood up and headed toward the briefing room with his bodyguards in tow.

Petrov had recently insisted on having a set of bodyguards with him twenty-four hours a day, regardless of what he was doing. He'd also doubled the number of guards protecting his family, which he had moved to a well-furnished dacha near the Urals, far away from the American bombing attacks.

As Petrov entered the briefing room, everyone rose from his or her seat out of respect before he signaled for them to sit. Surveying the faces of the men and women at the table, Petrov could sense their unease. They squirmed in their seats.

Not beating around the bush, he jumped right in. "How did the British and Americans uncover our deception with Prime Minister Chattem? And what has happened to our man, Maksim Sokolov?" he inquired. He stared icily at his senior advisors, the men who had assured him this could never happen.

Ivan Vasilek shifted uncomfortably in his seat. The tables had been turned. Ivan was usually the one assaulting his subordinates with these types of pointed questions. However, he obviously did not enjoy the feeling of being put on the spot himself.

With all eyes looking at Vasilek, he sighed deeply before eventually looking Petrov in the eyes. "We were betrayed. *I* was betrayed, and for that, I am supremely sorry."

Taking this in, Petrov's eyes burned with rage. "Betrayed! How? Who?" he demanded.

"Major Petr Yelson, a young and very promising officer in my British directorate," Vasilek responded, hanging his head low. "He was assigned to work for Sokolov and handle his reports and electronic files here in Moscow. He also met with him on a number of occasions prior to the war, so they knew each other personally. In his role, he knew everything about the Chattem deception, from the political assassinations to the domestic attacks, the role the Antifa organization played in inciting domestic destabilizations, to our *Red Storm* social media disinformation campaign. From what I've been able to learn, somewhere in the last month or so, he became disillusioned with the war and found a way to reach out to Alexei Kasyanov."

There was a collective gasp. Then grumblings and curse words were muttered throughout the room as the full magnitude of this betrayal became clear. Petrov stood up, not saying a word, and paced for a second, too angry to talk. He then burst out in a tirade of profanity at Vasilek for allowing this to happen. Petrov was so enraged that he grabbed a nearby pitcher of water and threw it at the wall, shattering it in a loud crash.

"I ought to have you *shot!*" he yelled at Vasilek, whose eyes suddenly grew large as saucers. "You realize, this leak, this betrayal, has compromised our entire war effort! The entire war plan and strategy has essentially been given to the enemy. This Major Yelson will be a veritable treasure trove to the Allies for years to come!

"I want this man's family rounded up and executed," Petrov ordered. "Video the execution, and make sure it's sent to whoever he defected to. I want him to know that his actions have consequences. He's betrayed his country and cost the lives of countless thousands—his family's death doesn't even begin to make up for the damage he's done to our country!"

The others in the room looked aghast as they, too, suddenly realized that nearly a decade's worth of time, effort, and planning had just been revealed to the enemy. Their looks of shock turned to looks of anger and betrayal. Several of them seemed to be drilling holes into Vasilek's skull with their eyes.

Taking a moment to calm himself down and collect his thoughts, Petrov spoke again, more softly this time. "What is being done to minimize the damage?" he asked.

Foreign Minister Dmitry Kozlov joined the conversation at this point. "Sir, as of this morning, the British opposition party introduced a no-confidence vote in the government, and the Home Secretary issued an arrest warrant for Prime Minister Chattem. He's currently under house arrest until he's officially removed from power. The public outcry at the realization that he had helped to orchestrate multiple Tory assassinations and the cruise missile attack that hit five British cities has enraged the public. There are already calls for the British to rejoin the Global Defense Force and restart hostilities against us."

"How is this affecting our operations on the continent right now?" asked Petrov. He wanted to know if their offensive could still accomplish its goal or if they would have to start playing defense again.

"For the moment it has had no effect," answered Alexei Semenov, the Minister of Defense. "However, if the British do reenter the war, then we are going to see their fighters return. It will take time for their ground forces to redeploy, but within a month we could expect to see large British ground forces again. Putting aside the possible return of British forces, I believe that militarily, our larger concern is the destruction of our oil refineries and pipeline near Volgograd and Makhachkala on the Caspian Sea. These two attacks just severed more than 40% of our entire petroleum production. This is going to cut our fuel stocks at the front by significant margins." The poor man looked very worried, like he had just swallowed a rotten bowl of borscht.

"How far have our forces reached?" asked Petrov.

"In the south, our forces captured Trnava, Slovakia, roughly 57 kilometers east of Bratislava and Brno, Czech Republic," answered General Boris Egorkin, the Army Chief of Staff. He pulled up a map on his tablet. "In the center, with great help from our Indian counterparts, we broke through the Allied lines and captured Kraków. However, the GDF has hit us repeatedly with counterattacks, and I don't believe we'll be able to hold the city for more than a few days, maybe a week. In the north, our forces were stopped cold just north of Lublin. We have been unable to break past the German and French forces there."

President Petrov ran his fingers through his hair, calculating his next move.

"Generals, I want a plan by tomorrow on how we are going to hold on to our gains while Minister Kozlov works to put an end to the war," he announced. "We will try to secure an end to hostilities, with us retaining control of eastern Ukraine in exchange for withdrawing our forces from the captured territories. We'll see if President Foss is willing to save the lives of his countrymen, or if he will continue this war."

Petrov then angrily looked at his FSB Director. "As for *you*, you and I are going to have a private conversation. Dismissed."

Chapter 8

Counteroffensive

Wadowice, Poland

The sky had turned gray. Another storm looked to dump even more rain on the already-saturated ground. After rain that had lasted for most of October, the cavalry men were hoping to catch a break, so they could get back into the fight. The last month had been a frustrating series of fighting withdrawals, one after another, under relentless Russian attacks. Those attacks, however, appeared to have faltered. Perhaps they had finally come to an end.

Lieutenant Colonel Grant Johnson, of the 1/8 Cav "Mustangs," walked over to a table in the tent with several thermoses of black liquid gold, pouring himself a second cup of coffee before heading over to brief his company commanders on the latest set of orders they'd just been given. They were finally going back on the offensive. Intelligence reported a major fuel shortage in the Russian Army right now, and the division commander believed this would be a good time to hit the enemy.

"Listen up, everyone," Johnson announced. "Division has finally given us the green light to attack. Our battalion has been given the task of slicing through the countryside to hit an Indian regiment marshaled roughly 116 kilometers to the southeast of Kraków. The goal is to position a blocking force behind the Russian units in the Kraków pocket and either crush them or force them into surrender. I want everyone to take a few minutes and review the maps and the disposition of the enemy units in the area. The battalion is going to move out in the next hour, so get your men ready to roll."

His men smiled from ear to ear. They were obviously excited to finally get some payback for all the harassing artillery fire they'd had to endure the past week while being holed up in the rear, waiting for their chance to pounce.

****

Captain Jason Diss had been the Delta Company commanding officer or CO for nearly twenty months. He was the senior captain in the battalion and would probably be promoted to major at the rate the division had been losing officers. The only reason he hadn't already been promoted was that the battalion CO needed him and the other senior captain to continue to train and mentor the never-ending supply of second lieutenants who were arriving to the brigade fresh from Armor Basic Officer Leader Course. Big

Army was pushing through officers of all stripes at a prodigious rate, which meant there was a lot of pressure on the captains and majors to help get these young officers up to speed.

Walking back to where his company had been staging, he quickly huddled his platoon leaders and NCOs together so he could go over their objectives and the battalions' objectives. He wanted everyone on the same sheet of music when the band started to play. Once the shooting started, plans had a way of going out the door, so it was imperative that every one of his officers and NCOs knew what the overall plan was, so they could adjust accordingly when needed, in case his own tank was hit or disabled.

After finishing his brief, Captain Diss trudged over to his tank and proceeded to take care of a few hygiene needs and grab some chow before the festivities started. When he got to his tank he yelled up for one of his crew members to throw him one of the MREs from the case they just brought back from supply.

Catching the pouch of food, he looked at the menu number. "Hmm…what mystery meal did I get?" he mused. "Hell yeah, it's number four—spaghetti with beef and sauce."

With his breakfast in hand, Jason sat down with his back against the tank skirt to have a quick meal and read the most recent letter he'd received from home. When he opened the large envelope, what he found was actually a combination of several letters. Both of his daughters had written to him, and one had included a picture she'd drawn. Every time he read their letters, he couldn't help but get a little emotional. They were so little—just five and seven years old—and he wanted nothing more in life than to be back home with them in Texas.

Suddenly, Sergeant Dakota Winters plopped down next to him with his own MRE in hand. Captain Diss quickly wiped the tears out of his eyes.

"You'll see them soon enough, Sir," said Winters. "We all will."

Diss turned to look at his sergeant. "I know we will," he replied. "It's still hard sometimes. You know it'll be Thanksgiving soon. It's one of the few times my entire family is all together at one place. This is going to be the second straight year I'll have missed it."

Winters nodded as he ate his first spoonful of food. "I think this is going to be the last Thanksgiving we'll miss. We're practically to Russia right now. I can't see them holding out much longer."

"You're probably right, but let me ask you something. The Russians still have thousands of nuclear weapons. You really think they're going to surrender and not use them?" He shook his head. "I just hope my family stays safe," he added. "I have a bad feeling that Petrov guy would rather burn the whole world down than lose the war."

The two sat silently for a few minutes as they continued to eat their MREs, not talking about the upcoming battle. They both knew it was going to be more than a skirmish; it would be historical clash.

A voice suddenly intruded in on their thoughts. "Hey, Captain, you ready?" inquired their loader. He'd been monitoring the radios for them inside.

Looking up at him, Diss responded, "Yeah, we're ready. Let's get this show on the road!" He climbed onto the turret and dropped down the loader's hatch. In short order, Captain Diss then ran through the standard procedures, getting them and the rest of the company ready to roll out.

"Radios are set on the right frequencies," confirmed Sergeant Winters, "and targeting computers are up and running. Ready."

Tanner, his driver, chimed in. "I've got all our navigational waypoints entered, Sir. Ready."

Changing to the company net, Captain Diss called out, "This is Black Six to all Mustang elements. We're moving out in five mikes. I want a wedge formation with Blue Platoon in the middle. I want everyone to stay frosty and keep your heads on a swivel. We're going up against the Indians, and from we've been told, they will have air support, so look out for it. Acknowledge and send Redcon status."

Steadily, everyone reported in their status, letting him know all the tanks were up and running. Thankfully, none of his tanks looked to be having any morning troubles that might keep them down for maintenance.

"All right, Mustangs, begin your movement," Captain Diss ordered.

The platoon of tanks sprang to life, dutifully forming a wedge as instructed. They rumbled down Highway 28, headed toward the small village of Zembrzyce. The Bradleys tagged along, filling out the rest of the formation.

Captain Diss couldn't help but think back to when they'd arrived as a fresh unit, before they'd suffered and lost so many men. Their unit had arrived in Europe at the start of the New Year. By that time, the major fighting had largely ended, and the battle lines had stabilized. The war in Korea and China had stolen the attention from Europe, placing most of the European forces on defense. In the meantime, the constant probing attacks and retreats had cost their battalion more than a few tanks. Each time it would appear like they could punch through the enemy lines, they'd been ordered to withdraw. The division had not been given permission to go on the offensive. From the perspective of the soldiers, this was nothing more than wasting lives and tanks, testing the enemy lines without being able to exploit vulnerabilities when they were found.

The sound of several friendly attack helicopters overhead snapped him back to the present day. "Captain Diss, how many enemy tanks do you think we'll find after those choppers get done with them?" his gunner asked.

Diss smiled. Sergeant Winters was clearly hoping they wouldn't miss out on getting some payback. After months of sitting around, waiting for the summer offensive to start only to have it cancelled, the men were ginned up for a fight.

"From what the colonel said, there's an entire regiment up there, so I'd say there'll be plenty of tanks for us," Captain Diss answered. "We just need to make sure they don't get any lucky shots off at us."

"As long as we don't run up against any of those new Russian tanks, I think we'll pulverize this unit," said

Sergeant Winters assertively. "They're using T-90s, and we've already proven we can defeat them."

Captain Diss retorted, "You'd better hope they're using the Russian T-90s and not those new Arjun Mk-2 tanks. I heard they had a lot of help in developing those tanks from the Israelis in the 2000s, and the Israelis know how to build a tank."

Twenty minutes went by uneventfully as their tank rumbled through the rolling hills and lightly forested area. Suddenly, the roaring sound of a jet engine caught their attention. "Whoa, what was that?" asked Specialist Trey Mann, the loader.

"Probably just a jet on his way to attack the Indians," replied Winters, trying to calm the young kid. Specialist Trey Mann was the newest member to their platoon. He'd arrived as a replacement roughly five weeks ago.

Captain Diss popped open the hatch and stuck his head out for a moment to survey the scene. At first, he didn't see anything, even though he could hear several jets. Then he spotted a fighter plane, right before it exploded in a spectacular fireball. The flame of the explosion was so bright, it felt like he had just damaged his retina.

A voice came over the battalion net. "All Mustangs, enemy planes in the vicinity. Expect enemy contact at any time."

"Heh, you think?" he remarked snidely in a low voice.

As he kept observing his surroundings, Captain Diss suddenly caught sight of the silhouette of rockets heading in their direction. He popped back down, slamming the hatch closed.

"Mustangs! Incoming rocket artillery!" he warned over the company net.

The ground around them began to vibrate wildly, though none of the rounds seemed to be hitting close enough to their tank to cause any real damage yet.

Seconds later, Sergeant Winters yelled out, "Tanks to our front, 3400 meters!"

Captain Diss peered through the commander's sight extension. Sure enough, a line of tanks was shifting from a single file line to a full battle line and was headed straight toward them at a rapid clip. When he looked a little closer, a knot formed in his stomach. Those were not T-90s—they were all the Indians' best tanks, the Arjun Mk-2s. He let out one deep, long sigh.

"Mustangs, Arjun Mk-2 tanks to our front, 3,400 meters," he announced. "We are moving to engage. All units fall in on our position and move to a line formation. We're going to snipe at them while they advance. When you see my tank fire, engage!"

Diss made a quick call to his FIST team to request a fire mission. He needed some artillery support fast. Turning to the battalion net, he sent a quick message to his commander, asking for air support.

"Captain, those tanks are charging!" Sergeant Winters yelled. "Crossing 3,200 meters now."

Within seconds, he and his team had zeroed in on the Arjun that was most likely the battalion commander's tank due to all the antennas and had launched a sabot round at it. Diss watched it lob gracefully through the air, landing right between the turret and the chassis. It ripped the turret off, flinging it like a ragdoll.

"That was textbook, guys. Let's keep this up," said Captain Diss excitedly.

The rest of Captain Diss's troop took their cue and began to fire at will. He watched several of the rounds as they whizzed toward the enemy. Although a few missed, many more successfully began to pick off the enemy tanks, one by one.

"Sabot up!" shouted Captain Diss's loader, who pulled up on the arming handle.

"Fire!" ordered Diss.

"On the way!" yelled Winters. He depressed the firing button again.

Once again, their round found its mark, this time along the left tracks of the enemy tank. It blew the tread clean off the body of the tank, tipping its body to the side and leaving it dead in the water. The hatch opened up, and Indian soldiers scurried out, making a hasty exit. They obviously hoped to avoid the certain death that awaited them if they stayed inside what had become a steel trap.

While Captain Diss's company was steadily picking off the attackers, a steady stream of incoming enemy artillery rounds continued to land ever closer to their tanks. Tanner instinctively backed them up to move over to another firing position.

"Mustangs, pop smoke and fall back two hundred meters," Diss directed.

"*We need cover!*" he thought.

"Those tanks are now at 2,800 meters!" Winters yelled. The artillery grew louder and louder.

Captain Diss got back on the battalion net. "Sir, I need an air strike on the enemy force advancing on us," he urged.

His tank suddenly started shaking like it was sitting along the San Andreas Fault during an earthquake. Many dull clangs overloaded his senses as his tank was smacked with shrapnel. Captain Diss whacked his cheek against the commander's extension and instinctively pulled his left hand up to the side of his head. When he pulled it away, he noticed some blood on it.

"*I must have cut myself,*" he realized, still somewhat dazed.

"That was close!" yelled one of his crew members. "That artillery round was probably not more than ten meters away!"

His battalion commander overheard what was happening. "Delta Six, I'm ordering your unit to fall back to Rally Point Beta, is that understood? Get out of there now!"

Captain Diss didn't have the energy to argue, so he simply answered, "Yes, Sir," and went about the task of notifying his unit of their new orders.

Tanner plugged in the coordinates, and they began a fighting retreat. They eventually fell back behind the next line of American tanks that was positioned to move ahead and continue the battle in their place.

Captain Diss took a deep breath. *"We've survived one more round, but who knows how long our luck will hold out?"* he thought. Once Diss's company was able to regroup, they'd charge right back into the action.

As Delta Company began the process of recovering their wounded and assessing their damage, his first sergeant's vehicle stopped next to his tank, and First Sergeant Keene got out and proceeded to climb up to talk with him. Captain Diss pulled his CVC off and stood up in the turret.

"How many did we lose, Top?"

Instead of answering the question, he shouted, "Get me a medic up here!" and pointed at Diss.

The captain held his hand up in protest. "I don't need a medic, Top. I'll be fine."

Keene shook his head. "You'll be fine, but we need to get that bleeder under control before we go back into action. Look at yourself—you're a bloody mess." He pointed to Diss's coveralls. The front shirt had blood smeared all over it.

The medic climbed up the turret. He wiped away the blood on the side of his face to get at the wound. He ripped open a pack of quickclot and doused the wound with it before attempting to place a makeshift bandage on it to cover it up.

"Hey, I still need to talk and be heard!" Diss said angrily to the medic.

Satisfied that his captain wasn't going to bleed to death, First Sergeant Keene finally replied to the initial question. "We lost four crews outright. Another six soldiers were injured—four of them can return to the fight now that the medics have them patched up. The other two we have to medevac out. Second Battalion is hitting those Indian tanks now. From what I can tell, we'll be ready to get back in the action as soon as you tell us to go," he concluded.

Captain Diss nodded.

Just then, they heard a series of propeller-driven planes fly over their position. The two of them looked up and saw the Air Force's newest tank buster, the AT-6 Wolverine. Underneath the wing pilons, they could make out four hellfire antitank missiles and two anti-material rocket pods. Next to an A-10 Warthog, the Wolverine was definitely considered a godsend.

"OK, Top, let's get everyone ready to move. I want to get us back into the action as soon as the colonel gives the go-ahead."

His first sergeant nodded, then jumped down from the tank and ran back to his own vehicle.

Five minutes later, their battalion commander came over the radio net. "Advance!" he ordered. Second Battalion had blunted the enemy attack after they had withdrawn, and now they were going to push past their sister battalion and attempt to overrun the enemy unit.

As they moved past their earlier firing line, Captain Diss spotted a couple of his own tanks, now charred burning wrecks. A few minutes later, his company pulled up to their sister battalion, which was still firing at the enemy, who was now retreating. Once Diss and his men came abreast of the of the sister battalion, they stopped shooting.

Their battalion commander came over the radio again. "Charge!" he shouted.

"You heard the man, Mustangs. Charge!" Captain Diss shouted. He had secretly always wanted to say that. His tank lurched forward and picked up speed, and they quickly closed the gap on the retreating Indian regiment.

Looking into the commander's sight, Diss spotted two Arjun tanks. One was hiding behind a burnt-out wreck of a tank, and the other one was hiding behind a burning BMP-3 infantry fighting vehicle. Captain Diss yelled to his driver, "Stop the tank!"

He quickly lased the first tank to get a quick read on it. Winters punched in the targeting data, but suddenly, their targeting computer spat out an error.

"Damn it! It looks like they have a dazzler. It just blinded our targeting computer," Winters said to everyone's horror. The gunner immediately switched over to his auxiliary sight and got them back in the action.

"Back up now!" Diss shouted to his driver. In a fraction of a second, their vehicle lurched back, just as a round slammed into the front glacis of their armor. The round bounced off, but it rattled everyone in the vehicle hard.

Diss instantly popped more smoke grenades, hoping to throw off the enemy's next shot, which was sure to be on the way soon.

Boom, bam!

One of his tanks had pulled alongside his to try and hit the tank that had just shot at him. Unfortunately, the crew failed to identify the second tank, which had been hiding behind the burned-out BMP, and was blown apart by it.

Winters found the tank that was sniping at them from behind the BMP and sighted in on it, calling the target out.

"Identified! Arjun tank," he exclaimed in a hurried voice.

Specialist Mann grabbed a sabot round and slammed it into the breech of the cannon and pulled up on the arming handle.

"Up!" he yelled.

"Fire!" screamed Diss, hoping with all that was in him that they took that guy out. He wasn't sure how many more times their luck would hold out. They'd already taken several direct hits, and so far, the enemy rounds hadn't penetrated his tank, but he recognized that it was luck at this point that was keeping them alive.

"On the way!" Sergeant Winters shouted urgently.

Winters depressed the firing button and prayed for a hit.

Boom!

The cannon fired, recoiling back inside the turret as the vehicle rocked back on the tank's springs. The spent aft cap of the sabot round clanged on the turret floor, joining the pile that was now cluttering the floor.

Diss watched the round cross the distance and slam right into the tank, which burst it into flames.

"You got it!" yelled Captain Diss to his gunner. "Quickly, find that other tank and take it out before he realizes we're still alive."

"Sabot up!" shouted the loader as he pulled up on the arming handle.

Seeing that they had found the last remaining enemy tank, Captain Diss yelled, "Fire!" He said a quick prayer as the round was released.

Boom!

The cannon recoiled one more time inside the tank, and they watched the round fly right next to the turret of the burning tank to slam into the side of the other Arjun tank. In seconds, the tank blew up in spectacular form, adding another billowing cloud of oily black smoke to the surreal scene around them.

Crump, crump, crump.

More artillery rounds landed near them, rocking their tank.

"Get us moving!" Captain Diss yelled at his driver. "We need to get out of here. The enemy artillery has us zeroed in."

Once they were speeding along, Captain Diss again returned his attention to the rest of the company. He needed to figure out how many more tanks he'd lost during this charge. He knew the one next to him had been destroyed, but he didn't know whose tank it was or if they'd lost any additional vehicles.

Ten minutes went by as they moved through the area, past burnt-out wrecks of Arjun tanks, BMPs and BTR armored vehicles. Several Apache helicopters flew ahead of them, looking for more targets to take out. Just as Captain Diss was starting to feel somewhat safe about having them around, one of the Apaches exploded in midair, hit by some unseen missile. Then he identified the sound of more fighters overhead. An aerial battle was now in full swing above him.

****

Mons, Belgium
Global Defense Force HQ

General John Cotton, the Supreme Allied Commander, stormed into the briefing room.

"Why haven't we broken through the enemy lines in the south of Poland yet?" he demanded. He singled out his operations chief, a German officer, and practically shouted, "Our forces in the north have routed the enemy—they pushed the Russians out of Poland and back into Belarus— we may very well capture Minsk in a few more days. What is the holdup with our forces in the south?"

Lieutenant General Wolfgang Kholman was not fazed by Cotton's abrupt manner. He calmly responded,

"The situation is still fluid at the moment, Sir. Despite being surprised by the Indian use of the Arjun Mk-2s, I just received a report that the US 1st Armored Division and the German 9th Panzer Division broke through the Indian positions there, and the Indians are now conducting a fighting retreat back to the Ukrainian border."

Seemingly satisfied with his J3's response, Cotton took a short breath and signaled for the others standing at the table to take a seat. "All right, everyone, we need to get the rest of the midafternoon update. I have a secured video teleconference with the President before dinner, and I need to be fully caught up on everything."

Two captains sitting against the wall pulled out their notepads, ready to take detailed notes on the meeting. They had the dubious task of creating the slide deck to be presented to the President.

"OK," said Cotton, now more poised, "if the 1st AD and the German 9th Panzers broke through, then what's happening to the small contingent of enemy troops that are trapped in the Kraków pocket? Do we have an idea of how many enemy soldiers we're facing?" Cotton asked.

Major General Sarah Tyndale, his intelligence officer or J2, took this question on. "We've been going over a lot of drone footage to analyze the numbers on that, Sir.

We've also been combing through a lot of interrogation reports from prisoners taken near the city. The best we can tell is that at least one battalion of Indian infantry is still trapped in the city, along with a Russian motorized rifle regiment. We estimate it's 5,000 enemy soldiers, give or take."

General Kholman added, "We've been hitting their armored vehicles with precision strikes as best we can. Right now, they don't have enough armor or other vehicles to force a breakout in any particular sector. I can order the 9th Panzer Division in, but my concern is we'll end up destroying a lot of the city trying to root them out."

General Tyndale nodded, then asserted, "Sir, I'd recommend we let the PSYOPS guys have a crack at it. The enemy has been on defense for a while; they're getting hit from the air, snipers, and artillery. If we can't convince them to surrender by the end of the week, then we can look at sending troops in."

General Cotton put his two index fingers together in the shape of a steeple as he thought that over. Sending troops in now would surely result in a bloody street fight that would cause significant damage to a historic city. *"I could give them a week,"* he finally determined, *"but no more."* Without enemy units in their rear, a longer delay just didn't make sense.

"OK, General Tyndale, your intel guys have one week," General Cotton instructed. "If you can't convince the enemy to surrender, then I'm going to have General Kholman send the 9th in. I can't have that division stuck encircling Kraków trying to starve them out. I need their armor to help press home the attack elsewhere. Understood?"

She nodded, smiling slightly. General Cotton knew her well enough to understand that saving a beautiful city from destruction meant something to her.

Cotton moved on to the next topic. "Slovakia—have we pushed the Russians out?"

"Yes," answered General Kholman. "It didn't really seem like they planned on holding the country. We sent one Italian division, one Croatian battalion and two Austrian battalions in there, and all they encountered were two Russian motorized infantry regiments and one armor battalion. The Russians barely fought. They did carry out an effective fighting retreat, which tore up a lot of the country's infrastructure. Nearly every bridge they crossed, they destroyed. It's going to make launching any offensive operations from Slovakia a mess until we can get those bridges repaired."

General Cotton snickered. "That was the Russians' entire plan, Herr Kholman," he said with a smile. "They were never going to hold Slovakia, but now they've denied us its use as a launchpad to invade Ukraine. They want to force us to face them from Poland, where they've built an in-depth defense for us."

General Kholman nodded and pulled up a map on PowerPoint. "Right now, Sir, the enemy defensive line stretches from Košice, Slovakia, to Nowy Sacz, Poland, in the south. In the center, they hold at Lublin, Poland, and in the north, their line stretches from Baranovichi, Belarus, to just east of Riga, Latvia." A bulge in the enemy lines in the center had clearly developed.

Seeing the opportunity before him, General Cotton sat up straighter in his chair and announced, "I want Fifth Corps in Belarus to break off from their attack and shift south. Move the French division we have in reserve to take their place. I want Fifth Corps to drive south and capture Kovel, Ukraine. If they can capture that city, it'll cut the entire Russian center force off from resupply and place an entire corps in their rear area. We'll collapse the entire Russian front if we can pull it off," he said excitedly.

"This might be the ticket to ending this war if we can make it work," Cotton thought happily.

Kholman looked at the map and paused. He scattered some notes on the paper in front of him, and Cotton surmised that General Kholman was calculating the distances. Suddenly, he frowned. "Herr General, I agree this would cause the Russian lines to collapse. However, I'm not sure if you are aware, but that would be roughly a 320 kilometer drive south, largely behind enemy lines. We would in all likelihood not be able to resupply them for several days, maybe even a week, depending on whether or not the enemy cut through our own supply lines," he explained.

"What do you believe we'd need to have happen to make this plan work?" inquired Cotton. He really wanted to finish the Russians off there in Poland.

Kholman thought about that for a second. He looked at the units in the nearby area and consulted the map one more time. "Herr General, I'm not sure if the British are going to return to the war soon, or if they will at all, but if they did, we could probably complete the maneuver you requested if we could have the 16 Air Assault Brigade carry out a combat assault and secure Ivanava, Belarus, and Manevychi, Ukraine. I believe they would be able to keep our supply lines open and make sure Fifth Corps didn't get cut off or surrounded." He gestured to the locations on the map as he spoke.

General Cotton needed a moment to consider this option. No one spoke for a little while, although several of the people scribbled notes, apparently making their own calculations. Finally, Cotton replied, "I'll talk to President Foss about that when I speak with him tonight. It's only been twenty-four hours since the new British government was sworn in, and I'm not sure how quickly they'll want to get back into the war."

Looking now to his naval counterparts, Cotton said, "Changing subjects, are we ready to launch Operation Polar Bear yet?"

Operation Polar Bear was going to build on Operation Nordic Thunder by leveraging a naval task force to sail around the Kola Peninsula and finish off the remains of the Russian Navy. Once the *Admiral Kuznetsov* and the rest of the North Fleet were sunk, the amphibious assault portion of the operation could commence. The goal was to land a regiment of French Fusiliers Marins, the French version of the Marine Corps, who would assault Severodvinsk, Russia, in the White Sea, which would open up their access to the strategic city of Arkhangelsk. The French Marines would be supported by Princess Patricia's

Canadian Light Infantry. Between the three Canadian battalions and the French forces, General Cotton believed they should have more than enough strength to secure this critically important Russian seaport and open it up for future offensive operations once spring thawed the winter snow and ice.

French Admiral Denis Béraud, who would be leading the expedition, responded, "The task force is ready to sail within seventy-two hours of your giving us the order." He crossed his arms, hesitating. "However, if I could, General Cotton, I would advise that we wait to see if the British are going to rejoin the war. If they do, then I recommend we hold off on deploying the task force until we can get the British to join us."

Admiral Béraud pulled up a screen with a summary of his naval forces. "Right now, we have the Italian carriers *Cavour* and *Giuseppe Garibaldi*. Combined, these carriers have thirty-eight vertical takeoff aircraft. Then we have the Spanish *Juan Carlos I*, which can carry twenty-eight VTOL aircraft. Then I have my own carrier, the *Charles de Gaulle*, which can carry forty aircraft. We also have three amphibious assault ships that could carry additional aircraft, but I have intentionally left them to be dedicated helicopter assault ships to support the ground invasion. If we add in the

USS *Kitty Hawk*, the USS *Enterprise*, and USS *John F. Kennedy*, it will bring our naval airpower to over three hundred aircraft. However, if the HMS *Queen Elizabeth* is able to join the fleet, it'll add another fifty aircraft. Plus, we'll be able to add the Royal Marines to the ground force. It'll make our offensive much more effective."

A smile spread across General Cotton's face. "Admiral, I'm impressed. You've been given an incredibly difficult job of cobbling nearly a dozen navies together to form the largest allied fleet in the Atlantic since World War II, and you've done it. Again, I'll speak with the President tonight to see what the status of the British is and if we may be able to count on them in this coming operation. Was there any trouble getting the American carriers manned and ready?" he asked. "I know they'd just recently been pulled out of mothballs, so they needed a lot of work done to them."

Admiral Béraud nodded. "Yes, they needed a lot of work to get ready for this operation," he replied. "However, I'd like to commend America on its ability to get these ships ready for war in such a short timeframe. In less than fifteen months, your shipyards were able to rewire them and install the most current defensive systems, targeting computers, and radars. It truly was amazing."

General Cotton, who was now feeling much more optimistic than when he'd entered the room, concluded, "Thank you, everyone, for your hard work these past few days. We're close to defeating the enemy. We need to stay focused on the task at hand and finish these snakes off."

Then he got up and headed back to his office. He needed to prepare for his brief with the President, which would take place in two hours.

****

Arlington, Virginia

Pentagon, National Military Command Center

The air was thick with tension and apprehension as the men who would decide the fate of the free world sat at the table in the large room of the National Military Command Center, deep in the bowels of the Pentagon. From this very room, the launch orders to unleash America's nuclear arsenal could be generated and executed. The men and women that manned this room on a twenty-four-hour basis at times felt the weight of the world on their shoulders as six nuclear-armed powers waged war against each other. They never knew if one or all six would at some point unleash those horrid weapons of mass destruction.

Sitting at the briefing table was the Chairman of the Joint Chiefs, Admiral Meyers, the service chiefs of each branch of service, the Secretary of Defense, the National Security Advisor, several of the intelligence directors and the President. They had just concluded a teleconference with the newly sworn in British Prime Minister, Rosie Hoyle, who'd just informed them that the United Kingdom would be resuming their participation in the war against Russia. She'd promised that her government was going to do everything they could to reinstate the military buildup and the prior deployments of the military to the continent. This was obviously welcomed news.

They didn't have too long to revel in this happy development, though. A technician walked into the room and walked over to the colonel who would be leading the next brief. "Sir, the guys in Europe are ready for you," he announced.

The colonel nodded, and the technician gave a thumbs-up to someone in the rear of the room to activate the screen. A second later, the image of General Cotton and a couple of his advisors were shown on the large screen.

"Good evening, Mr. President," General Cotton said to the group. It was still technically lunchtime in the US, but he greeted him based on local time.

"Good afternoon, General. I hope things are progressing well on your end," Foss replied.

"Things are good on this end, Mr. President. As you'll note from the slides we sent over, we have finally achieved a breakthrough in several sectors." There was a slight pause as the group thumbed through their printed handouts. Cotton allowed a moment for review, but he was not one to waste time, so he cut to the point. "However, Mr. President, as you'll see on slide fifteen, I'd like to know if we're going to be able to include the British in our coming operations."

The President smiled. He exulted in being the bearer of good news for once. "As a matter of fact, yes," he answered. "We just spoke with the new British Prime Minister right before this call. She has assured us that Britain will return to the war. They have several of their senior officers on the way to your location to begin coordination of whatever forces you need for the coming offensive."

It was clear General Cotton was breathing a sigh of relief, even over the grainy video feed. He replied, "Excellent news, Mr. President. Once I've conferred with them, do I have your permission, then, to proceed with the proposed operation we presented on slide twenty-eight, the use of the British Airborne and V Corps to slice deep behind enemy lines?"

Despite only working with General Cotton for a short bit, President Foss had really taken a liking to him. He was proving to be a real tactician. He'd been making do with little in the way of support and reinforcements for the past year, and somehow, he'd still managed to help train a massive Allied army to fill in the gaps in his own forces.

"Gates was right, this guy will win the war in Europe for us," Foss thought.

"General, we've been going over the details since you sent them over. I believe the Joint Staff have some additional questions, which I'll let them ask offline. However, I'd like to move forward with the plan. They just want to sort a few items out, but otherwise, this looks like a sound strategy. If it works, you might be able to force a very large portion of the Russian and Indian forces into surrendering before the end of the year."

"Thank you, Mr. President," General Cotton responded. "We'll get things sorted out then with the Joint Staff and proceed. When I meet with the British LNOs, we'll have a better idea of how soon we can start our offensive. We'd planned to start the naval action in a couple of days, but we'll postpone a little longer so we can integrate the

British fleet into our own. If you don't have any further questions, then we'll take the rest of this offline and keep you apprised of any significant changes,"

Seeing no obvious questions, the President indicated that they were good, and the call was ended.

President Foss smiled. His day had just gotten exponentially better. With the British back in the war, the operational tempo was about to increase tremendously going into the final two months of 2018.

Chapter 9
Operation Nordic Fury

Norwegian Sea

Commodore Robert Cornell, the captain of the HMS *Queen Elizabeth*, had just poured himself a fresh cup of tea when the storm suddenly opened up on them. He sighed. He didn't want this winter storm to derail the start of this very important operation.

The wind had been howling for a while, but now the windshield wipers on the bridge were in full swing, batting back and forth against the rain, which was coming down so quickly that it still made it nearly impossible for them to see. Looking to the right of the bridge, Cornell could see one of the destroyers rising as it crested a solid ten-meter wave before racing down the back of it into the trough and subsequently being hammered by another large wave.

"The troops in the transports are probably retching their guts out right now. Land lubbers," he thought with a smirk.

Commodore Cornell turned to look for his weather officer. "How long is this new storm supposed to stick around?" he asked.

Lieutenant Commander Jonathon Band replied, "It should clear up in about twenty-four-hours, though we are still going to experience some rough seas for at least two or three days. The latest satellite report shows we should have about five days of clear, good weather before the next storm hits the Barents Sea and moves down into the White Sea."

Cornell thought about that for a moment. At their current pace, they'd be in range of Russian air and missile defenses in three days, but they'd need at least two or three days to clear themselves a path for the troop ships to round the Kola Peninsula into the White Sea. That left them roughly twenty-four to forty-eight hours to land the troops and secure the area before the next storm hit and put an end to both air and sea support operations.

"This next storm—can you give me your best estimate of how long you think it'll last? Are we talking a couple of days, or maybe a week in length?" he pressed.

The weatherman paused. "Sir, weather prediction is tricky, especially when you're talking about a week or more in advance. I can give you a better estimate in four or five days. However, right now, if I had to estimate, I would guess it should last around three, maybe four days. But that's a guess right now. It could be shorter or longer. What I can assure you of is, when it does hit, we'll be hard-pressed to carry out any air operations and certainly wouldn't be able to support any amphibious operations unless the ships were already in the White Sea."

This was about as close to a definitive answer as he was going to get. "OK, Band. Thank you for the insight," Cornell responded. "If you can, please make sure you're coordinating your assessments with the French and Americans in the fleet. Let's hope the weather gods will smile on us long enough to accomplish our mission."

Seeing that he wasn't really needed on the bridge, Commodore Cornell made his way to the air operations tower to see how his air operation planners were progressing with the next phase of the operation. They still needed to hunt down and destroy the Russians' remaining aircraft carrier and what was left of the Russian northern fleet.

****

The storm had been battering the HMS *Albion*, which had been carrying three commando brigades of the Royal Marines, for more than a day. While many of the men were used to being holed up on an amphibious assault ship, they were not as used to having twice as many Marines crammed into the same space. It made for some uncomfortable living conditions, and all the men were eager to get ashore and fight the Russians.

Sergeant Philip Jones was one such Marine. He was far more at home in the woods or mountains, stalking an enemy that could kill him, than being cooped up on a ship in the middle of the ocean with no way to defend himself. The constant battle drills the ship captain kept running the crew through only reinforced his belief that he was safer on land than stuck on the transport. The thought of a Russian submarine torpedoing their ship was unnerving and terrifying. With the frigid temperatures of the waters they were sailing through, there was little chance of survival for very long if their ship was sunk.

As the waves kept rolling up and down, he drifted back to thoughts of how he'd gotten to be in this situation in the first place. This was Sergeant Jones's seventh year in the Marines. He'd joined at the age of just eighteen, shortly after his mother had passed away from breast cancer. Jones was an only child, and his mother was the only real family he had ever known. His father, an abusive drunkard, had left him and his mother when he was just nine, abandoning them to fend for themselves. As a young boy he'd grown up in government housing, with a mother who loved him dearly but spent most of her time working, trying to make sure her only son had a chance at life. His mother had sacrificed so much to ensure he was able to attend a good primary and secondary school, knowing that education was going to be his way out of the low-income ghetto they'd found themselves living in.

When his mother was diagnosed with breast cancer, he had just turned sixteen. He opted to finish school early and quickly found a menial labor job to help bring in some money to help cover the mounting medical bills. Private insurance and specialists were expensive. When his mother became too sick to work, Jones looked for other ways to make money, eventually turning to one of his childhood friends who ran with the wrong crowd. His friend, George, was two years older and had been working for a local gang who made their money in the drug trade. It didn't take long before Jones was working a corner, peddling their products to earn some extra cash. However, he was a lot smarter than the average street thug. In a short period of time, he'd moved up the ranks from street peddling to running his own network. Jones knew the real money to be made was not on the street, but in the financial district.

A friend of his from school had a father who worked for Barclays as an investment banker. When his friend's dad caught them smoking weed one day after school, rather than chastise the boys, he joined them. Through a little prodding, Jones was able to learn that his friend's father had other colleagues who would be interested in finding a confidential source for some drugs. Jones assured him that he could provide a steady source of cocaine if he wanted it. Because he didn't know who these people were, he'd sell the drugs to his friend's father, and then he could sell the drugs to his friends. That way it made things easy.

For six months, this little arrangement worked out well. Jones was making more money than he had ever dreamed of and he made sure his mother was given the best care and medicine money could buy. Unfortunately for Jones, he was paying for specialized care that was way above the national coverage his mother's meager wages could have afforded. This behavior, along with a few unnecessary purchases, eventually caught the attention of local law enforcement. One day, a pair of detectives paid Jones and his mother a house call. They'd been observing him for nearly a month and had built quite a case against him. His mother was appalled once she learned of how he'd been earning his money; it broke her heart to see that he was squandering the future life she had worked so hard to give him.

The police detectives saw some potential in Jones, and in consultation with the Justice Department, agreed to not press charges against him if he provided the names of who was supplying him the drugs and who he was selling them to, and then enlisted in the armed forces. The prosecutor had served in the Royal Marines for a stint and told Jones that it had helped to set him on the straight and narrow, and he was willing to give Jones the same opportunity if he'd take it. During this ordeal, Jones's mother had passed away from the cancer, and with no one else in his life, he agreed to take them up on their offer of redemption.

A month before his eighteenth birthday, he'd joined the Royal Marines and left for recruit training. Seven years later, Jones had served in both Iraq and Afghanistan, along with a few other hotspots around the world. He had one year left in his enlistment, though he'd decided the Marines was it for him. He'd enlist again and this time make it a career, not just an adventure.

One of his corporals pulled him out of his memories. "Sergeant Jones, how far do you think we are from Russia?" he asked. The rest of his men were just as antsy to get off the ship.

"From what I've heard, we're roughly four days away from the Kola Peninsula and then the White Sea. How are the men holding up?" Jones asked.

The corporal shrugged. "They're holding up fine. I'm working them as hard as our limited space allows. Lots of time in the gym, etcetera."

Before the two of them could say anything further, the warning klaxons sounded general quarters again. Thinking this was just another drill, they turned back to continue their conversation before they heard and felt an explosion. It didn't quite feel like their ship had been hit, but something near their ship definitely had. This clearly was not a drill, and something terrible had just transpired. Sergeant Jones jumped up and made it his mission to find out what had happened.

****

The HMS *Duncan* was one of the newest British Type 45 Daring destroyers, and a pivotal part of the *Queen Elizabeth* strike group. With the American strike group in the center and rear positions of the fleet, the *Duncan*, along with three other Type 23 or *Duke*-class frigates, was responsible for protecting the European carriers and their French counterparts. There were over sixty warships in Task Force One, which made up the bulk of the fleet's striking power. In Task Force Two, there were an additional fifty-two warships, though these mostly comprised the amphibious assault ships, troop transports, and additional roll-on, roll-off or ro-ro ships. It was an enormous fleet, and by far the largest concentration of Allied warships.

"Any word on that underwater contact yet? Is it moving toward the fleet?" asked Commander Mike Shepherd, the captain of the *Duncan*.

Lieutenant Martin Nibs looked up at the captain, replying, "No word on the possible contact in sector G3. However, the *Portland* just registered a possible underwater contact in D5. They're moving to investigate it further right now."

They were all a bit on edge. Several of the frigates had detected an underwater contact at the outskirts of the fleet's protective zone. Unfortunately, the storm was preventing them from launching their helicopters or calling in for land-based support from their antisubmarine planes, which meant they were left with their passive and active sonars. One of the frigates would pound the water with its active sonar, while the other ships would sit in passive mode, trying to see if they would hear the sonar pulse reflect off the hull of an enemy submarine.

The terrible weather had also prevented them from being able to effectively deploy their towed sonar array, making it much more difficult to differentiate the sound of heavy rain and waves crashing around them from the noise of an electric pump or propulsion used on a submarine. For the last hour, they'd been picking up faint signals, only to lose them again in the clutter of the storm and then suddenly have them spring up again much closer to the fleet.

Commander Mike Shepherd scratched his head as he looked at the map for himself. As he saw where D5 was in relationship to G3, it just didn't make sense. "That new contact is way too far away from G3 to be the same contact," he asserted. "We're most likely looking at a new contact, if that is in fact what it is," he replied to the lieutenant, his targeting officer.

Lieutenant Nibs's brow furrowed. "Sir, if this is a new possible underwater contact at D5, then that contact is well within our protective bubble. Shoot, they're almost within torpedo range of the *Queen Elizabeth*, if it is a sub," he explained.

"*Damn this storm. We need our helicopters!*" thought Commander Mike Shepherd. He clenched his fist, frustrated that the pounding rain was blocking their sensing capabilities.

One of the petty officers who was manning a sonar display nearby suddenly turned in his chair. "Multiple underwater contacts!" he shouted.

Everyone's heads turned toward the captain, who shouted, "How many and where are they headed?"

"It's that possible contact in D5. It's a sub. Holy hell, the contact just multiplied. We've got five confirmed submarines!" shouted Petty Officer Lee Davies. "The identification is coming in now…they're *Akulas*," he said. Seconds later, he yelled, "Torpedoes! I count eight torpedoes in the water, Sir. It looks like one is heading toward the *Portland*, and another toward the *Lancaster*. The other six appear to be split evening between the *Queen Elizabeth*, the *Charles de Gaulle*, and the Italian ship, the *Cavour*."

"Sound general quarters!" ordered Commander Shepherd. "Send a message to the fleet admiral and let him know what's happening." He hoped that somehow the frigates and other ships would be able to launch enough decoys to confuse the enemy submarines.

"How could the Russians have gotten so close to us?" he wondered in awe. He figured that there was no way that all five contacts were enemy subs—there had to be decoys. There was simply no other way to explain how an enemy threat had been able to penetrate so far into their perimeter.

Lieutenant Nibs finished a phone call. "Sir, the *Lancaster* is engaging the enemy submarines with their torpedoes, and the *Somerset* is moving to engage the enemy as well."

Before either man could say anything else, Petty Officer Davies signaled for their attention again. "What is it, Petty Officer?" demanded the captain. He and Lieutenant Nibs quickly walked over to his sonar station.

"I'm picking up more torpedoes, Sir," he answered. "They appear to be from one of our submarines. It's engaging the underwater contacts. After listening more closely, it sounds like there's probably only one *Akula*, not five. It sounds like the other *Akula* noises were decoys launched by the original submarine to confuse us."

Both officers let out an audible sigh. Commodore Shepherd wiped his forehead. The volume of torpedoes five submarines would have been able to shoot at them would have certainly guaranteed some hits. As it was, they still had eight torpedoes heading toward the fleet.

They waited anxiously through every second for the next several minutes. One by one, they received reports from the sonar officer on whether or not the torpedoes hit their intended targets.

"Sir, I can confirm that the torpedo launched at the *Lancaster* went after the decoy and blew up harmlessly," announced Petty Officer Lee Davies.

Several seamen nearby let out an excited half-yell, half-grunt. However, the battle was far from over.

Davies had another announcement. "Sir, the *Portland* wasn't so lucky. The torpedo missed the decoy and definitely connected with the ship."

Lieutenant Nibs got on the horn to find out what their status was. He looked a bit pale when he hung up. "Commodore, they did pick up the phone, so at least they weren't immediately sunk. However, the torpedo sheared off most of the front part of the ship, and they're taking on a lot of water. They don't know for sure if the engineers will be able to repair the *Portland* enough for them to make it."

Petty Officer Davies spoke again. "One of the French destroyers must have been able to move their decoy into the path of one of the torpedoes that was headed toward the *Charles de Gaulle*. It just exploded harmlessly."

Every second felt like an eternity at this point to Commodore Shepherd.

"Commodore, the second torpedo headed toward the *Charles de Gaulle* did connect with the ship," explained Davies.

Moments later, Lieutenant Nibs announced, "That last torpedo that hit the *Charles de Gaulle* must have been a wave runner since it traveled right in their wake. It blew up against the stern. There's a small fire in engineering, but so far, they seem to be stable."

One of the radar operators suddenly waved for attention. "Sir, the *Kent*—it's moving right in the path of those torpedoes!" he shouted.

"*My God, he must've realized that there was a wave runner and now he's trying to obscure the torpedoes' guidance picture*," thought Shepherd. It was a very risky move, and he wasn't sure if he'd have had the stomach for it himself.

Petty Officer Davies announced, "Sir, the *Kent* just took a direct hit."

Seconds later, everyone heard an enormous blast.

The XO called down from the bridge.

"What just happened?" asked Shepherd.

"Sir, the first hit must have damaged the boiler room. As soon as that icy water hit, the entire stern was blown clean off. There's a third of the ship missing. There is no way they're going to make it. Let's just pray that some of the men can make it onto the life rafts before the *Kent* sinks beneath the waves," the XO explained.

"We're going to need to organize a rescue party," Commodore Shepherd said.

However, before any action could take place on that matter, Petty Officer Davies announced, "Sir, the second torpedo that had been headed toward the *Queen Elizabeth* just connected with the hull."

"What do you see, XO?" asked Shepherd.

"This does not look good, Sir," responded the commanding officer. "The torpedo hit the underbelly of the ship, and she's likely taking on a lot of water. She's already starting to keel over to one side. They're slowing down. They must have a lot of flooding. I see fires springing up all around. My God…I hope I'm not watching while the pride of British fleet is sinking."

A knot formed in the pit of Commodore Shepherd's stomach. He had never anticipated that this day could ever end this way.

Over the next few minutes, he learned that the *Akula* had been destroyed by the Allied torpedoes and that the Italian ship had skated by without any damage. However, it didn't remove the awful feeling of knowing that many lives had been lost and that Her Majesty's namesake was in danger of slipping to the bottom of the ocean.

****

Vice Admiral Mitch Lindal sighed. The fleet was four days into their operation, and already, they were experiencing a number of problems. Aside from the storm that was battering the aged ships that comprised his fleet, the *Kitty Hawk* was experiencing a series of engine problems that under any other situation would have meant she would have returned to port. But her aircraft—even the limited ones she was carrying—were needed for the coming operation. Two of her eight boiler rooms were experiencing problems that were affecting her propulsion systems. She was unable to maintain full speed, and while that wasn't a problem right now, when it came time to launch their aircraft, it could become an issue.

"*I wasn't even supposed to be here*," he thought in one of his rare pessimistic moments.

After thirty-two years of military service, Vice Admiral Mitch Lindal had been five days away from starting his terminal leave and his retirement from the Navy when the war with Russia had started. His retirement had been postponed for ninety days to allow the Navy to determine how serious this new war was. Once the *Bush* carrier strike group had been destroyed, a second carrier sunk by the Chinese, and a third severely damaged, it had quickly become clear the US was going to need to pull several of their older carriers out of retirement to fill the gap. World War III had arrived, and it was all hands on deck to defeat the powers bent on destroying them.

Once Admiral Lindal's retirement had been rescinded, he'd been placed in charge of creating a new carrier strike group that would defeat the Russian Navy and help end the war. In that pursuit, he was placed in charge of reactivating the USS *Enterprise*, which had recently been stripped of her electronics, reactor fuel rods and most of her other critical systems. An army of nearly three thousand contractors had been brought in and had worked around the clock to get the ship brought back up to speed.

In addition to getting the *Enterprise* reactivated and ready for war, he also had to ready *John F. Kennedy*, which was in a similar state. Both ships had been in the process of being made ready to be turned into floating museums, which was fortunate, given that at least they weren't in the process of being broken down for scrap.

Getting the *Kitty Hawk* seaworthy was practically going to require an intervention from the Almighty. However, instead of divine intervention, Admiral Lindal has been given an army of contractors. The carrier had just started the process of being broken down for scrap when the war started. It had taken nearly ten months to get her seaworthy and ready for combat. Even in her deployment to England, she was still flooded with an army of two thousand contractors who were getting the ship's electronics, weapons, and aviation functions ready for war. It was not until ten days prior to this deployment that the ship had received her full crew, munitions, and aircraft. Bringing these three carriers out of retirement and ready for war in essentially ten months had been nothing short of miraculous.

In addition to getting the three carriers ready for war, Admiral Lindal had also had to assemble the support ships that would be needed to escort this aged fleet of warships. After combing through the naval inactive ship maintenance facility in Philadelphia, his staff was able to identify thirteen of sixteen *Oliver Hazard Perry*-class frigates that could be brought back up to service for this newly designated fleet. His planners had also identified two *Ticonderoga*-class cruisers and six amphibious transport ships. In Pearl Harbor, they'd looked at the eight amphibious assault transports and had wanted to incorporate them into their Atlantic fleet but had been told they had been slated for use in the Pacific. Admiral Lindal had only been allowed to pillage through the Atlantic reserve fleet. Rumor had it the Navy was even considering reactivating the two remaining *Iowa*-class battleships, purely for their sixteen-inch gun platforms.

It had been a long few months for Admiral Lindal, to say the least. He poured himself another cup of coffee and stared blankly out the window at the storm.

Captain Donna King had a similar idea. She emptied the current pot of coffee on the bridge into her mug, and after setting the next one up to brew, she found the admiral, who was looking outside. "Remind me why we're launching this operation now, instead of a few months from now when the ship and the fleet would be better prepared," she said in a hushed tone only loud enough for the two of them to hear.

Admiral Lindal grunted in reply before turning to look at the newly promoted captain. Donna King had just pinned on captain when the war started. She was going to assume the role of Commander Air Group on the *George H.W. Bush* when it had been sunk. When the Navy had made the decision to reactivate the *Enterprise,* she had been Admiral Lindal's top pick to take command. Aside from being a brilliant aviator, she had served as his aide during his obligatory Pentagon tour. He knew if anyone could light a fire under the butts of the engineers to get the ship ready for combat, it would be her.

Ever since he'd met her sixteen years ago, Admiral Lindal had taken a liking to King. As a young F/A-18 Hornet pilot, she was aggressive and tenacious, but she was also a big thinker, someone who saw the grand strategy. That singled her out as an officer who would make flag level one day. He had taken it upon himself to help mentor her and guide her through the perils of the Navy officer selection process. When he had been given the herculean task of building a new carrier strike group out of mothballed and reserve ships, he'd sat down and gone through his rolodex of officers he had personally groomed and mentored. He had orders chopped and people transferred around as he sought to build his leadership dream team. He would do his best to make sure these officers were rewarded following the war.

Smiling as he looked at Donna, he responded in a similarly hushed tone. "If we wait, we won't be able to move until spring. Before we left port, I had a telecom with the SecDef. He told me that between the ground offensive and our amphibious assault, they believe the Russian Army may completely collapse. We could end this war within the next two or three months."

Captain King sighed but nodded. "Did you hear about the boiler room problems on the *Kitty Hawk*? I'm glad we don't have that issue to deal with," she said, changing the topic.

"Yeah, I've been hearing about a host of mechanical problems from different ships throughout the fleet. I hate to admit this, but I'm glad we brought a few tugboats along. Some of the transport ships are really having a hard time keeping up. I've already had to detail off a couple of frigates to help guard two transports that broke down and are currently trying to get back underway."

"Did you ever think in 2018, a carrier fleet would be traveling with several tug boats? We're as bad as the Russians," she said with a slight chuckle. Prior to the war, the Russian carrier was often seen traveling with a tugboat. It was notorious for breaking down and having to be pulled into port.

"The *Kitty Hawk* was commissioned in 1961. I served on her in the 1980s. I never imagined leading a fleet of ships that had largely been part of the Ghost fleet."

Before they could continue their conversation, a call came through, requesting their presence in the combat information center. They both headed down to the CIC to see what was going on. When they entered the room, they saw several underwater contacts on the big board screen.

"Torpedoes in the water!" announced one of the senior petty officers who had been manning one of the operations desks.

Before anyone else could speak, Admiral Lindal demanded, "Where are they headed?"

"The torpedoes appear to be aimed at the European ships," he replied. "We're well outside of their range."

"Admiral, we're receiving a message from the *New Hampshire*," the underwater LNO explained. "They say they're moving to engage an *Oscar*-class sub. They said it sounded like the *Oscar* was preparing to fire her cruise missiles."

"Let's go ahead and bring the rest of the fleet to battle stations and prepare them to respond to a possible cruise missile attack," the admiral ordered. Despite the new threat, he trusted that his people and their ships would be able to handle the evolving situation.

****

Bear Island, Barents Sea

Admiral Feliks Gromov smiled to himself as he watched the waves crashing. The storm raging in the Barents Sea couldn't have come at a better time if he'd planned it himself. Things were going much better than he had anticipated.

Their intelligence sources in both Britain and Norway had confirmed the departure of the Allied fleet four days ago; when they'd discovered the Allied plans for

Operation Nordic Fury, his officers had scrambled to figure out how they could stop the American fleet. It was clear they were going to try and end the war before the conclusion of the year, and if the Allies were successful in landing troops at Severodvinsk, they had a good chance of succeeding.

A major high-profile defeat like that would be nearly impossible for the media to spin, and it would cause the Russian people to question how well the war really was going. In general, the average Russian citizen knew the Allies were still carrying out sporadic strategic bombings across the country, but the news from the front was still regaling them with victories, tales of pushing the Allies completely out of Ukraine, and their army driving deep into Poland and even Slovakia. An Allied invasion of the Russian mainland from the White Sea would call all of that into question.

When the war with the Americans had started, Admiral Gromov had petitioned to have upgrades to the *Admiral Nakhimov* rushed, and to have his own flagship, the *Pyotr Velikiy*, equipped with their new 3M22 Zircon anti-ship missiles. NATO had called these missiles the SS-N-33, and they were petrified of them. While the Russian Navy had not been able to use them in the war up to this point, they would be heavily used in the coming naval battle.

Admiral Gromov had marshaled his meager fleet, which consisted of the lone Russian aircraft carrier, *Admiral Kuznetsov*, two *Kirov*-class battlecruisers, his two remaining *Slava*-class cruisers, and the one remaining *Sovremennyy*-class destroyer the Allies had not sunk yet in an occupied Norwegian fjord. The Russian rocket forces had successfully shot down a few Allied satellites that were providing them with real-time intelligence over this area of the Barents Sea just for this operation. He also had three additional *Udaloy*-class destroyers for antisubmarine warfare support.

In all, his fleet comprised eight surface ships and four submarines—not much considering the fleet they were supposed to intercept, but what they had that the Allies didn't was a hypersonic anti-ship missile capable of carrying a 2,500-pound warhead at speeds in excess of Mach 5. His fleet was equipped with a total of 120 of these missiles, and depending on how many of them made it through the Allied air-defense screen, his little fleet could still force the Allied fleet to turn around and head back to Britain.

Gromov's greatest fear right now was not that his fleet would fail, but that Petrov might authorize the use of tactical nuclear weapons to destroy the Allied fleet if it came down to it. Many of the Russian military leaders were desperate to keep the war conventional, even if it meant they ultimately lost. After seeing how the American president had responded to the use of nuclear weapons by the North Koreans, there was no question as to how the US would respond to a second use of these dastardly weapons against their forces. Even in defeat, Admiral Gromov and his men would still have a home to come back to. However, if the war turned nuclear, there was no guarantee any of them or their families would survive, and that kind of victory was not worth having.

Once the Allied fleet left their British and European ports and formed up in the North Sea, the meteorologist reported that a large winter storm would descend from the North Pole and converge into a nasty storm over the Greenland Sea and then make its way down to the Norwegian and Barents Seas. During this period, it would be nearly impossible to conduct air operations, and the dense storm cloud coverage would hamper drone surveillance after the Allies lost their satellites. The loss of the satellites would only guarantee him a day, maybe two tops, before either new ones were launched or satellites already in space were redirected to cover the Allied fleet. If Gromov rushed his fleet from Tanafjorden, where he currently had them laid up, into the opposite side of Bear Island, he just might catch the Allied fleet by surprise.

As he continued to watch the waves crash around him, his mood soured a bit. *"These rollers are horrendous,"* he thought. Launching an attack in this severe of a weather pattern was very risky. If the targeting officers weren't careful, the missiles could very well fly right into a wave before they even hit an American ship.

He sighed. If they waited for calmer seas, the Allies would be able to use their Air Force and drones, and his fleet wouldn't last an hour against the Allied airpower.

"No, we need to use this horrible storm and hope for the best," he determined.

Turning to face his weapons officer, Admiral Gromov nodded. "Order the fleet to begin firing our missiles," he announced.

Gromov glanced down at his watch; the submarines would begin launching their attack within the next ten minutes. If they timed things correctly, the Allied fleet would be dealing with torpedoes and missiles from the submarines when their swarm of hypersonic missiles showed up on their radar screens.

Bright flashes of light appeared on the front section of the battlecruiser as the first missiles fired out of the vertical launch system. Forty Zircon missiles packed enough punch to severely cripple a strike group—at least that was what the military developers in Moscow had told the Russian armed forces.

****

"Vampires! Vampires! Vampires! We have inbound missiles bearing 113, one hundred and thirty kilometers, traveling .9 Mach," shouted one of the air-defense officers aboard the USS *Enterprise*. The team of radar and defensive weapons personnel were picking up handsets and shouting all sorts of information as they tried to begin the critical coordination of the fleet's defenses.

The watch commander in the CIC turned to face the admiral. "Sir, the *Gates* is asking permission to slave the fleet's air-defense systems. What should I tell him?" asked Commander Lipton, holding the receiver to his shoulder while he waited for a response.

Captain King gave the admiral a pensive look that said it was a gamble. While the *Thomas Gates* was a *Ticonderoga*-class guided missile cruiser, she had also been pulled out of mothballs and given a hasty upgrade to make her seaworthy. There were a lot of concerns about her targeting computer's ability to properly slave and integrate the air-defense weapons of the fleet's destroyers and frigates. In normal times, none of them would have questioned this decision. They would have had a system in place where the cruiser would have taken over and immediately engaged the enemy threats with the fleet's missiles.

Admiral Lindal made eye contact with King. He must have seen her nervous look, but he straightened up. "Permission granted," he ordered. "Have the *Gates* take control of the air-defense systems immediately. Tell Captain Tappal he'd better take those threats out."

Captain King felt nervous, but she gritted her teeth and went about her job.

"*I wish I had as much optimism as Lindal,*" she thought. Then she realized that the admiral had known Captain Tappal for a long time and most likely trusted him to report any potential problems before now.

She turned to her air boss. "Captain Adel, is there any possible way we can get some aircraft in the air? I have a feeling there are going to be a lot of missiles being thrown at us soon."

The CAG looked at her for a second and then at the weather screen and readings. "I'd advise against it, Captain, but I'll ask for volunteers. Are you thinking of a Growler flight?"

"Yes, I want to get as many of our Growlers in the air as possible. I know the weather's terrible, but my gut says there's at least one or two *Oscars* out there that are about to make life tough for us. With the *Queen Elizabeth* and the *Charles de Gaulle* sitting still while they assess their damage, I want to make sure we have some electronic countermeasure assets airborne."

No sooner had she finished her sentence than the lieutenant commander who oversaw their air-defense system shouted again. "Vampires, Vampires!"

She turned to look at the radar display. As she watched, she saw the original six anti-ship missiles headed toward the fleet suddenly turn into forty new contacts. Before she had any time to figure out what had happened, a second wave of twenty missiles appeared from a new heading and suddenly split into sixty missiles, further throwing her off.

"What the hell is happening, Commander Lipton? How are these missiles multiplying?" Captain King asked, confused.

"They aren't multiplying," answered Lipton. "They're projecting decoys to throw off our defenses." The irritation in his voice showed just how angry he was at the Russians for employing this new trick.

Minutes went by as they observed the fleet's missile interceptors start to converge on the enemy threats. One by one, the enemy missile count was starting to go down, though they were still getting close to the fleet. The British and French warships now joined the fray, firing the next round of interceptors. Once the enemy missiles reached forty kilometers from the fleet, they increased speed as they headed in for the kill. The targeting computers were still struggling with determining which missiles were ghosts and which ones were in fact missiles, so interceptors were being launched at each contact, just to make sure.

As the enemy remaining missiles zoomed into the last layer of defense, a new set of missile contacts showed up on the screen.

"Those must be more ghost contacts. There's no way an enemy missile could travel that fast," Captain King thought. Her eyes grew wider as the targeting data showed that the new threats were traveling at speeds of Mach 5.2. At that rate, they would close the distance between them very rapidly.

She turned to face her watch commander. "Where are these missiles coming from? And tell me that's not their true speed," she demanded.

Commander Lipton didn't say anything.

Admiral Lindal picked up a receiver near him. "Tappal?" he confirmed. After the slightest of pauses, he yelled, "Tell me those missiles aren't traveling at Mach 5.2!"

Captain King saw Admiral Lindal hit the speaker button so everyone could hear the answer.

There was no response on the other end for a few seconds, but everyone could hear a fair bit of shouting and loud voices in the background. "Those speeds are accurate, Admiral.," Tappal finally said. "They appear to have come from the Bear Island vicinity, or at least that's our best guess. I didn't think the Russians had deployed them yet, but these must be the new Zircon missiles. They can travel at speeds in excess of Mach 5 and carry a 2,500-pound warhead."

Captain King suddenly felt nauseous.

"Tell me you can shoot them down or have a plan to deal with them," demanded the admiral.

"The two Growlers you guys just launched, we're going to try and see if they can jam the missiles until they hit our defensive perimeter," said Captain Tappal. He paused. "I'm not going to sugarcoat it, Admiral, we'll get one shot at taking them before they come in range of our point defenses. Once they enter that zone, I'm not confident our systems will swat them down. I'd prepare the fleet to absorb some hits, Sir." His voice sounded bleak.

Admiral Lindal sighed. "Do what you can," he answered. "Hopefully, this is the only barrage they have."

Just as Captain King thought the situation couldn't get any worse, the initial wave of hypersonic cruise missiles was suddenly joined by a second, and then a third wave that were rapidly closing the distance between them.

Turning to the watch commander, the admiral asked, "Did we sustain any hits from the first barrage of missiles?"

Commander Lipton replied, "A couple. One of the frigates took a direct hit. The ship is still afloat, though she has a serious fire to her aft section. Two of the destroyers were hit. None fatally. I'm more concerned by this new set of missiles. I don't think we've ever encountered something like this. I have no idea if we're going to be able to shoot them down."

Minutes ticked by as they watched the Growlers use their ECM jammers on the missiles in an effort to help confuse and blind them from the hundreds of interceptors heading toward them. When the first wave of interceptors converged on the hypersonic missiles, they scored a number of hits, but of the forty missiles in the first wave, thirty-two continued on. Then the second wave of interceptors converged, and another ten more missiles were destroyed. At this point, the Zircons were traveling so fast that they were on the fleet before a third wave of interceptors could be fired, and it was now up to the point defense systems to do their job.

Dozens upon dozens of RIM-116 and ESSM missiles from the carriers, destroyers, and frigates joined the fray, adding hundreds of additional interceptors, all trying to stop the hypersonic threats from hitting the fleet. Fractions of a second later, the Phalanx CIWS guns joined in.

"Brace for impact!" yelled someone in the CIC. Seconds later, the ship shook violently, throwing several sailors to the ground who were not strapped in. A thunderous boom reverberated throughout the ship.

"Damage report!" yelled Captain King.

Before anyone could respond to her, the CIWS opened fire a second time. The next wave of hypersonic missiles had already begun to arrive.

"Brace for impact!" someone else yelled.

Thud!

The ship lurched as another missile hit their carrier. The lights flickered off briefly, creating a moment of panic before they switched back on.

Captain King had been thrown the floor and hit something on her way down that temporarily knocked the wind out of her. She watched Admiral Lindal help himself back up from the deck and walked over to one of the action officers. "What's the status of the fleet?" he asked.

From her perch on the floor, King could clearly see the look of fear written on the young lieutenant's face.

"*This is probably his first time being shot at*," she realized. It was an unnerving experience, one she wished they were not going through right now.

The lieutenant examined his computer screen, which was being refreshed with the status of each ship in the fleet. Although she couldn't see very much from the floor, Captain King did note that there were several names highlighted in red and many more in yellow.

The young lieutenant answered, "Three ships have been destroyed, Sir. I'm showing fifteen more with damage. We'll get the actual damage report on how bad they are soon."

"What about the carriers? How many were hit?" Admiral Lindal demanded.

One of the petty officers tried to use the external cameras to see if they could spot any of the carriers and see if they had any visible damage. "Sir," he said, "while the winds from the storm have died down the past hour, the rain is still heavy. There's enough of a mist that it's difficult to get any clean images. From what I can see, there are a lot of fires in all directions around us."

"Satellites are back up!" yelled one of the petty officers manning the air-defense system. Bad weather had been interfering with their reception for several hours.

Captain King finally managed to catch her breath and went about the task of getting a damage assessment of the ship. However, she also kept her ears open to overhear what was going on at Admiral Lindal's end. She managed to pick up that the enemy ships were making best speed to the coastline, and heard Lindal order, "Send a message out to the fleet to engage the enemy ships with our Tomahawks. I want those ships destroyed."

A few moments later, Admiral Lindal walked over to join her. "Captain, satellites are back up. We've identified the location of the enemy fleet. Can you get your birds in the air to finish them off?" he asked.

Captain King looked at the admiral and shook her head. "We're a no for further flight operations, Admiral. One of those missiles hit the hangar deck. We've also got one of the catapults down right now, and the port-side elevator is out. More reports are coming in now, and it looks like we took a lot of damage to the aircraft down there as well."

"This isn't good. How many casualties?" he asked.

King tried to stay strong and keep her composure as she responded, "No idea just yet, but it's going to be high, Sir."

Captain Adel interrupted them. "Ma'am, I've got four F/A-18s that were already on the flight deck before the attack. We can launch them now if you want," he said.

She nodded, and the CAG ordered the fighters launched. They'd link up with the others that had already been able get airborne and go after whatever Russian ships remained after the Tomahawks did their job.

****

Admiral Lindal thanked Captain King and then moved over to his action officers. "Have the Tomahawks launched yet?" he asked.

Chief Morris looked up at him. "The *Ramage* and *Cole* are launching their missiles now. However, Sir, the *Laboon* was sunk, and so were the *Carney* and the *Gonzalez.*"

"*My God, that was sixty percent of our Tomahawk capability,*" Admiral Lindal thought. He suddenly realized just how many sailors had perished at sea. He shook himself—there wasn't time to dwell on it. He could mourn the dead later.

Changing subjects, Lindal ordered, "Give me the battle damage assessment of the fleet."

A senior chief spoke up. "Sir, the *Charles de Gaulle* is gone. She was nearly dead in the water when the hypersonic missiles converged on the fleet, so she had no way of being able to maneuver. She took nine direct hits, several to her magazine rooms. Once her missiles and bombs started to go off, she completely blew up. I don't know how, but both the Italian and Spanish carriers sustained only minor damage from the first cruise missile attack by the Russian subs. They are moving to try and conduct search and rescue operations of the ships that have been sunk."

Admiral Lindal shook his head. This was not good.

The senior chief continued his report. "The *Queen Elizabeth* appears to have taken seven hits. I'm honestly not sure if she's going to make it. She's almost completely ablaze, though the rain does appear to be helping to tamper down the fires. Who knows, maybe the cruddy weather might actually save the ship by putting out some of the fires. The *Kitty Hawk* is going down. She hasn't sunk yet, but she's burning out of control. I spoke with someone from their CIC a few minutes ago, and he said the captain had given the order to abandon ship. They took a hit to engineering, and they were already having problems with two of their boilers.

When the missiles arrived, one of them hit just at the waterline in the engineering section. Aside from the blast tearing the place up, once the icy waters hit the boiler room, everything exploded. It blew the aft and lower section of the ship wide open."

As if to add emphasis to what he was saying, the senior chief pulled up a camera feed that showed the *Kitty Hawk*. Admiral Lindal crossed his arms in frustration. Not only was a good portion of the *Kitty Hawk* on fire, but the aft section of the ship was sinking—nearly the entire bow of the ship was raised out of the water.

"How about the *Kennedy*?" asked Lindal.

"No damage," said the senior chief. "I don't know how, but they didn't take a single a hit." He paused a moment. "Sir, I know this doesn't bring any of our guys back, but the Russians fired 120 of those hypersonic missiles at us. Only 46 of them actually scored hits. Without the Growlers we launched prior to the attack and some seriously fancy shooting by the *Gates*, the Brits, and French destroyers, this could have been a bloodbath. Plus, none of the troop transports or amphibious assault ships sustained any damage."

Admiral Lindal grunted and uncrossed his arms. "I suppose that's one way to look at it, Senior. You guys did a good job through all of this."

Lindal patted the senior chief on the shoulder, then walked over to the workstation he had been occupying and sat down for a second. He needed to collect his thoughts before he phoned back to higher headquarters to let them know what had happened.

He rested his head on his hands. *"It's going to take a while to scoop up the survivors,"* he thought. However, he realized that at the end of the day, despite the loss of ships, they would still be able to carry on with their original mission. This war was going to end, and the troops they were escorting were going to make it happen.

Chapter 10
Winter Warfare

Moscow, Russia

Looking outside his office window, Petrov saw that the snowfall that had started out as a light dusting that morning was starting to pick up pace into a full-blown winter storm.

"It's beautiful watching the snow drift down like this across the city," he thought, almost nostalgically. He allowed himself a couple of minutes to just let go of the world around him. For a moment he forgot the weight of the war, which was beginning to become like a millstone around his neck.

That burden had become a constant drone in his mind as of late. The Americans had again rejected Minister Kozlov's latest peace proposal, further limiting Russia's options to end this war on his terms. This new American president was hellbent on finishing the work his predecessor had started.

The nagging thoughts came back. *"We were so certain that the elimination of President Gates would lead to a cooler-headed president,"* he groaned to himself. He had been absolutely convinced that Foss would see reason and end the war to stem the threat of a major nuclear conflict. *"Well, if the Americans believe I will simply surrender power and my country, they have another thing coming,"* he thought as he clenched his fist. Russia still possessed over five thousand nuclear weapons, and he was not afraid to use them given the right conditions.

After looking at the report from yesterday's naval battle in the Barents Sea, Petrov had begun to think very hard about authorizing the release of a tactical nuclear strike against the Allied naval task force before it reached his shores. The sinking of three Allied aircraft carriers was nothing short of spectacular, but more than half of the new hypersonic missiles were jammed and unable to hit their targets. He was still irate that the engineers had been wrong in their assessment that the new Zircon missiles would not be susceptible to jamming.

"Had all of those missiles hit their targets, the Allied fleet would have been defeated," he mourned.

His senior leadership had conflicting opinions about what to do next. Admiral Anatoly Petrukhin, the Head of the Navy, had requested permission to hit the Allied fleet with several nuclear weapons before they offloaded their troops, but General Egorkin had objected strongly to this idea, even offering his resignation if he authorized the strike. Egorkin's logic had been very simple—if the Russians used these weapons against the Allied fleet, the Allies would use them against his ground forces. With no Russian Navy left to speak of, it would be his forces that would bear the retaliation.

"Egorkin does have a point," Petrov thought as he continued his inner conflict about what to do next. The Russian Army still held on to Ukraine, Estonia and Latvia. If several of their formations were nuked, it could cause the entire front line to collapse.

Knock, knock, knock.

Petrov turned away from the window and the falling snow and saw his aide standing near the doorway, letting him know that it was time to head over to the morning meeting. He grunted slightly as he got up from his chair, beginning to feel every bit his sixty-two years of age.

He followed his aide down the hallway until they entered the briefing room. Everyone in attendance snapped to attention. He signaled for them to take their seats as he made his way to the center of the table.

He nodded first toward his admiral; he thought he'd let him lead off with the morning brief. Petrukhin obliged. "Mr. President, last night, the Allied fleet in the Barents Sea hit our naval facility in and around Murmansk with 160 Tomahawk cruise missiles. Our missile defense system was able to shoot down 54 of the missiles. Unfortunately, most of the naval facility has been rendered useless and destroyed. We had thought the Allies would leave them intact, hoping to secure them with a ground invasion—we had expected to battle them on land and had planned accordingly. Once they destroyed the facility, we noticed the fleet was not slowing down to take up positions offshore. Rather, the fleet continued at top speed, and it now appears the Allied fleet is actually heading into the White Sea. This is a guess, but we believe the fleet is going to land their ground forces at Severodvinsk and will then move on Arkhangelsk."

This turn of events perplexed everyone in the room. It made no sense for the Allies to try and land forces that far north, at the start of the very long northern Russian winter. The White Sea, if not patrolled heavily by icebreakers, was frozen over for most of the winter.

Scratching his beard, General Egorkin asked, "How many troops are estimated to be in the Allied landing force?"

The admiral flipped through a couple of papers to find the number. "Eh the British committed two divisions, the Canadians one division, the French one division, the

Brazilians one division, and the Americans two divisions. So, roughly 70,000 troops."

"So, we'll have seventy thousand soldiers in northern Russia?" Egorkin verified.

Admiral Petrukhin nodded.

Egorkin held up a hand up to forestall any disagreement or outburst by anyone else. "This is a good thing," he asserted. "These soldiers are roughly 1,100 kilometers from St. Petersburg, and 1,200 kilometers from Moscow. They're also going to be socked in for at least four months during the winter, which is just now starting in northern Russia. The Allies will have to keep these forces fed and supplied during that four-month period, which will be incredibly hard to do considering much of the White Sea freezes over during the winter. No, gentlemen, this landing is not a disaster, it's a blessing in disguise. It will drain critical resources from the Allies' army in Europe, which will only help our cause. Those 70,000 soldiers that will capture Arkhangelsk will be 70,000 soldiers we won't have to face in Europe." A genuine smile spread across his face and he leaned back in his chair, putting his arms behind his head briefly.

Petrov grunted. "I don't think I'd thought of it that way, General. You bring up a very valid point. What forces do we have there to defend the city right now?" he inquired.

"Not much, Mr. President. We never thought the Americans would invade that far north, so we don't have a lot of units in that area. We have roughly one brigade of soldiers in that district," answered Egorkin. "They are ready to defend the beaches if you'd like them to."

The president shook his head. "No, General. Don't have them die meeting the enemy at the shore. Have them plan on fighting an insurgency throughout the winter. Let's make them bleed, General," Petrov said with fire in his eyes.

Changing subjects, he asked, "What's going on in Ukraine? Last night you informed me that the Allies had launched some sort of new operation into Belarus."

Egorkin sighed. Instead of taking the question himself, he nodded toward Lieutenant General Mikhail Chayko, the ground force commander in Europe, to answer.

Clearing his throat before responding, General Chayko started, "Mr. President, the Allies made use of the newly arrived British forces and secured several key road junctions in Belarus and Ukraine. This was quickly followed by an all-out assault by the American Fifth Corps, which was recently augmented with an American armored division and a British armored brigade. They successfully punched a hole through my lines at Brest, Belarus, and are presently driving toward Lutsk and Rivne, Ukraine. It's a 280-kilometer drive to their objective. Surprisingly, during the last twelve hours, they've managed to travel a little more than half of that distance. At their current pace, they will reach Rivne by tonight."

The generals and admirals looked at the map and the projected path of the Americans. It quickly became apparent that this would place a substantial number of troops more than three hundred kilometers behind their front lines. It would effectively cut off the supply lines to their army group along the Polish-Ukraine border and threaten to isolate more than 380,000 Russian and Indian troops.

Petrov leaned forward, his eyes locked on to General Chayko's. "What are your plans for dealing with this force in your rear area, General?"

Chayko suddenly looked sweaty. He used a finger to stretch his collar at the neck. "With your permission, Mr. President, I plan on wiping them out, and then continuing to hold the current battle lines through the winter," he said.

Taking the bait, Petrov asked, "You said with my permission—what are you asking permission to use to wipe the Americans out? And don't tell me it's a nuclear weapon.

We've already determined that any nuclear attack would result in a nuclear attack on our own forces."

Leaning forward as he replied, Chayko said, "I'd like permission to deploy our Novichok-5 nerve gas and saturate the American positions in Rivne once they arrive. The attack will devastate their ability to operate as an effective fighting force. My reserve divisions stationed in Zhytomyr will then move in and finish the enemy off."

Minister Kozlov interjected, "Mr. President, I must adamantly disagree with General Chayko. If we use this weapon in the quantities that will be needed to kill this military unit, we will also kill 500,000 civilians—maybe even more. I know the war isn't turning out how we had hoped, but we can't stoop to this level. We cannot use this weapon!"

Petrov was taken aback. Kozlov was speaking with more conviction than he had ever shown in any previous meeting.

Chayko jumped back into the conversation, countering, "If we don't use this weapon now, the Allies will force me to give up our current positions or be cut off from our supply lines and encircled. This needs to be a military decision, Mr. President, not a diplomatic one. If we don't do this, then we're going to have to give up our current positions and withdraw. It'll mean giving up more than 400 kilometers of captured land—land my soldiers have fought and bled over for the past year to give Minister Kozlov the time and bargaining position he said he needed to get a negotiated peace settlement."

The meeting then shifted from a civil discussion of what to do next to an outright shouting match, with insults and threats of violence between the differing parties being screamed at full volume. Petrov sat back for a moment, not saying anything and just listening to the chaos unfold.

Essentially any suggestion of using a WMD, whether nuclear or chemical, seemed to cause this heated divide among his generals. He bristled thinking about what Vasilek would have said to him if he were there, that they could cause a "fissure" within the military that he might not recover from.

"*Well, that traitor's brains are still splattered against the wall outside my building*," Petrov thought, dismissing the idea that Vasilek's opinion should have any meaning to him.

This arguing had gone on long enough. He held up his hand up to settle everyone down. "As much as I want to use these weapons to defeat the Allies, I fear their use would necessitate an overwhelming response by the Americans," he announced.

Half the room suddenly seemed very happy while the other half glared at him. Petrov took a deep breath in and slowly let it out through his nose. "General Chayko, I don't believe we should give up our hard-fought ground willingly. That said, looking at the map, I don't see any other course of action. However, that doesn't mean we have to give the enemy anything useful as we withdraw."

General Chayko's left eyebrow rose skeptically, but he said nothing.

"Here's what I want to happen," President Petrov began. "I want our forces to begin a staged withdrawal back to Kiev. As our forces retreat, I want any captured electrical substations, powerplants and major power distribution nodes destroyed. I want any critical roads, railways, and bridges demolished as our forces fall back. I want us to do to the Allies what we did to the Nazis during World War II and initiate a scorched-earth policy. We can create a humanitarian crisis far worse than using chemical weapons. With the coming winter, the Allies will suddenly find themselves responsible for taking care of the Ukrainian people, who will struggle during the winter weather with no electricity, natural gas, rail or road infrastructure across their country. If the Allies won't come to some sort of end to this war, then we will reduce the rest of Ukraine to nothing as we withdraw back to our own borders." An evil look filled his eyes.

"If they won't end the war on our terms, then we will have no mercy. They will wish they had ended it when they had the chance," he thought.

Chapter 11

Operational Security

Pushkino, Russia

The kettle on the stove whistled as the water started to boil, letting Alexei Kasyanov know it was ready. He quickly got up and turned the burner off. He pulled a mug out of the cabinet, stuffed his metal tea ball with leaves and plopped it into the water. With his tea brewing, returned to his previous task, logging into the internet through a complicated series of proxy servers that masked his activity and changed his IP address.

Looking at the latest news reports, he was heartened to see the Allies had successfully landed a substantial military force in the White Sea, capturing the city of Arkhangelsk. *"The invasion of this historic Russian city would play well on his evening broadcast,"* he thought as he wrote a few notes down on his pad of paper. Another article from the BBC talked about the Russian withdrawal from most of eastern Ukraine. It showed a number of maps of the Russian retreat and the new battle lines near Kiev. It also talked extensively about how the Russian and Indian armies were systematically destroying the infrastructure of Ukraine as they retreated back to the Russian borders.

A soft knock broke Alexei from his train of thought. He looked up and saw Gunther Brinkbaumer, his BND handler, and Mitch Lowe, his CIA handler, both standing near the rear door of the small house. He walked over and quickly unlocked it, letting them both in. As he walked inside, Mitch dusted the snow off his shoulders and unwrapped his scarf, hanging it on the hook near the door.

Smiling, Alexei said, "This must be important if you both are here to see me."

Mitch nodded, and without saying anything, he guided them down the stairs to the basement quiet room, which was impervious to electronic eavesdropping. While they were talking, the two sentries on the first floor would continue to look cautiously outside, making sure there was nothing suspicious, while a third man would watch a set of cameras that monitored the surrounding neighborhood. Security for Alexei was of paramount concern to Mitch, and something neither he nor the CIA chinsed on. They had even rented a house two doors down with a direct-action team inside, ready to pounce in case an unwanted visit appeared to be imminent. Not to mention they had several alternate locations they could move Alexei to should the need arise.

As the three of them sat down on the chairs in the "quiet room," Mitch started by asking, "How did the meeting go yesterday with your new source?"

Alexei smiled. Mitch and Gunther knew this guy could be the linchpin to making a coup work, and they were more than eager for information about him. "I know I haven't told you a lot about this new source, and I suppose it's time I come clean and tell you exactly who he is. The man I've been in contact with is Oleg Zolotov, the head of the FSO and Petrov's security detail." He watched amusedly as Mitch and Gunther's mouths dropped to the floor.

Gunther was the first to respond. "How did you two make contact? Does he know where you're staying? Is this location still safe?" he asked, speaking quickly and nervously.

"I can't believe you actually met this guy face-to-face last night," Mitch said, speaking in a tone that was a mix of horrified and angry. "Had I known who you were meeting with, I never would have agreed to let you go without backup."

Alexei waved his hands as if to dismiss their concerns. "When I met with him, he told me the key to seizing power was getting Grigory Sobolev on board," he answered. "Oleg said if we can convince Sobolev that a coup can work, then the two of them could make it happen and bring an end to the war."

There was a moment of tense silence. Mitch leaned forward in his chair. "Is this a deal you would accept, and your supporters?" he asked. "If not, then there's no point in moving forward. The coup needs to hold the country together, not splinter it into regional warlords."

Alexei had wanted to become President, but he also wanted to see his country succeed and become a thriving democracy. If he had to back a dictator for a couple of years and accept an occupying force, he'd do it. "It's not the grand plan I had envisioned," he admitted, "but it's probably the only plan that realistically would work. I back it, and I'll do my best to make sure my supporters do as well."

Mitch looked at Gunther who shrugged, then turned his attention back to Alexei. "OK, I'll brief this back to Washington and work to get approval from the President. Until I get confirmation from Foss, don't communicate further with Oleg. We want to make sure we have our i's dotted and our t's crossed before you talk with him again. We don't know what kind of surveillance he's under, and we don't want to risk them finding you."

With the official business taken care of, Mitch and Gunther left to head back to their own safe house and transmit what they had discussed back to Washington and Berlin. It would now be up to the President and his team to determine if this was an acceptable end to the war or if they would press for a full dismantling of Russia.

Chapter 12
World on Fire

Washington, D.C.
White House

The midterm elections were finally over, and by all accounts, President Foss should have been elated. Traditionally, the ruling party tends to lose seats in the election. However, when it became known who was responsible for the assassination of Gates and the political motivations behind the attack, the election had turned decisively in Foss's party's favor, giving them a supermajority in both the House and the Senate, at least for the next two years.

Still, Foss was immensely saddened by the turn of events. He had personally never envisioned himself becoming President. He'd wanted to be the guy behind the scenes helping to get things done, not the primary political target of the opposition party and the relentless personal attacks by the pundits and other talking heads in Washington and around the country.

"I have no idea how Gates was able to weather this kind of public beratement, let alone this catastrophic war that is consuming the world," he thought.

He looked down at the report in front of him to distract himself but ended up scratching his head in confusion. He still couldn't understand what could possibly make the Indian government willingly choose to join the Eastern Alliance. It made no economic, military, or political sense.

He read through the bullet points and the highlighted portions of the brief. The overarching tone of the report suggested that the alignment of India with the Eastern Alliance had more to do with the perception that the US and Europe were in a considerably weakened state, and that if Russia and China pushed hard enough, the West would collapse, leaving them as the new world powers. By joining the Eastern Alliance, India must have believed that they were throwing their lot in with the winning side and stood to gain from an American defeat.

Before he could finish reading through the details, his Chief of Staff, Josh Morgan, walked into his study. "Are you ready for our guest?" he asked.

The President nodded, knowing he'd probably get more answers from the people he was about to meet than from reading a report put together by the CIA. Josh had pulled some strings to make this consultation happen so quickly.

In walked Aneesh Dayal, the US Ambassador to India, Vivek Chopra, a prominent businessman from New York who was deeply involved in the Indian-American community, and Neal Biswal, a cofounder of a major Silicon Valley IT company.

President Foss stood and walked toward his guests. He shook their hands and gestured for them to take a seat on the couches and chairs in the center of the room. He had wanted to meet with them in his private study as opposed to the Oval Office because he wanted the setting to be informal and more inviting. He needed honest answers if they were going to figure out how they were going to handle India.

"Thank you all for meeting with me on such short notice," he said.

A steward finished pouring everyone the drink they'd requested, and a sandwich tray was also brought in and placed on the table in front of them. It was lunchtime, and Foss figured breaking bread with people, even those who adamantly disagreed with his politics, was a way to open things up.

"When the President requests a meeting to speak with you, you meet with him," Vivek replied with a smile as he helped himself to a half an egg sandwich.

The President returned the smile briefly. "I'm struggling with some aspects of this war," he began. "Mainly, how did America find itself at war with India? We've traditionally had good relations with India. I'm still trying to figure out exactly what happened that changed that dynamic."

"I'm not a good person to ask that question, Mr. President," answered Neal Biswal. "Most of my friends and employees were killed when the nuclear missile hit the Bay Area. The only reason my family and I are alive is because we were vacationing at Disney World in Florida when the attack happened. I believe this war started because your predecessor was a bloviating idiot who didn't know what he was doing. I think India is at war with America because they see America as a global threat to world peace, and after our defeats in Europe and Asia, they saw an opportunity to pile on and take us out." Neal Biswal spoke with anger and heat. His beliefs, and those of his company, were well known to the President, but Foss had still wanted his perspective.

"You don't believe North Korea or China bear any blame for launching the nuclear weapon that destroyed

Oakland?" the President bristled. Although he'd known what to expect from Neal, he was still shocked that the man before him blamed Gates for the destruction of Oakland when he had done everything in his power to save it.

Holding a hand up in surrender, Neal clarified his response. "You're right. Gates didn't launch the missiles at America, and I know the military did its best to try and shoot them down. I guess I'm just mad that of all the missiles to get through our missile defense shield, the Bay Area ended up taking it on the chin."

"We're all irate about that, Neal," said Ambassador Dayal. "It could've been a lot worse if the interceptors hadn't hit the other missiles though. We could have lost New York, Chicago, Washington D.C., and a few other cities."

The President allowed Neal to vent for a few minutes, nodding as he listened. When he had said his piece and gotten some of his anger out of his system, the President moved in to prod for more information.

"Neal, you're a businessman, and you seem to have a good grasp on the politics of what's happening. When the Indian government first joined the war against us, the situation looked bleak for America. However, a year has passed, and the tides of the war have changed. Their military suffered a catastrophic defeat in the Russian Far East, and they've sustained heavy losses in Europe. Do they still believe they can defeat America? That they're still on the right side of history in this war?"

Neal leaned back in the chair for a second to think. "I don't have a lot of contact with people back in India, for obvious reasons, but I believe the initial optimism about a quick victory has evaporated. I think the reality of what it would take to fight and defeat the United States has started to set in. The initial war hawks in the Indian government and military are now facing the reality that their allies, Russia and China, are not in nearly as strong of a military position as they first believed they were."

"I agree," confirmed Vivek. "I think the initial optimism the government had about dethroning the US evaporated when their forces were soundly defeated in Siberia. I have some family living in Mumbai, and they tell me the average person on the street believes the war is a huge mistake. When the casualties from the battle were made known, a lot of people took to the streets to protest the war. They had been led to believe the war would be won quickly, and America was all but defeated—that it would be India, Russia, and China who would dominate the world. That belief has been shattered. I suspect when the casualty reports are released from the European battles that are taking place right now, any support within the government for the war will further evaporate."

Foss took the information in while he formulated his next question. "OK, so if what you all are saying is true, and I have no reason to believe it's not, how should we try to convince them to end their involvement in the war? I'd rather not have to launch cruise missiles at them, or potentially land troops near their borders. So how do we persuade them that staying in the war any further is not going to end well for them?"

There was a brief pause before Ambassador Dayal responded. "I propose we make them an offer. Give them an opportunity to end their involvement in the war peacefully, now. If they choose not to, then we start to use the Navy to launch cruise missiles at key aspects of their economy that are specifically supporting their war effort. Right now, the casualties they're suffering are far away from their borders. If they start to lose people at home, that might be the needed catalyst to force real change."

The President thought about that for a minute. He agreed with the ambassador's assessment. It was time to make the Indian government an offer to end the war or face a further escalation.

****

Following the lunch and continued conversations with his guests, President Foss went to the next meeting, eager to hear what his spy agency had to report. When he entered the PEOC, he saw CIA Director Jedediah "JP" Perth, Tom McMillan, his National Security Advisor, Admiral Peter Meyers, the Chairman of the Joint Chiefs, and Secretary of Defense Jim Castle all eagerly waiting for him. This meeting was intentionally being kept small. Once the President had taken his seat, Josh, his Chief of Staff and senior advisor, took a seat next to him and the meeting began.

"Sir, I've called this meeting to brief you on the latest developments with Operation Strawman," JP said, urgency in his voice. "I received a crucial message from our source in Moscow. There's been a major development, and we need to discuss it with you now."

The others squirmed a bit in their chairs, unsure of what awaited them.

"For the sake of the war, I hope you are reporting good news to us because my analysts are becoming increasingly concerned that Petrov may start to use his WMD in the very near future," said SecDef Castle. He narrowed his eyes at JP.

President Foss surveyed the faces in the room. They seemed as genuinely concerned with Castle's statement as he felt. The Russians had kept the war conventional up this point, but with the continued losses forming an ever-tightening noose around Petrov's neck, that could change.

Foss signaled for JP to continue. "Alexei Kasyanov, the political leader of the Russian resistance we've been cultivating to take Petrov's place, has been holding secret meetings with certain regime members as he's sought to build out his coalition of support against Petrov. We know the FSB Director, Ivan Vasilek, was executed by Petrov a short while ago for the failure of the British deception and for the progress of the war. His replacement, Lieutenant General Grigory Sobolev, has been a bit of an unknown to us. However, one of the men Alexei has apparently recruited to his side is a man by the name of Major General Oleg Zolotov. He's head of the Russian FSO, which is essentially the Russian version of the Secret Service."

This last part got President Foss's ears to perk up a bit as he realized this was one guy who truly had access to Petrov on a regular basis and was one of the few people allowed to be armed around him.

"He secretly met with General Zolotov the other day, and the general intimated that an effort to replace Petrov was not only possible but should be carried out sooner rather than later. He also told Alexei that General Sobolev was willing to support a coup against Petrov and sue for a separate peace from China and India with the Allies if he could personally secure and retain power," JP explained.

The group was silent for a moment. Tom McMillan commented, "On the surface, this sounds great. However, I fear we'd be changing out one dictator for another one. How is Sobolev going to be any better than Petrov? Right now, we're probably months away from defeating Russia. I'm not sold on this just yet."

Jim Castle interjected, "I say we go for it, and here's why. We're about to capture St. Petersburg, and the British are leading an effort in northern Russia that is driving on Moscow even as we speak. General Cotton is about to launch a several-hundred-kilometer-long offensive to drive the remaining Russian and Indian forces out of Ukraine and move on Moscow. As the war gets closer to Moscow, Petrov is going to become more desperate—so will his generals. His military leaders will advocate for the use of tactical nuclear weapons against our forces, or at least chemical or biological weapons. It's the only way he can stop our offensive. If backing Sobolev to take Petrov's place ends the war and removes the credible threat of the Russians using nuclear weapons, then I believe we should take it."

The room stayed silent for a moment. President Foss contemplated what Castle had just said. He had known the possibility of Russia using their nukes was out there, but no one had really given it a lot of credence before now, especially after how aggressive President Gates had been in his response to the destruction of Oakland. He looked up at the ceiling, saying a prayer that he would make the right decision at this juncture. Then he told the men in the room his counterproposal to Sobolev.

****

Later that evening, well past dinner, President Foss finished reading a long proposal from his cyberwarfare advisor, Katelyn Mackie, on what actions she advocated for in India. President Gates had still been formulating what he wanted to do with India when he'd been killed, so Foss hadn't had a lot of precedent to go on. Up until now, he'd been hesitant about going after India too hard as he'd hoped a peaceful solution could be found. However, after his afternoon lunch with several prominent Indian Americans, he realized he hadn't given India nearly as much attention or effort as he probably should have.

Katelyn had come up with a unique proposal that would limit the loss of life and hopefully get the message across to the Indian government that continuing the war would result in further debilitating attacks. Her plan centered around the rail industry; according to her research, a total of 8.26 billion passengers used the rail system in India annually, which meant the country was heavily dependent on this sector. President Foss shuddered in horror as he looked at photos of how horrifically overcrowded the commuter trains in India were. As he continued to read, Foss learned how vital India's rail system was in moving the war munitions that India produced, as well as the workers who commuted to produce the ordnance.

Of the 121,407 kilometers of rail tracks in the country, 49% were electrified, and through collaboration with a team of locomotive engineers in France, Katelyn's team had identified a vulnerability within the 2x25kV autotransformer system used in the Indian railways. By inserting a malicious code into a component of this system during one of the automated patch updates Indian Railways performed on a weekly basis, they had already successfully infected the electrified portion of the rail line with their code. All Katelyn needed was permission to initiate the attack, and India would lose access to half of their rail lines. The proposed cyberattack wouldn't destroy India's rail infrastructure or cause significant loss of life, but it would shut down the sector until the damaged components could be replaced, which could take them months, maybe even a year or more.

Foss had to smile at the ingenuity of the plan. Part of him wished that he knew more about cyberwarfare so that he could have come up with the idea on his own. Then a sobering thought hit him. *"If we can do this to India, I have to imagine China, Russia, or India could do this to us too,"* he realized. He made a note to discuss vulnerabilities in the homeland with Katelyn Mackie later.

He put his pen behind his ear for a moment as he thought over the implications of the proposal, and then he scribbled his signature on the authorization form to allow Katelyn's team to initiate the cyberattack. He placed the completed document and the brief in his "Out" bin.

President Foss had a chuckle at himself. Here he was initiating a complex cyberattack while utilizing what was arguably a very archaic filing system for his paperwork. *"They have their methods and I have mine,"* he thought.

With the final tasks for the day complete, it was time for Foss to collapse and get a few hours of shut-eye before he had to get up and do it all over again the next day.

Chapter 13
Battle of Huatung Valley

Dulan Forest, Taiwan

"I hate chili-mac," Sergeant Price said to no one in particular as he finished scooping the last spoonful of the stuff out of the MRE and shoved it in his mouth.

"Oh, come on, Sergeant. It isn't that bad. It comes with the jalapeno cheese pack," chided one of his soldiers good-naturedly.

Price sat against the trunk of a large tree. Around them, the birds in the forest sang their melodies and did their best to ignore the human intruders to their environment. In the distance, helicopters and the occasional fighter plane flew overhead.

Price spotted Lieutenant Martinez walking over toward him and the rest of his platoon. "Five minutes, guys! We're pulling out in five mikes, so get your gear ready!" he shouted.

"We finally got orders off this rock?" asked Sergeant Price.

The LT nodded and pulled out a map. "Yeah. The brass wants us to make our way down this ridge so we can patrol and clear this sector here," he explained, pointing to the location. "Word has it the enemy has a base camp somewhere on the opposite side of this river." Martinez waved for the other squad leaders to come over so he could show them as well.

Once their company had secured the air base on D-Day, their unit had completed the long trudge up to the top of the Dulan Forest. They'd been prepared to fight their way to the top, but once they'd pushed past the first set of defenses, the enemy had just evaporated. Granted, the Australians had had it hard taking the beach and securing the city, but once that initial fight had been won, the enemy had withdrawn into the countryside.

They'd spent nearly three weeks patrolling and clearing the ridge and low-lying mountaintops for enemy bunkers and hidden positions, but now they were coming up empty and it was finally time to move further inland. The terrain they had been battling on was brutal, similar to some of the mountains of Afghanistan. It had definitely been a challenge to traverse this area with eighty-pound packs and body armor. Sergeant Price would certainly not be alone in his excitement to get off the ridge.

The soldiers gladly finished stuffing any last items into their packs and prepared to move out. Sergeant Price noticed that one of his soldiers seemed a little less excited than everyone else to be moving on.

"Sergeant, you know the nice thing about being stuck on this mountain, patrolling through the woods like this?" he asked.

Price pulled his ruck straps tight. "No, but I'm sure you're going to tell me," he answered with a chuckle.

"We haven't lost anyone since the first day," the trooper replied with a somber look. Then he made his way down to one of the trails where the rest of the squad was forming up.

"*Man, he's right*," Price thought. "*Poor guy's still hurting over Tyler.*"

Like a lot of soldiers in their unit, Private Tyler had been killed during the combat jump on the first day of the invasion. He was a well-liked guy from Colorado, the sort of guy everyone wanted to hang out with on a Friday night. His loss had hit several of the guys really hard. Of course, it didn't help anything that they'd only had five privates join them during the three weeks they were in the field—they were still short six soldiers in their platoon and eighteen for their company.

They all slowly made their way down the mountain, until they came across a small family farm. At first, the sight of nearly a hundred heavily armed soldiers coming in their direction scared the family, who had been tending to their property. However, once the locals learned the soldiers were Americans, they were more than happy to greet them and talk with them.

The soldiers fanned out and secured the area, and then Sergeant Price brought their interpreter over so they could have a legitimate conversation with the man who owned the farm. Since they didn't have a Chinese linguist in their unit, their battalion had hired a few dozen local nationals to act as their guides and interpreters, at least until vetted contracted linguists could be brought in. The local national that was working with Sergeant Price's company had been a college student studying to be a doctor, so his English was superb. It sure didn't hurt anything that he was very physically fit, considering all the rough terrain they'd been traversing. He'd told the Americans to call him Mr. Lee, since none of them could pronounce his Chinese name without butchering it.

Mr. Lee warmly introduced himself, the major and the lieutenant to the farmer, who then began speaking very rapidly, waving his arms wildly and pointing toward the large river a couple of kilometers below their current position.

Major Adam Fowler, the company CO, told Mr. Lee, "Hey, get this guy to calm down so we can ask him some questions."

Mr. Lee nodded. "The man and his family really just wanted to thank you and your men for liberating them from the communists. He said they would prepare food for your men if you would like."

The officers nodded, not wanting to insult them. The woman set off for the house along with two of their children. Lieutenant Martinez and one of the other soldiers went with her, to make sure the house was clear of enemy soldiers, and to make sure the woman knew they would be paying them for the food. They wouldn't take from a family in need, and the company could easily write up a voucher receipt that follow-on units would honor.

Major Fowler changed the topic. "Mr. Lee, ask him where the communist soldiers went," he instructed.

The two men went back and forth for a few minutes before Mr. Lee turned to face Fowler again. "The man says the communists left the area shortly after we arrived," he explained. "The enemy soldiers moved to a fort they built nearby. It's over in that area there." He pointed toward what appeared to be a large hilltop across the river, at least seven or eight kilometers away from their current position.

Major Fowler nodded. "Ask the man if the roads and trails are clear of enemy soldiers until we reach the edge of this side of the river."

More banter went on between the two Taiwanese men before Mr. Lee once again turned back toward Fowler. "Yes," he answered. "The road and trails around here are clear of enemy soldiers. He said we don't need to take the hard way down the mountain. The communists left the area several weeks ago, and they've been using the roads and trails without incident."

The company stayed at the farm for an hour while they refilled their camelbacks and contacted battalion. They wanted to pass along the intelligence they'd found and see if any of the other units had heard the same thing about this enemy fort. Shortly before they left, the farmer's wife brought out some sort of chicken and rice dish for the soldiers, which they greedily ate every morsel of. With full bellies, it was time to get back on the road.

Continuing their descent to the bottom of the mountain, they encountered half a dozen other small farm plots. In each location, the people were eager to greet them and share what information they knew about the enemy with the men they viewed as liberators.

As they neared the base of the mountain, they came across a small village that sat just above the river they would eventually need to cross. Once they entered the village, several locals came out to greet them and talk with them. One of the locals who introduced himself caught the major's attention because he identified himself as the only police officer left in the local area.

"The other police officers were killed or taken away by the communists, never to be heard from again," Mr. Lee translated.

Mr. Lee and Major Fowler started talking with the man to try and gather as much intelligence as possible on this enemy fort they kept hearing about.

"He has confirmed that he knows the fort exists, but he doesn't have the exact details of how big it is or know how many soldiers are there," translated Mr. Lee. "All he knows is that most of the local villagers were rounded up many months ago to work on building it."

Given this new bit of information, Mr. Lee looked for volunteers to provide some more information. One of the villagers seemed particularly happy to divulge any information that might compromise their occupiers. "The bunker is built with reinforced cement—it's going to be hard to destroy," explained Mr. Lee. "He says its located at Luyeh

Highland, which has a commanding view of the river and surrounding area. If we are going to move further inland, he says we have to destroy it." The villager and the policeman confirmed on a map the location of the fort.

Sergeant Price had been listening to all the back-and-forth exchanges between the interpreter and the major. He hoped they would just make camp at this village for the night and try to probe the enemy fort in the morning. It had already been a long day, and it seemed like finding this fortified position could wait another day.

****

The following morning, their company made their way along the edge of the river, until they came to the Luanshan Communication Road, which spanned 300 meters in length across the river leading to Luye Township, south of Luye City. The bridge was situated at the mouth of the Huatung Valley, a critical piece of real estate they needed to capture.

Knowing there was a fortified enemy position nearby, Major Fowler had requested some armor support before they tried to cross the location on foot. Before long, a company from the 73rd Cavalry Regiment arrived with a dozen of their JLTV vehicles. A feeling of excitement permeated the group when they heard the sound of those joint land tactical vehicles approaching.

Several of the JLTVs had the long-range acquisition systems or LRASs on them, which allowed them to search for targets up to ten kilometers away and lase them for artillery or airstrikes. Using the LRASs, the vehicles quickly searched the high ground behind the township for potential enemy positions.

One of the privates operating an LRAS signaled for Sergeant Price to walk over. When Price arrived, the private told him, "Sergeant, check this out. There are several areas with a heavy concentration of radio antennas."

Price shared the news with his CO. "We must've found them," confirmed Major Fowler.

They set about making plans and preparations for how to proceed, and Fowler called in for additional support. Around midday, two squadrons from the Australian 14th Light Horse Regiment arrived with a squadron of Aslan armored vehicles, which were armed with 25mm chain guns. Sergeant Price smiled when he saw the squadron of M1A1 Abrams battle tanks they'd brought with them.

After everyone had been brought up to speed, Major Fowler sent a squad of Rangers to clear the bridge, making sure there were no explosives rigged to the structure.

Everyone collectively held their breath while the search took place, but eventually, the Rangers returned unscathed and gave the all clear.

The Ranger Commander spoke with the Aussies. "Can we get you to send two of your Aslans across the bridge? You all have heavier armored vehicles than us, and they could take the hits better than the ones we have here."

The Australian major in charge obliged, and soon two Aslans were rolling across the structure. Their journey was uneventful. Once they'd crossed over, they moved to either side of the road, roughly 100 meters ahead of the bridge exit to provide cover for the tanks. One by one, the Abrams tanks were sent over and took up positions on the opposite side of the river.

Something about this just didn't feel right to Sergeant Price. *"Why haven't they taken a shot at us yet?"* he wondered. *"They have to see us."*

The armored vehicles continued to cross the bridge one by one, and still no one had had any contact with the enemy. The rest of the Aslan vehicles and the 73rd Cavalry Regiment joined them. Not to be outdone by the armor and reconnaissance units, the rest of the Rangers also crossed the bridge.

Despite the continued calm, the hairs on the back of Sergeant Price's neck stood up. Then all hell broke loose.

Zip, zap, whoosh, BOOM, BAM!

Heavy machine-gun fire raked the infantry positions, and a fusillade of RPGs and antitank missiles sprang forward from Luye Junior High School directly in front of them and a Buddhist temple to their right. The tanks' antimissile defensive systems prevented the first barrage of missiles from hitting most of them. However, two of the Aslans exploded in spectacular fashion, throwing fire and shrapnel in every direction. The twelve tanks in the squadron fired several rounds into the buildings where the enemy fire was emanating from, silencing the attack as quickly as it had begun.

While the area was temporarily covered in smoke from the explosions and cannon fire, the Australian and American troops did their best to use that as cover to push further into the small township toward the enemy positions. As they rushed forward, Sergeant Price heard the dull thumping sound of mortars being launched. Then a higher pitched scream really caught his attention.

"*Crap, those are katyusha rockets*," he realized.

Boom, boom, boom, crump, crump.

The 82mm mortar rounds and 122mm rockets peppered the bridge area and the edge of the township. The Australian infantrymen and Rangers did their best to get into the town and seek shelter. Rockets and mortars began exploding all around them. High-velocity shrapnel whizzed past them, hitting nearby trees, buildings, and anything else in its path. Sergeant Price felt his heart pounding out of his chest as he raced to get out of the impact zone.

As Price looked up toward the elementary school to his right, he spotted movement in the tree line. "Contact front!" he shouted. "Two hundred meters to my three o'clock!"

"I see it! Enemy machine gun!" yelled one of the other soldiers, who leveled his M240G at the new threat and lit up the position. Seconds after firing into the tree line, a barrage of bullets flew right back at them from several enemy gun positions they hadn't spotted yet.

Pop, pop, pop, zing, zing, crack.

Several tree branches from the trees above Sergeant Price's position disintegrated, dropping leaves and chunks of wood on him. "Suppressive fire!" he yelled to his squad. They changed positions rapidly, instinctively following their training. A couple of guys threw some grenades at the enemy, and the others used their M4s and opened fire on the enemy positions.

One of Price's soldiers leveled his grenade gun at the tree line, where the heaviest concentration of enemy fire was coming from, firing the 40mm grenade and quickly ducking before a slew of bullets flew over his head.

Sergeant Price turned to look behind him and saw a cluster of Australian soldiers pointing in their direction. Then an Aslan started heading their way. A couple of the friendly soldiers motioned for them to take cover.

"Everyone down!" Price shouted, straining to be heard over the roar of gunfire.

Seconds later, the 25mm cannon on the Aslan tore into the tree line in front of them. When the vehicle had stopped shooting, Price stuck his head up and saw the area had been ripped apart. The Aslan had shredded the enemy positions; most of the trees had been cut down to stubs.

Sergeant Price recognized that there was an opportunity to seize while the enemy might still be disoriented. "Charge!" he screamed to his squad.

The Rangers jumped up and ran forward with their weapons at the ready. The Australian soldiers and the lone Aslan advanced quickly behind them, ready to provide support should they need it. When they reached the enemy positions, they found the dead and dying littered about in a chaotic mash. Most of the Chinese soldiers had been ripped apart by the high-velocity cannon shells. Some were missing limbs, desperately calling out for help. Price's lone medic began to help the enemy wounded where he could; then a couple of Australian medics came forward and also rendered aid.

"Staff Sergeant Price!" shouted his platoon leader.

"Yes, Sir?" Price asked as he turned to face Lieutenant Martinez.

"We're going to hold up here for the moment," ordered Martinez. "One of the reconnaissance units found the enemy fort that the police officer and farmers told us about. It's roughly two kilometers in front of us. One of the tanks was just hit by an antitank gun built into it." The LT waved in the direction of the stronghold.

"Please tell me someone is calling in an air strike on that location, LT," said Sergeant Price.

Martinez smiled and nodded. "Yeah. It's inbound now. Going to drop a 2,000-pound JDAM on them. The CO wants us to move over near the tanks and be ready to support them when they move on the enemy fort. It looks like you guys have this area cleared—why don't you leave it to the Aussies here to clean up? We need to get moving."

Price nodded and yelled out to his squad, "Follow me! Let's get moving."

A couple of Aussie platoons moved into the enemy positions they'd just cleared. They would hold this section of the town while the Rangers moved to the next location.

Once Sergeant Price's men reached the location where the tanks were currently sitting and waiting, they dropped their packs and broke out their boxes of extra ammo. His soldiers knew what to do without even being told. They would use their free time to reload their empty magazines and get ready for the next assault. While they waited for the Air Force or Navy to send a jet over to drop some bombs, some of the Rangers pulled out MREs and wasted no time chowing down on some food. The level of physical exertion they had expended in the last several hours had drained many of them, and food and water was one way to replenish some of that energy.

Thirty minutes after Price's squad had sat down to wait for the Air Force and the tanks to make their move, their company CO walked over to talk to them.

"Listen up, Rangers. There's been a change of plans," announced Major Fowler. "A brigade from the 63rd division is moving up here tonight. The Air Force is going to plaster the enemy fort tomorrow morning and the 63rd, along with the Aussies here, are going to clear it out, along with the rest of the valley. After nearly a month in the field, we're being pulled out and back to the airfield. I have no idea where we're going next, but let's enjoy the reprieve for the moment, because you can bet your paychecks they'll be sending us back into the thick of it soon enough."

Chapter 14

Battle of Fei-ts Ui Reservoir

Crack, crack, BOOM.

The sounds of war were ever present for the men of Echo Company, 2-6 Marines as they began the first day of Operation Spartan, a Marine-led operation to clear the Fei-ts Ui Reservoir, the last major enemy stronghold on the island.

This key location in the northern center of Taiwan provided the majority of the island's freshwater and was also one of the only routes left to the west coast of the island, so it was a critical piece of land. The reservoir and the entire surrounding area was heavily defended by the PLA's 121 Motorized Infantry Brigade, which was a specialized jungle unit, as well as their parent unit, the 123 Mechanized Infantry Division. These Chinese forces had spent the better part of six months preparing the area for this very battle, and their commanders definitely would have been aware that clearing the reservoir was one of the last major obstacles to the Allies in securing the island.

Captain Tim Long was feeling apprehensive about the upcoming hostilities. Unfortunately, just the day before, his new battalion commander, a freshly promoted lieutenant colonel by the name of Mohamed Abadi, had been killed along with his executive officer and two staff officers when their M-ATV command vehicle had driven over a tank mine on their way back from a division briefing about the operation. Despite the vehicle's armor, it had been completely obliterated, killing all of the men inside instantly. With only six hours left until the operation was slated to kick off, Colonel Tilman had placed Captain Long in the position of de facto battalion commander until another officer could be pulled from another unit to take his place.

Captain Long wasn't normally superstitious, but Lieutenant Colonel Abadi had been the second battalion commander that 2-6 had lost in the past three months, and he wasn't exactly thrilled to find himself in the same position. This sudden shift in responsibilities was also a lot for him to mentally prepare for in a short amount of time. He had a lot of intelligence and data to sift through.

Long pored over maps, memorizing the marks where there were potential enemy positions and fortifications. From what he was able to gather, there were a series of enemy forts built along Route 9 at multiple points and elevations. What he still didn't know was exactly how complex these fortifications were. He couldn't find any information on whether or not they had machine-gun positions, antitank or artillery cannons. He didn't know what type of infantry support they had or what type of antiair defenses they had in the area.

He sighed. *"I guess we'll find out soon enough once we head in,"* he thought, frustrated.

At 0530 hours, Captain Long found himself standing in front of the company commanders of Alpha, Bravo, Charley, Delta, Fox, and of course, his own company, Echo. He knew he should say something profound, even inspiring, but he was at a loss for what to say. The sudden unexpected death of their battalion CO had caught them all off guard. Steeling himself, he looked up at the group.

"We've had a rough couple weeks, and I'm not going to sugarcoat it and say this operation will be a walk in the park," Captain Long began. "This is probably going to be just as tough as the invasion, maybe tougher. We're finally moving inland, but we'll be attacking the enemy on ground of his choosing, not ours. That said, we can and will defeat them."

He stood a little taller before he continued. "Unlike the enemy, we haven't been abandoned by our country to fight and die on some island. They have. We are Marines—the greatest fighting force on earth, backed by the greatest country on earth. I've been assured by Colonel Tilman that we will have close air support from both the carriers offshore, and the Air Force, who's finally got themselves set up at the airfield in Toucheng, near the coast. He also said the 1-10 Marines have settled into Firebase Ripper, so we'll have both 105mm and 155mm artillery support for the duration of the operation. Their call sign is going to be Ripper One-One."

Long turned to another captain and signaled for him to step forward. "This is Captain Reich; he's our FSO. If your unit needs fire support, direct your request to him, and his team will relay that request back 1-10 for support."

Captain Long signaled toward a new face in the unit, a man wearing a different uniform from the rest of the group. "This is Master Sergeant Hill. His six-man team is on loan to us from the Air Force. They are our tactical air control party or TACP group who'll handle coordinating our close air support from both the Navy and the Air Force. If you need any airstrikes, get with your TACP, who'll call it in."

Long finished going over who their support LNOs were going to be, confirming the call signs and frequencies everyone would be operating on. Then he pointed to a spot on the map hanging on the wall. "We're going to move to this point here along Route 9. This is where the recon guys said is roughly the edge of where the enemy lines start. We'll disembark the vehicles here and move in on foot. This farm area is where we are going to leave the vehicles, and will become our base camp for the time being. The aid station will be set up here."

He turned to face his Fox Company commander as he continued his brief. "I'm not changing Lieutenant Colonel Abadi's plans from earlier. Your company will provide security for the base camp. You'll need to clear an area for medical helicopters to land and find a spot for your mortar platoons," he instructed.

The captain nodded.

"OK, guys. We all know our orders. We've gone over this plenty of times this last week in preparation for this operation. It's time to execute, so let's go make the Corps proud and kick the PLA where it hurts."

****

Two hours went by as the column of armored vehicles and trucks trekked through the winding mountain road known as Route 9 to their new base camp. They reached the small mountain city of Pinglin, where they disembarked their military vehicles and went to work on turning the area into a forward base camp. Alpha and Bravo companies were sent forward to the position the recon Marines had identified as the front lines to start identifying where the enemy was.

The remaining four companies worked to get a perimeter established, build up machine-gun positions, and clear a suitable flat area for helicopters to land. By midday, a Seabee unit also showed up, bringing their construction equipment with them to aid in the transformation of the area into a forward fighting base.

Toward the end of the day, Alpha and Bravo companies ran into the first of a series of enemy strongpoints. At first, the soldiers only had to deal with a few pop shots, but as both companies pressed forward, they ran into a series of fortified positions, which stopped them in their tracks.

Back at the base camp, Captain Long listened to the radio chatter of the two company commanders as they relayed what they were seeing and called in for artillery support. In minutes, artillery rounds began flying overhead, on their way to hit the Chinese positions. Outside the operations tent, the men in the base camp could hear the distant sounds of explosions and heavy machine-gun fire. The fight was on, and Captain Long knew it was just a matter of time before they too would join in.

As evening turned into night, Alpha and Bravo companies settled in to their positions for the night, facing the enemy. Thus far, the first day of the operation resulted in only eight Marines being injured, no fatalities. The following day would prove to be the real test. With their support base now operational, Captain Long planned on moving his other three companies forward to support Alpha and Bravo in the early hours of the morning. Come sunup, they'd launch their first major offensive.

****

Captain Long swatted at a mosquito before leading the way with his point man to link up with Alpha. It was still dark. He nearly tripped over some roots that seemed to be doing their best to grab at him, preventing him from moving forward. It was almost as if the undergrowth knew he was walking into danger and Mother Earth was trying to stop him as the roots and vines clung to him with each step.

Captain Long spoke into this radio to one of his fellow company commanders. "Alpha Six, this is Echo Six. Have your rearguard turn their IRs on. We're nearly to your position." The last thing Long wanted to have happen was a friendly fire situation, so he was grateful at the moment that they all had infrared goggles.

Seconds later, he and his point man saw the pulsing throb of the infrared light as it flashed every couple of seconds, guiding them toward Alpha Company's position. A few minutes later, they connected with the other Marines. One of the sergeants led Captain Long to link up with Captain Dave Mitchell, the Alpha Company commander.

Captain Long looked around as he walked, noticing how bright it was starting to get. The sun had just broken past the horizon a few minutes ago, forcing the darkness of the evening to retreat. *"Perfect timing,"* he thought. *"We'll get in position before the morning sun is fully up."*

Captain Mitchell had just finished eating one of his MREs when Long approached. He smiled as he stood and extended his hand. "It's good to see you, Tim. I hope the trek over here wasn't too bad," he said with a smile.

"It's good to see you as well, Dave," Captain Long responded. "You weren't joking when you said the terrain to get here was tough. I thought those vines and roots were going to pin me down so those mosquitos could eat me alive."

Captain Mitchell chuckled as he swatted at a mosquito himself. "Yeah, I think those things are the national bird around here or something—they're as big as a freaking quarter. Let's go ahead and get your guys filtered into our lines. I want to show you on the map what we've run up against." Mitchell made a motion to his senior NCO, so he would go ahead and get Long's men moving while they still had the cover of some darkness left.

Pulling out his map, Mitchell showed Long where the enemy positions where in relationship to the intelligence they'd been given. Captain Long pulled out his own map to write down the information as well. "Right here, this spot is one massive machine-gun bunker," explained Captain Mitchell. "We hit it with a number of 155mm arty rounds, but they couldn't get through it. No effect. From what we could see, there are at least five heavy machine guns in it and at least two antitank guns or light artillery guns. Roughly three hundred meters to the right of this position, which is over by Bravo Company, is a second fort just like this one. I talked with Captain Floyd, and he said there's a third fort just like these two, roughly four hundred meters to his right. That fort has an excellent field of fire over most of Route 9 through this point here."

Long looked at what he'd just been shown and grunted. *"This is going to be a lot tougher than we thought,"* he realized.

Captain Long asked, "What's behind these forts? Are there more fortifications we'll have to fight through once we clear these guys, or is this it?"

Captain Mitchell's face reddened a bit, and Long immediately surmised that he didn't know the answer. "I, um, I'm not sure," he stammered. "I let us get bogged down with these bunkers and didn't have anyone scout behind them."

"OK, then that's the first thing we need to figure out," said Long patiently. "We're going to focus on hitting these two forts this morning with an air strike. While that's happening, I want you to have one of your scout teams find a way behind this fort here," he explained as he pointed to the first fortification directly across from them. "Then we should have them move at least a kilometer behind the enemy positions before moving north to see what's behind them. We need to know if this is just the first layer of defense, or if it's wide-open country behind them."

"We can try and use some of the scout drones. They may get shot down or tangled up under the tree cover, but it won't hurt to try," one of the platoon leaders offered.

Captain Long nodded in agreement. Then he turned to Master Sergeant Hill. "I need to know if we can get some bombs on those forts," he explained. "Do you think you can try and make that happen?"

The Air Force master sergeant had been listening to the two captains talk and had made some notes of his own.

He looked down at the maps and nodded. "Shouldn't be a problem, but we need to make sure none of our guys move any closer. These bombs are going to be danger close when they land. We'll see if a 500-pounder does the job. If it doesn't, we'll hit it with something larger, but we'll need to make sure you pull your Marines back a few hundred meters if we're going to drop a 2,000-pounder."

"Make it happen, Master Sergeant. Let us know when it's heading our way," he ordered.

The next twenty minutes went by quickly as the Marines filtered onto the front lines and prepared themselves for the coming airstrikes. If the Air Force was able to smash the enemy forts, then they'd charge forward and seize the ground.

As jets rushed overhead, most of the Marines looked up at the sky. Captain Long heard a loud noise like a rocket engine.

Swoosh!

Two elongated objects shot up out of the ground toward the jets, filling the area where they had just launched with smoke. The objects rushed into the clouds so fast, they seemed to create a path of lightning as they traveled toward the jets.

Boom!

The jets broke the sound barrier and then sped off. There was a slow-motion second of silence before one of the platoon leaders shouted, "Everyone down! Bombs inbound!"

The Marines instantly buried their heads below any cover they could find and opened their mouths slightly, just as they had been told to do when a bomb was being dropped danger close.

The ground beneath them shook like an earthquake as it bounced the Marines an inch or two off the ground before throwing them back onto the hard surface. Then a massive gust of wind from the overblast rushed over them and the incredible sound of the explosion slapped their bodies. Debris fell down from the sky around them like rain from a storm, covering them in dirt, grass and vegetation.

Captain Long looked in the direction of the explosions and marveled at the sheer power and destructiveness of such a weapon. It never ceased to amaze him how such a small metal object could cause so much death and destruction. As the dust settled, they saw the bunker, largely still there, though it was clear it had suffered some serious damage. The northern part of the structure had a hole in it, and smoke was pouring out of two of the gun slits. Clearly the bomb had penetrated the structure and killed a lot of its inhabitants.

Lifting the radio receiver to his lips, Captain Long called out to the units on the front lines. "SITREP. Did all the bombs score hits?" he asked.

A minute went by and then, one by one, the various sections of their front line called in saying the bombs had found their marks. Each section reported a hit. Captain Long nodded in satisfaction at the news.

"Good job, Master Sergeant," Long said as he jovially patted the Air Force TACP on the shoulder.

"Thank you, Sir," Master Sergeant Hill responded. Then his face dropped. "Just so you're aware, we lost one of the F-16s on that strike," he explained.

Captain Long was surprised at the comment. Then he remembered seeing those two surface-to-air missiles fly up out of the tree cover. Long just nodded and returned a grim look as he acknowledged the sacrifice just made to help save his Marines.

Without taking too much more time, Captain Long turned to his radioman or RTO. "Corporal Perez, send the order for everyone to advance," he directed.

The Marines, who moments ago had been hunkering down for the airstrike, moved forward at a crouch toward the enemy positions. Captain Long signaled for his RTO and senior NCO to follow him forward. He wanted to be as close to the action as possible to better direct the battalion's resources. The Air Force TACP grabbed his own M4 and joined them as well, along with one of his junior airmen.

When the Marines got to within one hundred meters of the fortifications, they saw the bunkers were a lot more complex than they had previously thought.

The radio crackled. The scout they had sent out earlier was on the other end. "Sir, there's at least one more layer of forts behind this one, potentially more. It's hard for me to see that far through the dense undergrowth."

Crack, crack, zip, zip, BOOM.

One of the Marines in the lead had stood up a little too high as he tried to climb over a fallen log. The poor young man was ripped apart by dozens of bullets from one of the machine-gun bunkers. Then several grenades arched through the air in their direction, and they started taking fire from what appeared to be a light-caliber field cannon.

Most of the Marines leading the charge hit the dirt as they ducked to get out of the way of the barrage of bullets being fired at them.

"Suppressive fire!" shouted one of the sergeants to the Marines nearby, and the second and third line of Marines quickly obliged, giving the first group of Marines a chance to find cover and start returning fire.

"Get us some artillery fire up here!" shouted another Marine. More of the Marines' machine guns came online, adding to the roar of gunfire.

Thousands of hot metal projectiles flew back and forth between to the two groups of soldiers. The crisscrossing of red and green tracers added a futuristic laser affect to the battlefield as smoke drifted across the ground, further illuminating the tracers' effects. Captain Long crouched down behind a large tree just as a string of rounds slapped the trunk, chipping parts of it away.

"Crap, that was close!" yelled Corporal Perez as he crawled up to Long.

"Get me some artillery fire on those positions!" Captain Long shouted. His voice was barely audible over the roar of gunfire happening all around them.

Another explosion blasted loudly not far from them, and one Marine was sent flying sideways from the blast, slamming in to a tree before falling limply to the ground. Master Sergeant Hill, the Air Force TACP, was already on the radio with his counterparts, trying to determine if they had any fast movers loitering above them that might be able to lend them some support.

Corporal Perez handed Captain Long the radio receiver, yelling, "I've got Ripper One-One on the other end!"

Long snatched the receiver from Perez, placing it to the side of his face as he depressed the talk button. "Ripper One-One, this is Echo Six. Fire mission. Target Zulu One, one round HE. Stand by for adjustments!" he shouted.

"Good copy, Echo Six. Stand by for fire mission," came the reply from the fire direction center.

Normally he'd work through his fire support officer, but he knew the other company commanders would be calling him. Long was hoping to lighten the man's load and handle his own company's fire mission requests for the time being.

"Echo Six. Shot out," the fire direction center operator announced. A couple of minutes later, the round came sailing in right through the tree cover and landed just behind the fortified enemy position, throwing up a geyser of dirt and underbrush.

"Ripper One-One. Adjust fire, drop twenty meters. Repeat last fire mission," Captain Long ordered.

Just as Long finished speaking, an enemy explosion ripped through the Marine lines. The PLA was doing their best to keep the Marines from getting too close to their positions. Then the whistling sound of the friendly artillery round screamed in overhead, this time landing right on top of the enemy fortification. The structure shook, though it was clear the round had not penetrated the reinforced concrete.

"Ripper One-One. Good shot," shouted Long. "Give me one smoke round and two rounds HE on that same spot, and stand by for adjustments." Captain Long crossed his fingers and hoped this next set of rounds might get lucky. If nothing else, it should shake the enemy up and potentially be enough of a shock to them that the Marines might be able to bum-rush them.

Switching over to the company net, Captain Long shouted to his platoon commanders. "Listen up! When the next round of artillery hits the enemy bunker, I want everyone to charge the bunker as quickly as you can. We need to close the gap on them once we stun them."

When the next rounds came crashing in, the explosions seemed to blast the fortified positions hard, throwing debris high into the air. Then the smoke round burst open, throwing smoke canisters all over the enemy positions, temporarily obscuring their view.

"Charge!" yelled Captain Long. He tossed the radio receiver back to his RTO as he jumped out from behind his covered position and ran forward toward the enemy lines as quickly as possible.

Long jumped over some fallen trees and fought not to get tangled up by the hanging vines and other undergrowth as he struggled to catch up to the rest of his Marines, who were now running toward the enemy as fast as they could.

Slowly at first, a couple of enemy machine guns resumed their melody of death as they blindly crisscrossed the battlefield in front of them. At least their once-dominant view of the area was now obscured by the infrared-resistant smokescreen the artillery unit had laid down for Captain Long's men.

In a matter of minutes, several platoons' worth of his Marines had made it to within twenty meters of the enemy positions. Unexpectedly, a light breeze suddenly blew through the jungle canopy, dispersing the smokescreen that had been protecting his men. As the smoke dissipated, the enemy machine-gun fire became a lot more accurate as the PLA homed in their aim. Then, the field cannon in the bunker resumed firing, blowing parts of tree trunks apart and sending shrapnel flying in all directions.

Captain Long was now less than forty meters from the first bunker. He took a knee behind a large tree trunk as he aimed his rifle at the enemy. A round cracked right past his head, causing him to instinctively flinch and duck behind the tree for cover. He looked back and saw Corporal Perez, his RTO, wince in pain and grit his teeth as he momentarily dropped his rifle. He'd been shot in his left arm. One of the Air Force TACPs that was running next to him stopped, grabbed Perez and his rifle and pulled both of them behind a large rock as a string of bullets kicked up a bunch of dirt around them.

Long popped out from behind the tree trunk, aimed his rifle at the gun slit that was shooting at them and squeezed the trigger. His rifle barked several times as he fought to keep his rounds in a tight shot group, right where he knew the enemy machine gunner to be.

Out of his peripheral vision, Captain Long spotted a small cluster of Marines who had managed to crawl up to the bunker. He smiled. They'd somehow gotten themselves to the base of the fortified position without being seen and were readying to take it out. One of the Marines pulled the pin on a grenade, then held it for a second before he shoved it into the gun slit. A second later, Captain Long heard a loud explosion, and then the enemy position fell silent.

Further down the fortified position, the other machine guns and field cannon continued to fire on them. Hundreds of bullets were still ripping the trees around them apart, some of the bullets finding their marks and hitting his Marines. Even above the roar of gunfire, Captain Long could still hear the wounded call out, "Corpsman!"

Near him, Long spotted one of the Navy corpsmen assigned to them jump up and run under heavy enemy fire to give aid to the wounded Marines. Captain Long admired the man for courageously risking his own personal safety to help save others.

The group of Marines who had made it to the edge of the fortified bunkers steadily made their way down the structure, tossing grenades into the gun slits and firing ports as they went along. They had nearly made it to the end when an enemy soldier inside must have discovered what was happening and dropped a couple of their own hand grenades outside the bunker. Before the Marines could respond, the two grenades exploded, killing or injuring all four Marines who had been systematically silencing the enemy positions.

Several additional Marines charged forward to take their place and provide medical help to their brethren. Unfortunately, they were quickly cut down by an enemy machine-gun crew who had anticipated this action. One of the groups of Marines eventually did make it up to the bunker and finished the job the first group had started. In all, it had taken them maybe fifteen minutes to silence the enemy bunker once they'd charged it, but it had cost Captain Long's company the lives of six Marines, and another dozen had been injured.

The same scene played itself out at the other three fortified positions, with the Marines eventually capturing the enemy positions. Now that they had a better picture of what was waiting for them at the next line of enemy defenses, Captain Long insisted on the Air Force plastering the Chinese positions with their heavier ordnance. They'd hang back a kilometer or so away and allow the fast movers to hit them with the heavier 2,000-pound bombs. If things went according to plan, the enemy positions would be largely destroyed by the time his battalion was ready to assault the next position.

As the day wore on, the sound of explosions and machine-gun fire continued to fill the entire reservoir area as the rest of the Marine division pushed its way through the enemy lines. The fighting was fierce and often devolved into hand-to-hand fighting. In the distance, Captain Long observed as dozens of surface-to-air missiles that had been hidden in the jungle rocketed out of their covered positions to reach out and hit the Allied planes as they swooped in to provide desperately needed close air support. Long had no idea what kind of losses the Navy and Air Force were taking, but he was glad to see them continuing to support them despite the grave risks to themselves and their aircraft.

While Long's battalion waited for the Air Force to get around to hammering their targets, he fell more fully into the role of battalion commander. His time and energy began to be consumed with making sure the various companies had enough ammunition, the wounded Marines were getting brought out of the jungle and back to the medics at the basecamp, and overall coordination of his battalion's operations in relationship to the other battalions in their regiment. As the day turned to evening, Long had all but turned over operational control of his own company to his executive officer.

The battalion sergeant major came by and made Captain Long painfully aware that he needed to do what he could to visit the other company positions and check on them. There was also a regimental briefing at 2100 hours that he'd need to head back for. This was the part of being an officer Long hated. When he'd been an NCO, his only job was to make sure his squad and then platoon were taken care of. Now he was responsible for the lives of nearly seven hundred Marines; it was an enormous responsibility.

Thankfully, that evening at the regimental briefing, Captain Long learned that the executive officer from their sister battalion was being moved over to take command of the battalion from him. Long instantly liked the guy—Major Brian Noble was a hard-chargin' Marines' Marine. He'd started the war as a first lieutenant and moved through the ranks quickly, like a lot of Marines had given the significant casualty numbers.

Like Captain Long, Major Noble had a chest full of medals. He'd been wounded once and had received the Silver Star along with two Bronze Stars. Long had him beat with two Purple Hearts and the Navy Cross, but both of them were the type of leaders who liked to lead from the front, in the thick of the action with their men.

That evening, when Long and Noble got back to the basecamp, Major Noble pulled Captain Long aside. "Hey, I want to make sure that you'll be my second-in-command in case something happens," he asked.

"It would be a privilege, Sir," Captain Long replied.

"OK, when we return to the front tomorrow, I will embed with Alpha Company, and I want you to resume command of Echo," Major Noble directed.

"Sounds like a plan, Sir," Long answered.

****

Captain Long had only managed to get maybe two or three hours of fitful sleep. The previous day had been brutal. Their battalion had encountered a much larger force than they had originally thought would be there. They'd taken a number of casualties, forcing the regiment to shift another battalion over to assist them in breaking through the enemy lines.

Since he couldn't sleep, Captain Long silently crept around with his first sergeant, checking on each of his platoons before the morning light signaled the beginning of the new day. It was 0600 hours as the predawn light slowly crept over the mountains that encircled the valley and reservoir. In another thirty minutes or so, it would be light.

When he'd finished checking on his platoons, Captain Long took the opportunity to grab an MRE from his ruck, reminding himself that he needed to eat if he was to keep up his strength and energy. Looking at the mystery surprise, he saw he had pulled Menu 1: spaghetti with meat sauce.

"Hmm...at least it comes with the cheese spread," he thought. He opened the bag and began to assemble his morning meal. He hadn't had time to eat most of the day before and was paying for it with a lack of energy now. The

body can fight through a lack of sleep, but only if it is properly fueled.

Three bites into his meal, the morning silence was shattered by a large *BOOM* and the sudden chattering of one of their heavy machine guns. A number of other rifles were firing near the perimeter. Captain Long stuffed his spoon back in the food pouch and turned to his radioman, who seldom ever left his side. "Corporal Perez, get me a SITREP from Staff Sergeant Jenkins!" he ordered.

Within a minute, the gunfire died down and eventually stopped altogether. At that point, Staff Sergeant Jenkins came on the radio. "Sir, it appears a small team of enemy soldiers hit one of our trip flares as they moved parallel to our lines. Corporal Dungy triggered his Claymore as soon as he saw the enemy soldiers, then one of the other privates manning the M204G raked the area with gunfire."

"Did they return fire? Did we take any casualties?" Captain Long inquired.

"Negative, Sir. The enemy never had a chance," Staff Sergeant Jenkins answered. "I have no idea how many enemy soldiers are still out there, though, or how many we killed. It's still too dark for us to see much, and our night vision can't see through the thick vegetation. If you can send a runner over with the thermals, I might be able to get you a better answer."

The scopes were in high demand, and unfortunately, three of the five scopes assigned to their battalion had been destroyed in the first day of fighting. A fourth was destroyed when the lieutenant operating it had been blown up during an enemy artillery barrage.

"Copy that, Staff Sergeant. I'm sending Lance Corporal Able to you with the scope. I want a SITREP ASAP. We'll stand by to launch some illumination rounds once you've had a chance to use the scope."

Five long minutes went by before he received an urgent call from Staff Sergeant Jenkins. "Sir, we've got trouble," he said. "I believe that group of enemy soldiers we just smoked was the point element for a much larger enemy force. I can't get you a head count, but there have to be more than fifty soldiers fanning out into an assault line maybe two or three hundred meters to our front."

"Copy that," Long answered. "Start waking everyone up and tell them to get ready. I'm going to work on getting us some illumination rounds. I need you to relay to Corporal Perez some coordinates for the artillery, so we can get this information back to regiment."

Corporal Perez pulled out a pen and notebook from his pocket and took down the coordinates from Staff Sergeant Jenkins.

"Ripper One-One, Pit Bull Six. How copy?" said his RTO.

"Pit Bull Six, Ripper One-One. Good copy. What do you have for us?" asked the artilleryman.

"Fire mission. Troops in contact," explained the RTO. "Need one round illumination, grid TW 3456 4765, five-hundred-meter airburst. Break. One round HE, grid TW 3456 4765. Break. One round HE, grid TW 3469 4521. How copy?"

"Good copy on all. Stand by," relayed the artillery battery.

After a moment of silence, a crackle went over the radio. "Shots out," announced the artilleryman.

A couple of minutes went by, and then they heard the loud whistle of the rounds flying fast overhead until they slammed into their plotted positions. Looking beyond the perimeter, Captain Long saw the two bright explosions from the HE rounds impact and then the sudden blaring brightness of the illumination round, igniting a thousand feet above the location of the enemy soldiers. In another twenty minutes, they wouldn't have needed the illumination round at all.

What Long saw next was horrifying. The entire ground suddenly appeared to move as enemy troops advanced. Hundreds of little lights flickered, and then thousands of bullets zoomed through the air, hitting everything around Captain Long's perimeter. The barrage of enemy fire directed at their positions was relentless as many bullets found their marks. Wounded Marines called out for corpsmen.

The roar of hundreds of voices screaming at the tops of their lungs thundered as the Chinese charged forward. This roar was soon intermixed with thunderous booms as his Marines detonated their Claymore mines. His Marines steadily returned fire, tearing into the ranks of the attackers as they pressed their own attack forward, desperately trying to close the distance between themselves and the Marines.

Long was still holding the radio receiver connecting him to the division artillery, so he depressed the talk button and shouted to be heard over the cacophony of gunfire and screaming going on all around him. "Ripper One-One! Good hit! Repeat fire mission. Fire for effect. Five rounds HE. We're about to be overrun. Keep 'em coming!"

Corporal Perez interrupted him as soon as he finished talking to the artillery battery, shoving another handset at him. "It's Captain Flowers from Charlie Company!" he shouted.

"This is Long!" he yelled.

Captain Long heard rifle fire and explosions in the background of the radio as Captain Flowers tried to relay what was happening on his end. "We're getting hit hard on the right flank. I estimate at least a battalion's worth of enemy soldiers. We need artillery support—can you get us some?"

"Flowers, I've got a fire mission coming in right now across our entire perimeter," Captain Long answered. "Have one of your guys start to relay any additional coordinates you have to Corporal Perez. Hold the line no matter what, Captain Flowers. Help is on the way!"

Seeing a swarm of enemy soldiers nearly upon his perimeter, Captain Long raised his rifle and fired at a group of PLA soldiers who were charging right for one of his machine gunners. The first two guys he fired at went down quickly. Captain Long had shifted fire to a third guy, but he was stopped in his tracks when an RPG flew over the heads of the Marines he was trying to protect and slammed into a tree several meters to his right.

He winced in pain as he felt something hit his right arm and shoulder. Long steadied himself and again aimed at the PLA soldiers, who were now fighting hand-to-hand with his Marines on the perimeter. The machine gunner he'd been trying to protect was now lying on the ground on his back with a PLA soldier straddling him. The Chinese soldier was trying to press his knife into the young man's chest. Long aimed at the pair as they struggled for survival, depressing the trigger once. He watched his bullet hit the Chinese soldier squarely in the head. The man went limp on the young Marine, who proceeded to throw him to the side as he once again scrambled to get behind his M240G. In mere seconds, he was continuing to lay down suppressive fire.

Captain Long turned to look for his first sergeant and saw the man slumped against a rock, half of his face missing from the RPG's shrapnel. Corporal Perez was on the radio, calling for more artillery fire.

Snap, crack, boom!

Bullets continued to hit the tree he had been using for cover while others zipped past his head and to either side of the tree. A hand grenade went off near the machine gunner he had just saved a moment ago, killing the young Marine.

Captain Long's heart sank. He had to get that machine gun operational again. It was the only thing keeping the enemy at bay.

"Perez! Follow me!" he shouted to his RTO. He leapt up, his rifle pressed to his shoulder as he charged the enemy, systematically killing as many of them as he could with each shot fired.

It took Long a minute to rush the twenty meters to the fallen Marine's position. As he neared the machine gun, he dropped his empty magazine and slapped a fresh one in its place. Jumping into the hastily built foxhole, he grabbed the M240G and placed it snug against his shoulder. Then he proceeded to let loose a long string of rounds into a mob of charging enemy soldiers, while bullets zipped past his head and kicked up dirt all around him.

Corporal Perez jumped into the position next to him, reaching over to one of the fallen Marines and grabbing several of the one-hundred-round belts of ammo off him. Then he linked one of the new belts with the one Captain Long was chewing through. Searching around the position for more ammo, Perez found three more in the ruck of the assistant machine gunner, who was lying dead next to him. He also took a couple of the hand grenades from his dead comrade and began throwing them at the charging enemy.

Crump, crump, crump.

The explosions sounded small in comparison to the mortars and artillery fire being rained down, but they were doing the job of killing or wounding the enemy, who was steadily bearing down on them.

"Shift fire to our right, Sir!" shouted Corporal Perez.

A fresh wave of enemy soldiers had surged toward their position. At some point in the battle, his right flank had fallen apart as the Marines were simply overrun by the sheer numbers being thrown at them. Captain Long saw the wave of humanity, shouting and screaming at the top of their lungs with bayonets attached to the ends of their rifles…charging right for them. Leveling the M240G at the charging horde, he pulled the trigger, letting a string of machine-gun fire rip through their lines. He moved his aim back and forth across the enemy, and watched as many of them clutched at their chest, arms, and legs, falling to the ground before they were trampled upon by the following soldiers.

Turning his head slightly to Corporal Perez, he shouted, "Fall back!"

Perez, for his part, threw several grenades at the enemy and then bounded back five or so meters before turning around to lay down suppressive fire so Long could move. Sensing that this was his moment, Long stopped firing as he ran in a low crouch past Perez to another tree, where he once again opened fire on their attackers, all the while shouting for the others to fall back as well.

It took a few minutes, but more and more of his Marines heard his call to fall back and collapsed back on a rally point they had identified the day before. The enemy reached their previous positions and halted their advance for the moment, committing a fatal error in their attack by giving the Marines a moment of reprieve. Within seconds, a lot of the gunfire happening around them slackened as more of the Marines disengaged and the PLA stopped pressing their attack.

When they reached the rally point, Captain Long called back to battalion to let them know what had just happened. While he was on the radio, more of his Marines continued to filter into their positions, some carrying wounded comrades, others wounded themselves but still able to fight.

"Get a perimeter set up now!" Long shouted.

Captain Long took a moment to talk with higher headquarters, requesting a quick reaction force be sent to their position.

"Where's the first sergeant?" asked one of the other sergeants as he took the M240G back from him.

Pausing for a second, the captain looked solemnly at the sergeant. "He's dead," he answered. Then, without giving him too much time to process that statement, he asked, "Where's Lieutenant Simmons? I need to speak with him."

"I'm coming, Sir," shouted his executive officer. He was helping to lay a wounded Marine down near the center of their position. The company's corpsman was busy trying to stabilize and treat the numerous wounded men being brought in.

Once his XO made it over to his position, Captain Long asked, "How many men have we lost? Did all the platoons fall back to our rally point?" While he spoke, he was performing a quick head count of the wounded.

"I don't know what happened to Second Platoon. They were on the right flank. Last I saw, several artillery rounds landed in their positions and then the PLA had swarmed all over them. I was with Third Platoon. I've got them situated over there," Lieutenant Simmons explained as he pointed to an area roughly twenty meters away.

Lieutenant Scott walked up to them. "I've got Fourth Platoon situated on our right flank, ready to repel any further attacks," he said. "I have to admit, Captain, I thought you were a dead man. The Chinese hardly hit our platoon, so I brought a squad over to your position. When I saw you charge forward and grab that machine gun like that I figured you'd last maybe a minute. My guys did their best to cover your retreat—I'm glad you made it."

"The Chinese didn't hit your platoon's section of the line at all?" asked Long.

"No, Sir," Lieutenant Scott answered. "The attack appeared to be concentrated on Second and First Platoon positions. Like I said, my platoon was hardly hit. We only sustained one wounded. My guys are ginned up and ready for some payback. Do you want me to head back to where Second Platoon was and see if we can find any survivors?" he asked.

Captain Long thought about that for a moment before responding. Major Noble had told him that he was sending two platoons from Delta Company to help him. Part of him knew that he should probably wait and make sure they held their current position, but Long also didn't want to leave a platoon of his men alone. He could still hear the *ratatat* of several machine guns, M4s and AK-47s, in the distance.

"Lieutenant Simmons, how many able-bodied men do we have ready to fight right now?" Captain Long asked.

Simmons had just finished conferring with a few sergeants and a couple of other gunnery sergeants, scribbling something on his notepad. He looked up. "We've got a lot of wounded and missing-in-action guys from Second and Third

Platoon right now. We have maybe two full squads from First Platoon and three full squads from Third Platoon that are able to fight. Of the five squads, probably only three of them could assist Fourth Platoon."

Letting out a sigh, Captain Long turned to look at Lieutenant Scott. "Take your platoon along with a squad from Third Platoon with you," he ordered. "I've got to keep the others here to protect the rally point until our reinforcements from Delta arrive. When they get here, I'll send them your way."

With that settled, Lieutenant Scott called out to two of the gunnery sergeants, "Grab your men and head with me! We're going to go find and fetch Second Platoon."
****

When Lieutenant Scott's platoon got close to where Second Platoon should have been, they saw something even worse than what he'd expected. Not only was the area littered with the torn and mangled bodies of their fellow Marines, but there had to be close to three companies' worth of enemy soldiers filtering into the area, getting ready to move toward them.

Scott's platoon sergeant whispered to him. "Sir, it doesn't look like anyone survived. We should report what we're seeing and head back to the rally point. That force is too large for us to take on, and the company will be hard-pressed to beat back that large of an attack without us."

Lieutenant Scott knew that was the right decision, and he did have to consider the well-being of his own men, but seeing his fellow Marines lying there, dead, alone, and surrounded by the enemy like that, really burned him up. He shook his head and let out a sigh.

"Relay the message back to the CO and tell him we're heading back." With that settled, the platoon silently crept back to the rally point, readying themselves mentally for what they knew would be another withering attack when it came.

****

"Sir, you really need to let me look at that wound," said one of the corpsmen as he tried for the tenth time to look at Captain Long's shoulder and arm. The right side of his blouse had a lot of blood on it, and his Marines were starting to get concerned that he might pass out from loss of blood.

"Fine, just be quick about it," Long consented.

While the corpsman went to work on his arm, he used his other hand to signal for First Lieutenant Simmons to come over and speak with him. "Simmons, what's going on with Fourth Platoon?" he asked. "Did Lieutenant Scott find our guys?"

Simmons just shook his head. "They found them, but it appears they were all dead, or the enemy had moved the wounded and others captured back to their rear area. He also reported seeing what looked to be maybe two or three companies of enemy soldiers forming up for another attack."

Captain Long shuddered in disgust. At this point he had his body armor and his blouse off, and the corpsman began to cut his undershirt off to get at the wound better. Long shot the man a look of scorn. "You're lucky that wasn't my Under Armor shirt. I only have a couple of them left," he said.

Just as Lieutenant Scott approached them, they heard a commotion behind them. While the corpsman was wiping away some blood and pouring some iodine on the wound, Colonel Tilman and the regiment's sergeant major approached them.

"That looks like it hurts, Captain. You all right?" asked Colonel Tilman as he eyed the wound.

The corpsman had a pair of medical pliers out and proceeded to pull a small piece of metal out of Long's right shoulder before examining his arm to do the same. Captain Long winced as the pliers pulled the fragment out of his shoulder. While it hurt, his shoulder felt a lot better with the metal out.

Long looked at Colonel Tilman and shook his head. "It's not the first time I've been shot or hit with shrapnel. I'm sure it won't be the last time."

"That's hard core, Marine. Semper Fi," grunted the sergeant major before moving on to check on the rest of the troops.

"You shouldn't be here, Sir," warned Captain Long. "Lieutenant Scott's platoon spotted at least two or three company-size elements forming up for another attack. There're roughly a kilometer in that direction." He pointed toward the location of the enemy.

The colonel nodded. "Good," he replied in a voice that was almost too optimistic. "I've got Third Battalion deploying to your right flank as we speak. Lieutenant Scott, go with Major Allen here and relay what you saw and where they are. We're going to finish this battle today."

While the officers continued to talk, rocket fire from the high-mobility artillery rocket system or HIMARS battery screamed in the background until it exploded on the enemy fortifications that the regiment still had to secure. The thumping sound of helicopters also got closer.

One of the squads had tied some det cord around half a dozen trees to help create a clearing for one of the CH-53 Super Stallion to land so they could fly out their wounded, so fortunately, there was at least some patch of land for them to set down upon. When the helicopter landed in the clearing, half a dozen Marines rushed forward to help offload several crates of ammo and grenades, along with numerous five-gallon jugs of water. Just as soon as that had taken place, the corpsmen ran forward with their stretchers, bringing the wounded to the helicopter. Many other walking wounded also got on board before the helicopter lifted off, ready to head back to a high-level trauma center. When the Super Stallion was gone, a second one landed in its place and offloaded a fresh platoon, ready for action.

Colonel Tilman saw the fresh Marines getting off and commented to Long, "I've got eight more loads of fresh Marines coming into this position right now. We're moving the regiment's headquarters forward. I need to be closer to the fight." He paused for a second, watching the corpsman wrap Captain Long's shrapnel wounds. "Are you sure you don't want to go back to a field hospital and get that stitched up?" he asked. "We'll manage for a few days while you're gone."

Long shook his head. "No, I'll be fine. I'll wait for the regiment surgeon to arrive. He can stitch me up here and I'll get right back to it. I can rest and recover after we finish these guys off."

"All right, Captain, have it your way. For the time being, I want your company pulled back to provide security for regiment HQ. You guys need a break, and it's the best I can give you until the situation changes."

Chapter 15

Battle of St. Petersburg

Kirovsk, Russia

Oberstleutnant Hermann Wulf of the 21st Panzer Brigade could still hear the distant sound of explosions as he looked off in the direction of St. Petersburg. A few snowflakes fell in the afternoon sunlight as the sun's rays fought to break through the cloud cover overhead. The temperature continued to hover around 30 degrees Fahrenheit, not cold enough to require heavy winter coats, but just cold enough to require something to ward off the wind when it blew. The evening temperatures, however, would drop closer to the teens with the windchill. Still, it was only a preview of what the winter would be like once January and February came. A winter war in Russia was not something anyone was looking forward to. However, unlike the armies of the past, the Allies were better equipped to deal with it.

Surprisingly, Wulf's unit, the 35th Mechanized Infantry Battalion, had met little in the way of enemy resistance once the American heavy armor units had broken through the Russian lines two days prior. When he had been given the order to secure the city of Kirovsk on the east banks of the Neva River, he had breathed a sigh of relief. It looked like his command would largely avoid some of the hardest fighting taking place in the city.

To help accomplish the task of securing the critical P-21/E-105 Highway leading to St. Petersburg, his battalion had been augmented with a single Heron TP UAV, an Israeli-made ISR drone. The US V Corps was going to use his battalion as their eyes and ears while the main body of forces collectively crushed the remaining enemy forces in the city. With this last major Russian formation defeated, they would have a clear path to drive on Moscow some 710 kilometers southeast of their current positions.

Oberstleutnant Wulf was elated that his unit wouldn't have to partake in what he knew would be a bloody street fight in St. Petersburg, yet anxious at being at the forefront of the army group. His battalion, while largely still intact from the recent months of fighting, would largely be on their own until the major fighting in the city was concluded. His battalion had a force of 39 Puma infantry fighting vehicles, 42 Boxer armored personnel carriers, and two dozen Fennek reconnaissance vehicles. His battalion had also been augmented with a company of Leopard II tanks and a battery of Panzerhaubitze 2000, the newest self-propelled Howitzers. The 155mm artillery guns were providing near-constant artillery support to the American, Swedish, and Finnish soldiers fighting in and around the city of St. Petersburg. With all their vehicles and equipment, his force had been tasked with blocking any Russian reinforcements from traveling to the St. Petersburg pocket and preventing all enemy forces from retreating.

One of his captains approached him, carrying a map of the region. "Herr Oberstleutnant, one of the scout units has spotted a column of armored vehicles near the city of Chudovo," he explained as he pointed to a small city that was maybe twenty kilometers from their current position, well within artillery range of their little mobile firebase they had set up.

"Find out from the scouts how many vehicles they are seeing and what type they are," Wulf ordered. "Also, send a message over our artillery unit that we may have a new fire mission for them." he ordered. The activity around his command vehicle increased as his soldiers went to work processing the information coming in from the scouts and keeping the various units informed of what was happening around them.

With no real snowfall on the forecast for a couple of days, Wulf was making full use of the surveillance drones the Americans had provided his battalion with. The small, portable drones were providing his analysis with a constant stream of data. He observed some video footage of one of the scout drones as it took up position over the enemy unit traveling toward them.

"Sir, the scouts are reporting six enemy tanks and eight BTRs heading toward Kolpino. That'll put them at the Americans' southeastern perimeter. Shall I order our Panzers to intercept them?" the operations officer asked. Another soldier manning the drone overhead zoomed in to confirm the scouts' report.

As Wulf looked at the video feed from the drone, he saw an enemy company, possibly a battalion-sized element. *"Where's its parent unit?"* he wondered. *"That's what we need to find."*

He turned to face his operations officer, Stabshauptmann Manfred Hoffman. "What air assets do we have available?" he asked. "Let's see if we can't vector some fighters in to hit them first, and then we can send the Panzers in to finish them off. Also, I want some drones to trace the road that column came from—I suspect there is a larger enemy unit further back. We need to see what else is out there."

Stabshauptmann Manfred Hoffman was the senior captain and staff officer in Oberstleutnant Wulf's battalion. He'd been assigned to be Wulf's executive officer and lead the staff functions for the battalion because not only was he a superb staff officer, but he understood battalion and brigade level tactics as well. His only flaw was his temper, which had gotten the better of him on a couple of occasions. When he had been a company officer, he'd struck a soldier for insubordination, and then just as the war had broken out, he'd punched a superior officer when he'd failed to inform him of a pending air attack during the opening hours of the war in Ukraine. Had it not been for the war with Russia, and the fact that Germany had been attacked hard during the first week of the war, he would have been charged and served prison time, or at least been kicked out of the Army. As it was, his unit had fought with distinction in Ukraine with the Ukrainian and American Armies. While not all had been forgiven, his superiors had given him a chance to redeem himself by mentoring a young up-and-coming star in the German Army.

Stabshauptmann Hoffman nodded at Wulf's suggestion and looked at one of the whiteboards they had set up, which listed the available air assets and was updated every fifteen minutes by an Air Force LNO, a sergeant who was responsible for coordinating any requests for air support. Scanning the board, Hoffman saw there were two pairs of German Tornadoes, a pair of Norwegian F-16s, and four German Tiger attack helicopters available at that moment.

Getting the attention of the Air Force LNO, Hoffman ordered, "Sergeant, find out which of those aircraft can attack the Russian column, and have them do it immediately. Tell our helicopters that once the Air Force hits them, we have a mission for them."

Ten minutes went by as the drone continued to observe the enemy force, advancing ever closer to the American flank. Wulf had warned the Americans the Russian unit was coming and informed them that they had air assets inbound to deal with them. It felt like hours waiting for the fighters to get in position. However, in mere moments, the two Norwegian F-16s swooped in fast, releasing a series of CBU-100 cluster bombs and destroying a number of the enemy vehicles. The survivors from the attack scattered their formation.

As the F-16s pulled away, Wulf watched half a dozen smoke contrails fly up after them. One of the F-16s fired off a number of flares, which succeeded in luring a few of the enemy missiles toward them as they successfully escaped.

The second F-16 tried to do the same; however, one of the enemy missiles blew past the decoys and detonated near the tail of the aircraft, causing the back half of the fighter to blow apart. Seconds later, the entire plane exploded before the pilot had a chance to eject.

The Air Force sergeant coordinating the mission for them muttered a few curse words to himself. Then he picked up the radio receiver and began to make contact with the attack helicopters to let them know it was their turn to go in and finish off the enemy column. He also wanted to warn them that the enemy had a lot of MANPADs with them and was not afraid to use them.

A few minutes later, the drone that was providing overwatch footage for them spotted the attack helicopters moving in at just above treetop level. In pairs of two, they carefully made use of the terrain around them, moving behind a copse of trees or hiding behind a barn or other structure when needed.

Stabshauptmann Hoffman had their drone pilot talk directly with the helicopters, relaying what the drone was seeing and explaining where the helicopters were in relationship to the armored vehicles. Just as the attack helicopters were zeroing in for their attack, a pair of MiG-29 Fulcrums zoomed in out of nowhere, obliterating two of the helicopters in a spectacular fireball with air-to-air missiles before they even knew what happened. The MiGs banked hard and climbed in altitude as they headed toward the city of St. Petersburg, obviously looking for their next target of opportunity.

The Air Force sergeant pounded his fist on the table, letting loose a string of foul obscenities. Hoffman walked up to him, placing his hand on his shoulder. "It's not your fault, Sergeant. People die, and aircraft get destroyed. It's just the nature of war. Put it behind you and move on to the next objective. Everyone has a job to do, and we're counting on you," he said in a soft voice.

Looking up at the Stabshauptmann, the sergeant nodded as he wiped a tear from the side of his face. "You're right, Captain. Thank you for understanding. Do you want me to try and get another air strike to hit that enemy column?"

"No, order our other helicopters to retreat back to base. We'll send the Panzers in now to deal with what's left of the enemy," he ordered.

Then he turned to one of his other sergeants and ordered the tanks in. The four Leopard IIs and eight Pumas should be more than enough to finish off what was left of the Russian force.

The next twenty-four hours turned into an on-again, off-again battle of small company-sized elements of Russian forces as they tried to test Wulf's battalion, searching for a weak spot they could exploit. Once the Allies secured St. Petersburg, the entire force would shift in his direction as they looked to begin their long march on Moscow to bring this war to an end.

****

St. Petersburg, Russia

The two Stryker vehicles moved steadily down Novosibirskaya Street toward the intersection some two hundred meters away. A squad of soldiers moved slowly, carefully, on the flanks of each of the two vehicles, making sure they were never too far away from a covered position. The ground beneath them had a few centimeters of snow on it from earlier in the morning that the sun had not yet melted.

In the rear of the platoon formation, Command Sergeant Major Childers was talking with Second Lieutenant Drake, the new platoon leader for Second Platoon. As Childers was in the middle of getting a status update from Drake, the lead vehicle was suddenly hit by an antitank rocket and blew up. Hot shrapnel was thrown into the squad of soldiers nearby. There was a loud roar as heavy machine guns opened fire on the remaining soldiers, who had been dazed by the explosion. Seconds after the gunfire started, an RPG sailed out of one of the fourth-floor windows, narrowly missing the second Stryker vehicle as it flew right over top of it and blew apart a small civilian vehicle abandoned along the sidewalk.

Childers and the other soldiers of Nemesis Troop scrambled for cover and returned fire. He watched as one of the soldiers near him set up his M203 grenade launcher and aimed for the window that had been used to launch an RPG at them. They watched as the 40mm fragmentation grenade sailed right into the intended window, detonating inside.

"Hopefully, that just killed those enemy soldiers," Childers thought. That would make one less window firing at them.

The trooper reloaded his M203, but before he could fire it again, a single shot rang out from several hundred meters down the road, exploding the trooper's head like a dropped watermelon. His body crumpled to the ground.

Another soldier, who had been manning one of the platoon's heavy machine guns, the M240G, brought his weapon to bear on the location he suspected the enemy sniper was firing from and unloaded on the façade of the building. One of the enemy machine gunners returned fire, forcing the American soldier to duck for cover or get riddled with bullets. The remaining Stryker vehicle backed up down the road they had just turned down, while the turret gunner laid suppressive fire so the remaining soldiers could fall back.

Several of the troopers tried to grab their wounded comrades, only to be gunned down or wounded themselves. Lieutenant Drake, who must've seen that his platoon was being torn apart, yelled to one of his squads, "Lay down covering fire!"

He and a couple of other soldiers attempted to drag the wounded back to cover. The lone Stryker vehicle also stayed in the line of fire, so the turret gunner could continue to fire back at the enemy and hopefully draw the enemy's fire while their comrades worked to recover their wounded.

Pop, pop, crack! BOOM!

The lieutenant's head snapped back. His body fell forward from the momentum of running toward one of his wounded brothers, but he was dead, killed by a sniper round to the head. An RPG shot out from another elevated window, hitting the front of the Stryker vehicle and catching part of it on fire. The driver of the vehicle immediately gunned the engine, pushing the vehicle back and around the corner of the road to get away from any further enemy fire. The remaining American soldiers begrudgingly fell back to the side of the Stryker vehicle.

"Help! Please don't leave me here to die...someone...anyone...help," cried one of his wounded soldiers roughly thirty meters in front of them. When one of the soldiers tried to retrieve him, a sniper shot him, leaving him wounded and trapped in the street, fully exposed. The sniper had added one more to his casualties.

Seeing that Lieutenant Drake had perished in the fight, Childers had no choice but to take control of the situation. "Men, fall back on me!" he ordered. We need to find a better position to attack or we'll only add to the body count."

****

Several minutes later, Command Sergeant Major Childers shifted uncomfortably on his side as he lifted his pocket binoculars to his eyes and scanned the buildings further down the block, past the oily black smoke from the burning Stryker vehicle and car.

"Where are you, you little snakes? Ah, there you are," he whispered softly to himself. A smile spread across his face.

They had already tried a few other approaches, but every time they tried to get into a better position to attack the Russians, they were met with a barrage of enemy gunfire and RPGs. Clearly, the enemy had thought this ambush point through and knew they'd be able to inflict a lot of casualties on the Americans. Now the young soldiers in the platoon were all turning to Childers to save them.

"How do you want to do this, Sergeant Major?" asked one of the surviving senior sergeants as he spat a stream of tobacco juice on the ground.

"I'd like to put a tank round into the upper floor above that café at the end of the block," said Childers with a wry smile. "However, seeing that we don't have a tank, we're going to have to figure out how to get closer to the building. Give me your map, will you?"

The sergeant obliged, and Childers eagerly took the map of the city and placed it on the ground. He pulled out his pad of waterproof paper and scribbled down a position on the map. He then used his index finger to give a rough measurement of a landmark they had preplotted on the map with the location of the café where the enemy sniper was located.

The sergeant asked, "You going to call in an artillery strike on them?"

Childers nodded, eliciting smiles and nods from the other sergeants and soldiers around them. With no other officers present, Childers was the highest-ranking person on scene, and while he wasn't the platoon or even company sergeant, he was the battalion's senior enlisted NCO. Normally, they wouldn't be allowed to call in an artillery strike in a densely packed part of the city unless they knew there were no civilians nearby, but with more than a dozen of his soldiers dead and half that many lying in the street wounded and calling out for help, he wasn't about to let an arbitrary rule written by a lawyer prevent him from keeping his soldiers alive.

"It's easier to ask for forgiveness than permission sometimes," he thought as he looked for the call sign for the German artillery unit they'd been assigned to use.

After signaling for the radioman to call up the Germans, he waited. A minute later, the young specialist handed him the radio handset.

"Arko Three, this is Saber Six-Seven. Fire mission. How copy?" Childers said, speaking calmly into the radio.

The tension in the air around him remained high as the soldiers continued to hear their wounded friends call out for help. It was tearing them up not being able to rush out to help them, but they knew they had to wait until the enemy positions had been dealt with.

"Saber Six-Seven, this is Arko Three. Send fire mission over," responded a voice with a heavy German accent.

"One round HE. Grid SP 5765 7654. How copy?" Childers requested. He spoke clearly and slowly so their foreign partners would be able to understand him.

The German unit replied, reading him the grid coordinates again, making sure they had copied them right. A minute later the Germans let them know they had fired the shot. A couple of minutes went by before they heard the round sail over their heads and slam into the upper floor of a building roughly 100 meters to the right of where they wanted it to land.

"Arko Three, Saber Six-Seven. Adjust fire 100 meters to the left. Repeat last fire mission."

A couple of minutes came and went, then they heard the next round sail over their heads and slam into the upper floor of the building where the enemy sniper had been operating. The upper floor of the building blew apart, throwing bricks and pieces of wood in all directions.

"Arko Three, Saber Six-Seven. Good hit. Repeat last fire mission. Stand by for additional fire missions," Childers directed.

He turned to the remaining soldiers in the platoon around him. "When the next round hits, I want first squad to run out there and grab our wounded and bring them back. Third squad, you're to lay down suppressive fire and cover them. I need one of you guys to get on the radio and call for a medevac so we can get our wounded out of here," he said as he handed the radio receiver over to one of the sergeants.

When the next round hit the building, the entire structure blew apart, along with the two buildings next to it. In that instant, first squad darted forward to the wounded soldiers, grabbing them by the handle on the back of their body armor and dragging them back to safety. The soldiers of third squad unloaded on the façade of the buildings where the enemy had previously been. Even though the buildings had been heavily damaged from the artillery barrage, they were taking no chances of someone getting a shot off at their comrades.

With the last of their dead and wounded having been dragged back to safety, the medics in the group went to work on the injured. A low rumble started moving toward them down the road, and several of the soldiers looked up to see a couple of Stryker vehicles moving toward them. When the vehicles got closer, they stopped, and another platoon worth of American soldiers disembarked. A familiar face also appeared as he walked toward Sergeant Major Childers.

"I thought that was your voice and call sign I heard over the radio," Captain Jack Taylor said. He approached Childers, extending his hand. They briefly shook hands before Childers led him toward the wounded guys.

"I was on my way over here to check on Second Platoon when they were ambushed," Childers explained. "Lieutenant Drake was killed and so were three other soldiers. Unfortunately, five other soldiers were wounded and trapped out in the open, and the enemy was using them as sniper bait."

Captain Taylor shook his head in disgust as he listened to his mentor describe the scene.

"Thanks, Sergeant Major, for helping to get them back. I heard you call in some artillery. Do you think you nailed them?"

"I don't know, Captain. We should send your Strykers down the block and see if there are any additional holdouts once we get the wounded back to an aid station," Childers replied. Although he wanted payback, his first concern right now was making sure the wounded were taken care of.

The medics and a couple of the other soldiers loaded the wounded into one of the Strykers, which then turned around and headed back to the battalion aid station. Captain Taylor got on the radio and called back to battalion headquarters to see if he could get some armor support and then poked his head down the street where the enemy was located.

"Childers, I hate to see that Stryker vehicle down there burning," he said. "My company has already lost four Strykers since we entered St. Petersburg twenty-four hours ago—if we keep losing vehicles to enemy action, we'll be a light infantry unit on foot instead of a cavalry unit."

Childers just nodded. Things could definitely be going better.

Thirty minutes went by. Then they heard the unmistakable clatter of metal creaking and the cracking of tank tracks. The ground shook and vibrated as the noise got closer, and then they spotted the source of the sound. Looking down the road toward where the Allies' line was, Taylor and Childers saw two Finnish Leopard II tanks and four CV-9030 infantry fighting vehicles rumbling toward them. When they pulled up next to Taylor's group of six

Stryker vehicles, what appeared to be a Finnish officer hopped out of one of the vehicles and walked toward them.

"I'm Colonel Juho Heiskanen," the officer said, extending his hand. "I'm the Jaeger Brigade commander. I was told by your colonel that your unit needed some armor support." By his demeanor, he seemed very eager to go blow something up.

"I'm Captain Jack Taylor, the commander for Nemesis Troop, 4th Squadron Sabers. We've run into an enemy stronghold down the road there," he said as he pointed to where one of his vehicles was still burning in the road.

"I see. Can you point to me where the enemy positions are?" the Finnish officer asked as he pulled a small radio from his body armor. Taylor and Childers pointed to the locations where the enemy machine-gun positions had been located, along with the sniper nest.

The Finnish officer relayed the information in his own language, presumably to the tankers. Both of the vehicles lurched forward. Once they reached the turn in the street, they pivoted on their tracks, heading down the road the Americans had been ambushed on.

The turret on the first tank moved slightly, then recoiled as it fired.

Boom! Bam!

The gun turned slightly and fired again at the next target.

Boom! Bam!

Then the tank lurched forward slowly as it started to rumble down the street. The second tank also moved forward quickly, followed by the four infantry fighting vehicles, their turrets staggering from right to left as they provided cover for the tanks should any additional Russian units decide to show themselves.

"Holy hell, if those guys aren't cocky, Sergeant Major," Taylor said as a few of the other sergeants nodded and chuckled.

"We should get going, follow these guys in," Childers offered as he looked at Taylor.

Captain Taylor reluctantly said, "Yeah, I guess you're right." Then he turned to his men and shouted, "Mount up! Let's follow our allies forward!"

They all moved forward dutifully. When the first Finnish tank reached the end of the block, a massive explosion from underneath the road—possibly from the sewers—exploded skywards, lifting the 60-ton tank nearly fifteen meters into the air and flipping it over on its back. The explosion was so large, the shockwave pushed the other

Leopard tank sideways onto the sidewalk and shoved it into a café, collapsing part of the building onto it.

The shockwave from the blast knocked most of the soldiers who were not riding in the Stryker vehicles to the ground as the overpressure blew out many of their eardrums. Sergeant Major Childers found himself lying on the ground against the side of a blown-out Lada sedan. Looking up at the sky, through the haze, he saw debris, snow, dirt and parts of the road starting to fall back to the ground below. Childers rolled over to his side, then suddenly realized he needed to breathe. He struggled for air—his lungs burned. Finally, he was able to gasp and inhale.

It took him a moment to recover. As he did, he saw dozens of soldiers stumbling around him, also trying to collect their thoughts and figure out what in the world had just happened. Looking down the road where the Finnish soldiers had been, Childers saw an enormous hole at the center of the T-intersection, where the lead Finnish tank had just been a few minutes earlier.

One of the Finnish CV-9030 infantry fighting vehicles lurched forward toward the massive crater, driving as far away from the edge of it as it could while navigating around it to get at the enemy on the next block over. The 40mm Bofors autocannon fired away at some unseen enemy as the vehicle quickly advanced. The other CV-90s rushed forward behind the lead vehicle, adding their own firepower to the scene. Several of Captain Taylor's Stryker vehicles raced to catch up while twenty or so soldiers that were on foot continued to recover from the near-death experience of that massive bomb that had just taken out both Finnish tanks.

Once he had collected himself, Sergeant Major Childers attempted to rally the rest of the soldiers to move forward with him and try to keep up with the rest of the company. Sensing some wetness on his neck, Childers placed his hand near his right ear; as he moved his gloved hand away again, he spotted blood on his hand. Not a lot, but it was definitely coming from his ears.

"*Crap! My eardrums have probably been blown out,*" he thought angrily. He didn't have time to deal with that. At least that explained why he could barely hear the Finnish 40mm autocannons firing.

He indignantly trudged along, trying to keep up with the rest of Nemesis Troop. If his hearing didn't return shortly, he'd have no choice but to be medevacked out until he could hear properly. If he couldn't communicate on a radio or hear what was happening around him, he would be pretty useless in a battle scenario, and possibly a danger to himself and those around him.

When he came near the crater in the road, he saw the sewer system fully exposed, along with a lot of water and heating pipes. He was in awe, thinking of exactly how many explosives must have been placed in that sewer in order to create a crater this large.

Childers spotted a soldier yelling at him but couldn't hear anything that was being shouted. Then suddenly he found himself being tackled to ground. The vehicle he had been hiding next to just moments ago took some heavy-caliber rounds.

As Sergeant Major Childers looked up, he saw that the soldier that had tackled him was trying to say something, but he was having a hard time making it out. He shook his head and pointed to his ears. The soldier nodded and gave him a thumbs-up before guiding them to a position with better cover. His new friend said something to a few other soldiers, who nodded toward Childers; he must have been bringing them up to speed on his current condition.

****

A half an hour went by, and Childers's hearing was slowly starting to return to normal. He tried his best to shelter his ears by placing some hearing protection in them once he was sure they weren't still bleeding. He refrained from firing his own rifle and did his best to stay toward the rear of the fighting, focusing his efforts more on helping some of the wounded soldiers. When they had nearly a dozen wounded American and Finnish soldiers, Captain Taylor detailed off one of his Stryker vehicles to take the wounded back to the regiment aid station. He ordered Sergeant Major Childers to head back and get his ears checked out as well.

Nearly forty minutes later, Childers found himself comforting a lot of wounded soldiers at the aid station, doing his best to try and help calm them down and reassure them.

"Hang in there, soldier. You're going to be OK. You got yourself a ticket home," he said to one young man who'd taken a gunshot to the stomach. He stayed with him until one of the medics was able to give him some pain medication.

Childers moved to another soldier, a man who looked to be in his late twenties whose left leg was missing. The soldier still had the tourniquet tied on, since someone who had been more critically injured was being treated first. Childers looked at the nametape and saw that the man was a sergeant with the last name Brice. He walked up and grabbed the man's hand; he gripped back hard and looked at him with an intense expression of pain written across his face.

Unintentionally shouting because his hearing still hadn't fully recovered, Sergeant Major Childers yelled,

"Sergeant Brice, I want you to know how proud I am of you! You did the best you could. Now hang in there until the doctors can help you. You'll be back home with your friends and family soon enough!"

When he finished speaking, Childers saw a tear run down the man's face, though he couldn't entirely hear what the man said in response. Childers pointed to his ears, and the soldier nodded and mouthed, "Thank you."

A minute later, Lieutenant Colonel Schoolman walked into the aid station and quickly spotted his command sergeant major and waved to get Childers's attention. As he got closer, he pointed at his ears; Schoolman nodded and then signaled to one of the doctors. The two of them talked for a minute before the doctor waved for Childers to come with him. Once he sat down, the doctor examined his ears with a standard otoscope.

The doc dictated a note for him, which a nurse dutifully copied it down so it would be legible. "OK, so it looks like you did puncture your eardrums, but if we treat it properly, I don't think there will be permanent damage. I'm going to put some drops in your ears to help make sure it doesn't get infected. This might sting a little, but it's really important that you keep using these drops twice a day for the next two weeks. You're going to have to sit out for a week or two while your ears heal, but you should be able to rejoin the combat soon."

Childers breathed a big sigh of relief. For a little while, he'd thought he might be permanently deaf.

An army medic filled out some information about what had happened to him and what they had treated him for. The medic must have seen Childers's left eyebrow rise quizzically, because he suddenly explained, "This form makes sure you get your Purple Heart." Holding a hand up, he quickly added, "When you retire, you'll also want this noted in your medical jacket for the VA, so no complaints."

Lieutenant Colonel Schoolman patted Childers on the shoulder. "When I heard you'd been injured and taken to the aid station, I thought you might've been shot again. I'm glad to see it's only your hearing that suffered."

Shaking off his squadron commander's concern, Childers replied, "How's the rest of the unit doing?"

Schoolman's expression soured. "Rough," he answered. "We're taking a lot of casualties, but we've managed to push the Russians across the river. The regiment is going to hold operations at the edge of the river. We're not going to try and cross. It appears we've pushed a large portion of the Russian Army to either the Petrogradsky District or the southern half of the city. At this point, we're just going to keep them encircled and force them to surrender or run out of food and bullets."

Childers nodded at that assessment. "I like the sound of that, Sir. This city combat is brutal. We can't take much more of this, or we won't have much of a unit left when it's done."

"The hard fighting is over with for now, Sergeant Major. Why don't you stay here for a little while longer and keep consoling the wounded? I'll see you back at headquarters in a couple of hours, once you've had a little bit of time to recoup—and that's an order." He shook Childers's hand and then left to go tend to the rest of his squadron.

****

The fighting continued around the city as the Allies tightened the noose around the remaining enemy units in St. Petersburg. After the first thirty-six hours of block-by-block fighting, the V Corps commander had his forces keep the enemy encircled, but he refused to grind the rest of his fighting force into the ground in a house-to-house fight with the Russians. He wanted to keep as much of his combat power ready and available for the march on Moscow. The Russians, for their part, employed hundreds of snipers throughout the city and the surrounding suburbs, making sure the Allies knew they hadn't been defeated yet.

Chapter 16
Winter Wonderland

Near Vologda, Russia

The snow swirled around the column of vehicles, making visibility beyond half a kilometer difficult, if not impossible—not that there was much to see this deep into the Russian interior. After 40 Commando had secured the city of Arkhangelsk, the battalion pressed inland. Once they pushed beyond the beach and the port city of Severodvinsk, they met virtually no resistance. Now that they were ashore, the harsh Russian winter began in earnest, pelting them with subzero temperatures and wintery mixes of snow and ice.

"*How anyone can fight in this is beyond me,*" thought Sergeant Philip Jones as he lit yet another cigarette. Fortunately, the heater in the BvS 10 or Viking all-terrain tracked vehicles worked like a champ, pumping out hot air that kept the Marines inside nice and toasty.

40 Commando had been on the road now for six hours, and judging by where they were on the map, Sergeant Jones guessed they had another two hours of driving before they'd reach their first waypoint, the city of Vologda. Once there, they'd hold up for a couple of days to let their supply

lines catch up. The city would be turned into a logistical supply base as the Allies continued to advance ever closer to Moscow, their ultimate goal.

When they got to within forty kilometers of the city, the weather finally let up. The swirling snow stopped, and the sky started to clear. What the Royal Marines saw next caused them all to take a moment and admire. They were about to enter a forested area that looked like something out of a magazine cover or movie set, complete with a beautiful display of the eerie and colorful northern lights. The trees were iced over with a dusting of snow, providing an almost surreal look to them, alien to what they had been accustomed to seeing thus far. For a brief moment, they forgot there was a war going on.

After allowing everyone to take a short bio break and stretch their legs, the convoy started to move again. Two of the Vikings were in the lead, quickly followed by a pair of Challenger tanks and a pair of Ajax armored scout vehicles. Following the armored vehicles was a long column of Vikings, Ajax and Warrior vehicles intermixed with a few Challenger tanks and some air-defense vehicles in case some Russian jets decided to pay them a visit.

Twenty minutes went by as the convoy drove deeper into the woods, and they continued to follow the M-8

Highway. Sergeant Jones shifted uncomfortably in his seat, his right leg falling asleep from the lack of movement. They still had another ninety minutes before they were scheduled to take a short break to stretch their legs again. Just as he found a way to extend his right leg to try and stretch it in their cramped quarters, the tranquility of their journey was broken. A loud boom reverberated through the ground, the shockwave of the blast slapping their vehicle hard. They veered slightly to the right.

Looking out through the windshield, Sergeant Jones saw the lead Viking slam back into the ground in flames, emitting a heavy billowing smoke. Within seconds, another large explosion nearly knocked their vehicle over on its side and peppered the left half of the vehicle with shrapnel.

"Contact front! Everyone out!" he shouted to the squad of soldiers as they fought to get the rear compartment door opened.

One of the privates kept pounding on the door, but he couldn't get it to budge. "It's jammed! I can't get it open," he yelled, terror in his voice.

The other Marines now turned to look at Jones, who was momentarily perplexed by what the young man had just said. Then the solution dawned on him. "The turret—everyone, go out the turret!" he ordered.

The gunner, who luckily had not been sitting in the turret at the time of the explosion, opened the sealed hatch and climbed out. He grabbed his rifle and slid down the side of the armored vehicle, away from the shooting, and signaled for the others to join him. The other four Marines in the vehicle quickly climbed over the side of the vehicle and fell into the half-meter-deep snow, bullets cracking all around them as they sought cover.

Crump, crump, crump.

The sound of mortars landing nearby added further confusion to the scene.

Whoosh...Boom.

One of the Challenger tanks exploded from an unseen missile that struck it just as it had moved off the road to engage whatever enemy force was attacking them.

"Follow me, Marines!" shouted Jones. He led his small four-man team away from the vehicle further into the woods to the right of the attack. They needed to get away from the vehicle, which was now a sitting duck, and get a better picture of where the attackers were, so they could figure out what needed to be done.

The second Challenger tank that had been behind their vehicle also lurched to the right of the convoy. The tank fired a round that sailed right over their heads, impacting against what Jones had thought was a pile of logs heavily covered in snow. When the round hit, the entire area exploded and a nearby machine-gun bunker opened fire on them.

Jones hit the dirt, then yelled out to his Marines, "Return fire!"

He shuddered. The Challenger had just fired a shot that had, in all likelihood, saved their lives. Sergeant Jones watched as it gunned his engine and advanced toward the enemy position. Its main gun barked a second time, and the gun bunker blew apart, silencing the gun crew.

As he and his men advanced toward the enemy position, Jones heard lots of loud shouts around him. Other squads of Marines filtered into the woods further back in the column. One of the Ajax's 40mm cannons joined the fray, adding its own firepower.

Within a few minutes, though, the firing by both the Marines and the armored vehicles had stopped. Everyone took a moment to catch their breath and determine if they had killed all the attackers.

"If any of the Russians are still alive, they're either good at playing possum, or they've withdrawn further into the woods and disappeared," Sergeant Jones commented.

The Marines spent another thirty minutes checking the enemy lines, checking on the dead and making sure the wounded were tended to. The short ambush had cost them one Challenger tank and two Viking troop carriers. In exchange, they had destroyed a Russian BMP-3 vehicle and three antitank missile crews. A total of eighteen Russian fighters had been killed in the ambush, and three wounded Russians were taken as prisoner. With the attack over, the Marines piled back into their vehicles, shaking off the attack as best they could as they resumed their advance to Vologda.

Based on the results of the recent conflict, the Royal Marines switched around the formation of their convoy. A heavy scout element advanced several kilometers ahead of the main convoy, followed by two Ajax vehicles in the lead. Bringing up the tail were two Warriors, two Challenger tanks and two Viking armored personnel carriers.

No sooner had the unit traveled fifteen kilometers down the road than a series of IEDs detonated along the armored column on the highway. They must have been placed prior to the heavy snowfall, because there was nothing evident to give away the fact that they were there. The Russian spotters had allowed half a dozen vehicles to pass through their kill zone before they triggered the nine 152mm artillery rounds they had daisy-chained together.

The explosions tore through the convoy, severely damaging more than a dozen lightly armored Vikings and other armored personnel carriers. As the British soldiers attempted to recover from the shock of the IEDs, a separate group of Russians eighteen kilometers away began their part of the attack.

****

Chekshino, Russia

Standing inside the living room of the small home in Chekshino that his officers had commandeered, Colonel Yury Chirkin of the 74th Guard's Motor Rifle Brigade puffed away on his pipe, looking at the map on the table before him. What concerned him most was how rapidly the Allied forces had advanced inland, especially given that the Allies had had to traverse more than 1,400 kilometers of northern Russia in the dead of winter to reach Moscow. However, Yury had learned early on in his military career fighting in the Chechen War that one should never underestimate the resolve of one's enemy.

Letting out a puff of smoke, Colonel Chirkin looked up at Lieutenant Colonel Maslov, the commander of the 867th Separate Motor-Rifle Battalion and the lead element of his brigade. They were now the only real combat force standing between the Allies and Moscow. "Colonel Maslov, how confident are you that your units will be able to stop the British?" he inquired, giving the man one of his famous icy-eyed stares.

Maslov held his chin up and puffed his chest out like a proud peacock as he announced, "My men will hammer the British and send them scurrying back to Archangelsk."

Colonel Chirkin looked around the room at the other officers. "*This guy is just talking tough for their benefit,*" he realized. He didn't want smoke and mirrors, though; he needed an honest answer.

"I want everyone else besides Lieutenant Colonel Maslov to go take a break and stretch your legs outside for a minute," he ordered.

After everyone had filed out of the room, Colonel Chirkin turned his steely gaze back on Maslov. "So, how exactly will your men crush the British?" he asked.

With the other officers no longer present, Maslov's façade dropped. His face was somber. "Sir, we can't crush the British," he admitted. "There are too many of them heading down the M-8, and they are being quickly followed by a Canadian division and an American division. The best I can do is slow them down and bloody them up."

Colonel Chirken smiled since he had managed to get an honest answer and placed his hand on the younger man's shoulder. "Colonel, that is all we can hope to do. I don't expect you to hold the Allies with a single battalion of soldiers. I do need you to slow them up—bloody them along the way, sapping their strength as they trudge through the interior of mother Russia. We don't have much time, and I must be heading back to my own headquarters, so please walk me through your attack plan."

Lieutenant Colonel Maslov breathed an enormous sigh of relief and nodded. "I've placed several small platoon-sized ambush units along the M-8 to carry out a series of hit-and-run attacks. The weather over the next couple of days is going to work to our advantage because my ambush units have easily concealed multiple IEDs along the side of the road, near these points here," he said, pointing to a map. "The armored columns will be forced to stop and deal with the casualties from the explosives, and when they do, the real ambush will begin.

"These spots have been chosen because they are deep inside the forested areas of the M-8 and will leave the British little maneuver room for their vehicles. Along this second ambush point, we've stationed the battery of BM-27 Uragan rocket artillery trucks you've assigned to me. When the

British pass through this point, the rockets will blanket this entire three-kilometer swath of the highway with the 220mm high-explosive rockets.

"Once the battery has fired their volley, they'll relocate to Vologda, where they will reload and wait for orders. I anticipate that the British forces will push through the ambush and survive the artillery barrage. At that point, they will move to capture this very village within a half an hour to an hour, but then they'll run into a company of soldiers waiting for them in this forested area here," Maslov explained, pointing to two clusters of trees.

Colonel Chirkin looked at the positions, which would create a very effective crossfire, and at the composition of the troops. They were mostly equipped with antitank missiles and heavy machine guns. *"They'll do,"* he thought.

The battery of BM-27s was a godsend. Colonel Chirkin also had a battery of BM-21 Grad rocket trucks, but they were old and only fired the lighter 122mm rockets. This was unfortunately the only artillery he had assigned to his brigade until the higher-ups deemed his defensive effort worthy enough to properly reinforce and staff. For the life of him, he could not understand how those fools in Moscow didn't see the threat this Allied force presented.

Chirkin nodded his head in approval. "OK. This plan looks good. Execute it as best you can, and I'll hope to see you in Yaroslavl in a couple of weeks. I need to get going; my helicopter should be refueled by now."

Colonel Chirkin knew this might be the last time he spoke with his battalion commander. Once this attack started, Lieutenant Colonel Maslov would be very busy. Once the Allies reached Yaroslavl, the rest of Chirkin's brigade would make their final stand. Beyond their last line of defense lay Moscow, a mere 260 kilometers away. If road and weather conditions cooperated, the Allied forces could travel that distance in four hours.

****

M-8 Highway near Vologda, Russia

"Ripper Six, Ripper Six, this is Citadel Six. We've just been ambushed!" shouted the regiment commander, Brigadier Kyle Jenson. "We're being hit by enemy rocket artillery originating from sector G8. It's most likely coming from the village of Chekshino. We need your scout element to advance quickly and see if you can intercept the artillery unit. How copy?"

Lieutenant Colonel William Watkins looked at the map board he kept in his vehicle. Doing some quick math in his head, he saw that the location was roughly twenty kilometers from the current position of the main convoy, and maybe ten kilometers from his position. Grabbing the radio receiver tightly in his hand, he depressed the talk button. "Citadel Six, Ripper Six, that's a good copy. We're less than ten kilometers from that location. We'll move to engage them now. Out."

Watkins quickly turned to the vehicle commander and shouted, "Head to sector G8, Chekshino, at maximum speed. We're looking for an enemy rocket artillery unit. We also need to keep our eyes open for possible ambushes along the way."

He switched his radio frequency over to his little scout party of vehicles and relayed what was happening to the main column. When he was done, the vehicles started to move at a rapid clip, racing to the village in hopes of catching the enemy artillery unit still in the process of firing, and defenseless. The two Ajax vehicles led the way, quickly followed by the two Warriors, which had traded places with the two Challenger tanks. The two Viking armored personnel carriers pulled up the rear.

Watkins turned to Sergeant Jones. "Let's get the troop hatches open," he ordered. "Have two of your guys help look for smoke contrails and potential ambushes. We have no idea if we're racing into a trap or not."

When Sergeant Jones's Viking had been destroyed, Lieutenant Colonel Watkins had been kind enough to let his five-man squad pile into his command vehicle. He'd figured if he was going to be riding in the front of the armored column with the scouts, he might as well as take the Marines with him; he had the room and they needed a ride. Now he was glad he had—they might need their added firepower.

Looking at the map, Watkins spotted a potential enemy ambush point. He grabbed the radio again and called ahead to the lead vehicle. "Ripper One, we should be approaching the edge of this forested area in a couple of minutes. When we do, I want you to veer off the main road to the field on our right. Drive the rest of the way through this field and stay off the highway. There's a copse of trees near a truck park on the left-hand side of the highway, and I believe the enemy's hoping to ambush us once we cross that point. How copy?"

A short pause ensued, and then the radio crackled to life. "That's a good copy, Ripper Six. We're coming up to that point right now…we've left the main road and we're moving through the field. The snow is kind of deep over here, so be advised. We'll have to travel a lot slower."

Seconds later, Watkins's own vehicle veered off the main road, hitting a few hard bumps as they followed the rest of the vehicles into the open field that skirted the edge of the town.

"Contrails, Sir!" shouted one of the Marines who had been standing in one of the troop hatches.

The vehicle commander, who was also standing in his turret, also looked off in the distance. "Found the enemy artillery, or at least where they launched from, Sir," he announced. "I'd say we're probably two kilometers away. Heading that direction now," he added. The vehicle lurched a bit as it changed directions.

The eight vehicles in their little scouting party picked up speed again, tearing through the snow and this farm field as they raced toward the village. One of the Marines then shouted, "Missile! Ten o'clock!" as he pointed in the direction of the incoming threat.

The lead Ajax vehicle turned its turret in the direction of the missile and let loose a string of 40mm rounds. The missile operator must have either been killed or had to duck for cover, because the missile then veered off course and exploded harmlessly away from them.

Two more missiles jumped out of the copse of trees and flew right for Watkins's group of vehicles. Then they heard two loud explosions. Looking behind them, Watkins saw a splash of sparks hit the oblique-angled armor of one of the Challengers as the enemy tank round bounced harmlessly away. The second tank was struck near the rear half of the tank, and the engine exploded in spectacular fashion; the tank came to a creaking halt, billowing thick black smoke and flames. The Challenger that had survived the hit then moved its turret slightly and fired its own main gun.

Boom...Bang!

An enemy tank exploded. The turret was ripped cleanly from the chassis of the tank and rolled along the ground, flipping end over end. Then a giant fireball expanded into the sky. Seconds later, the Challenger fired a second round, slamming into the remaining enemy tank, exploding it as well.

BOOM!

The lead Ajax scout vehicle was hit, flipping end over end as it burst into flames, rolling several times until it came to a fiery stop upside down. A second loud explosion rang out as one of the remaining antitank guided missiles slammed into the trailing Viking armored personnel carrier, bursting it into a scorching cauldron of death for the Marines inside.

The turret on the Warrior opened fire on the cluster of trees, raking it with its 30mm Rarden cannon, shredding the trees and the enemy missile crews hidden within it. As he continued to take in the scene around him, Watkins grabbed the radio. "Keep going!" he shouted. "We need to catch that artillery unit!"

The remains of his armored vehicles surged forward into the snow-covered village, racing toward the remnants of the smoke contrails from the rocket artillery that been fired just prior to the shooting match they now found themselves in. Bullets were pinging off their armored skin as the vehicle commander swiveled his crew-served weapon, letting loose several bursts from the machine gun at the attackers.

"Sir, you should duck back down and let us return fire at the enemy!" shouted Sergeant Jones from the troop hatch next to the colonel.

Watkins nodded, knowing the sergeant was right. The last thing they needed to have happen was for him as the battalion commander to be shot. He ducked back into the vehicle, allowing one of the young Marines to take his place and fire back at the enemy. Their vehicle continued to race through the village, and the volume of enemy fire dissipated to the point that their vehicle was no longer being shot at. Minutes later, they rounded a corner and found themselves facing a BMP-3 that was in the process of setting up a roadblock on the highway.

The vehicle gunner immediately let loose several bursts from their 30mm cannon as the driver veered hard to the right, barely missing a string of cannon rounds that was fired at them by the BMP. The Warrior's 30mm rounds tore into the BMP, causing a small explosion when one of the rounds hit the fuel tank. Seconds later, the vehicle blew up, engulfing it and anyone inside it in flames. With the immediate threat neutralized, the driver gunned it as they zoomed past the burning wreck in hot pursuit of the enemy rocket trucks.

Once they rounded a slight bend in the road, the gunner shouted, "I found the first BM-27 rocket launcher!" He depressed the fire button, sending a three-second burst of cannon fire into the rear of the vehicle. The rocket artillery truck blew up and the flaming vehicle careened off the road into a tree. With the first vehicle destroyed, the gunner had an excellent view at the subsequent vehicle and let loose another short burst of 30mm cannon fire. That vehicle also burst into flames as it came to a halt in the center of the road, obscuring their view of the rest of the vehicles.

The Marine continued to gun the engine of their vehicle as he swerved around the burning wreck, revving the engine as they tried to chase down the remaining rocket trucks. The BM-27s were particularly nasty rocket artillery trucks; the 8x8 wheeled vehicles carried a rotating rack of sixteen rocket tubes that fired the 220mm rockets. The rockets could fire either high-explosive rounds or disperse antitank or antipersonnel mines up to thirty-five kilometers away.

"We have to catch those BM-27s!" shouted Lieutenant Colonel Watkins.

As the driver continued to gun the engine, the vehicle slid a bit as the tracks fought to grab traction on the snow-packed road. When the Warrior passed the second burning wreck, they caught sight of the third vehicle, roughly a kilometer in front of them. The gunner fired off another burst from their main gun, sending another barrage of cannon fire slamming into the rear of the vehicle. It, too, burst into flames.

"Keep going! We need to chase down that last vehicle!" yelled the vehicle commander to the driver.

While they continued their hot pursuit, Watkins received a radio update from the other members of their convoy. Behind them, the remaining Ajax scout vehicle, the lone Viking troop carrier and the Challenger tank were still engaging the remnants of the Russian soldiers left in the village. The Marines had disembarked from their armored chariots and were fighting in the streets. Bullets flew back and forth between the two factions of soldiers, riddling many of the houses with ammunition.

Moments later, as the Warrior zoomed past the third burning wreck, giving them a clear shot at the remaining BM-27, they hit a patch of black ice on the road that caused their vehicle to spin out of control and slam into a snowbank. It took a moment for the driver and the vehicle's occupants to collect themselves and recover from the near-death experience. In the meantime, the final vehicle they'd been chasing had gotten away. With no chance of catching up to it at this point, Lieutenant Colonel Watkins announced, "Good shooting, lads. Now let's head back to the village and support the rest of our mates in finishing these guys off."

Shortly after they made it back to the village of Vologda, the remaining Russian soldiers were in the process of surrendering, waving white handkerchiefs in their gloved hands and probably hoping they wouldn't be shot out of spite. When Watkins's vehicle pulled up to the largest concentration of enemy soldiers, they dropped the rear hatch of the vehicle to let the five Royal Marines exit and help secure the prisoners.

Surveying the scene around them, Watkins saw several burning vehicles, and half a dozen homes in the small village that were currently on fire. Now that the shooting had stopped, a lot of civilians began to exit their homes, many of them crying in agony at the sight of what had just happened to their tightknit community. A couple of fathers and mothers who were cradling young children in their arms rushed toward the British soldiers, pleading with them for medical help for their little ones who had been injured in the fighting.

This was the part of war Watkins hated the most— the innocent civilians who had no say in the fighting and became ensnared when the bullets start to fly between the two warring factions. A shoot-out in or near a city often resulted in innocent civilians being caught in the crossfire. He wiped a tear from his eye before anyone could see it.

The Marines motioned for the injured children and other civilians to gather near the back of one of the vehicles, while the only two medics in the group did their best to work on them. Fortunately, one of the Russian prisoners was also a medic and offered his services to help the injured civilians.

Sergeant Jones looked at Watkins, pleading with his eyes but not saying a word. Watkins nodded his approval, and Jones walked over to the Russians, pulling his knife from its cover and cutting the zip tie restraints on the man's hands. Then Jones guided him toward one of the injured kids. The Russian soldier spoke softly and soothingly to the child as he did his best to bandage his wound until he could receive proper medical care.

Looking at the damage, Watkins couldn't help but think to himself, "*This all could've been prevented.*" If they had had air support or helicopters to rely upon, none of these civilians would have been harmed. "*We need to slow down this offensive until we can get proper support,*" he reflected.

Once the Allies had secured the Russian port of Severodvinsk and captured Archangelsk, the British commander in charge of the Allied force had insisted upon a rapid advance of their expeditionary force toward Moscow, only 1,200 kilometers away. In nonhostile conditions and with fair weather, one could travel the M-8 from Severodvinsk to Moscow in roughly eighteen hours, so clearly the thought of rapidly capturing Moscow had been an alluring proposition that would have been hard to resist.

The challenge the Allies now faced was one of logistics. As winter continued to settle in, the waters of the

White Sea would completely freeze over, preventing them from bringing in more supplies from Britain or America. This part of Russia also suffered from a serious lack of infrastructure. There were no major supply hubs or petrol dumps the Allies could capture, and little in the way of airfields they could take over to establish their own proper airfields. The airport they had successfully seized, Talagi Airport outside of Archangelsk, was in a terrible state of disrepair, and now it was several hundred kilometers away from the rapidly changing front lines.

The next airport they hoped to seize would be in Vologda. Once they captured the city and airport there, the British anticipated creating a forward base, moving in a couple of squadrons of F-35s and F/A-18s from the carriers that were still operating in the Barents Sea, at least until additional aircraft could be flown in from Iceland and Norway.

Until then, the Royal Marines leading the Allied advance would have to make do with what they had, which unfortunately was not very much.

Chapter 17

Second Battle of Kursk

Kharkiv, Ukraine

The weather had finally turned brutally cold. Along with the lower temperatures came a stormfront that threatened to bring a few dozen centimeters of snow with it. Lieutenant Colonel Grant Johnson pulled his parka a bit tighter as he fought against a slight shiver. Lately, the temperatures during the day hovered just below freezing and dropped to -30 degrees Fahrenheit at night. *"To think the Germans thought they could brave this weather with little to no cold weather gear..."* he marveled, wondering what madness had possessed the Nazis during World War II. At least the 1/8 Cav "Mustangs" weren't *that* crazy.

Johnson walked back into his operations tent and saw his captains were assembled and ready. He'd wanted to hold one final meeting with his own commanders and leave them with some words of inspiration—this would be the last time he held a command briefing until after the battle was over. The company commanders were eager to get this next battle started; everyone could see the end of the war was within sight, and they just wanted to get it over with.

Lieutenant Colonel Johnson walked to the front of the tent and stood next to the map board hanging from some five-fifty cord. He cleared his throat to get their attention. "Listen up, everyone. Tomorrow morning, at approximately 0600 hours, we launch Operation Grim Reaper. This may in fact be the largest armored warfare battle of our generation. I'm sure the historians or higher echelons will tell us in time how many tanks and soldiers were involved, but what I can tell you is this—this is the battle to end the war."

He paused for dramatic effect. "Right now, I want you to ponder on this—seventy-five years ago, the Nazis launched Operation Citadel on this very spot. The Germans attacked the Soviet Army at Kursk with 780,000 soldiers and 2,900 tanks. The Soviets had 1.9 million soldiers and 5,100 tanks. These two armies fought for control of the same ground we are going to be fighting on tomorrow. We, however, are not going to meet the same fate as the Germans."

Seeing that he had their full attention, he continued, "We are facing the remains of the Russian 4th Guard's Tank Army, the 8th and 20th Guard's Army, and the Indian 2nd and 9th Corps. Intelligence says this combined force is roughly 1,260,000 soldiers when the Russian reserve forces are added in. We have the entirety of the US Seventh Army, which consists of 510,000 soldiers, and roughly 320,000 German, French, British and other Allied soldiers. I'm telling you all this because I want you to know that when we go into battle tomorrow, we are going into battle with the largest, best-equipped army ever to invade Russia. Our orders are simple: we are going to move to contact, find and fix the enemy, and destroy them."

Several of the men smiled and nodded, but he also saw a look of concern in their eyes. This was going to be a tough battle, one that would most likely result in a lot of casualties. A lot of their men were going to be killed, and they too might not survive the battle.

Johnson motioned toward Captain Jason Diss as he pointed at a spot on the map. "Captain Diss's Mustangs are going to lead the battalion. They'll advance to Waypoint Alpha at Oktyabr'ski, just across the Ukrainian-Russian border. They'll skirt to the east of Belgorod into the open fields there and advance to contact until they reach Waypoint Bravo at Mazikino. This will place our battalion roughly 140 kilometers southeast of Kursk. We'll hold up at Mazikino for the evening to refuel, rearm, and prepare for the next assault 130 kilometers northeast to Gorshechnoye, which will be Waypoint Charlie. Depending on how much resistance we encounter, we may continue on to our primary objective, the city of Voronezh 90 kilometers away."

He shifted as he pointed to a new area on the map. "A large part of the Allied forces is going to converge on the city of Kursk itself. Our focus will be on expanding the front and punching further holes in it as we line up for the thunder run to Moscow."

He paused for a second to look at his notepad. "We'll have the 3rd Battalion, 16th Field Artillery Regiment, providing us with constant 155mm artillery support, should we need it. They also have one battery of HIMARS if we encounter any large enemy formations. In addition to the artillery support, we're also going to have the 1st Battalion, 227th Aviation Regiment's Apache helicopters, so let's make sure we leave them something to destroy," he said, which elicited a few chuckles from the tankers.

"I also want you guys to keep an eye out for enemy artillery fire," he continued. "This isn't like invading Iraq; the Russians and Indians have a crap ton of artillery, as we've already learned, and they like to use it in spades. There'll be a lot of counter-battery fire happening, but don't let that detract from calling for artillery support. Our gun bunnies are good, and they can handle it." A few more men laughed.

Johnson saw the eager looks on the faces of the men before him. They were ready. Seeing that he had no further information or words of wisdom to pass down, he dismissed the group.

That evening, Captain Jason Diss briefed his platoon leaders and first sergeant on the battle plan for the coming days. They went over the map and the detailed plans for how each platoon would move and what they would do as they met resistance. Seeing that their company would be maneuvering through some tight areas, they settled on a diamond formation, with their FIST element situated in the center. That would give them the best possible position from which to spot and provide artillery and mortar fire. With the battle looming just ten hours away, the men tried to catch some rest in their vehicles with the heaters on as Mother Nature persisted in providing them with a fresh coat of snow.

****

At 0530, Captain Diss ordered the company vehicles started. With synchronized precision, they started the vehicles at nearly the same time to help distort the sound so that any potential enemy scouts nearby would have a hard time determining how many engines they had heard start up.

"You ready to get moving, Captain?" inquired his gunner, Staff Sergeant Winters. He was obviously eager to get started.

"Hell yeah," Diss answered, speaking over the internal crew network. "Get the systems up and running while I run through the company checks, OK?" He then switched to the company net, calling out to his platoons.

The crew knew what to do and went to work getting them ready for battle. This was their second major campaign of the war, so they had a better idea of what to expect in the coming battle. Still, it was daunting to think about the size and scope of what they were about to embark upon. The thought that this might truly be the battle that ended the war weighed heavy on everyone's minds.

"*We've survived up to this point,*" thought Captain Diss. "*Now we just have to make through this next big battle, and hopefully, we can all go home.*"

Making sure he got his driver's attention, Diss shouted, "Make sure you keep the heater going. It's freaking cold outside." His driver just grunted over the headset.

Within ten minutes, his company's platoons had fallen into the diamond formation he'd briefed them on, and they continued their march toward the Russian border. When they got within five kilometers of the border, Captain Diss spotted a series of defensive positions the infantry soldiers had been manning. Many of the soldiers gave them a short wave or other gesture of support as they passed through their lines. The First Cavalry division was the lead element for the US Seventh Army, and if anyone was going to see a lot of action this first day of the offensive, it was going to be them.

From his perch in the commander's seat, Captain Diss did his best to scan the horizon for the enemy. A gust of wind caught him off guard, seemingly seeping down to his bones. He shivered and pulled his scarf a bit tighter.

There was still a light dusting of snow falling, although it was nothing so heavy as to obscure his view. When they reached the official demarcation line that separated Ukraine from Russia and crossed it, Diss felt a sense of relief and joy—relief that they had not been attacked yet, and joy that they had officially invaded the Motherland. They were one step closer to victory.

In short order, they came across their first natural barrier and the first waypoint, the Siverskyi Donets River. With their attack helicopters zooming ahead of them to scout the area, they continued to move southeast of Belgorod into the open farmland that lay beyond the city.

As Captain Diss looked off in the distance, a thunderous roar of antiaircraft fire erupted from within the city. The heavy-caliber cannons spewed hundreds of high-velocity rounds in the direction of the Apache helicopters that were screening for his tanks.

Following a string of cannon shells and tracer rounds, Captain Diss saw the Apaches break hard to avoid the fusillade being fired at them. *"I wish we could go in there and take those enemy guns out,"* he thought. He crossed his fingers, hoping that the Stryker battalion that was slated to assault the city would be able to silence them soon enough.

Despite the frigid temperature, Captain Diss took the opportunity to open the hatch so he could get a better view of what was going on around them. Climbing up to his perch behind the M2 .50 machine gun, he watched and listened to the antiaircraft guns firing away a few kilometers to his left. Jets were roaring somewhere overhead. It was odd seeing the green tracers crisscrossing the morning sky, intermixed with the light dusting of snow. While he was taking everything in, an urgent call came in over the radio.

"Black Six, this is Avenger Six. Be aware, we have spotted what appears to be a Russian regiment-sized element, four kilometers to your front. We are moving to engage."

Dropping back into the turret and closing the hatch, Diss jumped on the company net. "All Mustang elements,

Avenger element is engaging enemy tanks, regiment-sized element, four kilometers to our front. Prepare for contact," he announced.

Minutes later, their vehicle crested a small hill that bordered a large copse of trees to their right. As it did, he spotted one of the Apaches as it pulled a tight turn and banked its nose down, letting loose a string of antimaterial rockets on the tree line. Half a dozen explosions erupted within the trees, followed by several secondary explosions.

Captain Diss began to search the tree line for threats but was interrupted when explosions erupted all around them. His tank was jostled from side to side as chunks of shrapnel banged and clinked off their armor. "Look for targets! They must be close!" he shouted over the thunder of artillery explosions.

"Tank, 1,700 meters, three o'clock!" shouted his gunner excitedly.

Captain Diss moved his commander's independent thermal viewer and spotted the tank lurking under a white camouflage net a few meters inside the tree line. "*How did Winters spot that thing?*" he thought in amazement.

"Gunner, sabot tank!" he yelled. His mind was now moving on autopilot.

"Identified!" exclaimed Winters, eager to fire.

Specialist Mann acknowledged.

"Fire!" screamed Diss. It was starting to get hard to hear anything over the racket and chaos happening outside.

Crump, crump, crump!

Enemy artillery rounds continued to follow them as they advanced closer to the enemy positions.

"On the way!" Winters shouted. He squeezed the hell out of the firing button, as if the harder he squeezed it, the faster the tank round would fly.

Boom!

The cannon fired, recoiling back inside the turret as the vehicle continued to race forward. The loader quickly rammed another round home and the gunner began scanning for the next target to shoot.

Returning his gaze to the front, Captain Diss caught sight of the silhouette of more enemy armor. Dozens of enemy vehicles had emerged from behind a bend in the nearby hill and from the forest to their right. The enemy vehicles appeared to be lining up for a charge.

Diss switched back to the company net. "Mustangs, we have a battalion-sized element 3,100 meters to our two o'clock. Company, change formation to a line position and advance to contact," he ordered. He wanted to bring all of his platoons forward, so they could effectively mass their fire.

Captain Diss contacted his FIST team next. "Black Eight, this is Black Six. I need a fire mission. Get us some arty on that copse of trees and that mass of enemy vehicles charging us!" he yelled.

Then Diss turned to the battalion net and sent a quick message to his commander, letting him know what they were seeing.

"Captain, those tanks are charging toward us now!" yelled Winters. "They've crossed 2,800 meters and moving fast." The turret turned slightly to the right as Winters started tracking their next target.

"Enemy missiles, three o'clock!" Diss shouted. He'd caught a glimpse of them zipping out of the tree line heading toward his tanks.

Before the missiles could get close to them, the forested area erupted into a ball of fire as dozens upon dozens of artillery rounds landed all throughout the area. Secondary explosions added further carnage to the already messy scene. Many of the antitank missiles still streamed toward his vehicles, scoring a couple of hits against his tanks and Bradleys.

Bam!

A large blast detonated near their tank, sending a concussion through the air. Then a voice came over the company net. "Blue Two is hit."

Diss had a sickening feeling in his stomach when he heard that announcement. He knew four of his troopers were most likely dead, judging by the intensity of the explosion.

Turning his attention back to the immediate threat to his front, Captain Diss saw the enemy formation begin to advance toward them. However, another volley of 155mm artillery rounds hammered the enemy positions, and a couple of tanks suffered direct hits, exploding in spectacular fireballs. Some of the enemy BMPs and BTRs were also taken out of commission.

Spotting over a dozen T-90s heading toward them, Diss yelled, "Gunner, sabot tank! 1,800 meters, eleven o'clock."

"Identified!" exclaimed Sergeant Winters. He had already found an enemy tank and placed the red targeting dot on it.

Specialist Mann tapped the loader's door lever with his knee as he methodically kept the gun loaded as fast as Winters was firing it.

"Fire!" screamed Diss. It felt like they could be blown up at any given second, and he was not about to waste time.

"On the way!" screamed Winters. The crew collectively fell back on their training to keep their tempo going of identifying targets, firing, reloading, and repeating it all over again.

He depressed the firing button. *Boom!* The cannon fired, recoiling back inside the turret. The more rounds they fired, the more the cabin filled with the sulfuric fumes of battle.

Continuing to press their attack, the Mustangs were now less than a thousand meters from the Russians as the enemy pushed their own assault.

Clang, clang, clang.

Three 30mm autocannon rounds from the BMPs bounced harmlessly off the turret of their tank. While the enemy rounds couldn't penetrate their armor, it was still nerve-racking to realize their tank was taking multiple hits from the enemy.

While the Mustangs continued to charge the enemy formation, several of their brigade's Apache helicopters let loose a string of hellfire missiles at the remaining enemy vehicles, destroying most of them. The helicopters then flew directly over their tanks, using their 30mm chain gun on the remaining armored vehicles as Captain Diss's tanks continued to press home their attack.

Seeing a swarm of infantry disembarking the BTRs and BMPs, Captain Diss yelled to his gunner, "Keep firing the main gun!"

He needed to get up in the commander's hatch and deal with the infantry. Swarms of infantry carrying RPGs were just as dangerous as an enemy tank if left unattended. Flipping the hatch open, Diss climbed up to his perch, unlocked the M2 .50 machine gun from its locking mount and trained the heavy weapon on a cluster of infantry soldiers maybe 800 meters to his front.

Depressing the butterfly button, he fired streams of .50-caliber rounds at the enemy soldiers, shredding many of them in seconds. One of the enemy soldiers had managed to set up an antitank missile with the help of one of his comrades—Diss sighted in on them and fired a short burst of fire in their direction. Afterward, all he saw was a red splattering of flesh and blood erupting, and then the missile they were trying to set up also exploded, adding its own shrapnel to the mix.

While his tank continued to charge forward, the main gun boomed nearly every eight seconds and they continued to nail enemy vehicles. As they got closer to the enemy soldiers, more bullets flew in his direction, many of them hitting the tank's armor but not far away from hitting him in his perch. Captain Diss knew he needed to get back inside the tank, but he couldn't resist the adrenaline high he was experiencing as his tank charged forward and he stood in the commander's hatch, firing away on the infantry with his .50-caliber machine gun. He felt like a god swatting away all that stood before him. However, when the gun ran out of ammo, he loaded another box in its place and then dropped down into the turret again, closing the hatch behind him.

Five more minutes went by as they finished off the remaining enemy vehicles and passed through the Russian lines, using their machine guns to finish off whatever infantry they came across. Captain Diss was under strict orders to press home their attack and keep going. Follow-on units moving behind them would clean up any stragglers or fortified positions they felt they had to bypass.

Once they traversed through the enemy lines, Diss called in a crew report to find out how bad their losses were. By the time his platoons had reported in, he discovered they had one tank destroyed to enemy artillery, two tanks disabled from the enemy artillery, three tanks destroyed by antitank missiles, and two tanks destroyed by the most recent enemy action with another tank disabled. His company had effectively lost fifty percent of their tanks, making them combat ineffective.

"Dear God—and we've only reached waypoint Bravo," he thought. Captain Diss shook his head in disappointment and sorrow at the loss of his men. He radioed in their losses to battalion, who ordered Charlie Company forward to take their place. For the time being, Delta Company was out of the fight until their disabled vehicles could get repaired and they could return to the battle.

Chapter 18
Humpty Dumpty

Moscow, Russia

President Petrov looked at the latest battle report from the front lines. He was not happy with what he was reading. *"How could things be unraveling so quickly?"* he thought. A year ago, the Americans and Europeans had been in their final death throes, and now it felt like the walls of the war were rapidly closing in on him. He wasn't sure Russia could still win without using nuclear weapons.

Sighing, Petrov depressed the intercom button on his desk. "Send them in," he said to his secretary, whose desk was directly outside his office.

In walked General Boris Egorkin, the head of the Russian Army, Alexei Semenov, the Minister of Defense, General Kuznetsov, the head of the Russian Air Force, and Admiral Anatoly Petrukhin. He'd wanted this meeting to be small and secretive for the time being. When the outer door closed, Petrov signaled to his Head of Security that he didn't want anyone to disturb them. The agent nodded and made sure the outer guards knew not to let anyone in, no matter who they were.

Blowing air out of the side of his mouth in frustration, Petrov began, "Generals, it's only the five of us in this room, so I need honest answers. I need to know how long we have left."

The other men in the room almost visibly deflated in their chairs. Perhaps they had believed their own lies, or the half-truths their subordinates had told them, but in that moment, they realized Petrov knew the jig was up. Defeat was all but assured at this point. It was just a matter of how and when, not if anymore.

General Kuznetsov was the first to speak. "Mr. President, I am not confident our air forces are going to be able to prevent the Allies from eventually dominating the skies. More than seventy percent of our fighter and ground-attack planes have been destroyed. We still have most of our strategic bombers, but I'm not sure how long that will last. We have to rotate their bases every couple of days to prevent the Allies from locating and destroying them."

He paused for a second, as if he was debating whether or not he should say what he wanted to say next. "Over the last couple of months, the Americans have used a new weapon to counter the advantage our S-400 had given us over the Allies up to this point. When they launch an attack on our integrated air-defense pockets, they send in multiple aircraft that launch a series of AGM-158 joint air-to-surface standoff missiles. These missiles have been specifically equipped with sophisticated jamming and electronic spoofing equipment. On radar, the aircraft appears to be an enemy fighter, which our SAMs rightly move to engage. While this is happening, the Americans release a series of small-diameter precision-guided glide bombs at our radar and missiles sites. These are small but effective little bombs they've come up with."

The general paused for a second and sighed. "This new attack strategy is proving to be incredibly effective, Mr. President. The Allies have managed to destroy more of our SAM sites in the last three months than they had in the previous twelve months. These are not sustainable losses. It's already having a hugely negative effect on our ability to protect our ground forces, as I'm sure General Egorkin can attest. We are working on figuring out how to counter this, but short of us completely disabling the world's entire satellite network, which I might add would obliterate our own satellite capability, there just isn't too much we can do."

Minister Semenov added, "At this rate, Mr. President, the Allies will be able to largely fly anywhere in Russia with impunity within a couple of months."

Clearing his throat, General Egorkin interjected, "When the Allies have full air supremacy, they'll quickly isolate and destroy our remaining combat formations, making it virtually impossible for me to amass any forces or launch any major counterattacks."

Admiral Petrukhin added, "Aside from our nuclear-capable submarines, we are essentially finished as a service. Our last major attack was at Bear Island in the Barents Sea. Those ships have since been sunk by the Allies; I have nothing left." He looked down in shame, then continued, "Despite our losses, I would argue that the operation was a major success in that we successfully sank three Allied aircraft carriers, along with a dozen other warships."

"And yet, the Allies still managed to land multiple divisions' worth of soldiers in Severodvinsk, establishing a large beachhead and enemy base in Archangelsk. Even now, those forces they landed are threatening Moscow," countered Petrov.

"Yes, Mr. President. But the sinking of those three carriers severely limited the number of aircraft that can support those ground forces. The loss of those Allied destroyers also limited the Allies' ability to launch cruise missiles at us," explained the admiral.

Petrov shook his head in frustration as he sat there listening to the raw truth his generals were telling him. His stomach churned a bit, and he felt a bit of bile build up in the back of his throat. Looking at his generals, he asked, "What are your suggestions? What can be done to turn the war around, or is there nothing more we can do?"

Minister Semenov hesitantly answered, "Unless you want the war to go nuclear, Mr. President, there isn't much we can do to turn things around at this point. We could make heavy use of tactical nuclear weapons and probably wipe out the majority of the Allied combat forces in or near our borders, but the Americans would surely respond in kind. We saw what they did to North Korea and China. President Gates didn't hesitate for a second in hitting China with a nuclear bomb once they confirmed the Chinese had provided the North Koreans with the ICBMs that hit their West Coast."

"We know how Gates would respond, but he's dead," said Petrov. "How would his successor, President Foss, respond? Does he have that same resolve? Would he really have the guts to use nuclear weapons? Especially if it were just soldiers being killed and not American cities being destroyed?" He searched their faces for an answer.

"Mr. President, I implore you not to consider using nuclear weapons," Semenov urged. "It will only lead to the complete destruction of our country. The Americans have invested too much into this war to make peace simply because we dropped some nuclear bombs on their military. They will level our remaining military bases and devastate our cities. We still have the support of our Indian allies and the Chinese. If we have to, Mr. President, we can move the government beyond the Urals and continue to wage an insurgency against the Allies."

Petrov shook his head at that suggestion. He wouldn't abandon Moscow, not while they still had the strength to fight. The Nazis had thought they could lay siege to Moscow, but they had lost that battle. "No. We won't relocate the government," he asserted firmly. "If we do that, we send a signal to the people and the military that we are abandoning them. They will lose heart in our cause and no longer fight. We'll stay here and make our stand. I'll speak with Minister Kozlov to press the Americans for a ceasefire. We will try to negotiate an end to the war, with acceptable terms that will allow everyone to save as much face as possible."

Some of the military leaders in the room might not have liked Petrov's decision, but they would never have contradicted him out loud. They had their marching orders. With the essential military strategy having been decided, the military leaders left to make sure the military could defend the capital. If that meant conscripting more people, handing them a rifle and a couple magazines of ammunition and dropping them off to guard a trench, then so be it. They would remind the Americans how deadly a street fight would be if they persisted in attacking Moscow.

****

Strogino District, Moscow

Oleg Zolotov poured himself another glass of Russo-Baltique vodka, a truly remarkable drink. As he filled the tumblers, he caught a short glance of his prized possessions playing with some toys in the living room, near the fireplace. His granddaughter, Eva, had just turned three, and his grandson, Ivan, was being cradled in his wife Katja's arms with his daughter looking on.

"I am truly blessed to have such a beautiful family," he thought.

He placed the tumbler on the end table between the two oversized chairs, where he could still look at the fireplace and watch the children and his wife and daughter from his private study. His son-in-law, Dmitry Chayko, took the tumbler, examining the liquid within before taking a sip. "This must be the finest vodka I've ever tasted, Oleg," he commented.

Oleg nodded, and he also took a sip of the extremely expensive liquid, relishing its rich taste before swallowing it. Seeing the apprehensive look on his son-in-law's face, he leaned to the right on his chair's leather arm, bringing his face closer to him. "What's going on, Dmitry? You seem preoccupied with something."

Shaking his head slightly, Dmitry looked like he wanted to say something, but he held his tongue. Sensing his hesitation, Oleg got up and walked over to the door of his study. He muttered something to his wife and then closed the study off. Before he returned to his chair, he walked around to his desk and pulled a small device from one of the drawers. With the click of a button, the shades on the windows closed and a slight electronic hum buzzed lightly.

Four years earlier, Oleg Zolotov had been promoted to major general and taken over as head of the FSO. This meant he was the man directly responsible for President Petrov's security apparatus, and he reported directly to Lieutenant General Grigory Sobolev. He was privy to a lot of closely guarded secrets within Petrov's office. Oleg and

Grigory had been old KGB buddies from the Cold War days and had personal relationships with President Petrov that ran deep. It had been Grigory and Oleg who'd advised Petrov to liquidate Ivan Vasilek, his predecessor, for his colossal miscalculation of the American's resolve to wage total war against the Eastern Alliance. His exposure as the mastermind behind the British prime minister's coup was the final straw.

As the atmosphere in the room changed, Dmitry looked at his father-in-law quizzically but dared not speak a word until Oleg explained himself.

"Don't be alarmed, Dmitry. When I took my new position as the head of the FSO in 2014, I had my home office turned into a secured quiet room, immune to electronic eavesdropping and surveillance. Anything we talk about in here right now won't leave this room. It will stay between the two of us. So, Dmitry, what is troubling you so much that you can't enjoy a rare day off with your family?" he prompted.

At the outset of the war, Dmitry Chayko had been promoted to the rank of colonel and given command of the Kremlin Regiment, which was responsible for protecting the Kremlin and other critical government buildings, in addition to the honor guard and ceremonial duties they traditionally performed during peacetime. When the war had started, the regiment had transformed itself quickly into a combat arms unit that would rival any other regiment in the army. When Dmitry's father, Lieutenant General Chayko, had defeated the Allied forces in Ukraine at the outset of the war, President Petrov had placed Dmitry in charge of the Kremlin Regiment, with the explicit orders to turn it into his own personal protective army as a check against the FSO and FSB, if it ever came to that.

Dmitry took his new responsibility seriously, especially after the Americans had nearly killed Petrov in the first couple days of the war with the attack on the National Defense Building. Dmitry had cycled his twelve companies through intense close-quarter combat training, urban warfare training and small-unit tactics, training with one of the Spetsnaz schools outside Moscow. His regiment was also equipped with the best weapons, body armor, and other equipment he felt they might need. On numerous occasions, President Petrov had commended him personally on how professional and fearsome his regiment now looked. Dmitry valued that praise, and he made sure his soldiers knew the President himself was proud of each of them. The esprit de corps within his regiment was high, and so was their loyalty to him personally.

Dmitry briefly eyed Oleg, as if he were not fully sure if he could truly trust him. He looked as though he were carrying a tremendous burden on his shoulders. He sighed, gulped down the contents of his tumbler, and whispered, "I received some disturbing news from my father yesterday. As you know, his army group has fallen back to just outside Kursk. They're preparing for another major battle with the Allies, but he isn't confident they are going to be able to stop them," he said in a hushed tone.

Oleg smiled. "I've been in enough meetings to know our army can no longer stop the Allies from invading our country, Dmitry," he said, almost relieved. "I'm also not hopeful about Minister Kozlov securing a peace deal that wouldn't humiliate our nation in the process. It's not a matter of if we'll be defeated so much as when at this point."

Dmitry shook his head. "No, it's more than that, Oleg," he insisted. "My father told me he had been issued an 'eyes only' order directly from Egorkin and the President to ready a series of tactical nuclear weapons to be used when the Americans attack."

Oleg felt like he had just been punched in the gut. He'd heard Minister Semenov implore the President not to use such weapons against the Allies. The man's logic and arguments were clear; the use of such weapons wouldn't save Russia. It wouldn't end the war on more favorable terms if anything, it would result in an overwhelming retaliatory strike by the Americans, and that counterstrike would necessitate yet another round of counterstrikes, each larger than the previous one until Russia and the rest of the world were obliterated.

"Dmitry, your father can't allow that to happen!" Oleg insisted. "If he uses nuclear weapons on the Americans, they will destroy us all. The President must have been mistaken in issuing those orders." A bit of fear was evident in his voice.

"You know my father, Oleg. He's a soldier, not a politician. He will do as he's told. If Petrov orders him to use tactical nuclear weapons, he'll use them in a manner that will best serve his army. I'm sure he'll only use enough of these weapons to accomplish his stated goal without going overboard," Dmitry countered. He seemed almost bewildered by Oleg's response.

Oleg sat there for a moment, absorbing what his son-in-law had just told him. He knew Dmitry's father to be one of the most competent military leaders in Russia. It was only through his father's tactical skill that the Allies had not already marched on Moscow. To hear that he was willing to use nuclear weapons if so ordered shocked him.

"I need another drink," Oleg announced. He stood and walked over to the wet bar in his office. Rather than pouring himself another glass, he grabbed the bottle and walked over to Dmitry, pouring him another tumbler and refilling his own, then placing the bottle between them.

Oleg sighed deeply. *"How much do I tell him?"* he wondered. He pondered what Dmitry would say when he learned the truth, and whether or not he would be turned in or arrested and shot.

"Dmitry, what do you believe will happen to Russia if your father follows Petrov's order and uses nuclear weapons against the Americans?" Oleg finally asked, taking a calculated risk.

Dmitry shifted uncomfortably in his seat.

Oleg understood the struggle his son-in-law must be experiencing. Even if he wanted to be honest, it would go against everything he had been taught as an officer. Softly, he asserted, "Whatever you say to me now will stay between us. I won't turn you in or have you arrested. You are my son-in-law, father to my grandchildren. This is a frank and honest conversation you and I need to have, and we need to have it without fear that either of us will report the other for his opinions. Is that understood?" A brief awkward moment passed as he waited to see how Dmitry would respond.

Finally, his son-in-law nodded. "If my father uses nuclear weapons, I'm confident the Americans will hit us back, and probably much harder than we hit them," he admitted. "That attack will cause an even larger response, and then the Americans will probably obliterate the rest of our country. I believe a nuclear attack on the Americans now will lead to the complete destruction of our country." He looked like heavy stones had just been lifted off his shoulders.

Oleg smiled. "That is right, Son. I was in the room when Minister Semenov pleaded with Petrov not to use these weapons. The Chief of the Air Force also made the case for us not to use them as well. That was two days ago. What has changed that calculus?" He paused for a second. "We can't win this war using nuclear weapons, nor can we win by keeping the war conventional. Right now, the best we can hope for Russia is an end to this war that doesn't result in the complete destruction of our country."

"And how do we achieve that? If the President has made his mind up, then there is no changing it. We are soldiers, we must accept our fate," blurted out Dmitry angrily.

"No, we don't have to accept that fate," Oleg insisted. "If the President is going down a path that will not only destroy our country but the rest of the world, then we as officers, sworn to the protection of our country, must stop him." He paused, calculating whether or not to say his next sentence. "We must remove him from power," he finally said.

Dmitry's jaw dropped, and his facial expression registered a mix of shock and horror. He struggled to say something in response, but all that came out was a garbled muttering.

Leaning forward in his chair, Oleg looked Dmitry squarely in the eyes. "I'm about to tell you something—something so secret, only a few senior officers know. With what you just told me about your father, I don't see any other course of action. We have to move now before it's too late. Do you want to save your country? Will you save your children from the holocaust that is about to be unleashed on the world?"

Dmitry inched away from Oleg for a second, apparently attempting to wrap his mind around what had just been said. A moment later, he leaned back forward and looked at Oleg. "What do you have in mind?" he asked cautiously.

Oleg smiled as he looked at his son-in-law with new respect. "You've heard of Alexei Kasyanov?"

"Yes, I've heard of him. No one is allowed to listen to him on the radio or the internet, but from the small pieces I've heard, he seems to have his facts straight on what's going on in the war. The state media is continually putting out counterinformation to what he is saying, but most of my officers don't believe the state news anymore. I'm finding more and more of my men tuning in to what he has to say."

Oleg nodded. "A handful of us have been in contact with him," he admitted. "We've been trying to figure out when would be the most opportune moment to remove Petrov, but with what your father just told you, it seems we don't have much time to act. When did your father say he might be ordered to use the weapons?"

Dmitry seemed to go into a sort of trance as he processed all of the information that was being shared. Oleg snapped his fingers to break him from his sea of swirling thoughts. "Hey, I know you may have a lot of questions about Alexei, but right now we don't have a lot of time. I need to know what your father told you."

Dmitry mumbled something, then answered, "My father said it would be at least two more days before the weapons were moved to his operational control. He wasn't sure how long it would take the other weapons be transferred to their regional commander's authority, but he was confident the Air Force was also being given access to nuclear weapons. He estimated that they could potentially be used in roughly 48 to 72 hours."

Oleg's mind raced. *We have even less time than I imagined,* he thought in horror.

"What is the status of your regiment? How loyal are your officers and soldiers to you?" he asked.

"You mean would they listen to me if I ordered them to secure the Kremlin and the various government buildings?" Dmitry asked, smiling coyly. Then his facial expression shifted, as though he weren't confident in his answer.

"If I order the President to be seized and placed under arrest, would your officers attempt to interfere with that arrest, or would they listen to you?" asked Oleg more pointedly.

"I'm not certain. There's something I need to tell you—when I was promoted to take command of the regiment, Petrov gave me and my executive officer a secret set of orders. Basically, we were told that our regiment might one day need to assume your office's duties should Petrov ever catch a whiff of disloyalty from the FSO. Some of my officers may come to Petrov's aid should you move against him, even if I ordered them to stand down. I could end up in a situation where I have some of my companies turning on each other to protect the President. How loyal are your FSO officers, and what would you do about Grigory and the rest of the FSB?" Dmitry countered.

"Remember when I said a handful of senior officers had been in contact with Alexei?" Oleg said with a crooked smile. "Grigory is one of those officers. He'll ensure the FSB doesn't interfere with our seizing of Petrov. Our main concern was how you and your regiment would respond. We had hoped we wouldn't need to use the Spetsnaz to go against you, but if you are on board, then the seizing of the Kremlin and Moscow would go significantly more smoothly. We could bring a quick end to this bloody war before it turns nuclear."

Dmitry shook his head in shock. Oleg understood the reaction—Grigory and the president had known each other for more than thirty years.

Dmitry held his hand up. "Why is Grigory involved in this coup? Surely he must be getting something out of all of this to betray Petrov."

Oleg nodded and leaned forward as he answered. "I understand your concern, Dmitry, and it is warranted. When the President is deposed, Grigory is going to take his place as interim president for a two-year period until a new election can be held. These are the terms the Allies have secretly negotiated with him in the event that he successfully deposes Petrov."

"Then what is Alexei getting out of this, if he is not going to become the new president of Russia? I thought that was the West's plan all along," Dmitry insisted.

"Alexei will become the president eventually. Grigory has cut a deal that will shield him and many others from criminal prosecution and other war crimes by the international community as long he doesn't run for president when his two-year provisional position is over with. He will work closely with the Allies and Alexei to ensure the country is ready to return to democratic rule."

He paused for a second. Sensing some hesitation by his son-in-law, he knew he needed to provide some context. "Dmitry, it has to be done this way. There's no one else that will be able to carry the respect needed to get the military to go along, and furthermore, we need to be sure the country doesn't break out in a civil war. Grigory knows he can never become a permanent president. He knows, as I do, that the only way to live out a long life and enjoy the rest of our time on earth for us and our people is to cut a deal, one that we can all live with. This is the deal that has been brokered by the West, and it's been agreed upon by Alexei and Grigory."

"What about you? My father and me? What would happen to all of us?" asked Dmitry.

"Your father will be offered to take over as the Minister of Defense, and I'll take over as the head of the FSB, at least until the transitional government ends. Once that happens, I'm not sure what will happen to us, other than I know we won't be prosecuted for war crimes or brought before any sort of international tribunal. This is a big deal, especially for your father. His army in Ukraine has not exactly been kind to the people there, and under Petrov's orders, they've been destroying the country's infrastructure, leaving millions of people without water, electricity, and heat in the dead of winter. This has not gone over well with the West. As to yourself, I suspect you will probably be promoted and will be around for many more years to come for your patriotic duty in supporting the coup," Oleg explained.

Oleg could hear the faint sound of laughter in the other room. "Think of your daughter and son, Dmitry. I know you believe as I do that they deserve a chance to grow up and live a long, full life. I know that there are risks, huge risks—but this is the only way that there is a legitimate chance for their future."

After a moment of contemplation, Dmitry answered, "OK. I'm in. You're right, we have to do something to save the country before it's too late. My father was pretty sure the authorization of nuclear weapons would be given within the next three days, and we can't allow that to happen. What do you need me to do?"

For the next couple of hours, they talked in detail about what they would do and when it would have to take place. The timeline for when they had to move was short, and they had a lot of things to get moving.

****

Moscow, Russia
Senate Palace

Vladimir woke up, startled by a vivid dream he'd had. In his dream, he saw himself being lined up against a wall with some of his key leaders and shot by his own Spetsnaz forces. The fateful trigger was pulled by his longtime friend and the new head of the FSB, Grigory Sobolev. Shaking off the bad dream, he leaned over and kissed his wife softly on the cheek. She gently stirred, smiling at him before snuggling deeper into her pillow. It was still dark out, but he couldn't sleep, not after a dream like that.

He glanced at the alarm clock. It was 0420 hours. *"Might as well as get up and do some exercises,"* he thought. It was going to be a big day.

As he swung his legs out of the bed, he looked around the bedroom, admiring the detail of how his wife had decorated the space. A frightening thought came into his mind. *"Will this room still be here a week from now?"*

He tried to shake away the idea as a holdover from his bad dream. Petrov proceeded to the bathroom and got ready to use the gym down the hall. During his workout, he kept replaying his last conversation with Grigory. His friend had urged him one last time to reconsider the use of nuclear weapons. He'd brushed off the warning and explained that they would only target the Allies' military units that had entered Russia.

"We'd be using nuclear weapons on our own soil— surely the West wouldn't view that as an attack on their own sovereign lands," he reasoned to himself again. He turned up the speed on the treadmill. There was no room in his mind for changing directions at this point—his army would destroy the Allied armies in Russia with these weapons and

then sue for peace. He would rebuild from the ashes and then try again in a couple of decades.

Still, he could not shake the dream, or his last conversation with Grigory. He knew it was preposterous to think that Grigory would depose him, but if there was ever a time he would do it, today would be the day. This morning, he was supposed to hold a special meeting with his senior military leaders to issue the release of nuclear weapons. Tonight, the Allied armies standing against Russia would be consumed in a nuclear fire that would hopefully end the war and return the world, or at least Russia, to peace.

"*I need to speak with Colonel Dmitry Chayko immediately*," he thought. His Kremlin Guard commander had turned the regiment into a highly trained killing machine, and if Grigory and his Spetsnaz were going to depose him today, they'd need to get through Chayko's men first. If that happened, Petrov wouldn't be able to get additional army units from the local garrison to come to their rescue. Chayko's men would only need to hold the fortress grounds for a handful of hours until help arrived.

"*Of course, I could just be over-analyzing a nightmare*," he thought, conflicted.

****

At 0530 hours, after a hot shower and breakfast, President Petrov was handed the phone, which he eagerly took. "Colonel Chayko," he began, "I want you to put your regiment on alert for a possible coup. You are to order your entire regiment to alert status, move the bulk of your forces to the fortress and prepare it to repel a possible attack. Is that understood?"

A slight pause took place on the other end. "Yes, Mr. President, at once," answered Colonel Dmitry Chayko. "I shall report to your office within the hour. Shall I alert your security detail that this is happening?"

Petrov thought about that. Oleg probably should be notified; he didn't want to alarm the FSO guards. If there was a coup, he'd need their help in repelling the attack as well. "Yes. Coordinate with Major General Zolotov, and report to me right away," he said and then hung up the phone.

Feeling better now that he had put his fears at ease, Petrov headed to his office to begin packing a few personal belongings he wanted to bring with him to the underground bunker. After he ordered the release of nuclear weapons, he would order the government to move to their various secured facilities while they hoped and prayed the limited use of the nukes wouldn't lead to an overwhelming retaliation by the Americans.

After finishing up his preparations, Petrov glanced at his watch again. It was 0750 hours, and the final meeting he'd hold in the Senate Palace was quickly approaching. At 0900 hours, his meeting with his senior military leaders would set into motion a series of orders and events that would either end the war by tomorrow or spiral it quickly out of control. It was a gamble, but if he hoped to stay in power and for Russia to prevail, he had to take it.

****

Kremlin Fortress

The air was cold, and a light dusting of snow blanketed the city as a column of eight T-90 battle tanks, twenty-six BTR-3s and thirty-two BTR armored personnel carriers made their way through the streets of Moscow. The morning rush hour was light since the city was still under a petrol restriction, but the sight of so many armored vehicles and tanks moving in the direction of Red Square certainly caught the eyes of many people, both on the road and on the sidewalks.

Colonel Dmitry Chayko had arrived at the Kremlin grounds at 0630 hours, appearing very much ready to repel an enemy force or coup should his men have to. He'd brought nearly all the armored vehicles and tanks assigned to his unit for this operation. Upon arriving at the Kremlin, he hopped out of his vehicle and approached his nightshift commander, a lieutenant colonel, and informed him of the increase in alert status.

He then proceeded to issue orders for his various companies to move the armored vehicles to encircle the Kremlin fortress in a defensive circle, ready to defend the grounds if so ordered. He had his soldiers expand the perimeter around the grounds and placed heavy machine guns and snipers in the various guard towers surrounding the walled compound. Next, he placed soldiers at every entrance to each building and made sure he had multiple quick reaction force groups ready to move to any potential breaches in their perimeter. They ran through this deployment of forces just as they had in their training scenarios; everything was running like clockwork.

Once his troops had been deployed, he met with several of his key lieutenant colonels and majors, who knew about the special instructions from Petrov but were clearly nervous about what it all meant. Several of them looked at him apprehensively. Dmitry knew he needed to allay their concerns.

"The President called me very early this morning. Apparently, he had a premonition or dream that he somehow might be deposed by some rogue army generals. Accordingly, he wanted me to have the regiment ready, in case his dream did in fact become reality. We're going to treat this like any other drill, and make our President feel safe and secure. As you know, my father-in-law is the head of the FSO. If there were more to this, then he would have told me so himself. So, please, let's use this as an opportunity to drill our men to be prepared for anything. I want everyone to go along with our initial plan we had for the day. The code word for the day will be 'morning glory.' When you hear that, initiate our prediscussed plans. Understood?" he asked.

A chorus of "Yes, Sir" echoed back from his officers.

All but one of them had been read on to the real plan. They'd all agreed that if the President's orders to release nuclear weapons were allowed to happen, their country, families, and everything they held dear would soon be destroyed. They had stood by and supported their President in the war against the Allies, but this next step was too much for them. If they didn't take a stand now, there wouldn't be a country left to serve or protect.

With the morning briefing done, his officers went about getting the fortress ready to repel an attack and tightened security around a variety of sensitive government buildings across the city.

****

Senate Palace

It was nearly the end of January, and the full might of the Russian winter was on display in Moscow. The temperature had dropped significantly, and a winter storm was threatening to blanket the city in heavy snow that was sure to add to the already-terrible traffic of a major metropolitan city. When Oleg Zolotov's vehicle stopped at the Borovitskaya Tower entry control point, he immediately noticed the increased security his son-in-law had warned him about. Instead of the eight soldiers that stood guard with a BTR parked at an angle that would allow it to close access to the Kremlin grounds, there was a BMP-3 blocking the road and a T-90 main battle tank, along with nearly a full platoon of soldiers.

The guard walked up to Oleg's vehicle. "Papers!" he demanded.

Oleg passed his official papers over, along with his driver's. The guard looked at the documents briefly, then snapped to attention and rendered a crisp salute before returning them. He twirled his hand in the air briefly to let the man driving the BMP know to move back so Oleg's vehicle could pass. Seconds later, Oleg's vehicle drove through the checkpoint and continued toward the Senate Palace, the personal residence of President Petrov and the seat of power in Moscow.

As the vehicle drove briefly past the Cathedral of the Archangel, they came to the Ivanovskaya Square, where he saw another four tanks and eight additional BMP-3s. It looked like Dmitry had moved a large portion of his regiment into the walls.

"*Good, he'll have plenty of soldiers here in case there's trouble*," thought Oleg.

His driver pulled up to a parking spot that was reserved for him. Getting out of the vehicle, he saw the first signs that the anticipated snowstorm was finally arriving. He set out at once for the Senate Palace, confident in the plan and what he had to do. When he reached the first checkpoint inside the building, he saw a number of his key guards present—men he had personally picked to work this specific shift. The outside of the building might be protected by Dmitry's men, but the inside was all his.

Making his way to the upper floor, where the President's office was situated, Oleg walked past several of his senior guards. They quietly cleared the floor, as well as the way to the bunker deep underneath the building. They needed to dispose of Petrov quietly, and thus contain any potential immediate fallout from his removal from office. When Oleg gave the order, his bodyguards, who protected the other senior members of the government, would also move into action, gathering them all in the basement bunker. Once everyone was present, his men would effectively remove them from office.

Oleg made his way to the small monitoring office near the President's residence. As usual, several of his men were looking at the various computer monitors, scanning them for anything out of the ordinary. Of the five men manning this room, four of them were already on board with the coup; the fifth man would either go along with them, or he'd be dealt with quickly.

Turning to look at the senior man on duty, Oleg asked, "Are all the parties present for the meeting yet?"

Boris nodded. "The senior military men have just started their meeting with the President. The other agents guarding the cabinet members have all reported in. They're ready to move when you give them the order."

Oleg nodded. He noticed the perplexed look on the face of the one man who hadn't been read in on what would be happening next, and decided it was time to find out where he stood. "Aman, the President is about to order the release of nuclear weapons so that tactical nukes can be fired upon the Allied forces currently inside Russia. When he does that, the Americans will surely retaliate with nuclear weapons of their own, and if they do, Petrov has ordered the military to respond with additional nuclear weapons aimed at the Allied countries."

Aman's eyes grew wide, and then a look of fear spread across his face.

Placing his hand on Aman's shoulder, Oleg asserted, "We can't allow the President to destroy Russia and the world. A plan has been put in place to make sure that would never happen, and now it needs to be implemented. Are you with us in ensuring Russia survives?" he asked. Of course, Boris had cleverly moved his right hand to his silenced pistol, in case Aman didn't respond to his liking, or anyone else chose to back out at the last second.

Aman looked a bit like an animal that had been backed into a corner. He gulped. "When you put it that way, General, there's only one choice to be made. We must protect Russia and prevent the world from being destroyed," he answered.

Oleg smiled and patted the man on the back. Then he took Aman's weapon from him and handed it to Boris. "Good choice. We'll keep your gun for the moment, until we know for certain that you are fully on our side. In the meantime, do as you're told by Boris, and we'll all live to grow old with our families."

Turning to face Boris, Oleg stood up straight and tall. "Initiate Morning Glory," he ordered. "Have everyone moved to the various bunkers around the city. Seize their phones and electronic devices at once. We need to make sure they're not able to transmit anything until it's time."

Boris immediately sent a coded text message to his heads of security and the bodyguards to round up their charges. The move to depose President Vladimir Petrov was underway.

Ten minutes later, Oleg was standing outside the briefing room, where Petrov was speaking with his senior military leaders. He waited until he heard the president give the orders to release nuclear authority to his generals, and then he sent a text message to his son-in-law.

A few minutes passed tensely, then he heard the sound of automatic gunfire and an explosion outside. That was his cue to rush in.

Bursting into the briefing room, Oleg shouted, "We have to move you to the secured bunker now, Mr. President!"

The bodyguards in the room quickly ushered the generals out into the hallway and down a set of stairs that led to the bunker. As they walked briskly, more gunfire went off, and then some soldiers yelled loudly.

"What is going on?!" demanded Petrov.

"There are reports of gunfire near Red Square, Mr. President," Oleg replied calmly. "I heard from one of my sniper teams on the roof that they spotted a column of vehicles heading to the Kremlin fortress from the Sokolniki District." They moved swiftly, ever closer to the bunker.

"Damn that Grigory! I knew my dream was a warning." Petrov cursed angrily under his breath as they made their way to the bottom floor of the building.

Once in the basement, Oleg's men led the President and the senior military members into the command bunker, which was already up and running, teeming with officers and NCOs updating the Allied positions on the various maps. The men in the room seemed surprised to see the President and the senior military leadership suddenly show up.

"Get me General Sobolev now!" demanded the President as he walked up to the operations officer in charge of the command center. Several of the other generals made their way to various phone banks to begin making their own calls.

"Sir, the phone lines are dead!" replied one of the young officers.

Petrov fumed with anger. He smacked his fist on one of the desktops. "Can you get through to Colonel Chayko with your radio?" he asked Oleg.

Oleg nodded. Had it not been for a series of upgrades to the FSO's radio systems, their radios never would have worked down there in the bunker. After a couple of minutes, one of his guards was able to track down Colonel Chayko and handed Petrov a receiver.

"This is Colonel Chayko, Sir," he answered. Through the radio, they all heard another short burst of gunfire in the background.

"Colonel, what's the situation? What is happening?" demanded the President angrily. The other military men looked on, attentively listening for the reply.

"Sir, it would appear General Sobolev's men are attempting a coup. I have the fortress on lockdown, and my forces are engaging his men outside the perimeter walls. We're experiencing a lot of signal jamming right now, so I'm not able to place a call to any other outside units. I've sent runners to those bases, but it will be some time until we're able to get some additional help. I recommend you stay in the bunker for the time being, until my men can resolve the situation," Chayko suggested.

"Keep us apprised of what's going on, Colonel," Petrov said.

He handed the radio back to Oleg. "You go find out what the situation is, and get us some additional help," he ordered.

Then the President turned to several of the other soldiers in the room, directing them to work with Oleg's men in securing the bunker, making sure no one else came inside.

Once Oleg left the bunker, he ordered his guards, "Make sure the door stays locked, and don't let anyone out." These men knew exactly what that meant. With the bunker effectively cut off from the outside world, Oleg and Grigory could assume control of the government and then liquidate the men who would have destroyed not just Russia but the entire world.

******

Lubyanka Square

Federal Security Service of the Russian Federation

It was 0750 hours as Grigory met with Colonel Gennady Troshev, Commander of the 45th Guard's Independent Spetsnaz Brigade. Colonel Troshev had just returned from the front lines when Grigory sent for him with a simple message: "It's time."

Grigory knew that his friend would have one of his most trusted battalions ready. Gennady shared Grigory's vision; he too did not want to see his country destroyed in a nuclear fireball. He'd fought too many years and lost too many friends since the fall of the Soviet Union to lose what remained of his country.

"Are you sure Oleg's son-in-law is going to be able to pull this off? I don't want to have to fight through his regiment if I don't have to," Gennady said as he looked at the city map of Moscow. He already had his men in their vehicles, ready to roll as soon as they were given the order.

It hadn't been an overnight progression that had brought Grigory Sobolev to be in this position. Ten years prior, the thought that he would be standing in that spot doing what he was about to do would've been completely out of the question. Grigory was fiercely loyal to Russia, to a fault.

Lieutenant General Grigory Sobolev had joined the KGB in 1975 and had worked in a variety of locations across much of Europe and North America. In the 1980s, he'd worked as a case officer in America, recruiting sources that would provide him with valuable information the KGB often used against the Americans. His main job was to oversee a small cadre of high-end escorts in the D.C. area. The working girls would secretly bug their clients' houses or have them come to hotel rooms his technicians had previously bugged. During the course of his escorts' interludes with their clients, many of whom were either politicians, defense contractors or military members, they would gather intelligence from these men, who would invariably confide in their mistresses and divulge some of their deepest secrets. This information would be used against them later on to manipulate or coerce them into giving up more secrets or face the possibility of being publicly exposed.

Grigory had risen to the rank of major when the Soviet Union collapsed and was considered a rising star in the KGB. His ability to develop an intricate honeypot trap in D.C., and then later in New York, had earned him many awards. When the Soviet Union had fallen apart, he had been ordered to return to Moscow. Many of the former KGB men were simply laid off when the great collapse happened, and Grigory thought that might've become his fate, but when he arrived, he was pleasantly surprised to see that not only was he being kept on, he was promoted and given a new assignment.

He was placed in charge of a counterterrorism directorate and given the mandate of rooting out those who sought to further break Russia apart. He took a leading role in creating a number of specialized Spetsnaz units to deal with the threat of terrorism and counterinsurgency operations, mainly focusing on the provinces of Dagestan and Chechnya. Throughout the 1990s and into the early 2000s, Grigory had built a name for himself as the go-to person when there was a terrorist group that needed to be dealt with. In the late 2000s and early 2010s, Grigory was promoted to major general and put in charge of FSB's European operations. He'd led many of the FSB's efforts in countering NATO's expansion into Eastern Europe as well the EU's effort to bring Eastern Europe into the Euro.

Throughout the many years Grigory had served the FSB, he'd constantly made sure his predecessor, Ivan Vasilek, and President Petrov knew he could be trusted. Like them, he was old-school KGB, and he wanted to see Russia return to its former glory. All three of their paths had crossed on many occasions while they'd served in the KGB, but unlike Ivan and Oleg, he had never served directly with

Petrov. When the war with NATO had broken out, Grigory had been named Ivan's deputy, and he was read on to Operation Red Storm for the first time. While the plan looked solid on paper, Grigory knew the Americans far better than Vasilek or Petrov did. He'd spent nearly a decade in America and traveled there on many other occasions, and he knew the Americans wouldn't be dictated to by Russia or China. He also knew the new American president, Gates, wasn't a person to be trifled with. He was a hothead, and when he became focused on something, he was like a pit bull that wouldn't let go.

When the tide of war started to turn against Russia, Grigory knew it was only a matter of time before things ended for the Motherland. He also knew Petrov wouldn't allow Russia to be defeated. He would use whatever weapons were necessary to win. When Vasilek's plan to depose the British prime minister fell apart and was exposed, Grigory knew this was his moment to seize control of the FSB and try to bring the war to an end in a way that didn't involve the destruction of the nation he'd spent his entire life serving.

First, he needed to get rid of Vasilek. His utter failure in the UK, along with his faulty assessment of the Americans and their willingness to wage war, gave him the opportunity he needed. With Vasilek out of the way, he could then work to establish a separate peace with the Americans that would save Russia, assuming, of course, that he was able to depose Petrov himself. After months of hunting down Alexei Kasyanov, he was finally able to secure a private meeting with the man. A secret pact was formed to bring an end to the war. Now it was time for him to put into place the means to do just that. He loved his country even more than the man who led it.

With the snow falling outside his window, Grigory shook off his memories. He looked at his friend Gennady, who he'd known for fifteen years. When he'd taken over command of the FSB's antiterrorism branch, he'd leveraged Gennady to help him build an elite antiterrorism unit within the FSB. As Grigory had risen in rank, he'd brought Gennady along with him.

Grigory nodded. "I spoke with Oleg ten minutes ago," he said. "Dmitry is with us and has the Kremlin fortress already on lockdown. No one will be able to get in or out of there once the plan goes into effect."

"I'm more concerned with what happens if one of the generals is able to make a call to one of the military barracks," Gennady countered. "If they're able to call for help, it could be a real problem for us."

"We'll cross that bridge when we get to it," Grigory answered. He stood and looked out the window. The snow was starting to fall more steadily now, and the BTR and BMP parked just outside his building were being covered in snow.

An hour went by, and then Grigory's phone chirped. "Begin Operation Morning Glory," the text message read. Grigory smiled. His time to seize power had finally come.

He looked at Gennady. "It's time," he announced. "Get your troops moving and let's secure the capital."

Walking outside Lubyanka, Grigory heard the sound of gunfire, right on cue. He walked over to the BTR that would take them to the Kremlin fortress and climbed in, closing the hatch. Through the thick outer shell of the vehicle, he heard more gunfire, and then a couple of explosions went off.

"*All part of the plan*," he had to remind himself. They had to make the President and the generals believe the Kremlin was under attack by the FSB. It was the only way to get them all into the bunker. By the time they realized what was happening, it would be too late.

Ten minutes later, his BTR and a couple of other Spetsnaz vehicles arrived at the checkpoint leading into the Kremlin fortress. The soldiers manning the roadblock

407

saluted smartly, letting them pass. Driving up to the main entrance of the Senate Palace, Grigory got out of the vehicle and was pleasantly surprised to see that Colonel Chayko had assembled a line of soldiers standing at parade rest, leading into the building. The soldiers snapped to attention, presenting arms as he exited the BTR and made his way to the entrance. Major General Oleg Zolotov and Colonel Dmitry Chayko were also standing there waiting for him at the entrance to the building.

After rendering a salute, General Zolotov extended his hand. "It's good to see you, Mr. President. Everything is in order," he said.

Grigory liked the sound of that. "*Mr. President*," he thought with a smile.

"I assume you have everyone locked up in the bunker?" he verified.

"Yes, Sir. I also have the rest of the cabinet members being rounded up and moved to the other bunkers as well. I should have confirmation in the next five to ten minutes that they have all been successfully secured. Once we have them in place, do you want to have them liquidated before or after you announce that you've taken control of the government?" Oleg inquired.

"I want all of them brought here to meet with me," Grigory asserted. "I'd like to address them as a group and explain why we've done what we've done. Anyone who is not willing to accept the truth and work toward a new Russia, I will gladly have you liquidate. As to Petrov and his central leadership in the bunker, I want you to bring them outside the building and have them shot. Line them up against the wall of the Senate Palace, video the execution and give it to me. We'll figure out how to use that video to our benefit to solidify our power. Once I've assumed control of the government and the armed forces, I have to make contact with the Americans and our friend Alexei. For that, I will be relying on you, old friend."

The two men talked for a couple of minutes while they made their way into the building. Oleg had the men in the bunkers disarmed and brought to the courtyard. Oleg and Grigory watched from the gazebo as the senior generals of the armed forces, along with the Minister of Defense and the President, were marched outside the building. It was amazing to see how these ruthless men of power, the very men who had ordered the deaths of so many tens of thousands of people, begged for their lives.

Grigory walked up to the former leaders of Russia, approaching Vladimir Petrov fearlessly. "You had a chance to lead Russia into the 21st century as a real world power," he said with disdain in his voice. "You squandered that opportunity on a war we had no chance of winning, and for what? To bring back an empire that will never rise again? Your time is over, Mr. President. We won't let you destroy our country and rain nuclear death upon us or the rest of the world."

In response, Petrov spat in his face. Grigory shook his head in disgust and walked back to the gazebo, pulling a handkerchief from his pocket and wiping away the saliva on his face. He nodded toward Colonel Troshev, who barked a series of orders to his men.

They held their weapons at the ready, waiting for the command to fire. Troshev looked at Grigory for the go-ahead, and he gave a slight nod. Then Troshev yelled, "Fire!"

His Spetsnaz soldiers unloaded on the former leaders of Russia. Each of them was riddled with bullets, collapsing into a heap on the ground. Colonel Troshev personally walked up to each of the bodies, firing a single shot to the head to make sure they were truly dead.

With the formalities of assuming control of Russia now complete, Grigory walked back into the building and proceeded to walk up to the former president's office, where he would make his call to the CIA contact that would put him through to the American president.

****

Senate Palace

Two Hours Later

Colonel Chayko's regiment secured the remaining members of Petrov's cabinet and gathered the remaining members of the government for an emergency meeting at the State Duma Building at 5 p.m. that evening. With the city effectively on lockdown, it would be hard for any Petrov loyalists to escape. General Sobolev had also placed several calls to some of the senior military leaders who had not been rounded up yet and told them they needed to report to the Kremlin immediately. While some of them balked at being ordered to meet with him, a few of them might have suspected they knew why and breathed a sigh of relief—no one more so than the general in charge of Russia's strategic rocket forces.

With the wheels of change in motion, Grigory Sobolev was ready to talk with the Allies and begin the process of ending the war. An aide had arranged for a 3 p.m. call to take place with President Foss—however, the one caveat to the call was that Alexei Kasyanov had to be present. Alexei was considered by the Allies to be a key part of this peace deal, and despite the Americans agreeing to Sobolev taking Petrov's place, the future of Russia would be Alexei Kasyanov and his Free Russia party.

Walking into what had previously been Petrov's personal office, Grigory saw Alexei there, along with several of his trusted aides, Colonel Chayko, and General Zolotov. "The call is connected, Mr. President. We're just waiting for the American president to join," explained one of the colonels.

Grigory nodded. He was glad to see that Alexei had been able to safely make it to the Kremlin grounds. The group chatted for a few minutes, going over some items that would need to be discussed when there was a click on the other end.

"Hello, this is President Wally Foss, the American president," Foss announced. "To whom am I speaking?"

Everyone looked at each other for a second before Grigory responded. "I'm Lieutenant General Grigory Sobolev, the Head of the FSB and now the current leader of Russia. I have several of my key advisors and military leaders present as well. Of note, Mr. Alexei Kasyanov is also present as requested." The rest of the people in the room introduced themselves briefly.

"General Sobolev, am I correct in assuming you have taken control of the military?" asked Foss.

"Yes, Mr. President. I've made contact with the senior leaders of all branches of the military, and all but a couple of division commanders have recognized my authority as the new president. The two units that have not yet specifically accepted my authority are based in the Far East. Let me cut to the chase—what I'm sure you are most concerned with is our nuclear arsenal. I have spoken with the head of our strategic rocket forces and the head of our naval submarine command, and they have all acknowledged me as the new president."

They all heard President Foss let out a deep breath. "General, this is good news. I'm glad the two of us are finally able to speak," he replied, clearly relieved.

"Mr. President, if I may, I would like to move forward with discussing terms of surrender. Our countries have bled enough; it's time to end this war before it spirals any further out of control," Sobolev offered.

"Yes. Yes, General, I agree," Foss answered. "I believe the CIA and Alexei presented you with the original terms of surrender. You, of course, will be allowed to remain for a two-year period as president of a caretaker government until a proper election can be held and a government can be formed."

The general grunted. "Yes, I remember the terms and accept. I do have one caveat—I request that my government be allowed to retain at least 300 of our nuclear weapons. I fear that a complete denuclearization of the Russian Federation would leave our country far too vulnerable to future enemies."

There was a pause on the other end of the line while the Americans discussed this. They couldn't hear every word, but essentially their sentiment was that, while reducing the number of nuclear weapons down to 300 would be a remarkable feat, the goal was complete denuclearization.

"General Sobolev, I understand the reasons why you feel you need to keep some nuclear weapons," Foss acknowledged. "However, I do have to question at what point you believe you would need to use them. Because this war has shown the world that their use not only is abhorrent but will lead to an escalation of further use. I don't see a future enemy of Russia against whom such weapons could possibly be needed. Do you?"

Sobolev took a moment to formulate his response. With the mute button on, he talked this over with General Zolotov.

"If we wouldn't use them now, at this juncture, then when *would* we use them, Sir?" Zolotov inquired.

"It's not that I want to use them, but I do want security guarantees," Sobolev answered. "I need to know that we won't be hung out to dry in a couple of decades when the wounds of this war have healed."

After some further discussion, General Grigory Sobolev took a deep breath, then depressed the mute button to return to the conversation. "Mr. President," he began, "if Russia is to fully denuclearize, then I need a security guarantee from the United States that if Russia is attacked by an outside power, the United States would be militarily obligated to come to our aid. I would like that guarantee to be in writing for up to twenty-five years, along with a $100 billion economic aid and reconstruction package for our nation. You are, after all, essentially buying our entire stock of nuclear weapons, which I might add is still quite vast."

The others in the room with Sobolev nodded in approval of his approach.

The Americans had clearly decided to utilize the mute button themselves, because a few moments of silence passed. Then, after a pause, President Foss came back on the line. "General Sobolev, I've spoken with my military advisors about your proposition. In principle, we agree with the security guarantee. However, I'm not willing to give Russia a $100 billion economic aid package. Our nation has suffered horrifically from this war, including the major cities on our West Coast that were completely obliterated. Millions of my people have been killed or displaced by the war. We can agree to give you $25 billion in hard currency to aid in your reconstruction. Is this acceptable for the complete denuclearization?"

General Sobolev looked at the men around the table. They all nodded in agreement, elated that they had been able to elicit even $25 billion in aid and a 25-year defense agreement. These two things would allow the country to focus heavily on rebuilding before they had to think about defense again.

"*Yes, this will be a win for the people of Russia,*" thought Sobolev. He hated to think about how much his own people had already suffered during the war.

"Mr. President, I can agree to those terms, and speaking for my nation, I thank you for allowing us to end this war on mutually agreed-upon terms that respect both of our nations." He paused for a moment. "Let's move on to the occupation and when that will begin. If I may, I would like to suggest a three-day cooling period before your forces move to occupy our cities. I would like to order my armies to return to their garrisons, where they will wait to be greeted by your forces. They can then work out the best way to manage the occupation," Sobolev proposed.

"General, these are agreeable terms," President Foss answered. "I will leave you with my generals and advisors to go over further details. I must excuse myself to consult with the rest of the Alliance and inform General Cotton to cease hostilities with your forces. I look forward to talking with you again soon."

The military leaders talked for a while longer, going over more details of the occupation. They agreed that a contingent group of Allied officers would fly to Moscow immediately to begin work on coordinating a full ceasefire across the country. It was time to end the war and stop the killing as quickly as possible. With millions of soldiers on both sides still locked in battle, it was critical that things start to deescalate.

Chapter 19

Victory over Russia

St. Petersburg, Russia

Command Sergeant Major Luke Childers couldn't believe the war was finally over. He gazed across the Bolshaya Nevka River at the Petrogradsky District of the city they hadn't captured yet. The bridges across the river lay in ruins, destroyed by the Russian Army as they continued to fall back. The river had finally iced over sufficiently that they could now cross it on foot, but the order never came to seize this last bastion of Russian resistance.

Two hours earlier, a message had been sent from headquarters letting them know that the war was officially over; the Russians had surrendered. When the news was disseminated to the rest of the Corps, the men broke out into spontaneous celebration. Many of them were elated that they had survived—yet the danger was not completely over. The Russians who were less than a few hundred meters away needed to be made aware of the surrender, and hopefully they would go along with it.

A brigadier general from the V Corps had assembled a small cadre of officers and senior NCOs near the edge of the Russian lines to head out to meet their Russian counterparts. Sergeant Major Childers joined the group as they raised a large white flag and approached the enemy. Several tense moments passed.

Finally, a small group of soldiers came to meet with the American contingent, who made their request to speak with the senior Russian commander. It took nearly half an hour for the Russian general to be tracked down and travel to meet them. When the group did finally gather together in the same room, the US delegation informed the Russian general of the formal surrender by Moscow.

At first, the Russian commander didn't believe the news. However, then he learned of the coup and read the transcript of the surrender between Lieutenant General Sobolev and President Foss. He sat down on a nearby chair, dejected at first, and then he couldn't help but cry for a moment.

As Childers watched this man fall apart before him, his own eyes got a bit misty. He understood the crazy mix of emotions the commander must be going through. His soldiers had fought and bled for their country for more than two years, ultimately losing. However, they had survived, and he must also be filled with relief that the war was officially over.

When he had had a moment to recover, the Russian general announced, "I will inform my soldiers at once and order them all to surrender their weapons to you and the other Allies."

The rest of the day went by relatively smoothly as unit after unit of Russian soldiers lined up in the streets to discard their weapons. One by one, they slowly grouped off into unarmed formations, where they waited for the Allied troops to enter their sections of the city and take possession of them. No one offered any resistance. Many of these soldiers were tired and underfed and just wanted to return home to their families.

****

Two days after the surrender, Sergeant Major Childers was walking through the Peter and Paul Fortress in the heart of the city as his regiment moved in to assume control of this critically important fortress. Judging by the fortifications he'd seen up to this point, the Russians had intended on turning this into a bloody contest if the Allies had wanted to seize it.

As he meandered through the cathedral and the museum, Childers was very happy they hadn't leveled it. It was a beautiful gem in the city. He was glad the residents would still have this piece of history to hold on to as they looked to rebuild their nation.

When Childers walked into the main building, he spotted a gaggle of officers, soldiers and NCOs going through the various rooms. At first, he didn't think much of it and figured they were touring and securing at the same time, just as he was doing, but then he witnessed some of them snatching up items they'd found around them—probably to take home as mementos.

He remembered what had happened in Iraq when Baghdad had fallen, and how the country's national treasures had been pillaged by the looters at an astonishing rate. He knew he had to get this situation under control immediately. Right now, two companies in his battalion were already present at the fortress, but by evening, the rest of the battalion and eventually the regiment would be there.

He quickly turned around and walked right back through the main entrance of the building before anyone else could enter. Swiftly, he unslung his rifle. He yelled at the soldiers near the entrance, "Stand back!"

Childers switched his selector switch to semiauto and proceeded to fire off several rounds, which obviously immediately gathered the attention of everyone around him. Those inside would have heard the shots, too.

He poked his head into the entrance, and in his loudest and angriest sergeant major voice he shouted, "Out! Everyone, get the hell out of the building and into formation *right now!*"

Instantly, the soldiers started falling into formation, and a few of the officers fell in with their platoons and troops. He saw Lieutenant Colonel Schoolman give him a bit of a bewildered look as he walked up the stairs to the entrance of the building.

"Did I miss something, Sergeant Major? What's going on?" he asked, confused.

Childers pulled Schoolman aside so he could speak to him without giving up his staunch demeanor in front of anyone else. "Sir, when I walked into the building here, I spotted several soldiers and officers starting to loot the building. While I know we just won the war, this building is a national treasure to the Russian people. When I invaded Baghdad, one of the big mistakes we made was not protecting the national museums. They were raided, and most of the items were sold on the black market. The items in this building, Sir, are worth hundreds of millions, maybe even billions. We can't let the men of our unit loot it. It wouldn't be right, and it would bring enormous shame on the 2nd Calvary and V Corps."

Schoolman nodded. "You're right. Thank you, Sergeant Major, for taking charge of this situation and bringing the men to formation. You might have just saved my career. We're going to nip this in the bud right now. I want you to have all the men searched, and I want you to personally oversee the security of this museum until we can get a proper unit to take over the task. Is that understood?"

Childers smiled. "Roger that, Sir."

Then he turned around to the rest of the soldiers, staring daggers at them.

Schoolman glanced at Childers as if asking to speak first, and Sergeant Childers tilted his head to defer to his officer.

Lieutenant Colonel Schoolman did his best impression of a bad cop. "Listen up," he said starkly. "I was just made aware of something egregious that was about to happen. This museum you see behind us is a historical heritage and landmark to the people of Russia. *Our unit* is not going to be the one that loots it. I won't have the 4th Squadron or the 2nd Calvary Regiment's name and reputation impugned by those who would seek to rob this place and bring home items to sell on the black market or hang up in their office as war trophies. Every one of you has fought with distinction in this war and brought honor to our country and your families. I won't have a few hotshots mess that up for the entire regiment. Effective immediately, I'm placing Command Sergeant Major Childers in charge of protecting this museum. He's going to search everyone who has already been inside the museum to make sure nothing has been taken. If you took something, then cough it up right now and we won't hold it against you. If we find it later, I'll have you brought up on charges and court-martialed. Troop commanders—if the sergeant major says he wants one of your platoons or squads for guard duty, you *will* give him control of them. Is that understood?"

"Yes Sir!" shouted everyone present in formation.

"Excellent," Schoolman responded, speaking a little quieter now. "Captain Taylor, you're going to work with the sergeant major as the OIC in charge of this task. When we get a proper unit to secure the museum, your group will be relieved and join the rest of the squadron in whatever duties the regiment has planned for us. In the meantime, I want camp set up immediately. I want guards posted throughout the facility, and I want EOD to make sure this place is safe. Tomorrow, I want NCOs and officers to begin writing up your AARs and award packages at once. The war may be over, but the Army will get its pound of flesh when it comes to paperwork. I want this taken care of at once before we get assigned some sort of occupation duty…and before you ask, I have no idea what that may be. When the rest of the squadron shows up, I want what was said here passed down to them. Is that understood?"

"Yes Sir," came the reply, a little more subdued than before.

"Dismissed!" he announced.

****

Schoolman moved out of the way while Childers took control of the search for artifacts. While that was taking place, he decided to tour the building himself and see if he could spot any obviously missing items. As he walked in this time, he couldn't help be drawn into all of the intricate details and the collections of beautiful historical items. After he finished his tour, he felt more than justified in coming down hard on his unit.

With the tasks at hand set, it was time for him to find out what the regiment had in mind for them, then he had to find some time himself to sit down and write up his own AAR and award recommendations. Sergeant Major Childers had already been awarded a Silver Star and the Distinguished Service Cross, but he wanted to push for him to get the medal of honor for his heroic action a week ago, saving those wounded soldiers trapped in the street by an enemy sniper. That might be a tough sell, but he'd try. The man deserved it for how he had led the soldiers of this squadron throughout the war.

****

Moscow, Russia
Ostankinsky District

Sergeant Philip Jones couldn't be happier now that the war was over. He had dreaded the idea of 40 Commando having to fight their way into Moscow. While their brush with combat had been limited to their last-minute dash toward Moscow from the northern port city of Severodvinsk, what he had seen was more than enough for one lifetime. Two of his Royal Marines had been killed, and three more injured during the fighting. However, by and large, his unit had come through rather unscathed compared to many of their army brethren who had fought with the Americans in Ukraine.

"Now those poor blokes saw some serious combat," Jones thought.

After a couple of days, Sergeant Jones was permitted to take a rare break from their now daily and hourly patrols through the streets of the Ostankinsky District. He and a few of his mates sat down at a comfortable café with a cup of tea and enjoyed having a beautiful waitress serve them. After the horror of war, it all seemed very surreal.

Chapter 20

Liberated

Taiwan

Victory Base Complex

Taoyuan International Airport

A cool breeze moved across the sprawling military encampment as the Marines of Echo Company focused on completing the last mile of an early morning run. Rounding the last stretch of the perimeter they were running along, Captain Long really opened it up, pushing himself as hard as he could. Few of his Marines could keep up with him as he ran for all he was worth. Once he reached the finish line, he slowed down until he came to a walk and then continued to amble along for a few minutes as he completed his cooldown. The rest of his Marines eventually arrived and followed suit, stretching their muscles and grabbing their canteens to rehydrate.

Looking to his left, Captain Long spotted a pair of C-5 Galaxies unloading several hundred new Marines, fresh from the States. *"I wonder how many of them are slated for my unit,"* he thought.

Once he finished his stretches, he trotted off to his tent to gather his gear to grab a quick shower and then head over to the mess tent for some breakfast. Today marked the third day his Marines had moved out of the field to a formal military camp. After months of hard fighting, the remaining PLA forces on the island of Taiwan had surrendered to the Allies. Now came the hard part—the rebuilding of the island and preparation for the eventual invasion of Mainland China.

An hour later, Captain Long walked into a tent that had been designated as his company headquarters and saw his platoon leaders eagerly waiting for him. "*Good, the new guy is here as well,*" he thought.

"You trying to kill us on that run this morning, Captain Long?" snickered his XO, a good-natured first lieutenant from Idaho.

"You guys are just out of shape, that's all," Long replied with a grin. He pulled out some ibuprofen from a bottle on his desk and tossed four tablets down his throat and then passed the bottle to his lieutenants. As he chased the pills down with water, they all broke out in laughter, though the new guy stayed relatively silent. Captain Long realized that he was the odd man out. The rest of the officers had all fought and bled with each other, but the newbie would still be unsure of where he fit in.

Checking his watch, Long turned serious. He took a seat and stared briefly at his platoon leaders. "Today is the start of day three we've been back in camp," he began. "We have a lot of work to do to get ready for what may be coming next. First, I need you to get on your NCOs to submit any award packets they want to write up from the Taiwan campaign. I also want the squad leaders and you platoon commanders to get me your AARs by the end of the day. During the regiment meeting last night, I was told the award packets from the Philippine campaign had all been approved and will be handed out in a ceremony on Monday by the division commander."

A few of the men smiled at the news. They were glad to see their Marines being recognized.

Captain Long looked down at his notes and then back at his lieutenants. "We have fourteen guys receiving the Silver Star, and two of them had their medals upgraded to Navy Crosses. Fifty-two Bronze Stars and sixty-seven Purple Hearts as well. Sadly, twenty-three of these medals will have to be awarded posthumously. Here's the official list of those receiving an award; make sure everyone knows who's getting what. Before I hand this out, I want to let each of you in this room know you're being awarded Silver Stars. That was a hard-fought campaign and we lost a lot of guys, but you held your platoons together despite some terrible losses. I want you each to know that I went to bat for you guys to get those awards, and every one of you earned them. You brought great honor to yourselves, this unit, and the Marines. Those paratroopers fought like demons."

Sighing, he passed the list over to his XO and then continued, "We're still short nine Marines. I was told the replacements should be arriving today, so when they do, make sure your sergeants get them integrated into their new fireteams and squads ASAP. Figure out with your NCOs what you want to do for team building exercises next week. We have a lot of new faces in the company, and we need to get them synced up with our veterans, so everyone starts to work as a team."

The leaders nodded.

"Today is Friday," Captain Long continued. "At 1800 hours, you're to dismiss your platoons until 1900 hours on Sunday. If they want to sleep in, go to the MWR, gym, or whatever else they want to do on base, let them. These guys need some downtime. Come Monday, we're going to be right back at it, training for the next mission."

First Lieutenant Buck Conlon, his XO, asked the question that Long realized must be on all of their minds.

"Do you know when the mission is? Are we going to invade the Mainland?"

The others sat silently, waiting to see what Long would say. "I'm supposed to meet with Colonel Tilman tomorrow. Hopefully, I'll know more after I see him. What I can say is we are most certainly invading the Mainland. Shoot, the Army's already invaded the Mainland in northern China—us Marines can't let the Army get all the glory."

Looking at his newest platoon leader, Second Lieutenant Miles Johnson, Long asked, "So, Lieutenant, why don't you give us the ten-second version of who you are and how you ended up in the famed Echo Company, 2nd Battalion, 6th Marines?"

Lieutenant Johnson stuck his chest out. "I'm from Atlanta, Georgia, and I joined the Corps right after graduating college. My brother served in the 2/3 Marines in Korea before he was killed. I asked to join Echo Company because I was told this unit saw more action than any other unit in the brigade."

"I'm sorry to hear about your brother, Johnson," Captain Long said. "I was in Korea when it all started, though I was in a different unit. Right now, Second Platoon is missing an officer, so that's where I'm going to stick you. You have an outstanding platoon sergeant, so basically listen to what he tells you as you get your bearings. We're going to run through a lot of drills and exercises the next few weeks, so that'll be a good time for you to learn how to lead the platoon before we're thrown right back in the fire. Just don't try to rush things right away; take your time to get to know your men and your sergeants. You'll do fine. If you have any problems or questions, ask any of these guys for help, or you can ask me."

With the company business out of the way, Captain Long passed things over to his XO while he and the first sergeant got caught up on the few remaining details—mostly promotions and award packets that had to be finalized for the battalion.

"There may be a war going on, but by God, your paperwork had better be in order," Long thought, nearly laughing out loud at the absurdity of it all.

****

The following evening, Captain Long found himself sitting next to Lieutenant Colonel Noble, his battalion commander. Colonel Tilman had invited his battalion commanders and a couple of captains to come along with him to a newly opened restaurant just outside the camp, and he'd reserved a large table for them in a private room, his treat.

"Gentlemen," Colonel Tilman began, "we've gone through hell together and lost a lot of friends along the way. I wanted to take some time out of our busy schedules to just relax, eat, and drink some beers together before we worry about the future. Right now, just enjoy this moment and the comradery we have with each other. When this war is over, these are the memories you'll look back on and long for again." He raised his beer, taking a very long chug before he sat down and joined his men as they broke bread together.

Long wasn't sure how it had happened, but he'd ended up being seated opposite Colonel Tilman. He tried not to overthink the seating arrangement and downed a beer like everyone else. After some good grub and another beer, he was starting to have a great time, just like everyone else. Then Tilman suddenly leaned forward. In a very serious tone, he asked, "Captain, do you plan on making the Corps a career, or are you going to get out at the end of the war?"

Judging by the seriousness of the colonel's question, Long knew his immediate future probably rested on his answer. He'd been thinking about that very question for a few months now. He was on year eight in the Marines, and usually at year ten you had to make a firm decision as to whether you were going to stay in until retirement or get out. This conversation felt like it was speeding up his timeline a bit.

"At first, I planned on getting out when the war was done," Captain Long admitted. "However, I've given that a lot of thought, and I think I want to stay in and see where my career takes me." The colonel's demeanor immediately changed from serious to happy, and he knew he'd given the right answer.

"Glad to hear it," said Tilman. "With your record and all those medals, you'll go far. As a matter of fact, I'm going to promote you to major. I'm short staffed officers right now, and I need some people I can trust to take command of a new battalion we're forming up. As we near the final stage of the war, the size of the Marines is still growing. All the Marine divisions are being given a new regiment, and the regiments are being given a new battalion, and the battalions are getting another company. It's all part of this massive buildup leading to the invasion of China. I'm sure once this is all over there'll be a huge demobilization like they did at the end of World War II, but for the time being, this is a great chance for you to get some higher-level command experience. When the time comes, I'll do my best to shield you from any demobilization." Tilman spoke like a father whose son had just joined the family business.

"Until the men for the new battalion start to arrive, I want to move you to my staff so we can spend some time getting you ready to take command," Colonel Tilman explained. "You know the field side of command, but we need to get you up to speed on the garrison side of running a unit. We'll be back in combat by spring, but until then, you'll be spending a lot of your time getting your new unit ready to fight."

Captain Long's brow furrowed as a reflex as he thought about the enormous weight of responsibility. Tilman must have seen the change in his expression. "Listen, Tim," the colonel said, "I know you're nervous, and rightly so. But I'm going to take care of you. I'm going to give you your current battalion sergeant major to help you run things. I'm also going to make sure you are assigned half of your officers from those who fought in the Philippine or Taiwan campaigns, so you won't have an entirely green command structure. This position is definitely going to force you to grow, but we need competent combat veterans in command, not guys who have the right rank but have never seen battle. My regiment is the toughest, most combat-tested regiment in the Corps right now, and I want to keep it that way."

Captain Long nodded. If the colonel was going to look out for him, then he knew he'd be OK. "I heard a rumor that you might be taking over the division. Is there any truth to that Sir?" he asked.

Tilman snickered for a second, then leaned in closer. "Between you and me, it's true. They aren't certain on the timing just yet, but yeah, I'll be taking over the division for the invasion of China. I still have no idea when or where we'll be fighting, but I do know this next round of fighting is going to be bloody, probably bloodier than anything we've seen up to this point. That's why I'm going to need commanders who know how to fight and win when the time comes."

****

Taipei City, Taiwan
Presidential Office Building

President Hung Hui-ju was horrified as she walked along Bo'ai Road toward the capitol building. The glass windows of nearly every edifice nearby had been shattered, and the shards lay on the ground below. Debris from the torn and blown-out buildings was also strewn about, littering the sidewalks and street. Seeing such destruction was unnerving.

As she thought about all that had happened to her beloved city, she could not help but cry. She could only hope the other parts of the city and the rest of the country had not sustained such appalling devastation as well.

Even now, crews of waste management workers were out doing their best to clean up the debris. Several large trucks had dropped off enormous dumpsters at varying intervals to give the work crews somewhere to collect the debris. As she observed a few more moments, President Hung was reminded that the cleanup effort was in fact an international one.

With Taiwan's economy in tatters, many of the government services were in complete disarray. Tens of thousands of contractors from the US, South Africa, South America and many other countries had been being flown in to help stabilize the country and get it back on its feet. The US, for its part, was providing a steady supply of food, fuel, and other support to aid the remaining people still on the island.

Despite the devastation around her, there was still hope. Many of Taiwan's citizens who had fled prior to the fighting were starting to return, bringing with them their intellectual capital and know-how to get parts of the country running again. It would be a slow process getting the country moving again, but many nations had pledged support, and in time, it would happen.

Wiping away her tears, President Hung stood up tall. She resolved herself to rebuild the country and prepare to become the eventual leader of a unified China once the communists had been defeated.

Chapter 21

Occupation Duty

Russian Provincial Authority
Kremlin, Senate Palace

Ambassador Ava Hicks cleaned her desk. The clutter on it was distracting her, and she could not afford to walk into this next meeting with General Sobolev unprepared.

The new ambassador to Russia was a stunning woman with an impressive work and academic background. Ava had been born to a working-class family in Michigan in 1972, during the high time of the automotive industry. Her father was a union member who'd worked on the Ford assembly line, building the Ford F-150 series trucks. Her mother had worked as a middle school teacher in Canton, halfway between Detroit and Ann Arbor. Growing up, her father instilled in her, "You can be anything you want to be, Ava, if you work harder than everyone else and take the jobs no one wants. You just have to try your hardest and never give up, no matter what obstacles get thrown at you."

When she was a senior in high school, she'd applied to the University of Michigan, Ann Arbor, to study civil engineering and had been accepted. Unfortunately, that was also the year that her father was diagnosed with stage four lung cancer; he died just weeks after she'd graduated high school. With the death of her father, her mother was not able to pay for her college as Ava still had three younger siblings her mother had to think about. Not wanting to give up on her aspirations, she'd joined the Reserve Officer Training Course or ROTC on campus. Her plan was to finish college, go into the military for her obligatory four years, hopefully in civil engineering, and then get out and pursue a career in the automotive sector like her dad.

What she hadn't counted on was being deployed to Bosnia during the height of the Bosnian-Serbian War in 1995-96. As a first lieutenant in an engineering battalion, her job was to help rebuild roads, bridges, schools, and medical clinics. She couldn't believe how brutal and savage the warring parties had been to each other. Every chance she got to do something kind for a child, or family, she did. She also worked with her family and church back in Michigan to send care packages, school supplies, clothes and anything else she could give away.

While building a school in a small city outside of Sarajevo, she'd met a cadre of people from an organization she knew little about, the United States Agency for International Development. They brought with them experts and funds to help rebuild the small community. During the remaining time her unit was deployed to Bosnia, she routinely worked with USAID, making many new contacts and friends within the organization.

When her contract with the military expired in 1998, Ava went to work for USAID for several years before later joining the State Department and becoming a political officer in 2002. During her time at the State Department, she'd spent four years working in Iraq, three years in Paris, two years in Moldova and two years in Belarus before she'd returned to headquarters in D.C.

She'd become a bit of a Russian expert over the years and moved quickly through the ranks by following her father's advice and taking jobs no one else wanted. All those years volunteering to work in Iraq, Moldovia, and Belarus had let her shine. She became the youngest ambassador when she was sent back to Moldovia, and she was on the fast track to become a deputy assistant secretary when President Gates became president. When the war with Russia started, she immediately became the go-to person for all things Russia, especially after Ambassador Duncan Rice had been assassinated in Ukraine.

When President Gates approached her about a postwar Russia plan, she was thrilled to have been chosen to lead what could arguably be the largest occupation and political restructuring of a nation since the end of World War II. The Allies' approach to postwar Russia was complex yet doable. Throughout the war, the CIA, MI6, and BND had found and cultivated political opposition groups to the Petrov regime. As a credible leader became clear, they worked with that leader to begin identifying and recruiting a postwar government.

When Lieutenant General Grigory Sobolev seized power and brought an end to the war, the plan had effectively started, and she'd flown to Moscow to meet with General Sobolev and Alexei Kasyanov to set up the Russian Provisional Authority or RPA that would administer the government of Russia in coordination with General Sobolev while a new constitution was written and then voted on by the people. New political parties had had to be created, and a new Justice Department was developed that would enforce the laws as they were written.

The first governmental meeting had taken place two months ago. A lot had happened since she'd set up shop. In some areas of Russia, it had taken nearly a full week for combat operations between the warring factions to subside. Once that had been achieved, the Allied armies had quickly moved in and occupied the major cities across the country.

Unlike what had happened in Iraq, the military and local police were not disbanded or dismantled. The RPA kept them intact and planned on using them to help stabilize the country; in fact, they'd placed them on the Allied payroll to make sure they were paid and continued to work. Allied Forces would work more as advisors and mentors with the Russian military as the country began the process of rebuilding and healing the wounds of war.

When Russia had surrendered, a total of two and a half million Allied soldiers had moved into the country. Once the occupation was fully up and running, nearly half of those soldiers would continue to stay on in Russia as part of the occupying force. The rest of the soldiers, along with their equipment and planes, were being transferred to fight in Asia against the Chinese and, if the Indians refused to surrender, then against them as well.

So far, her meetings with Russian leadership had gone very well, but Ambassador Hicks knew that the situation was still tenuous at best. Every encounter was a walk into the lion's den, and she had to be prepared for every possible scenario. She put on her headphones and listened to some Bach as she studied every imaginable angle.

****

Sitting across a conference table with General Sobolev, Ambassador Hicks began, "General, before we turn to the civilian sector of this meeting, I need to ask for your help and assistance in the Russian Far East."

He shot a glance to General Zolotov before he spoke. "What can we do for you, Ambassador?" he asked.

Hicks looked at General Cotton, the Allied Commander in Europe, and the man who was overseeing the military occupation of Russia. Cotton then turned to speak directly his counterpart, General Zolotov, who had taken over as the Minister of Defense.

"I'm having some problems with General Chayko complying with some of our requests," explained General Cotton. "I was hoping you might be able to intercede on our behalf and help get things moving."

The new head of the Russian Army had been causing some waves. While General Mikhail Chayko had taken over command of the Russian armed forces after the coup, he was not at all happy about or accepting of his country's defeat. He still felt that he could have won the war, or at least ground it to a stalemate, if he had been allowed to use tactical nuclear weapons. Now that he was in charge of the military, he'd been doing his best to slow walk and throw up as many obstacles as possible to the successful implementation of the occupation.

General Zolotov nodded. "I understand. I have people keeping tabs on him as well, and I'm aware that he has not been as cooperative as he should be. I'll speak with him at once and remind him that if he's not going to comply with the terms of the surrender, then he will be replaced."

Sobolev interrupted angrily. "If he won't comply with *my* orders, I'll have him lined against a wall and shot tonight!" he shouted as he pounded the table. "I won't have my presidency or the terms of this transition period undermined by members of the military or political elements. I'm determined to get Russia back on the right track and return us to a thriving economic member of the world."

"I don't know that we need to go to that extreme just yet, Mr. President," Hicks said cautiously. "Everyone is still going through a period of transition right now, figuring out their roles and what's going to happen. It's going to take some time to heal the wounds of war and move past the conflict."

Sobolev was still fuming a bit, but he reached over and grabbed his cup of tea. After a sip and a deep breath, he turned his attention back to General Cotton. "What specifically do you need help with, General?" he asked.

"I need some of your engineers to help us with the fuel farm situation outside of Irkutsk and Chita. Our engineers are linking your rail lines to connect with our deployed forces in Mongolia and northern China, but there some aspects of your railroads and fuel storage facilities that we are not familiar with." General Cotton handed over a couple of documents that were written in Russian, explaining the technical specifics of what they needed.

Sobolev perused the paper briefly, but seeing that it was more technical than he could understand, he passed it over to Zolotov to have taken care of. "We'll see to it that this is corrected," he asserted.

"If we can, I'd like to talk about domestic issues," Sobolev said, changing topics. "We have a lot of ground to cover, and that's a far more pressing area if we're to make the occupation successful."

Ambassador Hicks nodded. Getting Russia back on its feet and able to feed its people again was critical, as was repairing their electrical grid, roads, railway and other critical aspects of the country's infrastructure. The Allies had done a real number on these areas as they'd readied themselves for the final assault on Moscow. She was glad it hadn't come to that. St. Petersburg was a mess from the siege, and she couldn't imagine how bad Moscow would have been.

"Excellent," Ambassador Hicks began. "We have some ideas on how to get your electrical grid fully operational by summer."

The group talked for many more hours as plans were drawn up, and timelines set for activities to begin. It seemed that Hicks's classical music ritual for her preparation toward this meeting had helped.

****

10 Downing Street, London
Cabinet Room

Prime Minister Rosie Hoyle rubbed her temples in frustration as she listened to an argument between the Secretary of State for Defence and the Chancellor of the Exchequer. The war with Russia was barely over, and already they were clamoring for their forces to be returned home. *"Will these fools never learn?"* she thought.

The two of them were blathering on about the costs of the war and the size of the military. The American occupation plan for Russia called on the Allied nations to commit troops to Russia for up to ten years, and now the Americans had shifted the entire Alliance's focus to dealing with China and India.

Once these two had finally paused long enough to take a breath, the Secretary of State for Foreign and Commonwealth Affairs, Damian Hunt, added to the chaos. "We need to convince India that they have to withdraw from the war," he insisted. "They can't continue to support China and be a part of this Eastern Alliance any longer."

Liam Clark, the Secretary for International Trade, replied, "We're already facing a lot of backlash from the Indian community here in the UK over this issue. If we have to participate in any sort of military action in India, it's certainly going to inflame people's sentiments at home."

PM Hoyle pushed her chair back and stood, causing the others at the table to stop bickering and look at her. "Enough. The people of Britain have been lied to and deceived enough," she insisted. "We've suffered horrific civilian and military losses thanks to Michael Chattem and been humiliated on the global stage. We as a nation are going to regain our self-respect and trust within this Alliance, and we will do our part. Britain will commit to the Russia occupation for as long as needed. *If* the Americans and the rest of the Alliance deem an attack on India necessary, then our military will be a part of it."

She took a deep breath and let it out. "Right now, the focus is shifting to China. I implore Mr. Hunt to use whatever political options we have to help persuade the Indian and Chinese governments to come to terms with the Alliance for the sake of all of our people, but we will not back down from our obligation, or this fight," she said adamantly.

She took her seat again before she continued her lecture. "Look at social media, what the Chinese and Russians have done to our people, the youth of our nation. This brand of technocommunism they are propagating across the internet has turned our youth into mindless supporters of a form of government that would take away our free will as individuals. The development of a thought police, a way to publicly shame people into groupthink conformity, developing social scores for people—it's not only absurd, it goes against everything we as a free society stand for."

She smacked the table with her ring, making a loud cracking noise that startled everyone. "No, this war is much bigger than just defeating the Eastern Alliance. This is about the minds and souls of our youth and the next generation.

This is a battle that must be fought, and one that must be won, or we are looking at the death of everything we hold dear. Please, for the sake of the nation, let's put aside our pettiness and focus on the common good. When the war is won, if you all want to throw me out as PM, I'll gladly leave. Right now, we need to focus everything we have on defeating this depraved Eastern Alliance and their ideology before it has time to take root in our societies."

Most of the cabinet members nodded in agreement. Some even smiled as they relished having a strong PM to stand up to their political foes. Not since Thatcher and Churchill had they seen a PM so resolute in a single cause. With the trial of Michael Chattem now underway, public sentiment toward the Labour Party had dropped precipitously. With the evidence of what he had done laid bare for the people to see, many voters had turned away from Labour, demanding a cleaning of house. The people held regular protests in the streets, insisting on answers from the other members of parliament as to who else was involved, and who knew what.

Chapter 22

Indian Squeeze

Guam

Naval Station

After the long flight from Hawaii, Admiral James Lomas stretched his legs. It sure felt good to move. He took in the sights around him and stopped in his tracks when he saw several of the carriers that were anchored in Apra Harbor.

"I wish I were still sailing with the fleet," Admiral James Lomas thought longingly.

His hand rubbed across his abdomen, where his scars were itching him. Some days the area still ached. He counted himself lucky to have survived the opening day of the Korean War; many of the sailors in his fleet had perished, yet he'd survived.

His protégé, now Vice Admiral Michael Richards, had done well in his absence. He couldn't be prouder of Richards for how he'd handled the ship when he'd been injured, and then during the subsequent battles against the Chinese Navy. When the Secretary of Defense and the Secretary of the Navy had asked him in the hospital who should take command of the Seventh Fleet, he'd flatly told them Admiral Richards. He knew Richards had just been selected for admiral the day before the attack, and of the senior officers in the Pacific who truly knew how the Chinese would fight and how to battle them and win, the pick was easy. It had to be Richards.

Admiral Lomas finished his walk and found himself in front of the Navy Gateway Inns & Suites. His staff had rented out the facility for his upcoming conference with his senior NCOs and officers. It had been a rough two and a half years for the Navy. Many of them had lost friends and colleagues they'd known for years, some their entire careers. His goal in renting out the facility was to give everyone a more relaxed environment as they collectively talked about the next phase of the war. During the day, they would hold a series of briefings and strategy sessions; at night, the plan was to celebrate promotions and awards over some delicious BBQ and beers, letting the men and women relax and enjoy each other's company.

As he reached the front door of the building, the sentries snapped a smart salute and held the door open for him and his bodyguards—they never left his side, even for morning walks. He took a few minutes to freshen up in his room and put a fresh uniform on before leaving to head to the conference room.

When he walked into the main meeting room, everyone stood at attention as he made his way to the front lectern. "At ease," he ordered.

Surveying the room, Lomas saw a lot of familiar faces, but also a lot of new ones. With the war ended in Europe, the bulk of the Atlantic fleet had been moved to his command for the final phase of the conflict. Sensing the energy in the room, Lomas took a deep breath in before letting it out. "Gentlemen, the greatest war our generation has ever fought is in the final stages. We have before us one last great task—the defeat of both India and China. This morning, we're going to begin with our strategy concerning India.

"The President has given the Indians an ultimatum: they are to make peace with the Allies and leave the Eastern Alliance in seven days, or face severe consequences. In preparation for the need to swing the hammer, we have been ordered to prepare a series of military strikes aimed at two areas of their economy. However, in order to go after their economy, we'll first have to neutralize their navy. Although their navy has been largely absent from the war to this point, we will begin actively hunting them down and sinking every

Indian-flagged vessel we find, to include their merchant marine ships.

"Once the navy has been removed as a threat, we will pursue the assault on their economy. The first domain we will target is their steel industry, going after a series of steel mills and manufacturing plants. India has been providing China with vast quantities of military war stocks, and the fastest way for us to put a dent in the Chinese ability to wage war is to remove India from the war production equation. The second industry we'll be going after is their railway infrastructure: major rail junctions, railyards, key tunnels, bridges, and repair facilities. This will restrict their ability to move materials to support China and prevent them from moving against the Allied forces in Southeast Asia as we continue to liberate more nations."

He paused for a second, letting some of this sink in. This was probably many of these officers' first chance to really see the big picture of the war and how their efforts were shaping the outcome. In many cases, soldiers, sailors, and airmen are told where to shoot and who to shoot, but seldom given an explanation for why or told how their actions impact the grand strategy. Now that Lomas was the Pacific Commander, he wanted to do things differently. He wanted them to know the end state, so they could help him craft the best means to meet the President's stated goals.

"The purpose of the strikes at these two sectors is to seriously impede their ability to wage war while minimizing the loss of life as much as possible," Admiral Lomas continued. "Our attacks will take place in the dark of night, when most people will be asleep, and will be coordinated to hit as many targets as possible during an upcoming three-day holiday. These actions will also coincide with a massive cyberattack that CyberCom and the NSA will be launching."

Many of the officers were scribbling some notes at this point, as well as looking at the maps shown on the wall behind him. "We are forming Task Force 92, which will comprise two of our *Ohio* submarines, six *Virginia* submarines, twelve *Ticonderoga* cruisers, twenty-two *Arleigh* destroyers, and the carriers *Ford, Stennis, Nimitz, and Roosevelt*. The fleet will be escorting an Australian Army division and two US Army divisions, which may or may not set up a ground base in India to establish and protect the creation of a series of airfields for the Air Force to operate from. This task force will leave in seventy-two hours and will move at best possible speed to get in position in case the President gives the order to proceed."

Admiral Richards raised his hand to ask a question. Lomas nodded toward his protégé. "Sir, if we are forced to engage India in direct combat, will that delay or derail the invasion of Mainland China, and do we know where the landings will most likely take place?"

"Those are excellent questions, Admiral. Yes, if India doesn't surrender immediately, it may push back some of our timelines for when we had wanted to launch the final ground war in China. However, it won't impede our preparation of the battlefields. We're going to launch three seaborne invasions. The first two are diversions and will have a limited scope and mission. The third invasion will be the main attack and will coincide with the Army's three-pronged attack they will be launching from the north."

Admiral Lomas signaled for General Roy Cutter, the Marine Ground Commander for Asia, to come forward. They briefly shook hands and said a few hushed words before the Marine signaled for his first slides to be brought up. "I'm going to briefly give you the outline for the seaborne assaults, as many of you will start the preparatory attacks in the coming weeks."

Cutter turned slightly to verify that his first slide was properly displayed, then refocused his attention to the navy captains and admirals before him. "The first attack will be against Shantou, which is slightly southwest of Taiwan. It's a short distance for our forces on the island to have to move, but more importantly, it allows our force to threaten the Hong Kong-Guangzhou industrial sector to the south, as well as the critical port city of Xiamen directly opposite Taiwan. A landing of Allied forces in this location is going to force the PLA to commit a large number of their divisions down here in order to prevent us from tearing into their industrial heartland."

He nodded to the captain who was manning the computer with the PowerPoint presentation on it. "Our next landing will be near Wenzhou, another major Chinese port and industrial center. Our goal is not to capture the city or even to threaten further inland. The objective is to make them *believe* that is our goal and, again, commit a large concentration of forces to the area."

The next slide showed Lianyungang, just opposite South Korea. "This is our primary landing zone. We're going to land the majority of our Marines here and then drive on Jining, some 300 kilometers inland. This force will be the primary blocking force for the Army as they drive on Beijing. We'll go into more detail on these landings in the near future as we get closer to when they will take place.

With that, I'm going to hand it over to General John Bennet, the overall Ground Commander for Allied Forces in Asia."

General Bennet walked up to the lectern and surveyed the room. This was the first time he'd briefed an all Navy-Marine crowd, and it did feel a bit odd. However, if his plans for defeating China were to come to fruition, he'd need their help, especially with the Marine landings. The Marines needed to be such a perceived threat that the PLA would move most of the forces they would have arrayed against him to the south.

"Captains, Admirals, thank you for allowing us Army guys to talk with you today," Bennet said, which elicited a few chuckles from the crowd. "As Admiral Lomas alluded to earlier, we're going to hit the PLA with three prongs. The first is going to be Army Group One, which is currently snowed in in Mongolia. A large part of the Army forces from Europe have been moved to this location. They're going to perform two functions—one, they will go after the Chinese nuclear assets in west China and capture or destroy them, and two, they will attack Beijing from the interior of China." As he spoke, he used a laser pointer to highlight a couple of items on a large PowerPoint map.

"Army Group Two is going to attack the Jinzhou-Fuxin Line, which stretches from the coast here to this location here." As Bennet motioned with the pointer again, they could all see just how large this fortification was. It had essentially become the Chinese version of the French Maginot Line.

"Army Group Three will attack Harbin and thread their way through Tongliao in Inner Mongolia, which will hopefully open up a line of attack around and behind this massive fortification the PLA has built. The hope is that we won't have to actually punch our way through the Jinzhou-Fuxin Line and get enough forces behind them to force them into surrender. Once we've opened this area up, it's 470 kilometers to Beijing."

He paused for a moment and nearly laughed when he saw the expressions on the faces before him. He could see that some of the officers were glad they were going to be on a ship and not having to fight the ground side of this war. "Lord willing, President Xi is going to come to his senses and call an end to this war before we have to proceed this far into the plan. If we do have to fight, this land invasion is not going to be quick. We're estimating the Chinese will fight a lot harder for their actual homeland than they did in the occupied territories. Unless there are no questions, this concludes my portion of the brief."

One of the captains raised his hand. "Sir, what is the timeline for the Army's ground fight?" he asked.

"Tentatively, we're looking at July, but that will largely depend on when the Marines are able to start their seaborne attacks and what happens in India. If the Indians don't surrender, then we've been directed to seize the port city of Chennai on the Bay of Bengal and turn it into a beachhead for potential future combat operations against the Indian government," replied General Bennet. He didn't want to get too far into detail about the operations just yet.

Walking to the front of the room, Admiral Lomas addressed the group. "Thank you, General Cutter and General Bennet, for giving us an overview of the coming operations. Gentlemen, ladies, I wanted to give you the big picture of what's going on so we can discuss how we're going to make this happen. It's an enormous task our Commander-in-Chief has given us, and I need your help in figuring out the best means of achieving it. This afternoon and tomorrow, we will break up into smaller groups, and that is exactly what we're going to do. With that said, let's break for lunch and then get right to it."

The next several days, the senior officers discussed the best course of action, and more specifically how they were going to achieve each task. The next six months would change the course of the world, and thus its future.

****

New Delhi, India
Rashtrapati Bhavan

President Xi would normally never leave China during a time of war, but his meeting with Prime Minister Vihaan Khatri was best held in person. With the demise of President Petrov and the capitulation of the Russian Federation, Xi needed to make sure his remaining allies stayed strong and didn't jump ship.

The air was cool as President Xi walked toward the location of his little assembly, and the aroma of the gorgeous flowers nearby saturated the Mughal Gardens, which surrounded the grand Indian palace. He heard the noise of a group of people walking behind him and looked back to see Prime Minister Khatri walking toward him, a bright smile on his face. "President Xi, good morning," he called. "It's so good to see you in person. I hate using those video teleconference devices." He finished his approach and the two shook hands.

"Likewise, Mr. Prime Minister," answered Xi. "I'm glad we were able to meet and discuss these important matters of state in person. I hope you don't mind my suggestion that we meet in your lovely gardens? With the flowers in bloom and the air so fresh, I couldn't escape their beauty. The clean air helps to clear the mind." The two men began walking down another row of blossoms.

"Not at all," responded Khatri. "The flowers are beautiful, and I'm sure you must miss being able to stroll around wherever you choose." This statement was a nod toward the security precautions President Xi had to take in China. If the Allies caught wind of where he might be, there was a decent chance a cruise missile would find its way to the location.

Turning to look at his counterpart, Xi started the conversation. "I felt it important for us to speak in person to discuss the war. I was shocked and aghast at what happened in Russia. Who could have imagined Petrov's own head of personal security and the FSB turning on him like they did? This never would have happened had Ivan Vasilek not been replaced."

Prime Minister Khatri grunted before he replied. "It's terrible. The surrender of Russia also sent nearly 140,000 of our soldiers into captivity, and a large part of our air force is also interned. Between our military losses in the Far East and western Russia, our armed forces have been greatly degraded. It will take us many months before we are able to replace the losses in tanks and aircraft."

The two walked for a few moments as Xi digested what Khatri had just said. *"Is he subtly telling me India is not going to continue the war?"* he wondered.

"I won't lie, there have been some major setbacks in the war," President Xi admitted. "It hasn't turned out how we had thought it would or how our planners had predicted. However, it's far from lost. While some of our initial objectives are no longer feasible, many others still are. China still maintains control of Southeast Asia and some parts of the Philippines and Malaysia. The South China Sea is still firmly in our grasp." He paused, looking at Khatri before continuing. "If India continues to stay with us, we can defeat the Allies when this war turns into a ground campaign. They can't occupy us or hope to defeat our vast militia force."

Khatri thought about that for a moment. Their alliance had certainly lost some major battles. They still possessed some of their initial gains, though, and the war-weariness of the Allies would soon begin to sap them of their energy. If the conflict dragged out for several more years, then there was a good chance they could force the Allies into accepting a peace that favored them. The question his colleague, President Aryan Laghari, continued to ask was how much longer the people of India would continue to support the war. With the loss of their armies in both western and eastern Russia, there was a growing undercurrent of unrest among the wealthy members of society.

The prime minister sighed. "You know the Americans issued us an ultimatum last week. We have until tomorrow to end our involvement in the alliance and seek an alternate peace deal with the Allies or face severe retaliation until we capitulate." Despite the serious topic at hand, the two continued to walk at a slow pace through the gardens, pausing every now and then to admire a bed of flowers.

"The Allies have a fleet sailing toward our waters even as we speak," Khatri explained. "I have the support of the people right now, but that might change if we were directly attacked. Is there any chance the Allies will entertain a peace settlement now?" he asked, almost pleading for some tidbit of insight.

Xi took a deep breath in and out and walked over to another bed of flowers. Then he turned to look at Khatri again. "The only terms of peace we've received from the Allies are contingent on total and unconditional surrender. That is not something I, or the people of China, will ever accept. If the Allies would be willing to sign an armistice, we could end this war tomorrow, but a total capitulation is not something we will accept."

President Xi continued, "Prime Minister, I want you to think about something for a minute. Even if the Allies did attempt to land forces on your coast, India has such a vast army and population that you could simply overwhelm them at the beach. The Allies can attack you from the sea, but they can't threaten you on land. China still has some new superweapons that we will be unveiling against the Allies in the near future. I'm confident these weapons will change the dynamics of the war. When the Allies launch their ground invasion this summer, they will be met with such overwhelming numbers of militia forces that we will simply overrun them. Then our new superweapons will be unleashed, and we'll be able to severely damage their air force, the one branch that has prevented them from being completely overrun in Asia up to this point.

"The war in Europe and against us has destroyed more than 50% of the Allies' tier-one aircraft," President Xi explained. "These are expensive and complicated aircraft to produce and cannot be replaced overnight. As we degrade them further, the tide of war will change in our direction. I just need India to hold strong, at least until the end of summer. Then you can make a fair assessment as to whether or not our new tactic will have worked." Xi's voice almost pleaded with Khatri not to abandon the alliance, at least not right away.

Khatri studied Xi's face. He must have seen the look of sheer determination in his eyes because his own expression softened.

He nodded his head. "Fine," he responded. "We'll stay with the alliance for a short while longer, but your new tactic had better work. I'll issue the order to our navy to attack the Allies as best they can. We're going to lose what navy we have in this attack, but hopefully it will further hurt the Allies enough that they won't be able to properly threaten our country."

President Xi smiled. "There is one thing I should tell you as well. Our cyberwarfare division infiltrated one of the American banks."

Prime Minister Khatri gasped. It was exactly the reaction Xi had hoped for. "When I give the order, they will completely erase the bank's entire electronic records and their backup records at Iron Mountain," Xi said with glee. "This will cause considerable chaos in the American banking system. I hope this attack will help to persuade them into looking for more amenable peace terms."

The two leaders talked for a while longer before Xi headed to the airport and back to Beijing. Both parties had a lot of things to get ready for.

Chapter 23

Cyber Saturday

Tampa, Florida

JP Morgan Chase

Dennis Hall placed his Starbucks latte on his desk as he pulled out his laptop from his backpack and began the process of linking up to the corporate network. Between his three computer monitors, keyboard, and mouse, he was now officially ready for the day. This was the one Saturday a month he worked in his security department's weekend rotation.

Dennis loved writing code; he was fascinated with the concept of cyberattacks. To him, the ability of a single person or group to penetrate a company and completely run amok in their systems was amazing. He had been with JP Morgan for more than twelve years and had watched the organization evolve and grow, especially after the 2008 financial meltdown. He had just finished college the year before the collapse with a bachelor's degree in computer science and network administration, and he counted himself lucky to have landed the job when he had. When he'd started at the bank, he'd quickly risen through the ranks as a knowledgeable cyber leader, eventually becoming one of the department heads in charge of the bank's cyber defenses.

Logging into his system, he went through his initial checklist of things he usually performed when he arrived at work. He perused the incident logs and incident reports, looking for anything suspicious that one of his other teammates might have found. He immediately spotted a red flag in something that one of the analysts had posted a couple just a few minutes ago. Seeing that no one had fully looked into it yet, he grabbed the incident report to see what was going on.

As he read the report more closely, he noticed something unusual. An employee from the credit card side of the bank had gained access to the bank's records system.

"Hmm...you're not allowed to be in there," he thought. He immediately searched to see what the unauthorized person was looking for. Following the trail of the intrusion, he shadowed each click the person had made, taking him deeper and deeper into the credit card records— from records of individual credit card programs, to individual state records, to entire branch records. Then, to his horror, he discovered that the individual was systematically deleting millions of credit card records.

Dennis tried to intervene at once. However, as he tried to put a wrench into the intruder's actions, he saw that they had moved from the current live records to the backup files stored at Iron Mountain, their off-site backup vendor. *"How the hell is this guy accessing all of these records?"* he wondered. No one should have that level of access.

Dennis reached for his phone and hit the speed dial button to call the corporate security desk, which was manned twenty-four hours a day.

"Security, this is Jim," came a stern voice on the other end.

"Jim, this is Dennis at the insider threat desk. We have an emergency, and I need you to physically stop an employee who is currently inside the New York city office at once! He's sitting at desk 18E 12W."

"Oh, wow. OK, we'll send a couple of people up there now and lock his access card out," replied Jim. He immediately started to talk to a few other people nearby.

"Jim, you have to make sure this guy doesn't escape the building, and call the police," said Dennis urgently, praying the man on the other end could still hear him. "I'm calling the FBI and Secret Service. This is huge. Don't let him get away!" He stayed on the phone just long enough to make sure his message had been received, and then he hung up the phone and prepared to place an additional call to his own boss.

Standing at his desk, he waved for one of the other employees manning the twenty-four-hour office to come over. While talking to his boss, he pointed at his monitors. The employee bent down and looked at what was going on, and her eyes grew wide as saucers.

"Holy crap!" she exclaimed.

Dennis desperately tried to cut the guy's access to the system off, but nothing was working.

"What do you mean, you can't cut his access off?" his boss shouted angrily over the phone.

"He's got admin level access. I have no idea how he obtained it, but his access is above my own. I think it's even above yours," Dennis explained.

"I'm heading into the office now. Make sure security detains this guy, you understand?" The call ended abruptly.

A few minutes went by, and then Jim from security in New York called him. "Dennis, we've got a security team at that desk location, but there's no one there. It's empty. I've got my guys locking down the entire building, and the police are on the way. Can you see if he's still on the computer? Could he have remoted into this terminal?"

Dennis's mind was racing, trying to figure out what was happening. Maybe the intruder had hacked into this employee's account and was remotely logging in using a stolen admin login. Dennis looked at the admin code and quickly tracked it down to a bank's Chief Information Security Officer, his boss's boss.

"How in the world could these hackers have gotten the CISO's admin code?" Dennis thought. His mind was practically exploding.

****

Washington, D.C.
White House, Situation Room

"What do we know about this cyberattack taking place at JP Morgan?" asked Josh Morgan, President Foss's Chief of Staff. He wanted to get up to speed on things before the President joined the meeting.

Kevin Hampton, the Treasury Secretary, spoke up first. "It's a disaster is what it is. Whoever these hackers are, they managed to get inside the bank's credit card records, and they systematically wiped them out. They not only deleted the records, they managed to destroy the backup records at Iron Mountain, which is no small feat."

Josh looked at the Director of Homeland Security and the FBI Director for an explanation. Maria Nelson jumped in. "We're still gathering all the facts, but what we know right now is that someone coopted a work terminal in the New York office and remoted in from an unknown location to initiate the hack. Once they had gained access to the system, the intruder used the Chief Information Security Officer's administrative access, which gave them complete access to the entire bank's system. They then used that access to wipe out every trace of credit data on the roughly 43 million Americans who had a Chase credit card. At the time of the hack, those accounts had balances of roughly $274 billion."

Josh sat up a little straighter in his chair as he heard the number, then crunched his eyebrows a bit. "Are you saying JP Morgan just *lost* $274 billion?" he asked incredulously. "What happened to the money? Are the individuals whose accounts were affected still liable for their balance?"

"That's what I'm talking about, yes," Nelson confirmed. "As of three hours ago, JP Morgan effectively lost the records of $274 billion. It's gone. With no electronic record at the bank *or* their off-site locations, they have no way of saying how much each individual person actually owes. When word gets out of how severe this hack was and how much money essentially just evaporated at the bank, it'll collapse. Their stock will tank."

Molly Emerson, the DHS Director, added, "This is much bigger than just JP Morgan. If this could happen to them, who's to say it can't or won't happen to the other banks? For all we know, the hackers could have placed additional viruses or trojan horses in the Iron Mountain facility, just waiting to be activated. This could be the first domino to fall in the complete monetary collapse of our economy."

Kevin Hampton, the Treasury Secretary, moaned and rubbed his head.

Nelson shot him a look as if to say, "*You don't have to be so dramatic.*" She cleared her throat, then offered, "We think we might have a lead on who perpetrated the attack."

All eyes turned to her.

"You'd better be absolutely sure about that before you tell the President," Josh asserted. "He's going to want to respond to whoever did this to us, and I'm pretty certain he'll be using the military to do it."

Before Maria Nelson had a chance to reply, the President walked in, along with Secretary of Defense Jim Castle and Admiral Meyer, the Chairman of the Joint Chiefs.

Signaling for everyone to take their seats, the President said, "I assume the news about this hack is pretty bad for you to have called everyone in like this."

Josh looked at the President and nodded. "I'm afraid it is, Mr. President. I believe Secretary Hampton should probably give you the initial brief before Homeland and the FBI present what they know."

Hampton looked like he was going to be sick, but he nodded and then proceeded to get the President up to speed on what had transpired. The President, for his part, kept his poker face on. Then Homeland spoke, followed by the FBI.

Sitting back in his chair, President Wally Foss looked at the ceiling, not saying much, just thinking. Then he sat forward, placing his hands on the desk in front of him as he made eye contact with the Treasury Secretary. "Kevin, I understand the electronic records at Iron Mountain were destroyed along with the bank's internal electronic records, but if I'm not mistaken, there are printed copies of all the statements of these accounts kept as well. Surely the bank can reconstruct the accounts based on the written copies," he offered.

Secretary Hampton just shook his head. "That was true as of a few years ago, Mr. President. However, as part of many of the banks' efforts to 'go green' and cut costs, many of the financial institutions made several changes to their data storage procedures. First, they began storing data on their own electronic databases as opposed to using paper copies. Second, many of them have moved most of their databases to the cloud, thus cutting storage and security costs tremendously, since the cloud providers provide their own protection. Some banks use Iron Mountain as an additional safety mechanism to back up data on digital storage farms, but again, those are not physical copies. A few banks use a hybrid function where their records are backed up to the cloud at set intervals. *If* JP Morgan had been using a hybrid function, then yes, there would still be an alternative digital set of their records. However, when I spoke with the CIO at JP Morgan before coming to this meeting, he told me they had transitioned entirely to the cloud three months ago. With Iron Mountain gone, and their records at the cloud provider gone, they have no way of reconstructing them."

"OK, I'm not understanding something, then. I could understand how the records in the cloud were hacked and deleted—someone used the CISO's admin password to go into their files at the cloud provider and deleted them all. But how was that same individual able to delete the backups at Iron Mountain? Aren't there procedures in place to make sure something like this couldn't happen?" the President demanded.

"I can answer this question," FBI Director Maria Nelson said. She had previously been the Science and Technology Director at DHS, so she had a deep IT background. The President nodded for her to go ahead. "Several decades ago, Iron Mountain, along with several other cloud storage companies, began to build out a series of hardened facilities to handle large-scale data storage. In some cases, they were even acquiring decommissioned ICBM silos and turning them into enormous server farms, just like the three-acre server farm the FBI has in Clarksburg, West Virginia.

"The JP Morgan backups were stored at two separate locations. One is located in northern New York, and the second is in an old ICBM silo in Kansas. Both of these locations are impervious to EMPs, earthquakes, fire, flood and any other natural disaster. When the bank transmits their backup to Iron Mountain, it takes nearly eighteen hours to complete because of the size of the files, so it's done on a Saturday afternoon. When the data hits the New York site, Iron Mountain then promulgates the data to the second backup site at the same time. *That* is how the hacker was able to delete the entire backup. When the transfer started from the bank to Iron Mountain, the hacker was able to ride the connection from one location to the other and then delete everything. We've asked Iron Mountain to immediately stop any concurrent backups until we can figure out how deep and wide this penetration within the banking sector is," she explained.

Foss turned his head slightly and let out a soft sigh. "OK, clearly the damage is bad, and as of right now, it appears it's permanent unless something else turns up. What I want to know is, how is this going to affect the bank, and what can be done about it? Then I want to know who our suspects are, so we can figure out an appropriate response."

Secretary Hampton replied, "I've been thinking about how this is going to impact the bank, Mr. President, and there are multiple ways to look at it. JP Morgan essentially just lost $274 billion, and there is no way the bank is going to make up that kind of loss, so it's going to have to be written off. The problem is the bank's valuation is roughly $99.62 billion, so the loss is over two and a half times the institution's value—essentially, it's instantly going to be insolvent. This problem is huge, Mr. President. We aren't just talking about people's credit cards being affected. If the bank is dissolved, we're talking about tens of millions of people's bank accounts being wiped out, along with their mortgages, savings, and worse, all the investment accounts tied to the bank would also be affected. This is going to tangentially impact the majority of the country, and it could lead to a complete collapse of our financial system."

Hampton continued, "You see, banks lend money to each other, especially investment banks, which often share debts, loans, and investments with each other. These financial institutions have everything from mutual funds and EFTs to kids' 529 college funds. Because of the bank's current financial situation, their entire portfolio would have to be sold off at a discount, which means a *lot* of people are going to lose money. That's not to mention all the money people had in savings accounts at the bank or the value of the bank's stock itself. All of that will be at zero once word of this gets out. To make matters worse, Americans will likely fear this could happen at their own bank and will rush financial institutions all over the country just like the beginning of the Great Depression to pull their money out and make sure they don't also lose everything they own. Do you understand the scope of the problem, Mr. President?"

"I think we need to get Wendy Oliver from the Fed over here," the President ordered, tilting his head toward Josh to make it happen. "We need to figure this out before we leave this room, or it's going to be massive panic before the end of the day. What are we doing to make sure this information doesn't get out?" he asked. The gravity of the situation had now fully set in for him.

FBI Director Maria Nelson answered. "I've had my agents detain everyone involved who has any knowledge of what's happened for the time being. Right now, we've told them they're helping us figure out how this happened, and thus far, they're going along with that and have been a big help. Unfortunately, though, we can only hold them for so long before some of them start to protest."

The President nodded. He knew Director Nelson hated to use the FBI to hold American citizens without charges, but thankfully she'd recognized that it was for the greater good to keep this under wraps until they figured out what to do next. If this got out to the news before they had a plan in place, it would cause a mass panic.

"OK, we'll resume that discussion when Wendy arrives. Until then, I want to know who our suspects are."

DHS Director Molly Emerson spoke up. "The CISO, Preet Jindal, is of Indian-American descent, so we immediately suspected him. However, he came back clean. That still didn't explain away how his admin code had been obtained and used. It was his code that ultimately led to this catastrophe, so we dug deeper into his family to see what we could find. We managed to get a FISA warrant issued twenty minutes after we'd learned it was his credentials used in the attack. Using the warrant, we grabbed his entire electronic profile and that of his family, along with everyone he's been in contact with that in any way looked suspicious.

"This search led us to his wife, Aarushi. While Preet is a second-generation American, his wife was born in Mumbai and still has extensive family back in India. Preet and his wife met during a trip he made to visit family some twenty-six years ago. They've been married now for twenty-three years and have five children: three boys and two girls, ranging from twenty-one to sixteen. Their eldest son is currently serving in the Air Force as a linguist at the NSA. Their second son is in the Army, and he's currently part of 81st Infantry Brigade, which, ironically, is part of the ground force currently in the Bay of Bengal. Their other children are exempt from military service while the older two are currently serving."

"Hmm," said the President, in a tone that said, *"Could we please speed this up?"*

Molly flipped a page on her notepad, then continued. "The wife, Aarushi, has two brothers serving in the Indian Army. One was a colonel who served in Siberia—he was killed last October. Her second brother perished in the battle of St. Petersburg. Shortly after his death, she made contact with someone on an Indian chat board we regularly monitor. Combing through the chats and activity, we learned that she apparently met this person a couple of times in person. We used the Google geotracking on her phone to place her at several locations we've had under surveillance as known meetup locations for Indian intelligence. We believe it was at one of these meetings that she was recruited to their cause and then passed her husband's admin credentials to them."

"OK, so where is this person?" the President insisted.

"We have her under surveillance right now," FBI Director Nelson answered. "She's still at home with her family, and she hasn't tried to leave yet or done anything suspicious or out of the ordinary. Do you want us to grab her right now?" she asked.

"No, not yet," said the President. "We need to sort through things here first before we grab her. Taking her into custody is going to lead to speculation, and until we have a plan in place, we can't risk this information getting out."

Moments later, the Fed Chairman, Wendy Oliver, walked in. Seeing that she was late to the party, she plopped down at her seat next to Hampton. "I'm sorry I was late in getting here—traffic was brutal. I have, however, been on the phone with my team to discuss this problem, and I've read the quick blotter the FBI and DHS sent over to me. Can you guys take a minute to get me caught up?" she asked as she pulled out a pen and pad of paper.

Ten minutes later, the President asked the only real question he had for her. "What do we do, Wendy? Is JP Morgan salvageable, or what?"

All eyes turned to Wendy. She gulped, then blurted out the only real answer. "No, Mr. President, it's not. Not unless you want to do a 2008 style bank bailout."

The words hung in the air like many needles, piercing each one in the room.

"The best we can do as the Fed is make sure the FDIC honors its deposits and we do our best to help the bank unwind their holdings and sell them off," Wendy continued. "I'm sure we can get other banks to buy up parts of JP Morgan. It's not like they're an unprofitable bank, but they have no equity or cash to cover their current holdings, and no matter how much stock they're offered or what they sold off, it wouldn't equal the amount they just lost. If I may, I do have a recommendation that I believe will help to soften the blow to some people."

"Yes, please, what is your recommendation?" the President asked, desperate for anything that would ameliorate the situation, even a little bit.

"The FDIC only protects a person's deposits up to $250,000 per person at the bank. So, if Mom and Dad had a joint account in their names, they would be protected up to $250,000 each. While most people don't have that much sitting around in their bank accounts and are going to be fully protected, the wealthier individuals who do all of their banking and investing at JP Morgan are the ones who will be devastated. I propose that for this one specific instance with this bank, we increase the $250,000 limit per individual and raise that up to $1 million. In the case of a business account, I propose the limit be raised up to $5 million. While this won't recover all the lost monies that a lot of individuals and businesses will incur, it will help."

The President nodded. It seemed reasonable.

Wendy continued, "With regards to businesses, I propose that any business that had its accounts with the bank be allowed to borrow directly from the Fed at a 1% interest rate for up to five years. This will help make sure businesses both large and small are not suddenly without money and frozen out of the credit market. This will be critical to making sure we don't have an immediate economic collapse. Now, as to the investment side of the bank, their portfolios— we'll move to get them sold tomorrow to other firms who will take over the management and positions of the accounts.

Because the money was already invested, the individual holders won't lose anything. We just need to have the management of the accounts transferred to a new bank that is solvent to manage them going forward."

The President held his head in his right hand as he thought over everything that he'd just been told. At the end of the day, the bank was still going to become insolvent, and over 250,000 employees were suddenly going to find themselves unemployed. But if they moved decisively, they could prevent this one collapse from destroying the rest of the financial sector and the economy.

After nearly an hour, the President thanked the financial folks for their input and help, and then dismissed them to begin putting the plan into action. He signaled for the FBI and DHS directors to stay put as they turned their attention to the response to this brazen attack.

Looking each of the women in the eyes, the President asked, "You are clear there is no doubt that this attack was directed by the Indians?"

Both women nodded in agreement.

Foss turned to look at the SecDef and Admiral Meyer. "I suppose we have our response to our ultimatum, gentlemen. Admiral, I want our cyberattack to commence immediately. Jim, I want our naval assets to begin hitting their targets as soon as possible. I also want their navy hunted down and destroyed. Let's move forward with the immediate capture of Chennai. The sooner we can get some air bases set up on land, the sooner we can start to pound them into submission."

With the decisions made and the orders issued, the leaders of America's military began to get the wheels of their forces moving to crush India. The Indians might have just hurt the US economy, but the US was about to hammer their society by crippling their transportation sector.

Chapter 24

Operation Fight Club

Bay of Bengal

Sergeant First Class Conrad Price smiled a bit at the sight of so many of his men snoozing like babies. The hum of the engines on the C-17 had lulled most of the soldiers in the cargo bay asleep. Many of them had smartly taken the opportunity to grab some shut-eye before they had to get ready for the jump, but he couldn't sleep.

Once again, the Rangers of 2nd Battalion, 75th Ranger Regiment, were being called upon to capture an airport in a hostile nation. This time, they were going to seize the Chennai International Airport ahead of a seaborne invasion. This airport, unlike the past ones they'd seized, was a large commercial airport. Current intelligence didn't show there to be any military units present or even nearby, though that could change quickly once the enemy figured out where their little air armada was headed.

Flying advance for them were several airwings from the US Navy's Task Force 92. They had spent the better part of three days hitting every Indian air base within a 400-kilometer radius of Chennai to make sure there would be no enemy fighters to greet them. Flying several hours behind them was a long gravy train of 747 planes, carrying a brigade from the 82nd Airborne. Even further back were more C-5 Galaxy and C-17 Globemaster cargo planes, which would be landing their ground equipment.

Ninety minutes out from the jump, Sergeant Price roused the men from their slumber so they could begin to get their equipment ready. They all went over last-minute tasks and objectives for what felt like the hundredth time. Thirty minutes from the jump, the Rangers psyched themselves up for what should be an easy jump. Their past few jumps had been on hostile airfields that had been heavily protected, but the airborne gods appeared to be throwing them a bone with this one, or so they hoped.

Sergeant First Class Conrad Price walked the row, making sure his platoon of soldiers was ready for the jump, checking their equipment and also making sure the squad leaders were ready. The responsibility of his new position still weighed heavily on him. When their company had been pulled from the front lines in Taiwan back to the airfield, one of their trucks had hit a landmine, killing their first sergeant and his platoon sergeant in one fell swoop. It had been a devastating loss, especially since they had just been ordered to the rear. A few days later, Staff Sergeant Price found himself in the company commander's office being told he'd been promoted and would be taking over the platoon, along with a handful of new replacements fresh from training.

A week later, their unit was sent back to the front to do some deep reconnaissance for the Allies as they continued to hunt down the remaining PLA forces on the island. After spending another month in the field, they were pulled from the line and officially sent to Indonesia.

The memories were all jolted out of his mind as the jump master yelled out, "Five minutes! Get ready!"

Price walked up to his spot in the line, making sure he'd be one of the first to jump. He felt it was his job to make sure he was one of the first guys in the platoon to hit the ground and figure things out. The platoon leader would be the last to jump, making sure everyone got out the door, which suited their captain just fine. Not that he was a bad guy or anything, he just wasn't one of those types of officers who charged out in front of his NCOs in combat.

The next thing Price heard was the jump master shouting, "Go, go, go!"

He quickly followed the two guys in front of him out the door. The first thing he saw when he exited the plane was the runway below them.

"Wow, they're putting us right on the tarmac!" he thought. An extra adrenaline rush flooded his system, and his heart pounded wildly.

In minutes, his feet hit the ground. He tucked and rolled just like the previous jumps and came up ready for action. He quickly unsnapped his parachute and grabbed at his drop bag, pulling out his rifle and pack. With the basic essentials ready and no visible signs of danger, he wrapped up his chute and ran to a spot just off the tarmac, where he dropped it. Looking around, he saw a number of soldiers following his lead and heading toward him, rallying on him and dropping their parachutes there as well.

When he'd collected a dozen Rangers and still they hadn't received any enemy fire, he signaled for them to follow him quickly across the taxiway to the parking ramp and the actual airport terminals.

"Thank God we're doing this at night," Price thought. He was sure the place would have been crawling with people in the morning. He and the other Rangers continued to run toward the terminal, which still had half a dozen aircraft parked there. A dozen or so civilian ground crewmen were doing their nightly work on the aircraft.

As they approached the terminal, Sergeant Price's men swiftly took the airport workers into custody and secured the area. With one squad handling the prisoners, his other three squads made their way into the structure and started to clear the individual rooms and the terminal as a whole. Another platoon made its way around the outside of the terminal as they moved quickly to the airport entrances. Their goal was to lock down the entry points and ensure no one else tried to enter the facility.

Within an hour, the entire battalion had landed and secured not just the airport, but a several-block radius around it. Price's platoon found themselves perched on a hilltop that overlooked the entire airport, the Trichy-Chennai Highway, and the southeast side of the city. It was a lot of ground to have to secure with just a single platoon. Once the 82nd Airborne started to arrive, two additional companies of soldiers would take over control of the area, and his platoon would act more like a quick reaction force or QRF for them.

Already, a heavy weapons platoon was trudging up to join them with their equipment, bringing with them several mortars, antitank missiles, and several M2 .50 heavy machine guns. In a few hours, they'd turn that hilltop into a well-defended firebase, able to provide good support to the surrounding area and the airport.

******

Elliot's Beach, Chennai

The Stryker vehicle jostled a bit as the LCAC made its highspeed run toward the beach. First Lieutenant Slater figured they must be breaking some sort of rule or Navy policy, riding in their vehicles while packed on this hovercraft.

"If this thing takes a hit or starts to sink, we could all drown," he thought. Looking up through the troop hatches, he could see the moon was still high in the night sky. *"At least everyone should be asleep when we land."*

Seeing the nervous faces looking back at him, Slater knew he should say something. "It's going to be OK, guys. This is just like Indonesia. No one knows we're coming, and there won't be anyone waiting for us on the beach. We'll land, we'll head to our targets and we'll secure the area and await further orders."

The soldiers seemed to be put a bit more at ease and they nodded their heads. So far, their company had been lucky—they hadn't lost many soldiers in Indonesia and they'd been spared some of the heavier fighting in Asia thus far. The unit wasn't chosen to head into Malaysia or take on any of the Chinese units, the ones who would undoubtedly fight back. They'd been saddled with the Australian and

New Zealand Task Force, and up to this point, they hadn't had to fight it out like the soldiers in Taiwan, Korea or Russia. For that, Lieutenant Slater thanked his lucky stars, but that could easily change now that they were the tip of the spear in India.

Within ten minutes of leaving the troop ship, their LCAC neared the beach. One of the Navy personnel announced, "We're almost there."

Then the hovercraft left the water and gently glided over the sandy beach as it made its way up to the edge of the road that separated the beach from the city. Once they'd reached the end of the shore, they dropped the front hatch, and the four Strykers and two JLTVs of his platoon sped off. With his platoon off the LCAC, the hovercraft spun up its engines again and darted back to the sea to pick up the next platoon and bring them forward as well.

Slater ordered his men, "Move forward into the city as quickly as possible."

Standing up so he could see outside through the troop hatches, he got his first glimpse of the city they had just invaded.

"*What a dump,*" was the first thought that came to his mind. As they raced down the narrow road, he saw clusters of dilapidated shacks, stores, and run-down houses that lined the street and dotted the beach area. The next thing he noticed was the stench.

"Holy crap, Lieutenant. What the hell is that smell?" moaned Private Leiter, his heavy gunner.

The smell of feces and other unknown decay bathed their senses in its putrid odor, causing some of the soldiers to retch at first while others used a cloth to cover their noses.

"Get used to it, soldier," remarked Slater. "It's raw sewage. You see those steep cement cuts next to the side of each road?" he asked. The soldiers instantly looked down. "Those are the sewage pipes."

Several soldiers shook their heads and went back to scanning their sectors. Once they got away from the initial beach zone, the scenery around them changed dramatically. They entered a much nicer area, and the horrid odor left immediately. The road was now lined by small and medium high-rise apartments and looked to be in much better condition.

Fifteen minutes went by as they made their way through the area and eventually found what they were looking for. Their objective was to find and secure the Adyar police station and a large maintenance depot directly across the street. The maintenance depot would become the company headquarters by the end of the day, giving them a secured compound from which to operate and secure their vehicles.

When they approached the police station, they saw a handful of police cars parked in front of the small building and a few police officers milling around out front. Lieutenant Slater hopped out of his vehicle with his translator quickly following him. He made his way cautiously toward the police officers. None of them had made a move for their weapons yet, and Slater held his hands open and out to his sides to show that he meant no harm, and that he had not come to fight if it could be avoided.

The police officers squirmed a bit and suddenly became quiet as they saw dozens of armed soldiers with their faces covered in dark face paint. After all, they were fully clad in body armor and carried more weapons and grenades than the men had ever seen before. The soldiers immediately fanned out in the street. Some soldiers made their way around to the back of the police building, while others positioned their vehicles to block the roads and take up defensive positions. As Slater got closer to them, they all settled their gaze on him.

"My name is Lieutenant Ian Slater," he said slowly and calmly. "I'm with the American Army. We don't wish to fight you or harm you. Who is in charge?" His translator followed him, speaking rapidly to the men in their language.

One of the police officers spoke to the translator, gesturing angrily toward Slater and his men. The translator then turned to him, saying, "They want to know, if you are not here to harm them or fight them, then why are you here? What do you want?"

Smiling, Slater suddenly felt good about the situation. "*This just might work*," he thought.

"Tell him I would like to know if we can sit down and talk together. Tell him I've brought his men some food and American cigarettes as a peace offering," Slater announced. He turned and signaled for Private Leiter, his M240G machine gunner, to bring a small patrol pack to him. The police officers eyed Leiter nervously as the stocky giant of a soldier approached with his multihundred-round belts of ammo wrapped around his body armor and his giant machine gun. He also had some pretty hideous-looking face paint markings on that made him appear even more menacing, as did many of the men in Slater's platoon. It was somewhat of an adolescent ritual, but Slater didn't care as long as it pumped up the soldiers in his platoon.

Opening Leiter's patrol pack up, Slater pulled out a carton of Marlboro Reds out and tossed it to the man who appeared to be in charge. Smiles quickly spread across the officers' faces, and some of the initial tension relaxed.

The police officer jabbered on to the interpreter, who said, "The man says his name is Captain Aarav Anand. He thanks you for the cigarettes. He wants to know if you would like to come to his office and talk privately. He also is asking if you can have your soldiers lower their weapons while we talk. He assures us that no harm will come to us. They are police officers, not soldiers."

Slater turned to his platoon sergeant. "Tell the guys to stay alert, but we don't need to keep our guns pointed at them right now. Secure the area and get the depot locked down. I'm going to go inside and see if we can work out some sort of arrangement with the captain here."

"Copy that, LT, just don't let your guard down," Sergeant First Class Starr replied. "We're on their turf, and these guys might try to take you as a hostage."

Slater grinned as he answered, "Come on, Starr, when have you ever known me to let my guard down?"

The sergeant chuckled and then began to bark out orders to the other soldiers to get moving. They had a job to do, and it was already 0350 hours. The sun would be up soon, and that meant the city would start to wake up and it would become a real mess around here.

"Private Leiter, you're coming with me, along with Sergeant O'Neal. I want you guys as backup," Slater announced. "Oh, and try to be nice. Maybe smoke a few cigarettes with these guys and pass out some of the food we brought with us, will you?" He motioned for the police captain to lead the way, and his interpreter faithfully tagged along.

Once in the small office, the captain signaled for them to sit. Slater took the chair as opposed to the couch. With all this gear on, he wasn't sure he could get out of the couch quick enough, should he have to.

The captain opened the discussion. "One of my officers called and woke me up an hour ago. He said they saw landing ships heading to the beach, so I got dressed and came to the station immediately. Then, you guys show up. I want to know what's going on and why you Americans are here."

"Captain Anand, our president issued an ultimatum to your prime minister two weeks ago. India needed to withdraw from the Eastern Alliance and end the war, or India was going to face severe consequences. We are here to secure the city of Chennai and the port before we move inland to hunt down and destroy the remaining army units and force your prime minister to surrender," Slater explained.

The police captain shook his head before responding. "You realize we have over a billion people living in India. If we wanted you gone, it wouldn't take us long to drive you from our country. Putting that aside, what do you want with my police department? This was clearly the first place you came to."

"As I said earlier, we don't want to fight the people of India," Slater answered. "Our disagreement is with your government. What we want is your help. We want your police officers to continue to do their jobs. Arrest criminals, man traffic corners, and go about your daily duties. We're going to set up our headquarters across the street at the maintenance depot. I would like to coordinate the movement of other units through this part of the city with you."

The captain snorted. "I suppose you Americans are making this same proposal to other police stations around the city as well?"

"Yes, and to your local and city officials. Again, our disagreement is not with the people of India, it's with your government. Until your leaders end your alliance with the Chinese, we are going to stay here."

The two of them stared at each other for a few tense minutes, not saying anything as they sized each other up. Captain Anand eyed the oversized Private Leiter standing in his door and his huge machine gun. He shook his head.

"Fine," he replied. "My men will go about their normal duties, just like any other day. We'll work with you to keep our part of the city calm and under control. I can't control what happens in other parts of the city or what the government does."

"None of us want to see any more bloodshed, Captain. We have an opportunity to make the best of a bad situation. I hope you understand that. This situation will hopefully be resolved in with your government in a few days now that we've arrived."

Slater stood, then instructed his interpreter to tell the captain to bring his officers in so they could all be briefed on what had been agreed to and what they would be doing next. What happened in the next few hours could very well determine if their sector of Chennai would be peaceful or turn into a complete mess.

******

Chennai Container Terminal

Major General Alan Morrison stood near the terminal building as he observed the second RO-RO ship pull up to the dock to begin offloading its equipment. The first ship had docked half an hour ago, and already, 1st Armored Regiment had B Squadron offloaded and ready to go. The thirty-eight M1A1 Abrams battle tanks were even now moving to a marshaling point near the port entrance. Morrison's hope was to get his entire brigade offloaded before sunup, so the unit could begin to get their part of the city secured before the area became a zoo. The Americans would then move in with their own RO-RO ships and get the rest of their divisions offloaded.

"Any word yet from our scout units? Have they made it to the Ripon building and secured it?"

"Yes, General," replied a major who was coordinating the brigade's operations. "Captain Foster's unit just checked in. They're securing the building as we speak. He said we probably won't be able to make contact with most of the government officials until later in the morning."

"Good," said General Morrison. "I also want to know immediately when SAS makes contact with the mayor and the governor. They should be securing them both by now."

"Sir, the mayor and governor have already been secured and are being driven to the Ripon building as we speak. They'll be there waiting for you when you arrive," replied the major.

An hour later, as the light of dawn began to push away the night, Major General Morrison found himself sitting across a table from the governor of the state, the mayor, the head of police and a couple of other senior members of the city government. None of them looked very pleased to be speaking with him.

"I demand to know what you are doing in our country!" shouted Governor Bakshi, who looked disheveled and out of sorts. The SAS men clearly had not given him much time to throw some clothes on before they'd carted him away in a vehicle to be at this meeting.

"Governor Bakshi, please calm yourself," General Morrison said in his thick Australian accent. "Our quarrel is not with you or your city. However, until your prime minister renounces his unholy union with the Eastern Alliance and makes peace with the Allies, I'm afraid we are going to be turning Chennai into an Allied base camp of sorts."

This announcement generated a lot of looks of concern from the politicians.

"You can't simply occupy our city like this," countered the mayor hotly.

"I can't?" asked General Morrison, who was clearly enjoying himself. He waved his hands around and gestured out the windows. "I believe I already have. By the end of the day, I'll have 12,000 soldiers in Chennai, and in three days I'll have over 50,000…and more will continue to come. I'm not sure if you are aware, but the Allies recently defeated the Russians. Where do you think that large European army is headed?" he asked.

Wisely, the chief of police replied, "What do you want?"

A smile crept across Morrison's face as he surveyed the men before him. "I'm going to offer you two options, although I hope you choose the first one. In option one, we would leave you in power to govern your city as you see fit. In time, as we secure the state, you'll continue to administer it as you previously have. There would be no immediate changes. The police would continue to do their jobs, and life would go on as our army steadily makes its way to the countryside to do battle with your army. The second option is this—I will have you all removed and replaced with those that will comply with our requirements. You will be locked up as enemy prisoners of war until the war is concluded and prisoners are either released or swapped. I'll give you all five minutes to discuss this amongst yourselves, but I advise you to take me up on option one. Being a former Commonwealth member, I do hope we can keep things civil, but the Americans are not as understanding as I am."

He then stood up and left the room to let them deliberate for a moment and to check in on the rest of his units. The first six hours of this landing were critical. Either things were going to go smoothly, or there were going to get ugly quickly.

****

Chennai
Hill Five

The sun was fully up and so was the city. Hundreds of people had come out to see who these odd-looking soldiers were that had suddenly taken over this hilltop position overlooking the airport. The main highway running next to the airport had been closed off and so had nearly every entrance to the highways in the city. Tanks, infantry fighting vehicles, helicopters and fighter planes could be seen everywhere as the sleepy city woke up to suddenly find out it had been not only invaded by a foreign power, but seemingly been completely occupied without so much as a shot fired.

"Sergeant Price, what kind of plane is that?" one of his soldiers asked, pointing at a propeller-driven plane that was being offloaded. It looked like nearly a dozen of them were being pulled out of the cavernous bay of the giant cargo plane.

Lifting his pocket binoculars to his eyes to get a better look, Price smiled. "That, my friend, is our close air support. It's one of the Air Force's new Beechcraft AT-6 Wolverine turboprop ground-attack planes. It's a freaking beast."

The soldier grinned. "Good. We may need them if the Indians don't surrender."

"It'll work out, Specialist. If not, that's what we're here for," Sergeant Price replied good-naturedly.

His radio chirped. "Zombie Five, this is Zombie Six. How copy?"

Price depressed his talk button. "Zombie Six, this is Five. Go."

"I need you to report to my location," his captain explained.

"Copy that. I'm on my way," Price responded. He bade the group farewell as they continued to watch the Air Force offload additional helicopters, vehicles and other equipment they would need.

Trudging through the camp that the Airborne troopers had quickly begun to set up, he made his way over to what appeared to be a headquarters area. Spotting Major Fowler and Lieutenant Martinez, he walked over.

"What's going on, Sir?" Price asked.

Major Fowler replied, "We've got a new mission and some wheels. Major General Morrison—you know, the Australian general—he's given us a mission. We're going to head to a small village by the name of Voyalanallur a couple of kilometers outside the city here. Once we get there, we'll need to identify a suitable location for an artillery regiment to set up shop, establish a firebase, and create a base of operations for reconnaissance."

Sergeant Price looked at the map they'd handed him and traced his finger across it from their current position to where the little village was located. It was an ideal position to set up an artillery base; any guns set up there could provide support to any location in the city and twenty plus kilometers beyond it, which would certainly be helpful if they ran into any serious trouble.

"OK, sounds good. When do we leave?" asked Price.

"As soon as our vehicles arrive from the airfield. That said, the rest of the company is going to do this mission," explained Fowler. "I'm personally tasking you, your platoon and Lieutenant Martinez here with gathering intelligence on an Indian air base."

Price and Martinez exchanged a surprised look.

Fowler continued, "Arakkonam Air Base is roughly 75 kilometers from our current location. I need you guys to figure out what sort of military presence is still there and what condition the runways are in. I was told the Navy didn't crater the runways, just hit the aircraft hangars, etcetera. If the runways look to be in good condition and the base doesn't appear to be heavily occupied by the enemy, then the battalion may assault it and expand our military footprint deeper into the country."

They talked for a bit longer, making sure they had a fallback plan in case they ran into trouble.

Fowler concluded, "I was told by our Air LNO that within an hour, the first several Wolverines will be ready to provide close air support should we need it, and we'll also have some Apaches on standby as well."

With the meeting officially finished, Lieutenant Martinez and Price walked back to their platoon area to let the guys know about the new mission.

"LT, when are they going to give you your captain bars? I heard you made O-3 last week," Price said lightheartedly to Martinez.

Martinez shook his head. "No idea. I think I pissed the major off and he's holding my bars on me until he feels I'm good and ready for them. I don't really care. I checked my LES statement and I'm getting paid O-3 pay. That's all that matters."

Sergeant Price grunted. "Lucky you," he shot back. "I checked before we left, and they hadn't bumped me up from E-6 to E-7 yet."

When they approached the platoon area, the men crowded them, looking for info.

"Have we got a mission yet, or are we still on babysitting duty for the airborne?" one of the specialists asked snarkily. He obviously was not happy about being stuck on QRF duty.

Smiling, Martinez responded, "We have a mission, a *real* mission. We're going to scout out an enemy airfield and see if it's operational. If it is, then the battalion is going to capture it."

A few whistles and hoots could be heard from the men.

"Calm down, girls," said Sergeant Price with a laugh. "I need everyone to make sure your rucks are ready. I want three days' worth of food and a triple combat load of ammo.

We have no idea what we're driving into, and we're a long way from help. Understand?"

The guys nodded and went to work getting their supplies organized while they waited for their vehicles to show up. Twenty minutes later, eight SOF-outfitted JLTVs rolled up to their position, fully armed and ready to go. Unlike the conventional Army JLTVs, the SOF ones had machine guns mounted on special swivels on the sides of the two front doors, an M2 .50 or Mk19 grenade gun mounted on the turret, and a M240G mounted in a rear position in the bed of the truck. These small vehicles packed a whole lot of firepower and made for great scout vehicles.

Once their rides had arrived, the platoon started loading up their rucks and double-checking the weapons, ammo, water, and fuel. The few 82nd Airborne soldiers nearby just looked on, seemingly jealous of the exciting mission that they were missing out on and the sweet ride they were traveling on to get there.

The Rangers, for their part, made it look like this was just an everyday vehicle to them. Once the platoon had their equipment fitted out, Lieutenant Martinez called them all over to gather around him and began an impromptu mission brief. Since he didn't have a lot of information, or really even maps to show them, he used the GPS map built into the vehicles. For the most part, they'd stay on the highway since it would give them the fastest route to get there. Once they were roughly ten kilometers out, the platoon would break into squads and envelop the base from multiple positions, approaching as close as they dared to get a peek at what was waiting for them.

****

As the day turned to evening, the Rangers had taken cover in various locations around the air base and the surrounding city.

"It looks like the base is empty," Lieutenant Martinez said. Sergeant Price saw Martinez shoot him a look, asking for confirmation.

Sergeant Price pulled out his binos and surveyed the scene anew. "The runways look clear. The parking ramps and taxiways, however...well, they've seen better days." Burnt-out wrecks of several aircraft and helicopters dotted the area, along with the charred-out remains of the buildings on the base. "I think whatever enemy units were at this base have long since abandoned it. I'll bet our platoon could seize this base right now." Price lowered his binoculars. Night was almost upon them, and soon they'd have to switch over to their night vision goggles.

Depressing the talk button on his radio, Martinez radioed in what they were seeing. Sergeant Price smiled when he heard the lieutenant suggest that they attempt to take the base at nightfall. Some chatter took place between Martinez and Fowler for a few minutes while their options were discussed.

After a few minutes, Martinez walked back to the vehicle and singled out Sergeant Price. "You really think we can seize that base after dark?" he asked.

"The other squads have all checked in and they haven't reported any movement," Price answered. "We've watched the base now for several hours. Whoever was there has probably long since left after the Navy paid them a visit. I think going in after dark using the NVGs is the best approach."

Martinez thought about that for a moment and nodded. "OK. I'll let Major Fowler know we're going to do it after dark. He offered to get us some gunship support in case we need it. Do you think we should request it or just keep it on standby?"

Price didn't think they would need it at all, but having it on standby, ready to help them should they need it, couldn't hurt anything. "Let's keep them ready to assist in case we run into trouble, but I think we've got this, Sir," he answered.

An hour after dark, Sergeant First Class Price and half a dozen Rangers slowly crept along the outer edge of the base perimeter where it came closer to an access road. Once they found the point where the two ran next to each other, Price reached for his Gerber and began to cut the wire while the other men in the squad took up a defensive perimeter around him. In a matter of minutes, he'd cut the five strands of barbed wire that made up the external security and pulled the wires back to the nearest pole, creating a twelve-foot gap in the fence.

He depressed his radio talk button. "Zombie Six, this is Zombie Five. Entrance is open. Heading in now," he announced.

Price's thirteen-man team broke out into three four-man teams as they headed to their respective sections of the air base. Using their NVGs to see through the night, they quickly made their way past the outer perimeter of the base to the main facilities, stopping every so often to listen for sounds of movement.

Thirty-minutes after entering the base, Price's team found themselves sitting in a thicket of trees just opposite a road that led to the main headquarters building of the air base, or at least what was left of it. Pulling a thermal scope out of his ruck, Price turned it on and looked at the structures across the street for any signs of life.

He spent roughly ten minutes examining the entire area before he made the call that it appeared to be abandoned. Price ordered his team to move across the street so they could begin to search the structure.

Running past the base sign, he read, *Welcome to Arakkonam Naval Air Station. Home to the longest runway in Asia.* In minutes, his team was in the ground floor of the building, moving from blown-out room to room and finding nothing. They went to explore the second floor, but both stairwells had been destroyed, leaving them no viable way to access the upper floors.

Once this first building had been searched and cleared, they moved to the next set of buildings, and so did the other teams. It took them nearly an hour to clear through the building, but the only notable thing they found was the burnt-out wrecks of half a dozen Indian Navy Tu-142s, one newer Poseidon P-8I, and half a dozen helicopters. They also found a lot of dead and charred bodies in the various buildings and maintenance hangars.

Seeing no obvious signs of danger, he radioed in for the rest of the platoon to bring the vehicles on in. Twenty-minutes later, they consolidated their vehicles in the tree line, near the bombed-out headquarters building. With the rest of the platoon present, they finished doing a more thorough sweep of the buildings and the rest of the perimeter, ensuring Price's initial team hadn't missed something.

Lieutenant Martinez walked up to Sergeant First Class Price. "This place gives me the creeps," he said. "It's almost like something out of a zombie apocalypse or the *Walking Dead* TV series or something."

Price smirked. "You have a wild imagination, LT. It just looks like a bombed-out air base to me. Did you call it in yet? What did Major Fowler say?"

"I called it in ten minutes ago," Martinez replied. "He said congrats on the seizure and to hold on to it. He told me the rest of the company is stuck pulling security for that artillery firebase until they're relieved by another Army unit. He did say he passed our situation on to battalion, and they're going to see if a regular Army unit can relieve us. The Air Force is apparently eager to get this base operational; they want to move an engineering unit out here ASAP.

"In the meantime, I want everyone to try and get some sleep for now," Martinez ordered. "Once sunup comes,

I think this place is going to get a lot harder to defend. This is an enormous base, and we're just a platoon."

Price nodded, then went to work getting a guard rotation set up for the platoon.

****

Adyar Police Station, Chennai

It was nearly two in the morning when Captain Wilkes got a call from the battalion commander, ordering him to have his company stop everything they were doing and head out to a new location seventy-something kilometers outside the city. Apparently, a platoon of Rangers had seized an opportunity to capture an enemy air base, and now the brass wanted it properly protected so the Air Force could get it up and running ASAP. The following hour was a rush of controlled chaos as he ordered his platoons to wrap up whatever they were doing and join his position near the Adyar police station.

Wilkes felt lucky that the entire movement was happening in the wee hours of the morning, when the citizens of Chennai would still be largely asleep. Unfortunately, so were most of the soldiers, who now had to be roused from their slumber and made ready to fight. It hadn't even been twenty-four hours into the invasion of India and they were already receiving their first fragmentary order or FRAGO, and it was to go reinforce a platoon of Rangers deep in enemy territory.

Spotting Lieutenant Slater, Captain Wilkes walked up to him in a hurry. "Are your troopers ready, Lieutenant?" he asked, looking at his watch. "I think we're starting to fall behind schedule."

Slater nodded. "My guys are ready to roll, Sir. We're packed up. My only question is, since I've been able to establish a reasonably friendly relationship with the local police captain, do we know who's going to take our place? I'd at least like to tell them who they'll be working with."

"I don't have a lot of details. The battalion CG said something about a New Zealand unit moving in to take our place, but I have no idea what unit or who they are." He paused for a second as he guided the two of them away from the soldiers nearby. "Look, I have no idea who's running this mess right now or what's going on. All I know is I was at battalion headquarters to pick up some supplies and the commanding general was pipin' hot about something. One of the orderlies told me the brigade commander got a FRAGO order from the Ranger battalion that they were in some sort of trouble and had a platoon way out deep in enemy territory that stumbled onto an empty airfield and took the opportunity to seize it. Now the Australian general in charge of the ground operations here ordered it reinforced and turned into forward operation base. We're the first unit to head out there, but from what I gathered at battalion, it looks like the rest of the unit will be joining us out there over the next couple of days, along with a few artillery units."

Slater kind of slumped his shoulders at the news. Captain Wilkes understood; like many of the soldiers in their unit, he had hoped they'd be assigned to garrison duty in Chennai. That would have been a relatively safe duty assignment, and it would have meant they wouldn't see a lot of combat unless things completely turned to crap with the locals, which seemed to be relatively low-risk given their current relationship with the local government.

Slater shook out his shoulders, then stood up straight and tall. "Well, look at it this way, Sir," he said. "We've been selected to go save the Rangers. We'll be able to brag about that to these guys forever once we get back to Fort Lewis."

Wilkes laughed, and for a moment, the tension in the air was lifted. The captain had even more reason to avoid combat than Slater at the moment—his wife was expecting twin boys any day now. All he wanted to do was survive this war and get home to them. His poor wife was already trying to deal with their other two girls, ages two and three, and now twins. Thank God her parents had come to live with them while he was gone. He wasn't sure how she would handle it all.

"Thanks for lightening the mood, Ian," Wilkes responded. "I suppose I'm just distracted with the twins coming any day now. I know I need to keep my head in the game, but it's so hard right now. I just wish I could be there with them, and frankly, there isn't anyone I can really talk to about this." He wiped a tear away, making sure none of the men could see them.

Ian just nodded. "It'll be OK, Sir. You can always talk to me. I'm not going to judge you or think less of you. You helped me out a lot back in Washington when I was mentally heading in the wrong direction after I returned from Korea. For a while, I really thought I was going to go AWOL or shoot myself. You gave me a mission and a purpose, and that helped turn me around."

The two talked for a couple more minutes, then headed back to their soldiers to get ready to meet whatever was waiting for them at this airfield the Rangers had captured.

****

The sun crept up slowly at first, then before Wilkes knew it, the sun was up, and the darkness of the previous evening was all but gone. Alpha Company continued to race down what was largely a deserted highway toward the Arakkonam Naval Air Station. With the brighter light, Wilkes, like the rest of his soldiers, took in the opportunity to see the Indian countryside.

Within two hours of leaving Chennai, they arrived in the city of Arakkonam with little to no fanfare. While they hadn't run into any enemy resistance up to this point, Captain Wilkes noticed they were getting the stink eye from the locals once they realized the soldiers were Americans.

It took them a few minutes of driving around to actually locate the airport, and eventually the front gate, but once they did, they rolled right up to a couple of Special Forces-outfitted JLTVs and a squad of Rangers who eagerly greeted them.

An officer was there to meet them, and he quickly directed them to where he wanted the company to marshal so he could speak to them all at once. Ten minutes after their arrival, they all milled around outside their vehicles, waiting for whoever was in charge of this little operation to come over and tell them what the plan was. Finally, someone walked up to Captain Wilkes to introduce himself.

"I'm First Lieutenant Martinez. I'm the platoon leader of the Rangers who seized this airfield." Martinez extended his hand to Captain Wilkes.

After they shook hands and finished introductions, Martinez got right down to business. "First, I want to thank you guys for getting here on such short notice," he said. "I'm sure you saw on the way into the base that we're not exactly looked upon very nicely by the locals here. I suspect it has something to do with the fact that we bombed the base into a stub before we got here. What I need from your soldiers, Captain Wilkes, is for them to establish a defensive perimeter around the base. We have to make sure this place is as secured as we can make it until additional soldiers and the engineers arrive to help us fortify it."

Captain Wilkes nodded.

Martinez continued, "Once your unit has the perimeter secured, my platoon needs to expand our footprint of the area and see if there are any enemy units in the area. We have a few surveillance drones up, but they have a limited range. Intelligence says there's an Indian army base roughly 120 kilometers from here. My unit needs to get eyes on it and see if we have any enemy units headed our direction." He paused briefly. "How soon do you believe your guys can get this place secured so my platoon can get moving?" he asked.

Thinking for a moment, Wilkes made the decision that he'd rather have these Rangers out scouting for possible enemy units than showing his men around the base. They'd figure it out soon enough. "Lieutenant, why don't you guys go ahead and go? We'll sort things out on the base," Wilkes suggested. "We've got the rest of our battalion arriving throughout the rest of the day, so we'll be fine. *If* you find any enemy units heading in our direction, please contact us. I'm going to assign my Fourth Platoon, headed by Lieutenant Slater here, to be your QRF if you need it. He's seen a ton of action in Korea and his platoon is hard-core— they'll be able to help you if you need it."

Slater extended his hand, and the two talked for a minute before the Rangers headed out. With the business of handing the airfield over complete, the men of Alpha Company went to work exploring their new home.

****

Bengaluru, India

Once it became clear the Global Defense Force was going to attack India, the Prime Minister ordered Lieutenant

General Nirmal Chander's XXI Corps to the south of India, so they could be rapidly deployed to deal with a potential Allied invasion force.

While many in the government didn't believe the GDF would *actually* invade India, General Chander was not going to take any chances. He moved his Corps headquarters to Bengaluru, which essentially placed most of his forces in the center of the country, where he could easily direct them to meet the enemy.

With a large percentage of the active Indian Army committed to the Russian front, the only other available forces to defend the country were along the Pakistan-Indian border, leaving only his Corps to defend much of the interior of India. Fortunately, his force had been heavily augmented by the activation of the Reserves and the raising of a citizen militia force. With most of the reserves having been assigned to his command, he had 350,000 reservists and roughly 200,000 citizen militiamen in addition to his regular Army force of 67,000 career soldiers. His biggest challenge was moving his forces to fight the enemy and making sure they were properly equipped, fed and housed.

A young major who was helping to run Chander's operation center ran up to the general and signaled for his attention. "General Chander, reports are coming in that the

Americans seized the Arakkonam Naval Air Station. Our intelligence says it's a very small unit that has taken over the air base, but they expect more Americans to show up soon. What do you want me to tell the scouts to do?" he asked.

General Chander held back his emotions so as not to give away his feelings in front of the young officer. *"The Allies captured that base a lot faster than I thought they would,"* he thought. Though he was cool on the exterior, he was panicking a bit inside.

"This is to be expected," Chander said nonchalantly. "The Allies will look to expand their forces inland now that they've secured a port. We need to move our forces quickly though to deal with them."

Chander turned to face the Commander of the 36th Infantry Division, Brigadier General Singh Ghuman. "General, you need to get your division on the move. Order your militia and reserves to attack the Americans at the naval air station. I'm going to have the rest of the Corps move around you to attack the enemy formations in Chennai before they're able to get themselves organized outside the city. Timing is going to be critical—rush your forces forward, even if it means sacrificing many of your militiamen. They need to tie the Americans down while we get the rest of our army in position. Is that understood?"

"Yes, General. We'll overwhelm them with our sheer numbers," General Ghuman responded with a wicked grin on his face.

Chapter 25

They Kept Coming

Banavaram Reserve Forest

It was nearly morning as First Lieutenant Martinez sat with Sergeant First Class Price, poring over the images being fed to them by their reconnaissance drone. They were nervously monitoring the movement of an enemy force heading toward them. The number of enemy soldiers and vehicles showing up was scary.

For the past twelve hours, Martinez had been watching the enemy build up around the city of Ranipet. On three separate occasions, he had tried to call in for an airstrike, only to be told the available air assets were busy dealing with an Indian armor unit further to the north. Desperate for some fire support to break up this enemy buildup, he tried to get some friendly artillery units to do the job. Unfortunately, the battery of 105mm artillery guns were still being towed to the airfield they had captured thirty-six hours earlier. While the capture of the airfield was a huge tactical boon, it had also placed them very deep behind enemy lines, well beyond the initial fire support bases the Allies had set up outside of Chennai.

"I wish we had armed drones. At least we could feel like we're doing something," said the sergeant operating their little surveillance drone. They watched several busses drop off another large batch of soldiers at the edge of the city.

Patting the guy on the shoulder, Sergeant Price responded, "The gun bunnies will be set up soon enough. It doesn't look like these guys are getting ready to move anytime soon."

"I can't believe how many enemy soldiers are amassing like this. If we had proper air assets available to us right now, these guys would be toast," mused Lieutenant Martinez.

The rest of the company had finally made it to the base twelve hours ago. They'd been working with the regular Army units getting the base perimeter expanded beyond the airfield to include enough flat ground for two batteries of artillery. An engineering unit had also arrived and was quickly working to get fortified bunkers, gun positions and trenches built, while an Air Force Red Horse unit was getting the airfield operational.

Lieutenant Martinez's radio came to life. "Zombie Four-Six, this is Zombie Six. What's the status of that enemy unit you guys have been watching?" asked their company CO, Major Fowler.

"Zombie Six, this is Zombie Four-Six," Martinez answered. "We have eyes on at least two battalions' worth of irregular militia forming around the city of Ranipet, roughly nine kilometers from our position. The militia appear to be outfitted with a series of pickup trucks and older-model army trucks as transports. Break."

"Several kilometers beyond the city appears to be one battalion's worth of mechanized infantry and one armor unit, count twenty-eight T-72 Ajeya main battle tanks, and thirty-two BMP-2s. No artillery support spotted. How copy?" asked Martinez after he'd read off their report.

"Good copy, Zombie Four-Six. We need to buy more time for the base defenses to be built and for the artillery units to arrive. I'm sending Third Platoon to reinforce your position. They're going to bring our mortar tubes and two hundred mortar rounds with them. If those forces move before we give you the order to fall back to the base, then I need you to try your best to bog them down and keep them busy to buy more time. How copy?"

Martinez and Price looked each other over, both obviously aware this was nuts.

Regardless, Lieutenant Martinez acknowledged the order and then got off the radio.

"Well...it looks like we're waiting on Third Platoon to arrive," Martinez said, using a tone that was half laughing, half ready to cry. "I guess we'd better work on getting our position as prepared as possible for an incoming enemy attack."

The Rangers of Fourth Platoon went to work, feverishly getting their positions ready as best they could to repel an enemy advance. They set their heavy machine guns up to provide interlocking fields of fire and prepared a couple of positions ready where they would place the company's five 81mm mortar tubes once they arrived.

Martinez and Price continued to talk on the side about the situation at hand, and eventually agreed that if any of those tanks or BMPs attacked their position, orders or not, they would fall back to the base. They didn't have any weapons that could stand up to a tank. At least on the base, they had those Strykers that packed TOWs, and some were equipped with 105mm and 20mm antitank weapons.

Morning turned to early afternoon, and then Third Platoon arrived with 48 extra Rangers and their mortar tubes. The added soldiers began to dig a series of three-man foxholes at the perimeter of the forest preserve and set up their three additional machine guns. Then the Rangers continued to wait for news that their artillery support had finally arrived so they could start to put a world of hurt on the forces building up before them.

"Zombie Four-Six, Zombie Six. How copy?" called their commander.

Lieutenant Martinez called back, "Zombie Six. Zombie Four-Six. Good copy. Send."

"I've just received word the air base is officially operational. Five AT-6 Wolverines are now en route to the base, along with a cargo plane bringing munitions and fuel for them. We'll have tactical air support available within a few hours. Break.

"The battery of 105mm Howitzers we've been waiting on will be ready to start fire missions within thirty mikes. A second battery of 155mm Howitzers will be operational in ninety mikes. Start prioritizing targets for the gun bunnies. Break.

"The base commander wants to keep you guys in your current location to spot for the artillery and ground-attack planes until closer to evening. Then we'll look to pull you guys back closer to the base. How copy?" confirmed Major Fowler.

Breathing a sigh of relief, Martinez was glad they weren't going to have to spend any more time in this position than they had to. "That's a good copy on all. We'll prioritize the enemy armor first, then work our way down to the troop concentrations. Is it possible to get any HIMARS support from Chennai?" asked Martinez.

"Negative on HIMARS. They're tasked with the battle in the north. Do your best. Zombie Six, out."

Lieutenant Martinez called Third Platoon leader, First Lieutenant Franklin, and Sergeant Price over to talk with them. A few minutes later, they gathered around the drone operator with a few pads of paper and their Air Force TACP and artillery FSO LNO to go over targets.

After reviewing the drone footage, the FSO LNO spoke up. "Sir, if I may, I'd like to recommend that artillery focus on hitting the lightly armored and nonarmored trucks and vehicles the militia appear to be using. If we can destroy their rides, then we can largely force them to move on foot. That would obviously slow them down and allow us to continue to harass them at will with remaining artillery."

This option drew the approval of everyone there.

The Air Force TACP suggested, "I think we should have the AT-6 Wolverines focus exclusively on destroying the enemies' tanks for the time being. We have zero armor support of our own to rely on, so taking out the enemy's armor has to be their top priority."

Martinez nodded.

The TACP continued, "Following the destruction of the enemy tanks, the Wolverines could focus more on going after the enemy troop concentrations, which are looking more and more intimidating as the reinforcements keep piling on." They all glanced at the drone feed. There was no denying he was right.

Lieutenant Martinez was on board so far. "Rather than starting our artillery barrage as soon as artillery support is available, I think we should hold off until the Air Force says they're ready on their end," he said. He held up a hand to preempt any questions. "That way, we hit the enemy hard all at once and cause as much confusion and disorganization as possible."

The other men nodded; it was a solid plan. At 1500 hours, with only maybe four hours of light left, all the pieces of the puzzle were finally in place. The five AT-6s had just lifted off from the airfield and were now moving in to hit the enemy armor. The planes would go in first, and then the artillery barrage would start in earnest.

****

5,000 Feet Above the Battle

First Lieutenant Kimberly "Sparkles" McNeal was both exhausted and excited. Her squadron, the newly created 359th "Death Dealers," had drawn the short end of the stick and had to ferry their planes from Indonesia to India while their sister squadron was able to have their planes disassembled and flown directly to Chennai. With four drop tanks of fuel, the Death Dealers had able to make the flight, but it had been a very long and arduous one.

Once they'd arrived in Chennai, she'd had little time to rest before her squadron had received orders to move out. Before she knew it, she was on her way to a small forward air base deep behind enemy lines to support a group of Rangers and infantry facing an overwhelming number of enemy soldiers.

She'd arrived at the spartan air base barely twenty minutes ago, and they'd already been briefed on their next mission and quickly sent back into the air. As Lieutenant McNeal flew toward her target, she looked to her left and then to her right and saw her flight mates, which made her feel much better about her first combat mission. Having only graduated flight school four weeks ago, she was eager to prove herself to her male counterparts. As the only female pilot in her squadron, so she'd been given the call sign "Sparkles," which suited her just fine.

She smiled when she looked briefly at her wings through the large bubbled canopy and saw the four AGM-65 Mavericks she was carrying. Sparkles relished the opportunity to destroy some tanks. She also had two rocket pods carrying seven 70mm antimaterial rockets for added punch.

Suddenly, her radio crackled to life. "Death Dealers, we're going to move down to 3,000 feet and line up for our attack from the east." While each of the pilots had their own call signs, they also went by DD one through five—a shortened version of Death Dealers—to keep themselves identified with their air traffic controllers.

"I want DD 1 and 2 to go in first, then DD 3 and 4 next, and I'll follow in last. Remember, our first pass is meant to go after the tanks," ordered their flight leader, Captain Adrian "Beaker" Adler.

Each flight of two moved to their loitering and attack positions, roughly fifteen kilometers away from the enemy they were about to attack. Thus far, they hadn't detected any enemy air defenses, but that didn't mean they weren't lying in wait for them either.

The first flight of Death Dealers swooped in out of the late-afternoon sun, completely catching the enemy by surprise. Both aircraft were able to identify and engage eight of the T-72 tanks, scoring hits before the enemy even realized they were under air attack. As the planes pulled away from their victims, a slew of antiaircraft fire erupted around them, giving chase to the fleeing aircraft.

The element of surprise had been broken, but the second wave of Death Dealers lined up for their own attack, this time angling from a different direction and altitude to throw off the defenders, who would now be waiting for them.

Checking the arming switch on her missiles, Sparkles felt confident going into her first-ever attack run on a real enemy. Her turbocharged engine roared hard as she picked up speed, fully opening the throttle up as she sped up to stay in formation with her wingman, "Hedge," who'd acquired his call sign based on his last name, Hedgerow.

The two of them swooped in like a pair of German Stukas as they activated the targeting cameras on their Mavericks. Her onboard targeting computer picked out four tanks to her immediate front, roughly ten kilometers away, assigning a missile to each of them. The computer also sent a quick burst message to her wingman as the two aircraft's targeting computer systems deconflicted their targets, making sure they weren't double-targeting a tank. All of this happened in fractions of a second as her heads-up display or HUD began to show green triangles over the targets her computer had found.

"Firing now!" radioed Hedge as he released his four missiles.

Sparkles depressed her own firing button once, then twice, then two more times as her Mavericks flew out in front of her toward their intended targets. Seconds after her missiles had fired, she saw a slew of what appeared to be bright objects flying right at her. Her mind instantly recognized this as incoming antiaircraft fire, and her training took over.

"Break right!" yelled Hedge as he broke to the left, dodging several lines of enemy rounds.

In the midst of her hard turn to the right, Sparkle's missile warning alarm blared in her ears. She craned her neck around to look for the possible threat.

"Enemy missile, enemy missile," announced the automated system. She pulled her plane into a steep climb and then banked hard to the left. Sparkles hit the flare button, firing out a series of flares every three seconds until all eight flares were spent.

She looked at her altimeter, which now read 5,500 feet. Then she looked behind her to see if she could spot the enemy missile that had been tracking her. "There you are," she said to herself as she saw the missile explode amongst her flares. She quickly leveled her plane out as she looked around for her wingman.

In a brief flash, she saw his plane spitting out a second batch of flares just as an enemy missile exploded nearby. His plane was blown sideways through the air and instantly spouted smoke from the engine.

Hedge radioed in. "I've been hit," he said. "I'm going to try and make it back to the airfield for an emergency landing if I can."

"Death Dealers, good attack run. Re-form on me," Beaker said over the radio. "Hedge, are you OK? Are you hurt?"

"I'm fine—a bit shaken up, but I'm fine. I'm losing oil and hydraulic pressure though. I've got some pretty big holes in my wings, but she's holding together so far."

"OK, good to hear. If you need to ditch your plane though, try to get as close to the airfield as possible. The rest of you, get ready for our next run."

"*Holy cow, that was awesome!*" Sparkles thought. The adrenaline coursed through her veins, and she couldn't believe she'd just survived. When she'd taken a few deep breaths, she paused and sent Hedge a prayer—she hoped he made it back to the base all right.

"On this next run, we're going to unload our rockets on the BMPs on the west side of the river," explained Beaker. "Since there are only four of us, I'm going to take over as Sparkles' wingman. Everyone needs stay frosty on this run. The enemy knows we're here and will be gunning for us."

"Beaker, or anyone else, do you guys know what kind of missile hit Hedge?" asked one of the other Death Dealers. "Was it a MANPAD or something else?"

"It was a MANPAD," replied Beaker.

A collective sigh of relief washed over them. It meant they were dealing with a much smaller missile, and one with a limited range. Their planes could largely survive a hit from a MANPAD, as Hedge's plane had just proven. If it had been a traditional SAM, they would have been in serious jeopardy.

Five minutes later, the flight of four Wolverines lined up from a different vantage point and descended for their second attack run on the enemy below. Sparkles saw the small cluster of vehicles she'd been assigned to strafe with her rockets and angled her fighter toward them. Once she was within ten kilometers of her prey, she increased her throttle, opening her engines up and pushing her plane to 530 mph. Her HUD indicated she was still a little too far away to release her unguided rockets on the cluster of vehicles, though she now saw her targets starting to scatter. They'd spotted her.

Seconds after the vehicles began to move, tracers flew right at her, attempting to blot her from the sky. She deftly banked her wings from left to right and made herself a harder target to hit by changing her flight path every couple of seconds. She continued closing the gap on her targets. With the enemy BMPs now scattering, she zeroed in on a group of four of them that were heading in the same direction. When the targeting reticle on her HUD turned green, she depressed the firing button on the stick, releasing two rockets every time she depressed the button. With six of her rockets away, she pulled up hard and banked to the right, while Beaker broke to the left in an effort to split the enemy groundfire.

"Good attack run, Sparkles. Did you happen to see those clusters of ground troops advancing toward the Rangers on the ground?" he asked as they both formed back up around 8,000 feet, several kilometers away from the hornet's nest they'd just stirred up.

"Yeah, I saw it. How many soldiers you think are down there?" she asked out of curiosity.

"I have no idea. But our next attack run is going to focus on them with our remaining rockets. This time, instead of breaking off, I want us to also strafe them with our guns— we have enough ammo to make a couple of strafing runs before we head back to base. You think you can handle a strafing run?" he asked.

"Yeah, I'm good. Let's do it," she replied, excitement evident in her voice.

Beaker radioed the other two planes in his flight and relayed their next attack plan. For the next twenty minutes, their flight of four Wolverines made two more passes at the enemy, pummeling them with rockets and .50 machine guns. Many of the enemy soldiers scattered when they saw the fighters swooping in, but the Death Dealers still scored plenty of hits. As they made their runs, a lot of ground fire flew up to meet them, but thus far, none of it had scored any critical hits.

When their ordnance was spent, they radioed back to the base, letting them know they had cleared the battlespace so the artillery guys could begin their own mission. When the fighters landed, Sparkles and the rest of the pilots were surprised to see their planes had sustained quite a number of bullet holes. The ground crews did their best to make sure nothing critical had been damaged and that the planes could get back in the air when the next mission was called for.

****

Banavaram Reserved Forest

It was nearly 1700 hours. With maybe two hours of light left, Lieutenant Martinez weighed their options. The last couple of hours, they had been calling in one strike after another on the advancing mob of Indian soldiers several kilometers in front of them. Up to this point, they had only been probed with a few small-scale attacks, but eventually, the enemy was going to try and bum-rush their positions.

They could fall back to the airport now that reinforcements had arrived, but giving up their forward position right now also meant the enemy would be that much closer to encircling the air base. The longer they held this position, the more they made the enemy react to them, as opposed to the other way around.

"Lieutenant!" the sergeant manning the drone shouted in an excited voice. "They're moving in," he said, showing him the image of a mob of undisciplined militiamen surging toward their position.

Before Martinez could say a word, they heard the whistling sound of mortars starting to fall on their positions.

"*Incoming!*" he shouted. The soldiers around him hit the dirt just as a series of rounds landed in the cluster of trees where they were hiding.

Crump, crump, crump, crump, crump.

Five explosions ripped through the forest, sending hot shrapnel in all directions. Then a guttural sound emanated from the gathering horde that was now roughly a kilometer away from their position.

****

Sergeant First Class Price poked his head up from his fighting position and looked for the militiamen rushing toward their positions. He turned to the Rangers to his left and right, and yelled, "Hold your fire, men! Wait until they get within two hundred meters and then cut loose on them."

More mortar rounds landed among their positions as they watched the enemy soldiers get closer with each passing second. Once the enemy left the smoldering ruins of the village next to the forest preserve, they had a brief hundred yards of open ground they had to cross before they edged into the wooded tree cover where the Rangers were set up.

Zip, crack, zip, zap.

Bullets whizzed over their heads, hitting some of the nearby trees and underbrush they were using for cover. Just as the enemy crossed into a stretch of open terrain that marked them to be roughly two hundred meters away, the Rangers cut loose with their M240G machine guns. The red tracers from their machine guns looked like lasers as they crisscrossed back and forth across their interlocking fields of fire, shredding the attackers. The first several waves of enemy soldiers were simply cut apart by the five M240s the Rangers had placed on this line of their defense.

Price raised his own rifle to his shoulder and took aim at the wall of enemy soldiers charging relentlessly toward them. Bullets were cracking all around him, but he zeroed in on each target and blocked out his other senses.

Bang, bang, bang, bang.

Sergeant Price just kept pulling the trigger. Time and time again, he scored a direct hit with nearly every trigger pull. However, despite every man he saw taken out by one of his shots, enemy soldiers just kept coming at him.

Price dropped his now-empty magazine, quickly slapping a new one in its place as the relentless horde continued unabated toward them, threatening to envelop them in a tsunami of bullets and pure suicidal hatred. Flipping his selector switch from semiauto to full-auto, he knew he needed to cut through the enemy ranks at a much quicker pace or they'd be on his position in minutes.

The chattering *ratatat* of the machine guns was almost nonstop as the gun crews did their best to cut down their attackers and keep them at arm's length.

Crump, crump, crump.

Friendly mortar and artillery fire hit the enemy ranks, throwing bodies and parts of bodies in every which direction, adding to the carnage unfolding before them.

"*How can they keep charging like this?*" Price thought, horrified. In that moment, he just wanted to be anywhere but there.

He reached to his right as a string of bullets flew right past were his head had just been, and grabbed the first clicker, depressing the button.

BOOM!

An enormous explosion occurred seventy-five meters in front of him as his Claymore mine detonated, flattening fifteen or twenty tightly packed enemy soldiers as the wall of ball bearings cut them down like a scythe.

When the enemy reached within 75 meters of their lines, more of the Rangers detonated their Claymore mines. As the fighting continued, many of the Indian militiamen were now using any cover they could find to seek shelter from the fuselage of bullets and ball bearings being thrown at them. The Indian militia began to take more accurately aimed shots at the defenders, finally scoring hits against the Rangers, who up to this point had been absolutely butchering them.

Price turned to the Ranger next to him to tell him to blow his Claymore when the man's head snapped back and disintegrated in a midst of blood and gore and his body collapsed to the bottom of their fighting position. Shaking the sight from his mind, Sergeant Price reached over and grabbed the Claymore clicker, detonating the last mine they had in front of them.

BOOM!

Another swath of enemy soldiers was cut down. His only remaining battle buddy threw hand grenades at the enemy like it was going out of style.

Crump, crump, crump. Shrapnel being thrown everywhere.

Just as Price thought, *"This is it—we're going to be washed over by the enemy horde,"* he suddenly heard dozens of whistles. The militiamen fell back—not to their original starting point, but several hundred meters away. Shooting between the two sides continued unabated, but the relentless charges stopped for the time being.

Lieutenant Martinez tapped Price on the shoulder. "We have to get the heck out of Dodge, or we're done. I don't know how we just survived that," he said in awe.

Price nodded. "It's starting to get dark, LT. The enemy probably pulled back to allow darkness to settle in, and then they'll resume their attack when it'll be harder to see them."

Martinez shook his head and then grabbed his radio. "All Zombie elements, fall back to the vehicles immediately," he ordered. "We need to get out of here ASAP. Leave the dead, but make sure we don't leave any of our wounded behind."

Sergeant Price was a bit impressed as he watched Lieutenant Martinez trot up and down the line to make sure everyone knew they were falling back. *"Those Rangers don't need to be told twice to leave,"* he thought with a smirk.

The lieutenant and Price met up on their way back to the vehicles, but Martinez made a critical mistake and looked back at the front line, where the enemy had been pushing toward them moments ago. He immediately grabbed his stomach and fell to his knees, retching. Price stole a glance backward—the carnage was unimaginable. The ground was practically covered in dead and mangled bodies all the way up to the edge of their positions.

"What kind of commander could order his men into such a slaughter?" asked Martinez as he wiped away the vomit from his mouth with his hand.

When they arrived at their vehicles, Price and Martinez discovered that a couple of them had been destroyed by mortars, and one was simply too damaged to be used. Martinez looked around the motley crew nearby and sadly commented, "Looks like we lost several Rangers in this last battle though, so there's no risk of leaving anyone behind from Third or Fourth Platoon."

Just as they were about to leave, a massive artillery bombardment slammed into both the enemy lines and their own lines, where they had just been a few minutes earlier. This was their fire support to cover their retreat as they sped away in their vehicles back to the airfield.

As he sat in the passenger seat of the SOF JLTV, Sergeant Price was exhausted. His hands were shaking as they sped away quickly to the protective perimeter of the airfield. The drive was short, roughly twenty minutes, but it felt like an eternity.

Eventually, they found the entrance to the newly built perimeter, and some of the infantrymen guided them in. Price was glad to see the familiar outline of the Stryker vehicles in the dusk, as well as the Army soldiers manning the various machine-gun bunkers. He was also happy to see the trenches that the engineers had managed to dig and at least one row of concertina wire that had been placed.

The convoy of vehicles made its way to the center of the airfield where the bombed-out hangar was that the Rangers had taken over. Major Fowler was there waiting to greet them. He gestured with his hand in a way that indicated he was performing a head count of the men, and his face dropped. Only sixty-two of the original ninety men had returned.

When the vehicles finally stopped next to the bombed-out hangar, medics rushed forward to help assist with the wounded soldiers. One of the medics announced, "We have helicopters inbound to evacuate the wounded."

Sergeant Price climbed out of the vehicle, and Major Fowler walked toward him. Price's right hand continued shaking as he tried to steady himself. Then he bent over and threw up. Unable to control the flood of emotions that was washing over him, he dropped to his knees and suddenly began sobbing.

Major Fowler stopped in his tracks for a second. A few of the other Rangers were reacting the same way. Despite his overwhelming physical reaction, Sergeant Price spotted Fowler waving down Lieutenant Martinez.

"What the heck happened, Lieutenant? Some of your men look to be coming apart," he said with concern in his voice.

Martinez paused for a second. "It was terrible, Sir…it was worse than terrible. It was pure murder. Whoever the enemy commander was, he just kept ordering these militiamen forward. They just kept charging and charging right into our machine guns, our Claymores, grenades and artillery. The entire ground in front of our position was awash in torn and mangled bodies, Sir," he explained. "It was pure murder," he repeated.

****

Major Fowler just stood there dumbfounded for a moment, not knowing with what to say or how to respond. He hadn't expected this, especially from his most battle-hardened platoon and Rangers. Looking at what remained of the platoon, he quickly observed that these guys were useless to him as a fighting force for the moment. He'd need to give them some time if he hoped to get them back into the battle anytime soon.

For the next half hour, he and his first sergeant spent their time just consoling and helping their fellow Rangers, calming them and letting them know it would be OK.

"This slaughter wasn't your fault," he told several of the soldiers. "You were just doing your jobs. If you want to blame anyone, blame me, or the enemy who placed those men in that position."

The battle for India was going to be much more difficult than he'd anticipated.

From the Authors

Miranda and I hope that you have been enjoying the Red Storm Series. We are on track to release the last book, *Battlefield China*, on December 16, 2018. You can preorder your copy on Amazon. Our audiobook versions of World War III are also coming along: *Prelude to World War III*, *Operation Red Dragon*, and *Operation Red Dawn* have been completed, and *Cyber Warfare and the New World Order* is currently in production.

We need your help. The two biggest ways that you can help us to succeed as authors are:

1. Leave us a positive review on Amazon and Goodreads for each of our books you liked reading. These reviews really make a difference for other prospective readers, and we sincerely appreciate each person that takes the time to write one.

2. Sign up for our mailing list at http://www.author-james-rosone.com and receive updates when we have new books coming out or promotional pricing deals.

We have really appreciated connecting with our readers via social media. Sometimes we ask for help from our readers as we write future books (we love to draw upon all your different areas of expertise). We also have a group of beta readers who get to look at the books before they are officially published and help us fine-tune last-minute adjustments. If you would like to be a part of this team, please go to our author website: http://www.author-james-rosone.com, and send us a message through the "Contact" tab. You can also follow us on Twitter: @jamesrosone and @AuthorMirandaW. Our Facebook website is also a good place to connect: https://www.facebook.com/JamesRosone/ We look forward to hearing from you.

You may also enjoy some of our other works. A full list can be found below:

World War III Series

Prelude to World War III: The Rise of the Islamic Republic and the Rebirth of America
Operation Red Dragon and the Unthinkable
Operation Red Dawn and the Invasion of America
Cyber Warfare and the New World Order

Michael Stone Series

Traitors Within

The Red Storm Series

Battlefield Ukraine

Battlefield Korea

Battlefield Taiwan

Battlefield Pacific

Battlefield Russia

Battlefield China (available for preorder, to be released December 16, 2018)

For the Veterans

I have been pretty open with our fans about the fact that PTSD has had a tremendous direct impact on our lives; it affected my relationship with my wife, job opportunities, finances, parenting—everything. It is also no secret that for me, the help from the VA was not the most ideal form of treatment. Although I am still on this journey, I did find one organization that did assist in the healing process for me, and I would like to share that information.

Welcome Home Initiative is a ministry of By His Wounds Ministry, and they run seminars for veterans and their spouses for free. The weekends are a combination of prayer and more traditional counseling and left us with resources to aid in moving forward. The entire cost of the retreat—hotel costs, food, and sessions, are completely free from the moment the veteran and their spouse arrive at the location.

If you feel that you or someone you love might benefit from one of Welcome Home Initiative's sessions, please visit their website to learn more: https://welcomehomeinitiative.org/

We have decided to donate a portion of our profits to this organization, because it made such an impact in our lives and we believe in what they are doing. If you would also like to donate to Welcome Home Initiative and help to keep these weekend retreats going, you can do so by visiting the following link:

https://welcomehomeinitiative.org/donate/

Abbreviation Key

AAV	Amphibious Assault Vehicle
AD	Armored Division
AKA	Also Known As
AWOL	Absent Without Leave
BND	Bundesnachrichtendienst (German intelligence)
BTR	Bronyetransporter (Soviet class of armored vehicles)
CAG	Commander Air Group
CG	Commanding General
CIA	Central Intelligence Agency
CIC	Combat Information Center
CIWS	Close-in Weapons Systems
CO	Commanding Officer
CVC	Combat Vehicle Crewman's Helmet
DHS	Department of Homeland Security
DIA	Defense Intelligence Agency
DoD	Department of Defense
ECM	Electronic Counter Measures
ESSM	Evolved SeaSparrow Missile
FAC	Forward Air Controller
FIST	Fire Support Team

FBI	Federal Bureau of Investigations
FISA	Foreign Intelligence Surveillance Act
FRAGO	Fragmentary Order
FSB	Federalnaya Sluzhba Bezopasnosti (Russian counterintelligence)
FSO	Federalnaya Sluzhba Okhrany (Russian Secret Service)
FSO	Fire Support Officer
GDF	Global Defense Force
GRU	Glavnoye Razvedyvatel'noye Upravleniye (Russian intelligence directorate)
HE	High-explosive
HIMARS	High Mobility Artillery Rocket System
HQ	Headquarters
HUD	Heads-Up Display
IR	Infrared
IT	Information Technology
J3	Operations Officer
JDAM	Joint Direct Attack Munitions
JLTV	Joint Light Tactical Vehicle
LCAC	Landing Craft Air Cushion (hovercraft)
LES	Leave and Earnings Statement
LNO	Liaison Officer
LRAS	Long-Range Acquisition System

MANPADS	Man-portable Air-defense Systems
MP	Member of Parliament
MPH	Miles Per Hour
MRE	Meal Ready-to-Eat
MWR	Morale, Welfare and Recreation
NCO	Noncommissioned Officer
NVG	Night Vision Goggles
PEOC	Presidential Emergency Operations Center
PLA	People's Liberation Army (Chinese army)
PM	Prime Minister
POTUS	President of the United States
PSYOPS	Psychological Operations
R & D	Research and Development
RIM	Rolling Airframe Missile
RO-RO	Roll-on, Roll-off
ROTC	Reserve Officer Training Course
RPA	Russian Provisional Authority
RPG	Rocket Propelled Grenade
RTO	Radio-telephone Operator
SAM	Surface-to-Air Missile
SAS	Special Air Service
SecDef	Secretary of Defense
SITREP	Situational Report
SOF	Special Operations Forces

TACP	Tactical Air Control Party
TOW	Tube-Launched Optically Tracked Wire-Guided
UPS	United Parcel Service
USAID	United States Agency for International Development
VLS	Vertical Launch System
VP	Vice President
VTOL	Vertical Takeoff and Landing
WMD	Weapon of Mass Destruction
XO	Commanding Officer

Manufactured by Amazon.ca
Bolton, ON

24402544R00306